ADVERSE POSSESSION

REBECCA ZANETTI

RAZ INK LLC

This one is for the Boyz:
Gabe Zanetti,
Ben Hoffman,
Jace Younker,
and Luke Hicks.
Thanks for the entertainment through the years, and we're so proud of all of you! Next time at the lake, drinks are on Big Tone.

ACKNOWLEDGMENTS

Thank you to everyone who helped to make this book a reality!

Thank you to Tony, Gabe, and Karlina for being the best trio of family any author could ever hope to have;

Thank you to Craig Zanetti, Esq., for the help with criminal law and procedure. Any mistakes about the law are mine and mine alone;

Thank you to Asha Hossain of Asha Hossain Designs, LLC for the fantastic cover;

Thank you to Debra Stewart of Dragonfly Media Ink for the wonderful edits;

Thank you to Jillian Stein for being the best social media guru in the history of the world;

Thank you to Anissa Beatty for being such a fantastic author assistant as well working so hard with Rebecca's Rebels, my FB Street Team;

Thank you to Stella Bloom for the fabulous narration for the audio book;

Thank you to Liz Berry, Asa Maria Bradley, and Boone Brux for the advice with the concepts for this new series;

Thank you to my incredibly hard working agent, Caitlin Blasdell;

Thank you to Sara and Gwen from Fresh Fiction, and Cissy and crew from WriterSpace for helping get the word out about this new series;

Thank you to FB Rebels Joan "Buffyanna"Lai and Jackie Baker for all of the fun, support, and encouragement;

Thank you to Rebels Karen Clementi, Heather Frost, and Kimberly Frost for the help with edits;

Thank you to my constant support system: Gail and Jim English, Kathy and Herbie Zanetti, Debbie and Travis Smith, Stephanie and Don West, and Jessica and Jonah Namson.

NOTE FROM THE AUTHOR

Howdy everyone! Thank you for so much support for his new series of mine. Sometimes, as an author, you have to write something a little different. This series is that for me.

I've loved the emails and FB notes about this series, and I'm happy to keep writing about Anna and her family. Sometimes we need a little bit of humor, right? This is a side note for the family with a full romance, which was fun to write.

Also, I am a lawyer, and I might live in a small town, but this is in **no way** autobiographical. It turns out that the name Albertini is a distant family name of my relatives, which is pretty cool. However, the story is all made up. The characters are all fictional and so are the towns and counties (like usual). Also, the law is correct. :)

I hope you like Anna's world as much as I do!

Also, to stay up to date with releases, free content, and tons of contests, follow me on Bookbub, Facebook, the FB Rebel Street Team, and definitely subscribe to my newsletter for FREE BOOKS!

Also, I like to pair up with other bestselling authors to cross promote and give away books in our newsletters, so I will be giving away copies of my friends' books coming up. Just go to my website (RebeccaZanetti.com) to sign up for my newsletter.

XO
Rebecca

CHAPTER 1

*M*y boyfriend was a sociopath.

Well, if he could be called a boyfriend. There was nothing boyish about Aiden Devlin, and it wasn't like we'd actually discussed whatever it was we were doing together. But at the moment, as I stared at the one full and one empty air-tight cereal containers in his new and fairly empty pantry, I had other things to worry about. "I can't believe you did this." I turned around in his quaint kitchen as I spoke, and then I forgot, well, everything.

Aiden lay shirtless on the floor with his head beneath the sink, doing something that clinked. What, I really didn't care. Jeans covered his long legs to his bare feet on the worn wooden floor, but my eyes remained on his very cut, very hard, very awesome chest. One that had more than its fair share of healed bullet and knife wounds.

The tattoo over his bicep always caught me. Sexy and jagged, it was a compilation of his life so far, all within the outline of a deadly Eagle. Military, ATF Agency, Ireland, and small town Idaho.

He wiggled his broad shoulders out from the cupboard, tossed the wrench into a battered tool case, and lifted one dark eyebrow. "Huh?" His blue eyes were so blue they always took my breath away.

My mouth watered and I cleared my throat to appear nonchalant. "Huh?"

"What did I do, Anna?" He sat up, shifted, and put his bare back to the dented dishwasher. His concentration was a hundred percent on me, and that always threw me, too.

"Uh." I looked around and caught sight of the cereal holders. Oh yeah. "This. You did this." I gestured toward the full one.

He stood and moved, his scent of leather and motor oil catching me as he looked over my shoulder. "I filled it. You said I had to have those plastic thingies to hold cereal, and that's what I filled it with." Then he wiped his hands off on his jeans and reached for a glass of water on the counter. "I thought cereal boxes were what you keep cereal in, by the way."

"You took *three* different kinds of cereal and combined them into *one* container. Three very different kinds. That's crazy." One was peanut butter flavored, one plain flakes, and one looked like waffles. I mean, who did that?

He leaned back against the counter, cocked his head, and gave me his signature Aiden look. The one that said he was partly trying to figure me out and partly wondering if he should take me to a shrink.

"Don't give me that look."

Both eyebrows rose this time. With his ruffled black hair and dangerous blue eyes, he was all Irish. Then he went in for the kill. "All right. What's bugging you?"

I hated that. I mean, I really hated that he was such a grownup and could see right through me. The problem was, I had no clue what was bugging me. Plus, combining cereals into one container when there was another empty one was just so…male. So Aiden. Ug. I sighed.

He crooked his finger in a 'come hither' motion. It was a move that should irritate me, but it was sexy and kind of sweet—and the look in his eyes was neither.

So I trotted across his uneven floor and let him gather me into a hug. Being surrounded by heat, male, and muscle was a very nice way for a healthy woman like me to spend a few minutes. When he placed a gentle kiss on my head, easily since he was about a foot taller than me, I relaxed completely into him.

"There you go," he murmured, holding me. "The opening of your law firm this week is going to be fantastic. Your help with my new place has been invaluable, even though I don't know why I need placemats or cereal containers. You're healthy, I'm healthy, and right now, nobody is shooting at us."

I laughed against him. He'd just closed escrow on the spacious cabin on the lake, and he seemed okay with the fact that it was only a few miles away from my cottage. His was a fixer-upper, and that seemed to make him happy. Who knew that the ATF agent was so handy around the house? It seemed like being able to go undercover for years and then shoot people before they shot him was enough talent, but no. He was good at house stuff, too. "I guess I'm just waiting for the next shoe to drop," I admitted.

He grasped my arms and held me away from him so I could meet his gaze. "It always does, Angel. Enjoy the good times. Trust me."

I'd dreamed about him my entire teenaged years as well as years into my twenties, and now here he was, and he was holding me. Life was sometimes too much to grasp. But he was right that we should enjoy the good times. It was a lesson we'd both learned while young. "Are you nervous about work tomorrow?" I asked.

"No." His grin was infectious. "I'm happy to be working out of the Spokane office. If they don't want my team there, we'll just find a satellite office here in Idaho."

His team was the only ATF special response team allowed to work out of a satellite office instead of one of the main SRT offices, and it was just an experiment. If it didn't go well, he'd have to move. Or he'd just go undercover again, and I wouldn't hear from him for years.

"Stop worrying," he murmured. "We control our lives."

Ha. I learned that wasn't true a long time ago, as well. It was sweet the alpha male thought so. Or maybe he had to think so in order to shoot people before they could shoot him. Who knew?

My phone buzzed and I tugged it out of my jeans to see a text from my sister, Tessa.

Aiden unashamedly read the text. "Quint 911?"

My heart sank, but I straightened my shoulders. "Yeah." I read the second text. *Meet at Tratto's at six. T.*

"Your cousin, Quint?" Aiden asked.

I nodded. "He's a smokejumper and also performs search and rescue missions. He's been in Cali at a fire looking for remains with his dog, and apparently it was a rough one, and he's home at the family barbecue today." I'd skipped the barbecue to help Aiden out with his new home.

Aiden turned me and pulled my back to his front, settling his arms around my waist. "When he gets home, you and Tessa check in?"

"Yeah. Donna, too." I stared at the floor that needed to be sanded and tried to ignore his hard body behind me. Both of my sisters were great at cheering people up or just listening to them. "When Quint has a rough one, we usually bug him until he gets back to his sunny disposition."

"I was in high school with Quint. Great wide receiver as well as golfer," Aiden said. "I didn't know he'd gone into smoke jumping. Doesn't he have a bunch of brothers? I played baseball with Rory until I got suspended from high school for a week."

"He has five brothers." The Italian side of my family procreated well. Heck. So did the Irish side. I had a lot of cousins. "Quint's girlfriend broke up with him right before he left, and then he had to find dead bodies in rubble, so he's going to need some meddling from us." As cousins went, Quint was a good one. He was also a good man, and he deserved some fun as well as peace. Plus, he was better with a project going on, so we'd have to think of something to preoccupy his mind for a bit. I looked around the kitchen that needed work.

"No," Aidan said, resting his chin on my head. "I want to do this myself."

I got that. Plus, the idea that Aiden was setting down roots gave me tingles in my abdomen. The more work he did himself, the more he'd want to stay put. "Maybe you guys could go golfing? Do you still golf?"

"Yeah. I went undercover in Mississippi at a Country Club dealing drugs and worked pretty hard on my handicap. I'll ask Quint to go golfing if that'd help." Aiden felt solid and sure behind me.

This was all too good to be true. We should probably talk about us or what we wanted or something. "Aiden—"

A pipe groaned beneath the kitchen sink and then water burst out.

Aiden moved instantly, setting me aside and dropping to his knees. "Damn it." He reached for the wrench and ducked under, swearing in Gaelic. "Hey. Hand me the plug wrench, would you?" His voice was muffled.

"Sure." I walked in the water pooling on the floor and dug into the toolbox, handing over the plug wrench. This wasn't my first leaking pipe.

"Thanks." Aiden fiddled as water continued to pour.

"Sure." Yeah, I was a little smug I could help fix the sink. I stepped over his legs and my heel caught on his jeans. Crap. I scrambled for balance but slid farther, landing on his legs and hitting my head on the side of the counter. Water sprayed me right in the face, and I turned away to cough.

Aiden grasped my arm and set me out of the spray. "You okay?" He didn't even sound surprised.

"Yeah." I shook water out of my hair and it sprayed everywhere. My head didn't even hurt. My entire front side was soaked, however.

A sharp knock sounded from his door.

"That's the pizza. Get money from my wallet." He ducked back under the sink, his muscles moving nicely. The spray of water trickled and then stopped.

I wiped water off my face and shook out my shirt before taking cash out of his wallet, which was on the counter. I'd pay, but I didn't have any personal cash right now. Even in the bank. Then I wiped off my feet before walking out of the kitchen and through the empty living room to the door. I opened it, more than ready for dinner.

"Hi." A stunning and very curvy redhead stood on the porch—without a pizza.

I blinked water out of my eyes, acutely aware of the feeling of mascara running down my face. "Hi." I wiped off my cheeks and looked past her for a pizza car. Nope. "Can I help you?" New neighbor? Wonderful. She really was pretty.

Her eyes were a light blue that matched her frilly shirt that was tucked into dark jeans. She had the ability to look dressed up in jeans, which was something I'd always admired. The Chanel handbag over her shoulder completed a perfect look, along with the four-inch red checkered wedges. When she spoke, she had the perfect southern accent. The one that sounded like warm molasses sliding over your skin. "I'm looking for Aiden Devlin. Rumor has it he lives here."

Of course she was. "Yes. Can I tell him who's here?" More importantly, I wanted to know who she was.

She smiled full and red lips. "Tell him his wife needs to talk to him."

CHAPTER 2

The entire world lurched to a stop, and my mouth went dry. My brain fuzzed. The woman's lips moved again, but I couldn't hear her through the wild buzzing of bees that somehow had gotten into my head.

She poked me in the upper arm. "Hello?"

The woman had *poked* me? Oh, hell no. I swallowed. Kind of. "Aiden?" My voice came out a whisper, and I cleared my throat. "Aiden!"

He emerged from the kitchen with the wrench still in his hand. "What? I said that the money—" He stopped cold. Water dripped down his muscled chest. "Sasha?"

I blinked. In slow motion. I think I heard the blink.

"Hi, Honey." She smiled and muscled past me, using her generous hips to do so. "We need to talk." She didn't spare me another glance. "Tell your Twinkie to get lost."

Twinkie?

Aiden looked at her, at me, and paused.

He fucking paused?

"How dangerous?" He looked all business now.

She tilted her head.

"Shit," he muttered.

It was at that point that I lost it. "What are you two talking about?" My voice most likely reached all the way across the lake through the screen at the open sliding glass back door. When my lungs kicked in, they did so with gusto. I whirled on Aiden, slamming the door shut at the same time. "You're *married*?"

His way too blue eyes narrowed, and I could actually see him thinking it through. I recognized that look.

My temper beat him to the punch. "No. Absolutely not. Do not protect me for my own good. Do not keep secrets from me. Whatever you're doing, stop it right now," I bellowed.

Sasha winced. "This one is a little feisty." With her cute southern accent, she made the insult seem classy.

I clenched my fingers into a fist. Unconsciously. Well, mostly unconsciously.

Aiden held up a hand. The one without a wrench. "Hold it a minute. I am not married."

Yep. He knew the exact right thing to pause me in what would've been a spectacular moment of Irish/Italian temper. "Explain," I grit out, my teeth actually hurting.

Sasha looked around the empty living room. "We need a sofa, darling."

Aiden exhaled loudly. "Stop it." He tossed the wrench back into the kitchen where it bounced loudly against the toolbox. "Anna Albertini, meet Sasha Duponte. Sasha, Anna."

Sasha turned to me, all smiles. "Charmed." She held out a hand.

I looked at her perfectly painted nails and reached out to clasp palms. Then I met her gaze evenly. "The pleasure is mine."

Whatever she saw in my eyes had her smile sliding away and awareness finally filtering into her gaze. The shake was quick. "If you don't mind, I need to speak with Aiden alone."

"I do mind." As my equilibrium returned, my feet settled, and I focused on her instead of the Irish hottie I wanted to kick in the knee.

"Aiden?" She turned back to him, and the way she said his name with her accent was…intimate.

He looked at me. Tall, broad, and possibly about to break my heart. "Nope. Anna can stay."

Sasha sighed, and even that sound was feminine. "We need to speak alone. It's dangerous."

His bark of laugh was unexpected but eased something deep down inside me. "I've learned the hard way that when I try to protect Anna at arm's length, I end up getting shot. Or she gets something blown up. Whatever is going on, she knows the full story. Period."

Sasha glanced at me again, and there was surprise on her face this time. "I see."

"That's good," I said evenly. "How about you start with your lie that you're Aiden's wife?" Now my voice was all sugar and sweetness.

Her smile was catlike. "Ah, good times. We need to reprise the role, Devlin."

Aiden leaned back against the now dry primer we'd painted on the wall two days before. "Sasha is ATF, and we worked an undercover operation a few years back."

"I already figured that out," I said calmly. I would not panic. If this very sexy woman wanted to go undercover as Aiden's wife again, I would not panic. Nope. Not a chance.

He eyed her. "How did you find me?"

"Official channels," she admitted. "Finally caught wind of Saber and he gave me your brand new address." She looked at the far screen with its several rips. "Are you already undercover?"

Saber was one of Aiden's ATF SRT members, and until now, I'd liked the guy. A heads up would've been nice, or perhaps he didn't figure Aiden needed one with Sasha. Just how close had they been? From the way she was eating him up with her gaze, pretty darn close.

"No," Aiden said. "I just moved home."

9

The way he said the word *home* made my stomach squishy because it felt like he included me in that statement. Maybe I just wanted that, but by the stiffening of Sasha's shoulders, she reached the same conclusion. Not that my mood depended on a man, but still. I felt a lot of things for this one, and I also felt no need to delve into those feelings quite yet. Right now, my curiosity began to filter into the irritation of the day.

"What's the case?" Aiden asked.

Sasha took one more look at me and then apparently gave up trying to get rid of me. "How blown is your cover with the Lordes motorcycle club?"

Aiden frowned. "Most members were arrested and I replaced members with my ATF team, but we busted a gun trafficking operation undercover after that, and I'd say the cover is shaky. Not blown and no public record tying me with the ATF, but anybody trying to connect dots would be suspicious if they had half a brain."

I thought the Lordes were in the past. Wishful thinking.

"Why?" Aiden asked.

"I have a line on Barensky," she said.

He pushed off from the wall. The tension in the room heightened. "Barensky went under after we busted most of his organization. What kind of a line do you have?"

"I met with his representative in Denver, and I hinted that I had connections to a motorcycle club that would carry out a campaign for a lucrative payment," she said. "I knew about your investigation with the Lordes, and the location is perfect. Barensky's client is going to hit certain locations in Seattle, and Barensky doesn't have the manpower to deliver because of us."

Aiden rubbed the scruff across his rugged jaw. "Has the Op been sanctioned by headquarters?"

"Yes," Sasha said. "The director wants to meet with us in Seattle Wednesday, but I thought I'd speak with you first."

I bet she did. I'd tried to be patient. "Who's Barensky?"

Aiden was taking the op. I could tell.

"He's a terrorist who likes bombs. A lot," he said.

Great. Just when things were calming down. I knew that shoe would drop, but I had no clue it'd involve bombs and arrive in the form of a sexy Louboutin wedge worn on the foot of Aiden's ex.

* * *

THERE WASN'T enough pineapple on the pizza. I sighed and looked out at Lilac Lake from sitting on the edge of Aiden's spacious deck. The worn wooden planks were warm beneath my butt from being in the sun all day, and it wasn't a bad way to eat a very late lunch. "You need furniture out here," I mused.

"Yeah." He munched on a breadstick, also watching the shimmering blue lake. He'd been quiet since Sasha had taken her leave with a kiss to his cheek. It was a good thing her red lipstick had been the stain kind, probably the expensive good stuff, and hadn't left an imprint on his face.

"Did you love her?" I asked, my own words catching me off guard.

He watched a boat pull a talented water-skier across the bay, just beyond his small dock. "No."

I tipped back my beer bottle and let the brew cool my throat. "Did you sleep with her?"

"You know I did." He reached for his beer and drank it down, his voice still thoughtful. "We met on an Op and started dating during it. It's against the rules." Not a surprise. Aiden wasn't much for rules.

"Did you continue dating after the Op?" I wasn't sure I had a right to ask all of these questions, but he was answering them, so why not?

"Yes." He angled his head to watch as the water-skier smashed head first into the waves. The guy popped up, his laugh reaching across the water. Tall pine trees cast shadows over us but framed the view to the lake beyond grass that needed to be cut.

I gulped down more beer, wishing I'd brought a bottle of wine. Beer wasn't my thing. "Was the breakup bad?" I turned and watched Aiden's handsome profile, wondering again how his face had been carved so perfectly. Or maybe I was wearing those proverbial rose-colored glasses. It was entirely possible, but he was handsome, no matter the yardstick used to measure that fact. "Aiden?"

He lifted one strong shoulder. "I'm not sure we really broke up."

I coughed out beer. "What?"

He turned toward me, the blue of his eyes unreal. "We both were sent on other operations, and we lost touch. There was never a scene."

Or a conversation. "You ended a relationship without even talking about it?" I set the bottle down. How was that possible?

"Yeah." Then he looked back at the water-skier getting back up. "Why?"

"I just want to know what I'm dealing with here," I muttered.

He moved then. Sometimes I forgot how quickly he moved when he wanted. He leaned over, grasped my hip and shoulder, and lifted me right off the deck to sit on his lap, facing him.

My eyebrows shot up and heat shot down to my abdomen. Surprise kept me quiet.

"You're dealing with me and I'm dealing with you," he murmured, his gaze dropping to my mouth. "I like the fact that a fading relationship confuses you because you'd never have one of those. You're all in, baby."

Sometimes he called me 'baby,' and I know I should get irritated about that. I'm a strong, professional, badass of a woman. But I melted instead. I've never thought I was completely sane, so who cared? "Are you all in?" I whispered.

"I am." He leaned in and kissed me, his lips firm but his movements gentle. Leaning back, he kept both arms around my waist, making me feel all secure and safe. "You and I are new, and we're just starting whatever this is. This is also the first time I've settled down in one place since I left town at eighteen, so let's not look for problems. Sasha is in my past."

"She's back," I said, humor gliding through me along with desire from the feeling of his firm thighs beneath me.

He kissed my nose. "I noticed. It's business, though."

It was sweet that he thought so. Sometimes the smartest of men were morons when it came to women. I'd seen women flirt with my dad before, and the guy had had no clue. I mean, none. While I believed Aiden to be a bit more aware, if he thought Sasha wasn't going to make a move on him, he was beyond clueless. It was my decision whether to trust him or not. Considering he'd saved my life when we had just been kids, I had always trusted him. Of course, that was before we'd started dating and I all but handed him my heart. "I did enjoy our three days of normalcy," I mused.

He laughed. Man, he had a great laugh. Deep and rolling with just a hint of Ireland in it. He'd moved to the states to live with his grandparents in his teens, and sometimes that brogue came through. "Three days is a record for us."

Wasn't it, though? "I'm not the jealous type," I said, mostly to myself. Yeah, Sasha was all curves and pretty eyes, but I was me, and I was fine with that. I'd never have curves like that, but I filled out a decently full B cup, my hips were a little curvy, and Aiden liked my eyes. They were a combo green/gray that looked plain to me, but he seemed to like them. Which was nice.

"You have nothing to be jealous about," he said, which was also nice. "I'll find out the details of this Op, and you and I will come up with a plan for us that works. If I have to go undercover with Sasha and the Lordes, it might get sticky, but if I've learned anything, it's that you can handle sticky. Or blow it up." He grinned.

Unfortunately, he wasn't wrong. I smacked his shoulder. "You're just relieved I'll be busy getting the law firm up and started."

"Yes, I am."

The sound of a large truck lumbered from the front of the cabin.

Aiden looked over his shoulder. "Finally. My stuff from the storage unit in Los Angeles is here."

"Furniture?" I asked hopefully.

He winced. "There might be a bar stool or two."

Great. Knowing Aiden, there'd be guns, sporting equipment, and probably a Kevlar vest or two. "We need to go furniture shopping." With our schedules? Yeah. We'd be sitting on the floor eating together in the coming autumn.

He stood and put us both on our feet. "Let's unpack the van."

I glanced at my watch. "You're on your own, pal. I have a cousin to rescue."

Aiden slung an arm around my shoulders. "I almost feel sorry for the guy."

Fair enough.

CHAPTER 3

I wore a light summer dress to Tratto's Italian Restaurant overlooking Lilac Lake, which was much larger than my sweet Tamarack Lake, although only twenty minutes away. Tratto's had been in business since the turn of the century, and it had the best restaurant lasagna west of the Rockies. My two sisters were already waiting on the deck with a bottle of Leonetti Cabernet breathing on the table.

"Somebody had a good month," I said, taking my seat and reaching to pour a glass.

"Not me," Tessa said, sipping delicately. Tessa looked like our mom and the Irish side of our family with her reddish-blonde hair and clear green eyes. She was the middle child, once the wildest one, and she'd always been good at sports. Right now, she was working as a waitress at Smiley's Diner, which was just a few blocks away in Timber City.

Donna sat back. "I sold a lake house to a family from California for double the asking price. Real Estate is going nuts in Idaho right now." Donna, the oldest of us three, looked like the Italian side of our family with her black hair and sparkling brown eyes. She was a realtor and had always been one of the smartest people in the room. Any room.

"Cool." I took a sip of the robust wine and felt my bones melt into happiness. I didn't look like either side of the family with my brown hair and greenish-gray eyes, and mailman jokes were a staple when people looked at the three of us. I was the youngest and wasn't sure how I would've navigated life without my two sisters plowing a way for me—at least until I decided to attend law school. At that point, I was on my own and now felt like I could help them out once in a while. It was a good feeling.

A twittering set up inside the restaurant.

Tessa chuckled. "Quint must've arrived."

Our cousin strode onto the deck, and my heart sank. Quint was a good looking guy with the Albertini genes. Dark hair, dark eyes, tall and broad. But now his eyes were too dark, they matched the circles beneath his eyes, and he limped slightly.

"Crap," Tessa said under her breath.

Right behind him came Zena, his beautiful black Labrador. She bounded up to me, knowing of our mutual love. I dropped from the chair and wrapped both arms around her, snuggling into her warm coat. "Heard it was a rough one, girl," I murmured.

She panted happily into my ear.

Then I stood and snuggled into Quint's chest. "Thanks for coming."

"Did I have a choice?" he asked wryly, hugging both of my sisters before dropping into a chair and motioning the waiter over to order a Moscow Mule.

I gave Donna a look. That was good. When Quint moved for Scotch right off the bat, it was a bad sign. A Moscow Mule was middle of the road for Quint-stress. Although the lines spreading out from his eyes and the tense set of his jaw still worried me. "So. What's new?" I retook my seat.

His grin eased some of my worry. "I'm fine, cousins. It was a bad one and we found a few bodies, which always sucks. But Zena is the best." He planted a hand on the dog's head, and she rewarded him by flopping down over his feet.

Donna cleared her throat. "I thought I'd also give you the heads up that Chrissy has been on a few dates with Trick."

I gaped. Trick was a distant cousin, and Chrissy was Quint's ex. "She has not."

Donna nodded. "Yeah."

Quint accepted the Moscow Mule from the waitress and drank it in three gulps.

Tessa winced.

I kept stoic. "She wasn't right for you, anyway." I liked the woman, but she just wasn't it for Quint. He had a dangerous job, and she made him feel guilty about it. If you loved a guy, you had to let him be himself. "You're better off single." But he wasn't. Quint was the type of guy who liked being with somebody, and he was a good partner for sure.

"You'll find somebody," Tessa said, patting his hand.

He looked down at his dog. "I have somebody." Then he grinned. "Zena's the best."

On that note, we ordered way too much food and enjoyed it way too much. By the time we finished with dinner, we were all nicely buzzed and thought going to Dunphey's Bar in town was a good idea. I was the best to drive because I'd been careful with the wine, so everyone piled into my small Fiat, and we wound along the lake road into town, where Dunphey's was hopping. I parked by the curb.

Quint untangled himself from Tessa and fell out of the car. "Why is the bar so busy on a Sunday night?"

"Beer Bingo," Tessa said, sliding her arm through his as she stood.

I followed them inside with Donna on my heels. We miraculously found a tall table toward the back, grabbed bingo cards, and ordered a couple pitchers of beer and a carafe of wine. The place smelled like wood, sawdust, and beer. Comfortable and homey.

Quint seemed better already, and the cute waitress kept flirting with him, so that was good.

I drank a couple glasses of wine and realized I wouldn't be able to drive anybody home, so I texted Aiden to see what he was doing.

The bartender rang a bell. "Shots only a dollar for five minutes."

I jumped up. "I'll get them." Who knows what Quint would've chosen? So I wound my way through the crowd to the bar and leaned over to speak to Joey, the bartender. "Four shots of Fireball." It was the safest bet.

"Sure thing." Joey was about fifty with a bald head, huge muscles, and an intriguing scar over his clavicle. He always had a smile for us, but nobody knew much about him. Well, except that his last name was Dunphey.

I managed to twist my fingers around the shot glasses with two in each hand and turned around to nearly run over Sasha. I paused. "What are you doing here?" It was then that I noticed the two women flanking her. Both wore black tank tops with the Lorde's logo on them and very short, way too short, jean shorts. They were in their late twenties, one blonde and one brunette—both taller than me. I kind of recognized the brunette as the old lady of one of the Lorde's members who'd been caught up in the drug bust and was now probably in jail. "Sasha?"

She elbowed closer. For tonight, she'd changed out of her fancy outfit into a jean skirt and low cut dark blue blouse. Her hair was sprayed high and a black choker wound around her neck. Her makeup was minimal except for the bright red lipstick. "I heard you were fucking around with my man while I was back visiting my dying grandma."

I'd had too much to drink to follow that. "What are you talking about?"

The two women with her sneered almost identically at me. Their glares trickled awareness through my very pleasant buzz.

Sasha leaned in, grabbed my hair, and yanked my ear to her mouth. "Go along with this. I'm sorry. When I punch, pull back, and fake a fall." She shook me and stepped away.

Oh, crap. My hands were full of shot glasses. "Sasha—"

She pulled back and punched.

I reacted instinctively, dropped the shots, and turned my face. Unfortunately, there was a tall guy next to me, and I didn't dodge very well. Her fist impacted my left cheekbone, and pain ricocheted through my head. I turned back to face her, gaping.

She quickly hid a wince. "That will teach you. Let's go."

"What the hell?" A female snap caught us as Tessa leaped through bodies and tackled Sasha into the bar.

"No," I yelled, just as one of Sasha's friends punched me in the mouth. Blood spurted from my lip. I turned and Donna took her down to the ground, my classy sister knowing how to fight dirty when necessary. "Stop—" I tried to yell.

The third woman screeched and grabbed my hair with both hands, pulling.

Pain ripped through my skull. "What are you doing?" I yelled as the patrons scattered to watch the girl fight. Donna and the woman on the floor rolled around in the sawdust and knocked over several bar stools. One landed on my foot, but I was too busy trying to keep my hair attached to my head. "Let go." I tried to grab her wrists.

She pulled harder and kicked me in the knee at the same time.

My temper finally blew. "That's it," I gasped, shooting my arms up and between hers to break her hold. "Don't pull hair in a fight, you jackass." When I had my head free, I reared back and punched her square in the nose.

She yelped, grabbed her nose, and doubled over.

I turned to help Donna up, but I underestimated my opponent. She grabbed me around the waist and threw me to the floor. Slivers cut into my palms. I flipped around quickly, just in time to see her drop with her nails aimed for my face. Yelping, I grabbed her wrists before she could do any damage. Grunting and swearing, we grappled. Sawdust covered my hair and flew across my face. She tried to get one leg over me, but I levered a foot beneath my butt and shoved us both over. I pushed her to the side and stood, trying to get my balance back.

Blood flowed from her nose. I think I'd broken it.

A camera phone came out of the crowd and took several pictures with a flash. I blinked stars out of my eyes and groaned when I saw that the phone belonged to Jolene O'Sullivan, a local reporter who disliked me as much as I disliked her. She smiled and took more pictures.

Donna stood up and yanked a bleeding woman up with her. Their hair was all over, and both were covered in sawdust and panting wildly.

Tessa and Sasha were going at it pretty well on the floor, and considering Sasha was a trained governmental agent, I was absurdly proud of my sister.

"Stop it." Aiden Devlin shoved through the crowd from the door. He must've gotten my text or had already been heading out to find us. Quint came from the other direction. Aiden grabbed Sasha while Quint pulled Tessa away from her and put his body between them. "What in the holy hell is going on?" Aiden's voice was dangerously quiet, and for some reason, he directed the question to me.

Sasha jerked free of him. "I heard about you two and had to do something about it." Her right cheekbone was already swelling, and her hair looked like it had spilled beer mixed with sawdust in it.

Aiden took in the scene as realization obviously dawned. He looked at Joey behind the bar. "Send me the bill for any damage." Then he pointed to the door. "Outside. Now."

Quint ushered Donna, Tessa, and me outside into the warm night, and we all stood near my car. Zena bounded out of the trees where she'd been sleeping and panted happily next to me.

Aiden brought Sasha and the other two women outside. "Sasha? I'll deal with you later. The three of you go back to the complex. Now." The hard edge of his voice made me want to go, too. Hopefully this was part of his cover. Yeah. It had to be. I swallowed rapidly.

Sasha lifted on her toes and kissed him on the mouth. I had to give it to her. She had balls. "All right, babe. Say goodbye to that bitch, and we'll move on from here." She motioned for her posse, and they all headed for a light blue convertible parked down the street.

Aiden waited until they'd driven off. "Are you okay?"

"Okay?" Tessa exploded. "What in the world is going on?"

I grimaced. "I didn't have time to tell you everything." Anything, really. We'd concentrated only on funny stories and childhood memories to ease Quint's mind during dinner. "It's okay."

Donna put her hands on her hips. "No, it is not."

Aiden hung his head. "Seriously."

Quint looked at him and then the three of us. He laughed, long and hard. Then he snorted. "It's good to be home." It was a real laugh, and there was humor in his eyes.

I smiled and ignored my pounding lip. Oh, to see Quint better, it was totally worth it. Then I caught sight of Aiden's expression.

Maybe it was worth it.

CHAPTER 4

J stretched awake in Donna's big bed and then winced as my face ached. Dreading the sight, I slipped out of bed and padded into her light pink master bathroom. Yep. Bruised cheek and fat lip. I took in a couple of the bruises on my neck. It had been a good fight.

Donna strode in, already dressed and ready for the day in a lightweight mint colored suit with yellow Naughty Monkey heels. Her dark hair was up, and makeup covered any bruises. She held two cups of coffee in her hands. "I can't believe we got into a fight."

I reached for the coffee like it was the answer to all questions in the universe. "I know. I'm sorry about that."

She bump-hit me with her hip. "I jumped in—made a choice." Leaning toward the mirror, she fixed her already perfect makeup. "Hopefully mom hasn't heard yet, but you know she will. For now, I can drop you off at your car if you're ready in fifteen minutes."

I took a drag of the strong coffee and felt the instant jolt through my system. "If I can borrow something to wear, I can be ready. We're just finishing the office for opening day tomorrow."

"Sure." Her eyes sparkled.

I took a deep breath. "How bad is the picture in the paper?"

"No picture and no article. Maybe Jolene couldn't write one since we all left and there wasn't anybody to interview?" Donna moved toward her spacious closet.

"I don't have that kind of luck," I admitted, following her.

I quickly showered and then dressed in borrowed jeans and a frilly shirt. I had my own toothbrush at Donna's charming crafts-man-style house and just used some of her makeup. After tossing my hair up in a ponytail, I met my sisters in the kitchen where they were still drinking coffee. "Has anybody heard from Quint? Did he make it home okay last night?" While Aiden had dropped us off at Donna's, Quint had seen a couple of buddies and had decided to stay and have another drink. He'd promised to call for a taxi home.

Tessa shook her head. "No, but he's probably sleeping it off." She had one bruise along her jaw and scratches on her left arm, but other than that looked all right.

"You were awesome last night," I said, nudging her in the arm. "Sasha is ATF. You kicked butt."

Tessa chuckled. "That was crazy." She glanced at the face of her phone. "Oh. We have to go. I have a shift in an hour and really need a shower." Yeah, she still had sawdust in her hair.

I looked longingly at the coffee pot.

Donna grinned and reached in the cupboard for a travel cup, which she poured to the brim and handed over. It was silver with a faded dog on it.

I took it. "I love you. If you ever need a kidney, mine is all yours. Any time."

"You already promised me a kidney," Tessa tossed over her shoulder as she walked toward the front door.

I sucked down more coffee and followed her. "You can fight over it. After last night, I don't know who'd I'd vote on winning it." Bottom line was that even though we were too old and hopefully too classy to get into bar fights, both of my sisters hadn't hesitated before jumping in when I was in trouble. "I love you guys."

Donna locked the door and followed us from the porch. "Have you noticed how much more interesting life has become since Anna came back from law school six months ago?"

"I truly have," Tessa chortled. "Rather, I hadn't realized how boring life had become before that."

I rolled my eyes. "Life is about to get boring again. I am finished with bar fights, shootouts, and going undercover for anything. Clark and I will have a professional and mellow law office where we figure out billable hours and budgets." Even as I said the words, I wondered if I could make that happen.

Trouble seemed to follow me sometimes.

Considering both of my sisters laughed—hard—I figured they'd need some convincing.

Donna drove a spotless SUV and first dropped Tessa off at her apartment before winding around the lake and stopping at the restaurant, where my old and trusty red Fiat awaited me. My grandpa had refurbished the car with me, and I loved it.

"Thanks," I said, jumping out.

"You bet. I'll see you at your opening tomorrow," she said, sliding her sunglasses back over her eyes.

I hurried across the heated asphalt to the driver's side door as she drove away. A truck parked beneath the tree right by the restaurant caught my eye. I squinted and looked closer. Wait a minute. It was Quint's truck. I dug my phone out of my purse and dialed his number.

"Yo, Annabella," he answered. "How's your face?"

"Fine. How's your head?" I returned, relaxing instantly.

He chuckled. "It's clear."

"Did you get a ride home last night?" I asked, looking at his truck again.

"Yeah. A buddy gave me a ride, and I'm getting the truck now.

Seriously, though. Is everyone okay today?" he asked, sounding like he didn't have a headache at all.

Those Albertini boys could drink. They really could.

I opened my door. "We're all fine. My face is the worst, but some decent makeup will cover it up. I'm sorry there was a huge blowout your first night back. In fact, that was my first bar fight." I could've gone my whole life without being in a bar fight, in fact. Oh well.

"Hopefully your last. Okay. I'll see you tomorrow at your opening. Bye, Cuz." He clicked off.

I breathed out. Good. Quint seemed okay now. Yeah, that's what a crazy night of family could do for a guy. I opened my door and let some of the heat out.

A black convertible BMW rolled by and pulled into the lot close to Quint's truck.

I paused.

Quint jumped out.

I looked closer to see Jolene Sullivan in the driver's seat. The Jolene Sullivan who'd once dated Aiden in high school and had most recently posted pictures of me in the paper that were not flattering. At all. My gut clenched.

She smiled, the sight calculating.

Quint turned, caught my expression, and winced.

Forget a night with the family helping him. Quint had gone home with my nemesis.

Well, one of them.

* * *

I ORGANIZED the file folders in the tallest cabinet in my office, which was at the rear of my law firm. While I'd initially chosen a different office suite down the hall for the firm, my Uncle Sean, who owned the building, ended up offering us this space, which was at the very end of the building and had more room. We would have to pay rent sooner, but that was all right to get the extra space. Clark and I had jumped on the opportunity. Right now, I didn't have time to count my fortunes. I could not believe Quint had gone home with Jolene Sullivan.

"Maybe they didn't sleep together," Donna said through the speaker on my phone, which rested on the windowsill.

"Ha. If Jolene took Quint home with her, it was for one reason," I countered. Normally I didn't care who my cousin played mattress hockey with, but this was Jolene. The woman who really didn't like me. Plus, she wasn't nice. "I'm totally into the sisterhood and supporting women and never cutting one down, but it's difficult with that one."

Donna snorted. "She has come after you a couple of times. It's okay to let go of the sisterhood with her." Considering Jolene had slept with Donna's prom date way back when, it wasn't a surprise to get this advice from her.

"Anna?" A deep voice bellowed down the hallway. "I have your desks."

I reached for the phone. "Cousin Rory is here. I'll call you back." Sliding the phone into my back pocket, I strode into the hallway and past two small vacant offices, the restrooms, two conference rooms, and Clark's office before reaching the reception area. I stopped cold at seeing my cousin Rory Albertini with his brother. Quint, the traitor.

Quint had the grace to blush. Maybe a little. Okay, I might've just wished he'd blushed.

"Quintino," I muttered.

He sighed.

Rory looked at his brother and then back at me. They had similar dark hair, brown eyes, and broad shoulders, but Rory was a few years younger than Quint. "What's going on?"

"Quint slept with my nemesis." I put my hands on my hips.

Quint's lips barely lifted in a grin. "You do not have a nemesis, and believe me, we didn't sleep at all last night."

I might've growled. Just a little bit.

Just then, my new law partner Clark Bunne barreled in behind them, his glasses askew and his jeans dirty. "All right. On the way in I checked out all of the storage areas in the basement, and believe me, we want to use the ones in our office here if possible." He paused. "What in the world happened to your face?"

I gingerly touched my aching cheekbone. "Bar fight last night —totally wasn't my fault."

Clark blew out air. His black hair was cut very short, which accented his angled facial features. His skin was a deep brown, and his eyes a shade darker with sharp intelligence shining in them. "You can't get in bar fights. We're starting a new law firm." He shook his head, and surprisingly enough, I felt like I'd disappointed him. Clark had been a public defender when I worked briefly as a prosecuting attorney, and we'd both been fired on the same day. He was patient, brilliant, and oddly cautious when it came to opening a law office with me. "Tell me you didn't get arrested."

"Of course not." I kept my voice calm. The last thing I needed was Clark ending our fledgling partnership. He was a good guy and he had more trial experience than I did. In fact, I barely had any. "It was a silly misunderstanding."

"You have a lot of those," Clark observed.

The guy wasn't wrong. "Clark Bunne, please meet my cousins, Quintino and Rory Albertini," I said. When all else failed, I'd learned to fall back on manners.

They all shook hands.

"We have your desks down in the van," Rory said. "They're all polished up per your requests, and you're gonna love them."

I bounced on my heels. Clark and I had found some great desks at an old antique store, and Rory refurbished wood furniture in his spare time, so we'd taken the furniture to him up in Silverville, which was a small mining town through the mountain pass where most of my family lived. "You have to send us a bill."

"It's on me as a congrats for opening your own law firm. Don't argue." Rory turned and headed out of the office.

We all followed. The office was on the third floor of a brick building holding all businesses. We unloaded the desks, and they were amazing. Mine was a light and polished pine with a glass top. It was delicate and sturdy at the same time, and it matched my file cabinets perfectly. Clark's was a more modern wood and cement desk, and the receptionist's desk was wide and I think a cherry maple or something like that. Rory did a fantastic job, and by the time we'd finished unloading everything, I had forgiven Quint.

Not that he'd done anything wrong to me. But still.

The Albertini brothers left while Clark and I perused the conference table. It was an old picnic table I'd borrowed from my Nana O'Shea. Compared to our desks, it looked pretty sad.

"We'll get a new one as soon as we have extra money," I promised Clark.

He nodded. "Are you ready for tomorrow?"

"Sure. It's just a cocktail party." One where our friends and families were bringing food and drink. I smiled. "My office is as good as it's going to get tonight. Do you want to eat an early dinner?"

His smile was a charming flash of white against his dark skin. "I already have plans."

Curiosity grabbed me. "Do tell."

"Not a chance. Go home, and I'll see you tomorrow after I finish with my office and then meet my friend for dinner." He patted my shoulder with his wide hand and then walked back to his office.

Interesting. Who was Clark seeing?

I retrieved my purse and headed down the hallway to the stairs, and then I turned for the back door where the private parking area in the alley was situated. The sun was going down, but considering it was August, it was still plenty warm. Donna's wedges were comfortable on my feet as I maneuvered around some cracks in the concrete to my car, where I opened the driver's side door to let hot air escape.

A truck screeched down the alley and stopped. Sasha jumped out with her two cronies. Then two more women slid out of the back seat. All of them wore black Lorde's tank tops and jeans, and under different circumstances, it'd be interesting to study the tattoos on a couple of them. Sasha reached into the truck, turned toward me, and pointed a potato gun at my chest.

A real potato gun.

Oh, crap.

CHAPTER 5

"*W*hat are you doing?" I asked calmly, focusing on Sasha and ignoring the other women. One of them cracked her knuckles, and the sound echoed back from the brick building.

Sasha hefted the long PVC pipe in her arms. "Making a point. Aiden and I made up last night at the Lordes' apartment complex, but I thought you and I should come to our own understanding. We were interrupted last night."

Was she undercover? If so, she was seriously good at it. However, I could always rat her out to her buddies. Surely she knew that.

I set my stance. "You know, you don't seem like the potato gun type, Sasha." True story.

"It's a potato cannon," she returned easily. "They fire farther."

I shook my head and studied the device. "In Idaho, they're all potato guns. Don't get fancy." Her gun was decent. The PVC pipe was a light gray and looked like it had been cut and primed fairly well. Growing up in Idaho, I'd made more than my fair share of potato guns to shoot at trees or into the lake. Sasha had what looked like four inch PVC pipe connected to two inch, which made the barrel. "You loaded?"

"Oh, yeah," she said, her smile gleeful. "Got a spud in the gun and I've already filled the opening with hairspray."

I pursed my lips. "That's called the combustion chamber. Good hairspray or the cheap stuff?"

"Cheap stuff," the blonde to her right said. "It's better."

That was true. When it came to igniting a potato gun, the cheaper the hairspray, the better. No question. "This close a potato projectile could cause some serious damage," I said. If Sasha didn't know that, she needed to understand.

"Good," she said, licking her lips.

All righty, then.

"Stay away from Devlin," she said. Her friend ignited a lighter and handed it to Sasha. She smiled.

Crap.

She stuck the lighter into the ignition hole.

The potato fired out and I ducked inside my car. The explosive hit the rear panel and dented it with a loud crunch. Fury caught me, and I leaned over to yank my gun out of my purse, stepping out and pointing it at her. "Drop the potato gun," I snapped.

Sasha's eyebrows rose. Both of them. "Hey. Give me another potato."

The blonde reached back into the truck. She still wore bruises from fighting with me.

"Forget the potato, lady," I ordered.

Sasha glared at my gun. "Put that down."

"No," I growled, stepping toward her with my hands steady on my gun. "Listen here, ladies. This is a Lady Smith & Wesson nine-millimeter, and it beats a potato gun any day of the week. Especially since my weapon is loaded and now yours is not. Get your asses back into the truck." I was so finished messing around with Sasha, even if she was undercover. She'd just dented my car. The car I loved.

They all scrambled back into the truck—except for Sasha. She moved toward me, her generous hips swaying. When she reached me, she let the potato gun dangle. "Sorry about this," she whispered.

"Me too. Drop the potato gun," I said, keeping mine now pointed at her leg. "I will shoot your foot." Ah, probably not. But she didn't know me well enough to make a determination.

She faltered.

Yeah, I knew how long it took to make a good potato gun, and losing one sucked. The Lordes men would not be happy to have it confiscated like this. She studied my eyes and then gently set the gun to lean against the dent in my car.

"You're taking this undercover crap a little far, don't you think?" I whispered, keeping my expression as mean as I could since the other women were watching.

"No," she whispered back, her lipstick still a bright red. "I need their trust and respect."

We were about the same height, but that was all. "Do you think you have it? With a freaking potato gun?" I asked.

"There was some sort of dustup between the guys last week, and they settled it with a potato gunfight. We've been drinking, and this seemed like a good idea at the time," she said. "Aiden mentioned last night that you were opening a law firm and to stay out of your way, so it was easy to find the location, and I figured you'd be here." She hiccupped. "Ug. Cheap booze."

Yeah, she did smell like whiskey. I shook my head. "What you all do to go undercover is a lot. Do you even know who you are any longer?" Not that it was any of my business. Well, except she did just shoot a potato at my car. I guess that did give me rights.

Her chin went up. "Oh, I know exactly who I am. In fact, I think I claimed my man last night at the complex, so yeah. Shooting potatoes at you is just the cherry on the top."

If she'd meant to throw me off, she failed. While I knew Aiden would do many things for an undercover operation, hurting me wasn't one of them. Sasha obviously wanted me to ask her about last night, and it wasn't going to happen. "Then I assume you're finished with this silliness?" I asked.

Surprise filtered through her expression that she quickly hid. "Not sure, but you made your point. I wasn't expecting you to be armed."

I'd been armed with some type of weapon from the day I'd been kidnapped as a ten-year-old and saved by Aiden Devlin. First knives and now a gun. "I think we understand each other, then," I said. "Right?"

"Right. Just agree to leave Devlin alone for the duration, and I'll say you gave in to my friends, and we'll leave you alone," Sasha said.

I studied her. "Is this all part of your cover?"

For the first time, she faltered. Just enough for me to notice. "No."

"That's what I thought," I said, my hold loosening a fraction on my gun.

"Devlin and I were good together and I want to see what we could have," she said evenly.

I respected the honesty, especially since she seemed to be playing games with the undercover crap. In addition, I did understand the Lordes motorcycle club, and she would need the respect of the members and their old ladies if she was going to get anything done, especially something dangerous with a terrorist. "I understand your job and the importance of it," I said quietly as the other women craned their necks to see us talking.

Her smile was a little catlike. "So you'll stay out of my way?"

Man, I was having problems with the sisterhood these days. I let her see me without the mask of anger. Without anything. "Do your best, Sasha. It won't matter if I stay out of your way or not."

Her shoulders hunched as if she were threatening me, and since the women couldn't see her face, it was probably a pretty good act. "You sound incredibly confident, Albertini."

I smiled, making sure I didn't look nice, just in case. "I am. You do whatever you need to do, play games, don't play games, whatever." I leaned toward her, and this time, I wasn't performing for the audience. "It doesn't matter. At the end of the day, at the end of *any* day, Aiden Devlin will choose me."

Her nostrils flared. "And why is that?"

I reached down, secured the potato gun, and tossed it in my backseat before slipping into my car. "Because I chose him."

* * *

I DROVE toward my garage near my peaceful lake, unsurprised to see the Harley sitting to one side. Stepping out of my car, I walked along the petunias I'd planted all around my homey cottage. I rented the guest house of an estate on the lake and loved my little place. Once inside, I caught wind of Aiden on the back deck by the grill, beer in hand.

I dropped my purse on the sofa, walked to the kitchen to pour myself a glass of Cabernet that was open and breathing on the counter, and then headed out into the warm early evening. "What's on the grill?"

"Steaks." He lifted the lid, studied the steaks, and then shut it before turning to me.

There was something about a hot guy holding a cold beer bottle. I don't know why. His black tee stretched across his broad chest, and his faded jeans led to badass motorcycle boots. His dark hair curled a bit beneath his ears and needed a good cut, while his eyes were a deep sapphire blue in the waning sun. "How's the face?"

"Fine," I said, taking a sip of my wine. "I don't think Sasha expected a fight when she punched me."

Aiden's cheek creased. "Not everyone understands the danger of the Albertini Three." He shook his head. "I've had more friends text me about the fight than you'd expect. Seeing Tessa and Donna fly through a crowd and tackle people was a new one on everyone." He moved toward me and ran a gentle knuckle down my aching cheekbone. "I also heard you gave better than you got."

I knew how to fight. "I tried to stop it, but then it was all too late."

"It usually is." He ducked his head to study my lip. The swelling had gone down, but my mouth was still tender. "You keep getting hurt around me."

"You weren't even there," I said reasonably, my body reacting instantly to his. "Sasha wants another chance with you." Might as well get it all out there and now.

"Yeah. I know," he said, tilting my head to the side by clasping my chin. "You have a bruise on your neck." He leaned down to kiss my cheekbone, fat lip, and bruised neck. "You know how much I dislike seeing bruises on you." Then he kissed them all again for good measure. "I told Sasha that you and I were together."

"I told her the same thing," I said, my wounds somehow feeling better just from his kiss.

One of his dark eyebrows rose. "You did?"

"Yep." I loved how gentle he could be with me.

"To tick her off?" He brushed my hair away from my face.

Surprise caught me. "No. Because it's the truth."

His grin showed a rare dimple in his left cheek. "I like you, *Aingeal*."

Aiden was as solid as they came, and yet, I still felt the sand shifting beneath my feet with him. He'd saved my life as a kid, and I'd harbored a huge crush on him for years, even though he'd all but disappeared. Then he returned, and we started something fast during several dangerous moments. It was way too early for the 'where are we going' insecurities, but I didn't feel settled.

"What's going through that big brain of yours?" he murmured, his brogue light enough to compete with the slight breeze.

"Too much," I admitted. Yeah, I needed to halt my horses and just relax into the moment. Enjoy the moment. We didn't have to get too serious or too deep right now, so why was I looking for problems? If whatever we had could be demolished by a sexy redhead who couldn't even aim a potato gun, it wasn't worth worrying about.

His phone buzzed and he tugged it from his pocket to place at his ear. "Devlin." No brogue. One eyebrow lifted. "I thought it was Wednesday. No. I need to—" He listened for several more moments. "Fine. Got it." He clicked off and faced me again.

Ah. I pressed my lips together. "Don't tell me. Your meeting with your boss Wednesday in Seattle was moved up to tomorrow."

One dark eyebrow arched. "How did you know?"

Good guess. So he was going to miss my law firm opening. Nice move, Sasha. "Don't worry about the opening tomorrow. It's just a cocktail party, and it's the same people you see at the Albertini family barbecue every Sunday. Mostly." There should be a few law colleagues and maybe even a potential client or two, hopefully. Aiden had already helped put the office together, and it wasn't like he'd miss anything.

"Are you sure?" He leaned in and kissed me, all strength and male.

"Yeah. Definitely." I kissed him back.

"Good." He pulled back, his eyes a deepening blue. "James Saber and I are headed over to pitch the operation because Sasha has something going on with the Lordes' old ladies. Her cover is good, and she's getting more info from the few real former members than I probably could."

I'm embarrassed to admit, even to myself, that I was pleased Sasha wasn't headed off to the Emerald City with Aiden. "Then we better make good use of our night." I grinned.

He sighed. "Raincheck. Let's eat dinner because afterward, I have to head to the Lorde's complex and help put the plan together that we're going to pitch."

Of course he did.

CHAPTER 6

I strode into my new law office, excitement, pride, and definite nervousness quickening my pace. I was a couple of hours early for the opening, *and my hands* were full of boxes.

"What do you have?" Oliver Duck rushed from the receptionist's desk to help me. Oliver was eighteen with short claret colored hair, broad shoulders, and bright red ears. I'd hired him to help out at the law office after defending him in court, mainly because he was a good kid without anybody in the world.

"Just some file folders and knick-knack things to place around the office." I dumped the remaining boxes on his desk.

Behind the desk, my cousin Pauley was organizing two of the four file cabinets. He didn't look up. "You have no money and should not be buying knick-knacks." Pauley was from the O'Shea side of the family and was already in college, even though he was only sixteen. He had dark hair, soft brown eyes, and I adored him.

"I only bought a few. How are the case files coming?" I pushed my hair back into a semblance of order.

"They're color coded." Pauley turned and looked at me briefly before breaking eye contact and returning to his task. He had autism with savant qualities and never kept eye contact for long.

Oliver started pulling business card holders out of a box. "Hey. I saw your and Clark's cards. Do Pauley and I get cards, even though we're only here part-time?"

I smoothed down my flowered navy blue skirt that I'd paired with a light white blouse. "Sure. Just order them separately from Cardley's online and use different email addresses for each of you, so you can get the first 500 free. They have free two-day shipping."

Oliver grinned, and his cheeks turned even redder. "Awesome. What should we put? Pauley?"

"I am a file clerk," Pauley said. "Perhaps office organizer?"

Oliver shook his head. "I don't want to put 'receptionist' on mine."

I waved a hand in the air. "Pick whatever titles that fit. Clark and I just have 'Partner' on ours, so make it simple. Have fun with it." I strode into Clark's office, where he was finishing placing his diplomas and law licenses on the wall. Aiden and I had placed mine a few days ago. "Looks great."

Clark turned around, today dressed in pressed tan pants, blue shirt, and fancy tie. "Thanks."

"You clean up nice, Clark," I teased.

"I know." He grinned. "Can you believe this? We're law part-ners in our own firm." Then he blew out air, and panic replaced the awe across his expression. "Our little start-up fund from the ATF won't last us long. We need clients and don't have any." He swept a hand around. "We just rented a huge office with no clients or income. What were we thinking?"

I smiled. It was reassuring that I was the calm one for once. "We'll get clients. That's why we're having a grand opening and have used our last few dollars to place ads in the newspaper and on Facebook." I partially turned to call out. "How's the website and Facebook page doing, P?"

"Good," Pauley returned, still working on the case files. "Oliver will take pictures tonight of the opening, and we will add those to both sites. I will not be taking pictures. No pictures. No crowds. No pictures. No pictures. No. Not me. No pictures."

"Perfect. Thanks," I said, turning back to Clark. "We've totally got this."

He put down the hammer. "You're totally full of it, you know?"

"I'm aware," I agreed, excitement still buzzing through me. "We even have staff. We're big time."

He snorted. "Our staff consists of your cousin and a kid working off a debt to you."

I bit the inside of my cheek. "The debt is paid off. We're paying them both." I couldn't ask Oliver to work for free, and I hadn't done much for him. He'd been arrested for trespassing on a farmer's land, and after I'd talked to the farmer, he'd actually hired Oliver part-time in exchange for room and board. They'd both been lonely, and I think it had worked out well.

Clark studied me. "We have to take paying clients, Albertini. You know that, right?"

"Of course," I said. I did enjoy eating, after all.

Clark didn't look convinced. "I mean it. At first, we really have to concentrate on getting lucrative. Then you can take pet projects and help out humanity. We have to keep afloat so we can help out people. Right?"

"Right," I said.

"You are such a softie," he muttered, but he didn't sound that unhappy about it. "That's good, but let's try and get a few corporate clients right off the bat. Transactional work is steady and will pay the bills. Then litigation will fill in the holes and hopefully give us bonuses."

I rubbed a smudge of dirt from one of the boxes off my arm. "One of us could specialize in estate planning. There's only one lawyer around here who does the bigger estates and trusts, and that's good money."

Clark nodded. "I agree. If we can figure out how to pay for it, I'd like to study tax law and take several of the estate planning seminars."

So we were on the same page. Excellent. "See? This is going to work out. We applied for a firm credit card. If we get that, we can pay for the seminars for you." I didn't want to practice in estate planning, so it was good that Clark was interested.

"I covered the picnic table with a tablecloth to make it look a little bit better, and folks can put the food there," Clark said. "We need to find something better. There has to be a business around here closing down that has a conference table. It'd be cool to get one with leather chairs."

"Let's not get too fancy." We couldn't afford anything like that yet.

"You-hoo," my Aunt Rachel called from the other room. "I have deviled eggs, napkins, and a couple bottles of Prosecco." She was Pauley's mom and one of my favorite aunts.

I turned and hurried into the room to help her with the goodies.

"Oh, you look lovely," she said, her light eyes beaming. "So lawyerly."

I laughed. "I'm trying. Let's hope this works out." I led her to the conference room, where Clark had indeed placed a tablecloth. It was decorated with the Seattle Seahawks, probably since he'd gone to school in Seattle. At least many of my family members were Hawk fans.

We set up the food, and more goodies arrived along with family members, colleagues, and business owners in the community. The food and drink flowed freely, and Clark impressed me with how easily he moved through the crowd and kept everyone's names straight.

Pauley disappeared before too many people arrived, but Oliver kept busy refilling glasses and collecting empties. The kid was really working out.

Quint showed up about half-way through, and damn it all if he didn't have Jolene with him.

He met me across the room before I could reach him. "She's covering the opening for the paper and would be here anyway."

I hesitated in smacking him. "Do you know what you're doing?"

He grinned, and the sight was so charming I could only sigh. "Yeah. I know you two have gotten off to a rough start, but she's not so bad. She's had a rough time of it and might've tried too hard with the new job and messed with you, but I think you two would get along great if you tried. Everyone makes mistakes, Anna Banana."

He always used that nickname to get to me, darn it.

Jolene made her way toward us, her pretty blonde hair up in some intricate knot. "Hi, Anna. This place looks amazing."

I smiled and held out a hand. "Jolene, it's good to see you." I tried to feel the words. "Quint said that you're covering our opening for the paper?"

She nodded. "If that's okay with you. We're doing a series on new businesses in the area, and this would make a great feature story. It might lead to some new clients for you."

Clark instantly popped up at her side. "I'm Clark." He held out a hand.

"Jolene O'Sullivan." She held out her hand, and they shook. She wore her customary pantsuit, this time in navy blue, and looked professional and chic. "It's nice to meet you."

"I've heard of you," Clark said, cutting me a questioning look.

I forced a smile. "Jolene is going to write a feature story on the firm."

Clark straightened. "That's fantastic news. Let me show you around." He drew her toward his office.

"Thank you," Quint said, snatching a beer from a stack on Oliver's desk. He looked typical Quint in dark jeans and a green T-shirt with a faded logo for search and rescue across the back.

"She's actually pretty interesting and has a great sense of humor. I'm hoping you two can bury the hatchet and start over."

For Quint, I'd do anything. Plus, if Jolene published a positive story about the law firm, it really would help us out. "You're lucky you're so pretty, Quintino," I drawled.

"Aren't I, though?" He waved at his mom, who was across the room with one of his brothers. "You look all grown up and lawyerly tonight, too." He glanced down at my feet. "I don't know anything about shoes, but if I did, I think I'd be really impressed with those."

I kicked back a heel and twisted my ankle to show off the design. "Yeah. They're pretty, right? I bought them on credit and should probably find a client or two soon." They were Prada heels with sparkly silver discs. I loved them, couldn't afford them, but bought them anyway. Life was short.

Clark and Jolene returned, and Jolene spent a few moments taking pictures with her cell phone. "I'm going to interview a few of the folks here," she said, moving toward a group of business-people in the corner. I think one of them owned the local cinema. I'd go introduce myself after Jolene finished asking questions, and Clark had already been there laughing with a couple of them, so all was good.

The party went off without a hitch, and finally, only Clark and I remained. My family had cleaned up before leaving, like usual, so the place was pristine.

We sat in his office sipping champagne.

"Life is good," Clark said, tipping back his glass. In the semi-darkness and his business clothes, he looked like a successful young lawyer.

"Yeah." The room was soft and so was my mood. "This is going to work out, Clark. Trust me."

"I do." He stood. "I have a couple of meetings tomorrow with prospective clients. You?"

I stood and stretched my back. "Same. I can't wait to dig in."

We locked up together and strode outside to the back alley. A streetlight had been installed directly above where we parked. It was new.

"You?" I asked.

Clark looked up. "Nope."

Aiden. He must've had it installed after I'd told him about Sasha, and he hadn't said a word. My stomach flip-flopped.

"See you tomorrow." Clark turned for Main Street.

"I can give you a ride," I called out.

He smiled. "It's a warm night and I want to walk. My apartment is just down the street. Have a good night, partner."

"You too, partner," I said, slipping into my car. My body was nicely tired and my brain buzzing with ideas for my meetings set for the morning. I headed home on auto-pilot with my window down, enjoying the late summer scents of flowers and lingering barbecue smoke.

I reached my country road and then the long driveway, pulling up to my garage. I had my winter rig inside along with different odds and ends, and I never used it during the summer for my Fiat. Even though I knew Aiden was planning to stay in Seattle for the night, it was still a disappointment not to see his motorcycle parked there. It would be a lonely night.

Shrugging off the silliness, I stepped out of the car and wound around the side toward my cottage. I stopped cold. My head reeled and a heaviness descended on my head. Gasping, I rushed toward the porch and leaned over.

Sasha Duponte lay on her side, blood pooled around her head and body.

I gulped and scrambled in my purse for my phone to call 911. "Hurry. There's a woman bleeding on my porch," I gasped.

"Is the woman breathing?" The operator asked.

My hand shaking, I knelt on the porch and leaned over Sasha. I didn't hear anything. I felt for the pulse in her wrist. Nothing, and her skin was cold. Very cold. "No. She's dead." I shined my phone closer to Sasha's vacant blue eyes. They stared blindly beyond me.

Shuddering, I gently closed them and then stepped back and away from the body. "Please hurry," I whispered into the phone.

Then I looked around at the shadows between the trees on both sides of my sweet house. Normally innocuous, tonight they seemed menacing. Threatening. Was there somebody out there watching me? I reached for my gun and pulled it free from my purse.

The hollow sound of sirens in the distance provided little comfort.

CHAPTER 7

Two uniformed police officers arrived first, and I didn't know either of them. One was a tall skinny man who looked to be about fifty years old, and the other was just as tall but a woman with long black hair. She escorted me to the end of the walkway and asked me to wait there as they secured the scene. Soon more emergency vehicles arrived, followed by Detective Grant Pierce in an unmarked generic vehicle that was a dark grey color.

He flicked a glance toward me and then continued to the scene.

I watched him go and took another look at Sasha. Her red hair splayed across my wooden deck, some of it stuck in the crevices. Blood had turned it a darker red than usual. She wore light jeans, black wedges, and a black tank-top. Her purse was next to her and close to my door.

I shivered.

Pierce took a flashlight and illuminated the entire porch area. Blood spatter glowed up the walls, along the door, and even across a window down the way.

Oh God. She'd been killed right on my porch. My breathing

quickened and a panic attack loomed. I smashed my palm against my solar plexus and breathed deeply several times, trying to calm my nervous system. The champagne and canapés I'd eaten earlier swirled around my stomach, and I had to swallow to keep from throwing up. The need to vomit hovered just on the edge.

Detective Pierce then wound his way through crime techs to me just as more spotlights were set up to illuminate the scene. "Are you okay?"

"No." I shook myself out of it and stood straighter.

"Take another deep breath." Pierce was in his late thirties or early forties and had that cop look with an edge. His hair was a dark blond tinged with gray, his eyes green, and his scent salty-ocean somehow. "Did you know the victim?"

I nodded. "Her name is Sasha Duponte, and she's an ATF agent. You're going to need to call the agency."

Pierce stiffened. "She's ATF?"

"Yes," I whispered, chilly in the warm evening.

Pierce's exhale was heated. "I suppose she knew Aiden Devlin?"

"Yes," I affirmed. Aiden and Pierce had been on the opposite sides of a couple of cases, and once Pierce had discovered that Aiden was an agent, he hadn't been happy at the concealment of that fact. It appeared he still wasn't.

"Great. Where is Devlin? I need to talk to him." Pierce looked around the area again.

I chewed on the inside of my lip. "Aiden is in Seattle meeting with his director about a case he was going to work with Sasha." I'd learned the hard way that lying to Detective Grant Pierce was a bad idea that just led to more problems. "They've worked together before."

Because Pierce was a good cop, he must've caught something in my voice. "They were just colleagues?" he asked.

I paused.

"All of it, Albertini," he said. "Don't mess with me on this one.

There's a dead body on your freaking porch, and you knew her. She was killed right here. Keep talking."

The world tilted around me, but I kept upright. Finding dead bodies was a shock to any system. "Yes. Aiden and Sasha were undercover at some point as a married couple, and they started dating. I don't know how long it lasted, but it fizzled away when they both moved on to other jobs." I needed to sit down.

Pierce pinched the bridge of his nose. "All right. When did you first meet her?"

I told him about her showing up at Aiden's. Oh, I'd give him everything about the fights with her if he asked, but if he didn't, I was going to keep those back for now. Blowing Aiden's undercover Op wasn't a good option, and I needed to talk to him before I revealed too much about it.

A shout echoed from the side of my porch, and an officer held up something. I squinted to see better and my stomach dropped. Oh, crap.

Pierce ducked his head to see better. "Is that a potato gun?"

I pivoted and hustled back to look in my car. Nope. No potato gun there. My thoughts reeled and I struggled to bring them in. Okay. I had to think.

"Anna?" Pierce followed me and then motioned for the cop to bring it over.

The tall woman who'd first arrived brought the gun over, her hands protected by gloves. "We photographed where it was found and all around it. Just need to bag and tag it."

I coughed and kept puke down. The potato gun was familiar, except it was covered in blood and what looked like brain matter. It was only PVC pipe, for Pete's sake.

Pierce leaned over to examine it better. "Recognize this, Anna?"

What would I do if I were representing myself? It was time to do what needed to be done. "I have a phone call to make." Turning away, I walked to the edge of the drive and dialed quickly.

"Anna? What the heck? Can't it wait until tomorrow?" Clark asked sleepily.

My voice shook. "I have good news and bad news. The good news is that we have our first client." Suddenly, I really needed to go to the bathroom. Now.

"What's the bad news?" Clark asked wearily, the sound of bedclothes rustling as he no doubt got out of bed.

"I'm the client."

* * *

IT WASN'T my first time sitting across from Detective Grant Pierce in a Timber City Police interrogation room, but it was the first time I was the one being questioned. Clark sat next to me, and it felt reassuring to have him there.

We'd waited about two hours until Pierce walked in and slapped a manila case file on the wooden table. He pulled out a chair across from us and sat. "Run me through your day. All day."

Clark sat straighter. "I want it on the record that my client is here voluntarily to help."

"It's on the record," Pierce said, his gaze remaining on me. "You're not under arrest, Anna. The sooner we clear you, the better."

It was reassuring that Pierce didn't think I'd murdered anybody. The idea that I'd found Sasha on my porch kept chilling me throughout. Why couldn't I get warm? "Okay. I woke up, went for a run, went home, showered and drank a lot of coffee." I might've had too much wine the night before. Even after Aiden had left, I finished the bottle. It had been a good bottle. I should probably stop drinking for a little bit.

"Were you alone this morning?" Pierce asked.

"Yes and all night," I said.

He made a notation on some paper. "Did you call anybody, get on a computer, or anything this morning?"

I shook my head. "No. I was unplugging and relaxing. What time did Sasha die?" She'd felt terribly cold, and when they'd moved her, it had been obvious that rigor mortis had set in. It usually set in within 2-4 hours of a death, which was a fact I'd unfortunately learned from real life and not television.

Pierce ignored the question. "Did anybody see you jogging?"

"I don't know. I ran along the old lake road, and I don't remember seeing anyone." Plus, I'd had my earbuds in, and I had been trying to go internal and just relax and enjoy the day.

"Then what?" he asked.

My skin prickled, and I looked beyond him to the two-way mirror. Was somebody watching us? "Who's in there?"

"Anna? What happened after you drank too much coffee?" Pierce remained calm but firm with his questioning.

"I, ah, sat out on the deck with a notepad making plans for the law firm. Then I made lunch, and afterward, I got dressed for the opening and ran a bunch of errands around town before heading to the firm to get ready for the party." I tried to remember every minute of the day, but it all blurred together.

"What time did you leave your cottage?" Pierce asked, still making notes.

"I don't know. Around two this afternoon?" I hadn't really looked at the clock since I had so much time before our party, which had started at six. I winced. That put me near the murder scene around the time of death. Maybe I should stop talking, but since I didn't kill Sasha, I wanted Pierce to have all of the information.

He looked up, meeting my gaze. "Tell me about the potato gun."

"It wasn't mine," I hastened to say.

His eyes darkened to the color of mature pine. "Have you seen it before?"

Numbly, I nodded.

"Like I said, tell me about the potato gun," he repeated evenly.

Clark leaned forward at this point. "She already told you about the potato gun. She does not own the gun." He stared at Pierce. "What is a potato gun, by the way?"

"Anna knows," Pierce said. "Right?"

I shrugged. "Most kids growing up in Idaho know about potato guns and how to make one. Was the one you found on my property the murder weapon?"

"In conjunction with somebody smashing the victim's head against your wooden porch," Pierce said, no emotion on his hard cop face. "That's just my opinion from viewing the scene, of course. I don't have the ME's results yet." He leaned back, looking all relaxed now. "Have you seen that particular potato gun before?"

It's amazing that a fleeting idea of lying to him ran through my head. Human nature, I guess. But I was a lawyer, and I knew better. "I think so. If the gun is the same one Sasha fired at me and I took from her, then I've not only seen it but touched it."

Clark stiffened next to me.

Yeah, that probably wasn't great news for my lawyer.

"Back up and run me through what happened," Pierce said. "This time, tell me everything."

I could feel somebody watching from the other side of the mirror, but it could be anybody in the station. Or it could be a prosecuting attorney. Interesting. My hands started shaking, so I clasped them together in my lap and relayed details of my interactions with Sasha to Pierce, including the bar fight and then the entanglement in the alley along with descriptions of Sasha's friends. Finally, when I wound down, I could feel the tension from Clark next to me.

Pierce took several notes. "You pointed a nine-millimeter at the deceased?"

"I was in fear for my life since it was five against one, and Sasha did dent my car when she fired the potato gun," I said calmly. "The second I was back in control and not in fear for my life, I put my gun away."

Pierce kept making notes. "How did the potato gun get from your car to the porch?"

"I don't know," I said.

He looked up, his gaze sharp. "Excuse me?"

My mouth went dry. Oh, this was bad. "I don't know, Grant. I tossed it in the backseat and pretty much forgot about it."

Clark made a slight movement that I interpreted meant it was time for me to stop talking. It was hard to think like a lawyer and a suspect at the same time. He cleared his throat. "I can tell you from experience that Anna never locks her car door. At her house, at the office, even shopping around town."

I swallowed. "That's true." I'd grown up in Silverville and then moved to Timber City, and there wasn't a need to lock my car door. Well, except that a murder weapon had been taken from it.

Clark set his hands on the table. "How bad is this?"

Pierce smiled, and it was his pissed-off smile and not the natural one. He had a great natural smile, but it was rare to see it. "How bad is it? Let's see. Your client and the victim had a public fight in a bar and then a semi-private one in an alley over a man who has ties to very bad people, even if Aiden is an ATF agent. The victim then died from being beaten with a weapon that was last in your client's possession—at your client's home. In case there's any question about this being the same potato gun, let me assure you that Anna's prints were found on the weapon. As you know, all lawyers are printed before taking the bar exam, so we already had her prints on file."

"Shit," Clark muttered.

I jolted. It was the first time I'd actually heard him swear.

CHAPTER 8

*M*orning light illuminated my office as I sipped my latte after a sleepless night. Aiden had remained in Seattle, and our conversation had been brief the night before because apparently, operation planning didn't stick to normal business hours. That was fine with me, though. I needed time to stew, worry, get mad, and then calm down about Sasha dying on my porch. Aiden had been quiet about the situation, and we'd have to discuss it when he got home.

Clark poked his head in my doorway. "Hey. Just got in. How are you doing?"

"I'm not sure," I admitted, twirling the cardboard cup in my hands. "I feel badly for Sasha and her family, if she has one. Also, if I didn't know I was innocent, I'd think I was guilty from the evidence." I was only partially joking.

"Me too," Clark said, his expression somber.

I sat back. "Come on, Clark. Detective Pierce is excellent at his job, and so is Nick Basanelli." Nick was our county prosecutor and my former boss. "They'll find out who killed Sasha and then prosecute that person. Don't worry. They both know me and know I wouldn't have killed Sasha." The woman had been so young, and her death was frightening and incredibly sad. Who'd want her dead?

Clark straightened in the doorway, today wearing gray slacks, a long-sleeved yellow shirt, and a darker gray tie. "Anna. We're talking about 18 U.S.C. Section 1114 here. Federal jurisdiction."

I choked on my coffee and then set it aside. He was right. "Sasha was a federal agent." My head spun. That might put her case under federal jurisdiction and not state. "Do you know the federal prosecutor? Any of them?" Panic tried to take hold of me, and I took several more deep breaths to keep from passing out.

Clark held up a hand. "Calm down. We don't even know if federal law applies. Let me go study the issue, and we'll see if we can keep this case at the state level. By 'we,' I mean Detective Pierce because you're actually not involved. Yet. I mean, unless you get charged. Obviously, you're a person of interest, but you—"

"Enough," I said, my knees going weak even though I was sitting. "Stop trying to make me feel better. You're freaking me out."

He pulled a folded up newspaper from his back pocket and tossed it on my desk. "More bad news."

Of course. The front page looked innocuous.

"Turn to the business section," he advised.

It was only a few pages away—we didn't live in a big city. Top of the fold showed a picture of our new law office opening...next to a photo of me getting in a bar fight the night before. The caption read: *"New Law Firm Comes Out Swinging,"* and the byline was Jolene's.

Clark chuckled. "It's not so bad. I kind of like the optics."

"Yeah, but wait until she writes the article about the dead body on my porch," I muttered. "It's doubtful those optics will be good for us." Not to mention poor Sasha. Who would've killed her like that?

My cell phone rang, and I pulled it out of my purse to read the screen. "It's my mother."

Clark laughed and turned back to the hallway. "I'll do some research on the federal issue." Then he paused and looked back over his shoulder. "Do not *do* anything on this case. No investigating, no calling in favors, no reaching out. Got it?"

I paused. Clark never got bossy, but he was my lawyer now. "Yes. I'll stay away from the case."

"Good." He then disappeared toward his office.

I answered the phone and dealt with my mom and the photograph of her youngest daughter being in a bar fight. Once I got her off the phone, I fielded calls from my sisters, grandmothers, grandfathers, a couple of cousins, and my dad. Finally, I'd finished telling everyone I was fine and not to worry about it.

I reached for my coffee again just as my phone dinged. "Hi, Oliver," I said after pushing the speaker button.

"Ms. Albertini? There's a client here for you," Oliver said, his voice deeper over the phone.

"Please bring them back," I said, rolling my eyes at the formality. I'd remind him to call me Anna later when there wasn't somebody in the waiting room. Then I straightened in my chair, anticipation licking through my veins. My first real client as a partner in the law firm. My own law firm. I couldn't help but stand and meet them at the door, where I masked my surprise at seeing Donald McLerrison ambling behind Oliver.

"Mr. McLerrison," I said, gesturing him inside and giving Oliver a look.

Oliver shrugged to show his confusion and then hurried back down the hallway when the phone rang loudly in the reception area.

"Come on in," I said, waving my hand toward one of the two leather chairs facing my desk. "I hope everything is okay." McLerrison was the farmer Oliver currently lived with, and he'd dropped the trespassing charges against Oliver.

"Sure." McLerrison settled his hefty bulk into the chair. For his trip to town, he wore clean overalls over a blue checked shirt and newish brown cowboy boots. His thick gray hair was slicked back with what had to be a pound of Brylcreem. "I told Oliver that I needed to speak with you about some mineral rights on the farm."

Mineral rights? Interesting. "All right. Are you thinking of just selling the mineral rights? What are we talking about here?" It wasn't usually a good idea to separate the mineral rights from a property, but I needed more facts first.

He shook his head. "No. That's just what I told Oliver."

I paused. "Okay?" Was Oliver in trouble again? My heart began to sink.

"Yeah." McLerrison leaned toward me. "Listen. When Twillie died, I was devastated and didn't care what would happen to the farm after I started pushing up daisies. Now that Oliver has lived with me, I've thought about what'd be best, and I'd like to have one of those Will and Testaments that leaves everything to him. But I don't want him to know about the inheritance until it's my turn to ride that pale horse into the sky."

How many euphemisms could he come up with for dying? My heart warmed. I reached for a legal pad and a pen. "That's no problem. I can draft up a simple estate, but if you want various trusts and so forth, I'd want to refer you to an estate planning expert."

"No. I want you. No experts." He settled his brown spotted hands on his knees.

I grinned. "All right. No expert here." Then I tapped my pen on the paper. "I'll need some information from you to draft the document, and we can go over it all afterward."

"I know." He reached into his back pocket and pulled out a couple pieces of folded paper. "Here's the legal description of the farm and my investments, which I haven't really looked at. They were Twillie's, to be honest. Oliver can have whatever she had in there."

I accepted the papers, which looked like they'd been kept in a barn. A piece of hay dropped onto my desk. "Thanks."

"Yep. The second paper has all of my personal information. I'm gonna need those back from you." He stood. "How much does a lawyer cost, anyway?"

Thank goodness Clark and I had come up with hourly prices. "Simple estate planning is three hundred dollars an hour," I said. "However, you get the friend and family discount, so it's a hundred an hour."

"That's a lot," McLerrison said.

Actually, it was really low for the area, but I also liked him. "Okay. How about fifty an hour?" Clark was going to kill me.

McLerrison waved me off. "No. Stick to your guns, girly. Even if it is highway robbery." He turned and sauntered back down the hallway.

I could barely sit still with my excitement. I had a client—a real one. Hopefully the old farm was worth something so Oliver could have a good start in life, but even if not, it was amazing that McLerrison wanted to leave him property. Also, I really hoped McLerrison stayed with real horses and didn't have to ride the one into the sky for a long time. He seemed like a great man. I gingerly unfolded the papers so I could start research.

My phone buzzed. "Hi, Oliver," I said, booting up my trusty laptop.

"Hi, Ms. Albertini. I have a client here for you and I'll bring her right back." Oliver sounded breathless.

"Okay." I still needed to remind him to just call me by my first name. I set the papers aside and met them at the door, surprised once again. "Kelsey." It took me a minute to regain my composure. "Thanks, Oliver."

"Sure." He lingered a moment, his gaze filled with Kelsey Walker. In her early twenties, she was very pretty with green eyes and dirty blonde hair, and she had a figure that filled out any clothing very nicely.

I gently shut the door and drew her inside. "How are you?"

She strode on pink flats to my guest chair to sit. The shoes looked perfect with her light blue skirt and flowered top. "Not good. I'm in trouble."

I walked around my desk and retook my seat, studying the woman. She was only four or five years younger than me, but I felt much older. The previous month, her sister had pled guilty to murdering Kelsey's ex-boyfriend and was already serving a prison sentence. The ex also had dated my sister Tessa a couple of years ago. "Tell me what's going on."

Her hands trembled. "The prosecuting attorney is charging me as an accomplice to Danny's murder as well as an accomplice for all of Krissy's crimes. I don't even understand all of them."

I sat back, stunned. Krissy had run a family funeral home where she'd trafficked in guns and accessories, in addition to having killed Danny. While Kelsey had worked at the funeral home, she hadn't been involved in any of it. "That's crazy."

Tears filled Kelsey's eyes. "I know," she whispered. "But I did work with Krissy with the secretarial type work, and she did kill my ex. The prosecuting attorney believes there's enough evidence to charge me as an accessory, and I'm afraid I'm gonna go to jail. I didn't do anything, Anna. I had no idea that Krissy was doing anything with guns. I swear."

"Okay. Let's take a deep breath." I needed to get some facial tissues for my office next time I went shopping. "Have you been arrested?"

She wiped her eyes off. "Yes. I met with a detective and told him everything last week, and he arrested me right there. I had something called an initial appearance, and some court lawyer showed up and requested a preliminary hearing. I fired him because he didn't seem to know what he was doing. My boyfriend posted bond and I have that preliminary hearing next Monday. I need you to be my lawyer there."

I perked up. "Is Grant Pierce the detective?"

"No. The guy's name was Detective Wilson. He read me those rights you see on television, but since I didn't do anything wrong,

I didn't ask for a lawyer, and then all of a sudden he was arresting me." She bit the nail on her ring finger. "I just don't understand this."

"I know how you feel," I said, meaning it. "I'm surprised you came to me, considering everything that happened with your sister." I'd helped put Krissy away and had even trapped her in a coffin until the police had arrived to arrest her.

Pink filtered into Kelsey's cheeks. "I know, but you were really sweet during all of that. My folks have pretty much disowned both me and Krissy after everything that happened. Even they think I've gone bad, Anna." More tears welled into her eyes.

I reached out and patted her hand, aching for her. The idea of my family ignoring me was painful and hard to even imagine. "I was with you during that whole case, and I believe you." The woman just couldn't get a break. "Have you talked to Krissy?"

Kelsey shook her head. "No. I'm still mad at her for getting me involved in that whole gun mess, and I loved Danny. She killed him." Kelsey's mascara pooled beneath her eyes in a black gob. "I know he wasn't the best of guys, and I'm seeing that shrink you recommended, but he didn't deserve to die." She dug in her purse for a Kleenex and blew her nose before continuing. "Maybe if Danny and I had gone to counseling together, he would've become a better person. He never got that chance."

I doubted Danny Pucci would've ever been better than a slug on concrete, but there was no reason to say so. "I'm glad you're getting help." Danny had liked to hit women, and it was good that Kelsey was attending counseling.

She reached in her purse and pulled out a wallet, Chapstick, lipstick, and then lotion to pile on my desk. Sighing, she dug deeper, yanking out a sunglass case and an unopened purple condom. "Geez. This is crazy. I need to get more organized." Finally, she pulled out a folded check to hand over. "I have some money in savings and hope this is enough to cover a retainer."

"It is." I didn't look at the check. Kelsey needed help and I was going to help her. I kind of felt like we were in this together.

She shoved all of her belongings back into the pink bag. It didn't look big enough to hold everything, but she made it work. "Thank you. What do we do now?"

I pushed the button on my phone.

"Hello, Ms. Albertini. This is Oliver. How may I help you?" Oliver asked formally.

I sighed. "Oliver, please call the court and get a copy of the case file against Kelsey Walker. You'll probably need to pick it up, and I'm sure they'll charge us for copies. See if we can set up an account there to be billed monthly. I think Clark has business credit cards for all of us." That reminded me that I needed to get mine from him.

"Yes, ma'am," Oliver said.

I grit my teeth. "Also, let's order lunch in, and we can have an office meeting." If he called me ma'am ever again, I was firing him.

"Yes, ma'am," Oliver said dutifully.

I briefly shut my eyes. Okay. I could make this all work.

CHAPTER 9

*C*lark walked into my office mid-afternoon with a couple of printouts. "You've hit the paper online and will be in the print edition tomorrow morning." He tossed them on my desk.

I read the newest headline featuring me: *Murder at Anna Albertini's Home.* "Wonderful." I quickly scanned the article, which more than hinted at my being a suspect. There was a lot of speculation, considering I'd been in a public bar fight with the deceased. "Fantastic. This is just great," I muttered.

"This probably won't bring us more clients," Clark said.

I tried to find a silver lining. "Sorry about this. I'm sure the police will solve the case soon, and we can move on."

"It'd be great if you could avoid being in the paper for a few days," Clark said as a parting shot. He retreated back down the hallway.

The article was written by Jolene O'Sullivan. At this point, she owed me half her salary.

I turned back to my paperwork and made diligent notes and plans for a good couple of hours. My phone rang just as I was shutting down my office. "Anna Albertini," I answered in my best lawyer voice, even though it was my cell phone.

"Have you washed your car lately?" Detective Pierce asked.

I frowned. "No. Why?" We hadn't had rain in a while and my car looked fine.

"I'm sending over a couple of techs to fingerprint it, just to see if we can find who took the potato gun out," he said, shuffling papers coming over the line.

I paused. His voice was at a slightly higher pitch than normal. "What's going on?"

"The case is probably going to get transferred to the federal authorities, and I'd like to get as much evidence as possible first." Now he sounded frustrated. "I'm being stonewalled by the Feds regarding the victim, so I don't even have a viable list of suspects. Well, except you and Devlin."

I leaned against the wall and flipped off the lights, my temples aching. All of my euphoria after the first full day at my new firm evaporated instantly. "Aiden was in Seattle, and I'm sure there's plenty of proof of that, including airline tickets and recordings from security cameras."

Pierce sighed. "Yeah. I figured. That leaves you, Albertini. You need to tell me who would've wanted Sasha Duponte dead."

"I have no idea," I admitted. "It's my understanding that she worked as an ATF agent for a while, and surely she has enemies. As for her personal life, I don't know a thing."

"When does Devlin return to town? I need to talk to him," Pierce said.

I cleared my throat. "He didn't say."

Pierce's sigh held the sound of heat. "That's quite the relationship you've got. Fine. Have him call me." He ended the call.

"We're just starting a relationship," I said to the empty room. Right? Weren't we? It wasn't like we'd had *that talk*, but we seemed to be on the same page. My feet ached a little in the wedges as I walked down the quiet hallway and leaned against Clark's doorframe.

He sat at his desk, rifling through papers. "It was a good first day."

I grinned, even though my limbs felt heavy. "Agreed. I have six new clients. How about you?"

He pushed his glasses up his nose. "Five and one of them is a corporation, so we might work out a retainer agreement." His eyes gleamed.

"That's great," I said. "Should we pick a day for office meetings where we can talk about our cases each week? I think the bigger firms do that usually on Monday morning."

He tugged his tie loose and leaned back in his chair. "That's a good idea. How about Friday mornings? That suits us better, and I don't want to do things like the bigger firms." He shuffled papers aside and pulled out a legal pad. "In fact, how about we don't schedule client meetings or events for Fridays unless we're required to be in court?

I stretched my feet inside my wedges. "I like that idea. We can have casual Fridays, where we just pump out the work." Having project days worked for me. Before I forgot, I handed over the retainers I'd collected that day. "We might need to get an office manager or accountant," I mused.

Clark reached for a different pen. "Agreed, but let's wait until we can afford one. I don't mind working the books right now if you don't mind handling all publicity and advertising. The logo you came up with for our website and cards looks fantastic."

"Tessa helped me," I admitted. My sister had always been artistic. "I told Oliver and Pauley that they could order business cards."

Clark shrugged. "That's fair. It's not like we're paying them very much."

I needed food. Like now. "All right. I'll see you tomorrow. Good job today, partner."

"Ditto," Clark said. "I didn't get a chance to research federal law but will get on that tomorrow morning."

"Thanks. Pierce called and said the case was probably going to get transferred." I just couldn't worry about it right now. The idea that I'd beaten Sasha to death by pounding her head into my porch and hitting her with a potato gun was just too ridiculous for me to take seriously. But the woman was dead, so it was a good thing Clark was doing the necessary research. "Night."

"Night." He turned back to his computer.

I strode down the hallway to the reception area, where Oliver was just shutting down his computer. "Great job today, Oliver," I said.

He grinned and looked like that young Opie kid from the old Maybury show on cable re-runs. "Thanks."

"I think we should keep it informal here and use first names. Also, please don't ever call me ma'am again. I'd really appreciate it." My voice stayed as gentle as I could make it.

He didn't seem put out. "I want clients to know you're a big deal."

Ah, the kid was just too cute. Too sweet. "I have E.S.Q. after my name on my business cards." I grinned. "They already know I'm a big deal."

"Okay. Why not the ma'am?" He sounded merely curious.

"It makes women feel old. Tip for the future? Never call a woman, ma'am. Use 'miss,' and you'll be golden." I turned for the door.

"Cool," Oliver said. "Hey, Anna? Is Kelsey Walker dating anybody?"

I paused and turned back around, every protective instinct I had flaring wide awake. Kelsey was a couple years older than Oliver and had more than her fair share of problems, and he was just a kid. Plus, she'd mentioned a boyfriend and had tossed a purple condom on my desk. "Yeah. She has a serious boyfriend." I might've pushed it with the 'serious' part, but who knew? "Why do you ask?" I tried to sound clueless.

"No reason." His face fell like he'd lost his best friend.

"Okay. See you tomorrow." I walked out of the office with my laptop bag slung over my arm and moved into the parking area in the alley, where two crime techs were meticulously fingerprinting my vehicle. I'd already forgotten. Sighing, I settled against the brick building to watch.

They shouldn't take too long.

* * *

THE TECHS HAD TAKEN FOREVER. By the time I drove into my driveway, my stomach was growling so loudly I figured a monster had taken up residence there. I had the top down on my car, which helped with the fingerprint dust because the faster I drove, more flew off.

I wasn't surprised to see a Harley parked next to my garage.

As usual, my breath sped up, and my extremities tingled. Nerves, anticipation, and energy. Somehow my body always reacted to the thought that Aiden was near. Would that always happen? It was interesting to ponder. I lifted my laptop bag and walked to the porch, where somebody had cleaned all the blood away. Even the crime tape was gone. Had Aiden done it? The porch still looked wet.

I took a deep breath and walked inside, where quiet met me. Dumping my bag on the sofa, I continued through the dining nook to the sliding glass door and found him outside by my table, kicked back on one of my comfy chairs with the daisy decorated cushions. He wore jeans and a faded red T-shirt, his feet bare and a beer in his hand as he looked out at the lake. I toed off my shoes and drew out the chair next to him. "Hi."

"Hi." He looked my way, a veil over his stunning blue eyes. "How was your first day at work?"

"Busy," I admitted, searching for the right words. "I'm sorry about Sasha."

He took a drink of the sweating beer bottle. "Me too. Do you have any idea what happened?"

"No." I couldn't gauge his mood, and that settled tension heavily over my shoulders. "Do you?"

"No." He finished the beer and studied the lake again. "Gorgeous pictures in the paper. I really liked the one of you punching a Lorde's old lady in the mouth."

I winced. "Yeah, I saw that. You can clearly see Sasha in the background."

"I'm sure the facts about her death will hit the front page tomorrow," Aiden said wearily, setting down the beer bottle. "She could fight and well. Whoever killed her was trained. Or lucky."

I was known to be lucky in a fight. "Could her death be associated with the Barensky case? Or a former case?"

"Sure. The ATF is going through all of her cases right now and looking for suspects. But Barensky is a sociopath who has a deep-seated need to blow things up. He would've found a more creative way to kill her, and as far as I know, he believed her cover."

"Is it blown?" I asked.

He lifted one strong shoulder. "We'll see. Right now, we're proceeding as if the cover isn't blown, although that just makes everything more dangerous."

"What can I do to help?" I reached for his hand and tangled our fingers together.

He gripped mine, surrounding my hand with warmth and strength. "You can stay out of it. From what I can tell, you're in enough trouble right now, and the ATF isn't going to do anything to help you out if it means blowing this operation."

I straightened. "Does that mean the federal prosecutor isn't going to get involved?"

"No. It means that the FBI is going to investigate Sasha's death and turn everything over to the federal prosecutor, but they're going to do it under the radar as long as we have an Op going. You're in trouble, Angel. We have to find out who killed Sasha on your front porch."

The body could've been there all day and nobody would've seen it, considering how far back I lived from the road. Plus, the attached garage that I rarely used blocked the porch. "Do you think she was placed here on purpose, or did somebody just follow her here?"

"I don't know," Aiden said, keeping my hand. "Why would Sasha come to your house?"

"Maybe to warn me off you again?" I asked. "She did want another shot with you." Although, after our altercation in the alley, it seemed doubtful she'd want to see me. "She was killed here, based on the amount of blood on my porch. Have you seen autopsy results yet?" Maybe she was drugged.

"They won't be available until tomorrow, I guess," Aiden said. "The feds called in their own ME to collaborate with the county coroner, so they wanted another night."

It was all so sad. Even though I hadn't liked Sasha, she'd been young and strong. "At least you're not a suspect. You'll be kept up to date with the investigation," I said.

"True."

"Did you clean up my porch?" I asked.

"Yeah." His gaze out at the lake was thoughtful.

This had to be weird for him. Even though they'd stopped dating or fizzled out, they'd once been close enough to sleep together. "Did she have family?" I bit my lip.

"One brother who died a few years ago from cancer," Aiden said. "The agency will take care of her funeral arrangements. We're going to bury her in the Timber City Cemetery on Sunday."

The lump in my throat just kept feeling bigger. "How are you, Aiden? Seriously. How do you feel about this?"

He turned to me, his eyes blazing. "Pissed off. I am going to find who killed her, and they're going to suffer. She was a friend and a colleague, and she deserved a lot better than this."

A chill wound down my spine. When Aiden was on a mission, nothing stopped him.

Even a bomber.

CHAPTER 10

J awoke in the middle of the night and snuggled into Aiden's side. Anxiety felt like buzzing flies in my veins, and I sucked down several deep breaths. He felt warm and solid behind me, and I took a moment to enjoy the quiet and his presence before sliding back into sleep.

The nightmare wasn't unexpected, but this time, my brain introduced new elements.

I was ten years old again, skipping rocks with my cousin at the river. Strong arms, skinny ones, pulled me into a four-wheeler and then tied my hands. I looked sideways to see Jareth Davey with his big nose and vacant eyes. Even years later, even knowing this was a dream, terror cut through me, and I might've held my breath while sleeping.

He took me to his cabin and looked at me. "We're married now."

A roaring filled my head as a teenaged Aiden rushed into the room and beat Jareth up. He took my hand and led me to safety, except this time, potato guns pointed at us from every tree. They all fired at once.

I gasped and sat up, my heart thundering.

Breathe. Just breathe. I dropped my head to my chest and let my heartbeat even out. Light streamed in through the sliding glass door, which showed a sparkling and deep blue lake. Aiden's side of the bed was empty.

I burrowed back down and curled around a pillow to watch the lake. A quick glance at the clock confirmed it was only six in the morning, so I forced my body to relax one muscle at a time. First my toes, then legs, and so on. By the time I got to my face, my heart rate had slowed and my breathing had evened out.

Usually when I had a nightmare, Aiden was there to talk me through it. Jareth Davey had been charged and tried in a court of law, but he'd been let go because of a technicality. Every year on the anniversary of the kidnapping and during Christmastime, he sent me a card. Right now, we had no clue where he was, but it was late summer, and I wouldn't worry about him until December.

Not consciously, anyway.

The front door unlocked, opened and shut. It was odd that I could recognize Aiden's footsteps, and the idea made me all warm and gushy again. He moved into my room, sweat dotting his faded gray tee and running shorts. "Morning." He kicked off his tennis shoes. "Want the bad news?"

I sat up and wrapped my arms around my knees, salivating at the muscles illustrated across his chest. "Sure."

Sweat dripped from his thick hair, down his angled face, to his shirt. "You made the paper."

I groaned and buried my face in my knees. "How bad?"

The bed dipped and his scent of male, leather, and motor oil tickled my nose. "Not too bad. Just that Anna Albertini of the new Bunne & Albertini Law Firm is a person of interest in the murder of Sasha Duponte. Jolene's article is pretty detailed about your fight at the bar, the argument in the alley, and then the death on your porch."

I lifted my head. "How did Jolene find out about the fight in the alley?"

He grimaced. "She interviewed two of the women who were

there that day."

I chewed on that for a moment. "Wait a sec. How did she—"

"Jolene has good sources at Timber City PD, it seems."

I jerked upright. Heat flashed down my torso. "Yeah. There are no good secrets in Timber City."

"I'm sorry you're involved with this." Aiden rubbed his hand through his hair. "By the women talking, it strongly associates Sasha with the Lordes and douses questions. Hopefully that will protect her cover as well as mine."

I studied him. That made sense. Oh, I didn't like it, but I got it. "All right."

Aiden cocked his head and that brilliant gaze wandered my face. He frowned. "You're pale." One knuckle nudged beneath my chin and he gently lifted my face. "You have that look. Did you have a nightmare?"

Butterflies winged through me. "Yeah, but I'm fine."

"I'm sorry." He leaned and kissed the top of my nose. "You usually don't have nightmares after three in the morning, so I felt fine going for a run. I would've stayed otherwise."

I leaned into his touch. "You know when I normally have bad dreams?"

"Yeah."

It was sweet that he tried to be there when I was scared. That day, so long ago, had marked us both. We didn't talk about it much, but I knew that Aiden was still trying to hunt down Jareth. The question was what would happen once Aiden found him, if he did. It seemed Jareth Davey was very good at staying off the radar.

"All right, sweet thing. I need to hit the shower and then head to the new offices in Spokane." With a tug on my ear, he moved off the bed and headed for my master bath.

Hmmm. Aiden very often made a move in the morning, and the fact that he hadn't lumped worry throughout me. He might still be dealing with Sasha's death, or he might be giving me space.

Either way, it felt off. *We* felt off.

I'd never been one to let things play out, which might be a character flaw or maybe a good attribute. Who knew? I slipped out of bed and ditched my T-shirt and panties on the way to the bathroom.

Aiden was already in the shower, and steam filled the small room.

I opened the glass door and stepped inside. While I definitely wore rose-colored glasses with him, Aiden Devlin objectively had a body that I'd only read about in romance novels. Hard and angled, scarred and muscled. He faced away from me, his head beneath the spray of water. A tattoo decorated his shoulder blade, and I reached out to trace the dark pattern with my finger. I'd noticed it as part of him, of course, but I'd really never studied the jagged edges of a bald eagle over a design, including a gun and rocks. "Why an eagle?" It was odd we'd never talked about it, although it wasn't like we'd had any downtime since we'd started dating.

He partially turned, letting the water hit my front. "An eagle for freedom and flying out of Idaho, the gun and rocks design for my first unit at the ATF. We know what it means, but anybody seeing it would not." He cocked his head and grinned. "Is it weird you don't know that?"

I relaxed and slid my hands up his chest. "Yeah. Kind of. Of course, we've been busy getting kidnapped and shooting people since we started dating." Had it only been just more than one month? That was nuts. "It'd be nice if things slowed down a little bit." What would we be like without all the excitement?

"Right. Slow down." He reached for me, lifting me right off the ground.

Excitement and desire slammed through me. I loved his strength. My hands curled over his shoulders out of instinct.

He pivoted and put my butt against the cold tile. "I don't see any slowdown coming, Angel." He leaned in, and his wet chest warmed my chilly one. My nipples perked right up against him. "We need a safety plan for you."

I blinked water out of my eyes. "Huh?"

He leaned in and nibbled along my jawline and up to my ear. Tingles spread through me, and I shivered, angling my head so he could keep going. "A woman was killed on your porch. You could've been here and you could've gotten hurt or worse. Have you even thought about that?"

It was difficult to think of anything at the moment. My thighs gripped his flanks, and being naked with Aiden was enough to make my brain just shut right down. Happily. "No." I was more worried about being charged with murder.

"Well, I have." He finally reached my mouth and went in deep and hard. Full on Aiden in full on naked control.

I shut my eyes and kissed him back, my nails digging into his skin. He could kiss. Mouth, lips, tongue...he used them all and drove me to a place of need only he could create.

His fingers slid down my side and across, finding me ready for him. The fact that he could hold me up with one hand against the wall while his other hand drove me crazy was almost as sexy as what he was doing with that other hand. Almost. "You're ready," he murmured against my neck.

"I usually am with you," I whispered, sliding one hand around to tangle in the back of his thick hair.

He leaned up, his eyes deep sapphires. "Sometimes you're so sweet you kill me." Then slowly, he started to penetrate me.

I'd gone on the pill weeks ago for this very reason, and at the moment, I was thanking the gods for the pill.

Then he was all the way inside me, moving fast, keeping us both in the moment and on the edge. For so long, just on the edge. Finally, when all I could do was hold on, he changed the angle of his thrusts and I went over fast. The climax roared through me, and I held on, riding through the storm safe with him.

He groaned with his own release and dropped his head to my

shoulder, still holding me aloft. "Now that's how to start a morning."

I laughed, feeling lighter than I had in days. "Totally agree."

He let me slide down his body and then turned me, letting the water douse me.

"Hey." I pushed against him.

He laughed and pulled me back before reaching for the shampoo. "Let me."

I paused. This was new. I let him shampoo my hair, and for some weird reason, that felt as intimate as what we'd just done. His fingers were gentle and firm, and I'd had no idea how good it felt to have somebody else wash my hair. Well, Aiden wash my hair. It was almost a massage, and my body relaxed from my head to my toes. "I like this," I murmured, my eyes closed.

"Me, too. I love your hair. Get under the spray." He nudged me and started working the shampoo out.

"My hair? It's brown." I kept my eyes closed and let him take care of me.

His fingers kneaded my nape, and I almost moaned from pleasure. "It's not brown. It's like my Gram's antique mahogany knick-knack table. Auburn, caramel, and coppery with just a hint of cinnamon." He pulled me back out of the spray. "It's soft and slightly curly, and it frames your heart-shaped face perfectly."

My heart thumped hard against my ribcage. Sometimes Aiden's romantic side slayed me. Were badass tough guys supposed to be romantic? That Irish heritage really came out sometimes. I turned and leaned up to kiss him again.

He grasped my wet hair and twisted my head to the side, taking the kiss deeper. So deep.

By the time we finished showering, the water had turned cold. Very.

But neither one of us cared.

CHAPTER 11

J was a little late for work but didn't think it would matter since I'd probably tanked our firm for good with the most recent newspaper article about me. So when I walked into our reception area to find people all but lined up, I stopped breathing. Smiling at a couple of folks to mask my surprise, I edged my way toward Oliver's desk.

Oliver was scrambling to type in information on his computer with a stack of client information forms next to him. "You're here." Relief filtered across his bright red face and he handed me a stack of papers. "You just missed Kelsey Walker. She dropped off her timeline for the day Danny Pucci was killed as well as a list of character references."

I kept my focus on him and not all the people behind me. "Sorry I missed her."

Oliver turned back to his computer. "We have appointments scheduled all day. Go get coffee and I'll bring the first client down."

I leaned toward him. "What is going on?" I whispered.

"Your article. People want a scrappy lawyer, I guess." He pushed my arm. "Go. Clark is already with his third client of the day. Get into your office." Panic sizzled in his eyes. "Hurry before somebody grabs you to talk."

Adrenaline flooded my body. I hurried through the doorway to our main hallway, waved at Clark in his office, and hustled to the kitchen where a nearly full pot of coffee waited. After pouring myself a cup, I walked to my office. Across from it was an empty office, and a quick look showed Pauley in there working on a folding card table.

I leaned in the doorway. "Hey, P. What's going on?"

He looked up and then back down at the case folders. "There are too many people in the reception area. I am working in here. In here. In here." He deftly stuck a label to a folder and gestured to the laptop next to him. "We are connected to the server. Oliver Duck puts information into the system, and then I create the case file here. Where it is quiet. Oliver Duck likes people. Duck is a good last name. Ducks are smart."

I rubbed a spot of tape off the doorframe. "All right. Thanks, P. I'll go meet with clients."

"Shut my door," he said, not looking up.

Fair enough. I shut the door and hustled across the hall to my office. True to his word, Oliver brought client after client in all morning, and I took several of the cases. I set aside some notes on the last case, which was a neighborly fight over land boundaries, when Oliver ushered in my Nonna Albertini.

I stood. "Nonna."

My Nonna was a stunning woman who looked like a mature Sophia Loren. She had thick dark hair, sharp brown eyes, and wonderfully Italian bone structure. She was several inches taller than me and today wore a smart linen pantsuit in the green pastel family.

I couldn't wear linen to save my life. I'd be a wrinkled mess by now, but not my Nonna.

She smiled and moved forward to take a seat. "Hello, Annabella Fiona. I'm glad it's time for my appointment."

I dropped into my chair. "Nonna, you never need to make an appointment. Never. I'll see you any time you want." I immediately moved all papers, notes, and case files to the side. "Please tell me you didn't have to wait to see me."

She shrugged. "I had a very nice time speaking with that Duck fellow. He's young, but he seems like a good person. I think your cousin Macy might need a date for prom next year. It's too early to know." She pushed her glasses up her nose. They were rose gold with a peachy colored tint.

"Okay." Duck was on his own with my Nonna. I wasn't going to cross her. Plus, he'd look great in a tux. "What can I do for you?"

She leaned forward. "I'm here to work on our plan."

"Oh." I leaned forward as well. "Okay. I think you should invite Nick to the family barbecue on Sunday." The two of us had banded together to match-make my sister Tessa with Nick Basanelli, the prosecuting attorney for the county. A couple weeks before, I'd puked into his potted flowers after being accidentally dosed with pot brownies, and he'd acted like the perfect gentleman, solidifying my opinion of him. "He has been to the barbecue before and knows a lot of our family."

"It's not enough." She waved one graceful hand in the air. "We need a more direct approach. Since you're such a successful lawyer, surely you have cases with him."

Only my grandmother would consider me successful considering I'd been fired from my one job as a lawyer and had created my own firm out of desperation. "Well, I have a couple of cases against him from this morning," I admitted. One was a minor in possession of beer and the other a trespassing case. "Not to mention my current case." Although the feds would probably take that one over.

"Perfect." She patted my hand. "You call him and have a business lunch at Smiley's." She dug in her monstrous purse, past the always present wooden spoon in there, and pulled out a carefully handwritten index card decorated with roses at the top. "Here's Tessa's waitressing schedule for the next week. I had her give it to me over the phone and told her I planned to shop in town at some point and wanted to know when I should pop by."

I accepted the notecard. "So you want Tessa to serve us?"

She nodded. "Of course. Tessa is a hard worker and is always smiling. Nicolo needs to see her in a natural environment. Plus, she has some hang-up that she's just a waitress, and he's a big-shot lawyer, and we need her to get over that. Actually doing her job will help."

Nonna had insight into people that was both unique and no-nonsense. Even so, Tessa was not going to like this. "Nonna, I'm not sure about this."

"I am." Her chin firmed. "How about you call Nicolo right now? Put him on speakerphone."

I hesitated. If Nick refused, there was no doubt in my mind that Nonna would jump in. "Um, okay." I dialed his cell phone instead of the office phone.

"Basanelli," he answered, his voice deep and distracted.

"Um, hey, Nick. It's Anna." I cleared my throat as my Nonna beamed. "I've ended up with a few clients, minor criminal charges, and wondered if we could meet for lunch and talk about them."

Nick was silent for a minute. "I don't have any misdemeanors on my docket. Who are the attorneys on the other side?"

I winced. "I, ah, don't have the case files yet."

Nonna frowned.

I held up a hand to keep her from ordering Nick around. "I also thought we could talk about my case."

"You don't have a case with me yet," he said. "In addition, if you're charged by my office, I've heard you are represented by counsel, so I could only talk with you if Clark were there. Is Clark coming to lunch?"

"No," I said quietly. Okay. This was not going according to Nonna's plan, and that was a mistake.

Nick audibly sighed. "I have a Zoom meeting with the governor in about ten minutes, Anna. What is going on?"

Think, darn it. "Fine. I thought we could just go to lunch and catch up."

More silence. "Aren't you dating Devlin?"

Considering my breasts still had whisker burn from that morning, yes. "I am. And I feel badly that you didn't know about his job, although he has to go under again, so we have to keep that a secret." Was that a good enough reason to go to lunch? Probably not, considering I'd just told Nick to keep Aiden's ATF status a secret.

"Got it. I'll keep that fact under my vest. I have to go, Anna. Talk soon." Nick hung up.

Nonna scooted her chair closer. "I need your phone." She flipped the office phone around and meticulously dialed in an Idaho number.

"Hello," a soft female voice answered.

"Gerty? It's Elda. Plan A was a bust. We have to go with Plan B," Nonna said.

I sighed. "Hi, Mrs. Basanelli." Nick's grandma was a hoot. She was a sweet lady, but she also was Italian and knew my grandmother well. "I'm not sure you two should have plans. Maybe we should let Tessa and Nick figure things out themselves." Unfortunately, getting them together had been my idea. I was totally at fault here.

Gerty snorted. "Those two would spend time being morons instead of giving us great-grandchildren. Plan B it is, Elda. See you tomorrow at noon." She clicked off.

Nonna set the phone back in the cradle. "You tried, Anna. Don't worry. This is just step one, and I'll need your help later on."

Guilt swamped me. "Nonna, I know this was my idea, but I didn't think you'd get Gerty involved."

"Gerty wants Nick married and she really wants great-grand-children," Nonna said reasonably. "Nick and his brothers need to settle down, and I see Tessa and Nick together. You're brilliant, and it's a relief to know that my match-making skills have been passed down to somebody."

I weakly held up a hand in protest. "No. I shouldn't be match-making. I wouldn't like it if Tessa did that to me. Let's reconsider this."

"Too late," Nonna said cheerfully.

I had no choice but to switch topics and grandchildren. Maybe I could get Nonna off Tessa and onto another one of the Albertini kids. I shouldn't. I mean, I really shouldn't. But having Quint mad at me was better than having Tessa angry. She could be volatile, and I wouldn't put it past her to cover my car with whipped cream or something. Tess was a sweetheart, but she believed in revenge. "I'm worried about Quint, Nonna. Since Chrissy broke up with him, he seems lost. He's dating the wrong women. Believe me."

Nonna stilled. "He is?"

I nodded vigorously. Jolene might've been just doing her job by nailing me in the newspaper, but she wasn't that nice, and Quint deserved somebody kind.

"Oh." Nonna sat back, obviously thinking rapidly. "All right, then. As soon as we get Tessa taken care of, we'll move on to Quintino. Do you have anybody in mind?"

"No," I burst out. "Nobody. I don't want to be a match-maker."

She stood up. "Too late, sweetheart." Then she ambled to the doorway. "Incidentally, how are things going with you and Aiden? Even though he isn't Italian, he's a good man."

"Great," I said quickly. No need for any interference from my family right now.

"Good. Is he going to be able to help with the fact that a dead body was found on your porch?" She turned at the doorway, the full force of her chocolate-brown gaze hitting me.

"Yes. Don't worry about that, Nonna." I'd wondered if she'd get to the newspaper article.

She sadly shook her head. "I can't help but worry. Also, why is that Jolene O'Sullivan always writing articles about you?"

"She doesn't like me," I said. As much as I wanted to help Tessa, I couldn't throw Quint under the bus a second time by telling Nonna that he was kind of dating Jolene. I was a better cousin than that.

"Then there's something wrong with that woman," Nonna said.

I grinned and stood to walk around my desk and hug my grandmother. "You might be biased." Slipping my arm through hers, I walked her into the hallway. While I hadn't known she'd made an appointment to see me, there was no way I'd keep from escorting my Nonna out of the office and to her car. My stomach growled. "I haven't eaten. Do you want to go grab lunch?" Oliver was going to kill me if I left him with all of those people in the waiting room, but I had to eat.

Nonna patted my arm. "Normally I would, but I have work to do today to prepare for Plan B. That reminds me. You and I are doing lunch tomorrow, so make sure you have an hour at noon."

Oh, man. I was now involved in this scheme. There was no way to argue with Nonna, so I didn't try. What had I gotten Tess into? I should probably warn her, but my schedule looked pretty packed for the rest of the day.

Thank goodness. Yeah, I'm a wimp.

CHAPTER 12

*A*t the end of a buzz-worthy day, I handed over all of the retainer checks I'd acquired to Clark. He sat at his desk, happily filling out the deposit slip and making notations. In fact, it was the happiest I'd ever seen him. "Good day?" I asked.

He looked up and his glasses slid down his straight nose. He pushed them back up. "We're making money. I can't believe it. That crazy newspaper article about the bar fight actually got us business." His office was decorated in navy hues that were calming, and the big tree outside his window added to the sense of peace. Even so, he all but hummed with excitement. "I don't suppose you could get in a bar fight once a quarter?"

"I don't suppose I could," I said dryly. "At least we'll be able to pay rent as well as the boys this month."

Clark nodded. "Yeah. Speaking of which, make sure you hand in billable hours end of the week, so I can transfer some of this money from the trust account to our actual account to pay those bills. We have to earn it first."

I winced. One of the best parts of being a prosecuting attorney was not having to worry about billable hours. I missed that set salary. Hopefully we'd still have salaries after the next newspaper article revealed Sasha's murder on my porch. "No problem," I said. "What time do you want to meet tomorrow morning for our first case management weekly session?" It sounded so official, and I loved it.

He reached for a nearly empty mug of coffee set neatly on a coaster. "If tomorrow is anything like today, we're going to be slammed starting at nine, when the office opens. How about seven? I'll bring lattes."

"Sounds good. I'll take a Chai latte with almond milk." I settled my laptop bag more securely over my shoulder. "I'll let Pauley and Oliver know to be here at 8:30 so they can catch the end of the meeting, and we can give them directions for the week. They're both doing a great job."

"Agreed," Clark said, happily turning back to his numbers.

"Oh. Also, I have a meeting in the morning at the prosecuting attorney's office at nine to go over Kelsey Walker's case. We just set it up an hour ago. But I'll get right back to help you with a crowd if we get another one." I hoped we did, and I wasn't going to feel guilty about a bar fight that got us there. Life was weird. "Have a good night, Clark." I turned and headed toward the door to reception, where I found Oliver typing furiously into his computer. "It's quitting time, bud," I said.

He looked up, his cheeks a cherry red. "I know. I was just finishing filling in your calendar for tomorrow and next week. We had twice as many calls for appointments as we did walk-ins. It's crazy."

I smiled at him and shook my head. It was crazy. "See you tomorrow at 8:30? You and Pauley can catch the end of our firm meeting."

"Sure. I'll put it on our calendars right now. Pauley checks his constantly." Oliver turned back to the computer.

"We're lucky to have you two," I said.

He blushed an even brighter red, which I wouldn't have thought possible. "Night."

"Night." I opened the door and strode down the quiet hallway and steps, where I found Kelsey Walker sitting on the floor by the back door. I paused. "Kelsey?

She looked up, her face pale. "Hi."

"What's going on?" I looked around.

So did she. "I don't know. When I left your office, I was going to work at the flower shop, and they called and told me not to come. They found out about the charges against me and fired me. I only had that job for a week and I liked it." She looked so lost and lonely on the floor. "So I just sat down. There's nowhere for me to go. My folks sold the funeral home, my sisters all live out of town, and Krissy is in prison. So I just decided to sit."

The poor woman had sat by the back door all day?

I set down my bag and plopped onto the floor. "Sometimes just sitting is a good thing." What could I do to help her? Life really wasn't being fair to her, not that I had many answers right now.

"What am I going to do?" she asked, plucking a string on her skirt.

The late afternoon sun beamed in through the windows, showing dust mites in the air. A sense of peace wandered through the quiet hallway, and the genuine and older wooden floor was warm. I took a deep breath and pushed my stress away so I could help her. She really needed help. "First thing you do is get up. Then go home and have a healthy dinner and then a decent sleep. After that, we'll figure out your case, and then you can get another job. How strapped are you for cash?" I didn't have any to share, but maybe I could find her a job if it was an emergency. Somebody in the family had to need something.

She finally smiled. "I have a good savings account, so there's that. I've always been a bit of a miser with money, so I'm financially okay for a little while." She bit her lip. "I can't go to the Caribbean or anything, but I'm not starving."

I nudged her arm. "See? That's a bright side. We'll learn more about your case during the preliminary hearing, and then we can come up with a game plan. Once we have a plan in place, you'll feel better. It's just this sucky state of limbo that causes so much stress."

"Totally agree," she said.

Yeah. It was the same place I was in with being a suspect in Sasha's murder. Kelsey and I had more in common than I liked, and so far, the legal system wasn't being fair to us. But I had to believe that it would all work out the way it should in the end. "I know how you feel, and everything is going to be all right." I couldn't tell her about my case, but I could commiserate a little bit.

"You promise I won't go to prison?" Her eyes were a meadow green in the mellow light, and she looked younger than her twenty-one years.

The temptation to guarantee her that and ease her mind was surprisingly strong. "No. I wish I could promise you that, but I can't. What I can say is that I'm good at my job and will do everything I can to make sure you don't go to prison. I trust our legal system, and you're innocent, so I believe this will all turn out okay. But I'd be lying if I made a promise I can't guarantee."

Her shoulders hunched. "I appreciate the honesty."

"Honesty sometimes sucks," I said, finally getting a laugh out of her. I pushed myself to my feet. "Did you drive here?"

"No. My boyfriend dropped me off. The flower shop is just around the corner, so I figured I'd walk to work." She stood and brushed dust off her butt.

I reclaimed my laptop bag. "Boyfriend, huh? When did that start?" I'd wanted to ask about the purple condom, but it hadn't pertained to her case, and I could only be so nosy.

"Not long," she said, smiling. "He's a good guy." She reached down and picked up her purse. "I'm sorry to be hanging out in your building. I just didn't know what to do, and it's warm and quiet here."

It really was. "These old buildings have a good feeling to them, don't they?" We should probably get a bench or two to put along the hallways, although each office was complete on its own. Potted plants positioned throughout couldn't hurt. The environment was perfect for plants. "How about I give you a ride home?" I'd been to her house a few weeks previous during a case. It wasn't on my way home, but it wasn't too much out of the way, either. "I'm happy to."

"Okay." She looked blindly around. "Thanks."

We walked down the steps and into the warm August early evening. Petunias scented the air, even in the alley. They overflowed planters all down the streets of Timber City, and this late in the summer, they filled the early evening with fragrance. My steps were light as I walked around a couple of cars and tossed my bag in back after opening the door for Kelsey.

She slid inside and tucked her purse at her feet.

Maybe I should ask her to dinner. She really did seem lonely. I crossed around the car to reach the driver's side door, wondering if Tessa was working at Smiley's. We could pop by there for a burger and shake.

A truck zoomed down the alley and skidded to a stop.

I jerked around. Crap. The driver was one of the Lorde's women from the other day, and a quick look at the passenger confirmed it was the other blonde. I jumped into my car and ignited the engine. Whatever they wanted wasn't good.

The blonde lifted a muted gray pistol to her window.

Kelsey turned around. "What is happening?"

I gunned my car and shot down the alley, away from the truck and the gun. "Um, hold on." They were blocking my way to Justice Road and thus the police station, but I could still get out the other end of the alley. "Call Aiden," I yelled at Siri on my phone.

"Calling Aiden Devlin," Siri said in the male Australian accent I'd chosen. He sounded so calm.

Kelsey slammed her hands against the dash.

My heart raced as I reached the end of the alley and zipped right on Acorn Road. I punched the gas, my mind spinning. Crap. The truck careened behind me, its brakes squealing.

"Hey, Angel," Aiden said over the phone.

"The Lorde's old ladies are chasing me in a truck and one has a gun," I yelled, my hands gripping the steering wheel so hard it hurt. "What is going on? Aren't you still the president of whoever is left in that stupid motorcycle club?"

"What? Just a second." He muffled the phone and yelled something unintelligible. Male voices came back. "Which old ladies?" he snapped.

Kelsey's mouth dropped wide open and she stared at me.

"I don't know. One blonde and one brunette. They were both with Sasha the other day." The light was turning red ahead of me. I glanced quickly to the sides to see cars coming, so I had no choice but to slam on the brakes.

Kelsey screamed.

My car lurched and I fell against the steering wheel. "Ouch! Seatbelt, Kelsey!" There wasn't time to get out of the car. Fumbling, I grabbed my seatbelt and secured it, looking frantically in the rear-view mirror as Kelsey did the same.

Hopefully they'd stop.

I could see the brunette's eyes widen. She must've pounded on the brakes because the truck hitched. It skidded loudly at the last second. Then her jaw tightened, and the truck sped up.

My instincts kicked in, and I grabbed the wheel but didn't have time to hit the gas and somehow get out of the way. The vehicle hit my car with a loud crunch of metal against metal. My body smashed against the seatbelt and then back, my head hitting the headrest. My ears rang.

The impact pushed my car into the intersection. Horns blared as cars swerved to get out of the way. I tee-boned a compact blue car, spinning both it and my Fiat around in a circle. The last thing I saw was a blond man slump over his steering wheel in that car. Oh no. Was he dead?

"Kelsey?" I whispered weakly. My ears rang and my vision went dark from the outside in. Then I fell into unconsciousness.

CHAPTER 13

I woke up in an ambulance, my head aching and my vision fuzzy. Then I went in and out until finally awakening completely in a comfortable bed, hooked up to hospital monitors. Santa Clause stood next to me. "Santa?" I whispered.

Santa smiled and looked closer into my eyes as he set a tablet aside. "No. I'm Dr. Springfield." He was in his mid-sixties with short white hair and a white beard. "You were in a car accident, young lady. I'm going to ask you some questions, and I need you to relax and answer them. What's your name?"

I answered all of his questions while taking inventory of my body. Nothing was broken, but everything was sore. Even my right knee protested. What had I hit with my knee? I couldn't remember the accident after the truck hit us.

Finally, he finished making notes on the tablet. "You have a slight concussion but I'm not horribly worried about it. You also have bruising along your ribcage, but nothing is broken. We'll keep you here for a couple of hours, but I think you'll be able to go home tonight with some directions." His smile really was Santa-like. "Is there anybody we can call for you?"

"Yeah." I gave him Tessa's number since she lived closest to the hospital. I'd rather deal with the rest of my family on my home turf and not in the hospital.

The doctor left just as Kelsey Walker rushed in, her eyes wild. "Anna? Are you all right?" She hurried to my bedside and grabbed my hand. A little bit of blood dotted her skirt.

I coughed. "Just a slight concussion and bruised ribs. How are you? Are you okay?"

A bandage covered the skin above her right eye and a few bruises stood out along her clavicle. "I'm fine and didn't even need to ride in the ambulance. There's a slight cut over my eye, but I didn't need stitches. It was crazy. Tell me you're okay." Her eyes filled with tears. "You've been through so much. Do you remember what happened?"

I frowned and tried to remember everything. "We were rammed by a truck." It didn't make sense. "Why did they want to hurt us? Where are they now? Are they here in the hospital?" I tried to push the covers off me.

She pushed them right back and pressed a hand to my shoulder. "Stay still and relax. I don't know where they are, and they're definitely not here in the hospital. They drove off after hitting us, but I managed to get their license plate and gave it to the police officers. There were two women in the truck, and I described them the best I could."

Man. Static filled my brain along with fog. "Are you sure you're not injured?" I asked.

"Yes." She looked at my face and then her shoulders relaxed. "I thought you were really hurt. At the scene, I tried to wake you up, but you were out cold. It was terrifying. Are you sure you're all right?"

"Um, excuse me?" A blond man stood in the doorway with bruises across the right side of his face and his left arm in a sling. He was about six foot, slender, and maybe in his late twenties? His eyes were a dark brown, and right now they were tinged with pain.

Kelsey moved more toward my head. "Oh. Hi. I tried to check in on you, but the nurse wouldn't let me. Said they were looking you over."

I pushed a button on the nearby control panel, and the bed sat me up. There was something familiar about the guy, and it took me a second to recognize him as the driver of the blue car in the accident. I gasped. Thank goodness he wasn't dead. We'd crashed right into the side of his car—on the driver's door. "You were in the other car. Are you okay? I'm so sorry about this." Yeah, as a lawyer, I should've never said those words. Right now, I didn't care. My car had been forced into his, and it wasn't either of our fault.

He limped inside, his jeans slightly bloody, and pain lines deepening on either side of his mouth. "Yeah. I'm okay. Just a bunch of bruises and a dislocated shoulder. I wanted to make sure you're all right."

Kelsey held out a hand. "I'm Kelsey and this is Anna." She blushed a light pink.

I thought she had a boyfriend? Must not be serious. Or maybe my slight concussion was just making life confusing right now.

He took her hand with his good one. "Teddy Thompson. Wrong place at the wrong time. As usual."

Kelsey drew out one of the two guest chairs. "You should probably sit down."

Teddy smiled at her and then sat. "You're a godsend."

She preened. I swear, she preened. But he seemed like a decent guy so far, and it'd be nice to see her flirt with somebody kind. Wow. Maybe I had inherited Nonna's matchmaking gene. "You should sit as well, Kelsey. We were all injured."

Kelsey sat next to Teddy, her worried gaze still on me. "Are you sure your brain is working? I've never seen somebody stay out for that long. Your head has to hurt."

"It does but not as much as I'd expect." I set the blanket more securely over my legs. Where were my clothes?

Teddy's eyes now sparkled through the pain. "The cops want to talk to us, but I wanted to make sure you both were okay first."

I finally started to think like a lawyer. This guy may sue me. So could Kelsey, for that matter. Although anybody seeing the wreck would know that it wasn't my fault. I'd been waiting at the red light, and the truck had deliberately plowed into me. One of us could've been killed. Anger filtered through the fog in my head.

A uniformed officer walked into the room, and I relaxed when I saw it was Bud Orlov. Bud had deep black eyes set into a hardened face. His hair was a short buzz, and he had more muscles than I could count. He'd been assigned to protect me earlier in the summer, and I'd accidentally gotten him shot once. I think he'd considered dating Donna but had changed his mind because of me and the dangerous situations that seemed to ensue. "Hi, Bud."

He walked closer. "Are you all right?"

"I'm fine. Bruised and concussed. Nothing new." Unfortunately a true statement. "It wasn't my fault."

Teddy leaned back in his chair. "Her car was hit by a Ford truck and pushed into the intersection, where we collided. She'd been parked at the light, and I had a green light, so I was proceeding through the intersection when she was hit from behind."

Relief sizzled through my arms and I completely relaxed. Teddy had seen everything that had happened and wasn't out to get me. Hopefully the women in the truck carried insurance. "That's all true."

Bud surveyed the room with his dark gaze. "That's what we've heard from witnesses on the sidewalk as well. We're running down the license plate number from Washington state. Can you tell me who was driving the truck or why you were targeted? This time?"

How much should I tell him? Aiden still was undercover, and I was a suspect in Sasha's death, but those women could've killed somebody. I went with the full truth. Well, almost. "I don't know their names, but I recognized the two women in the front seat as being friends of folks in the Lorde's motorcycle club." Bud wouldn't know about Aiden being ATF, probably. I think just a couple of the higher-ups and Detective Pierce were privy to that information right now. I hoped.

Bud lifted one thick eyebrow. "Aren't you still dating Aiden Devlin?"

I nodded and instantly regretted the movement when lights flashed behind my eyes with stabbing precision.

"Isn't he the president of the Lordes?" Bud asked.

"Yeah. I think the women were after me for some other reason." I wasn't sure where to go with this.

Teddy leaned forward. "Who are the Lordes?"

Kelsey patted my hand. "The Lordes are a motorcycle club out of Washington. They've gotten in trouble for running drugs and guns."

I bit my lip. Did Kelsey know that Aiden had been undercover with the ATF? I didn't think so, but the memory of the day everything had blown up was hazy. Her sister had been arrested that day, but I didn't remember either Krissy or Kelsey seeing Aiden with his ATF team. I'd have to discreetly question her when I got the chance. "I think the women are dating members."

"I don't see why any Lordes old lady would be targeting you. You don't have a bulls eye on your back. No way," Kelsey said, her eyebrow rising to the bandage.

Figured she'd know the lingo. "I'm very confused by this as well," I muttered.

Teddy tore his gaze away from Kelsey's pretty face to focus on me. "I don't understand. You're dating a motorcycle gang president, and girlfriends of his members tried to kill you?" He glanced at Bud and then back to me. "Maybe they're not dating? Does he want you dead? Is this how motorcycle gangs operate?"

Kelsey threw her hands up. "As far as I know. Especially one that works outside the law."

Bud set his shoulders back. "Have you and Devlin had a fight?"

"No," I said. It was too bad I couldn't tell Bud about Aiden's true job.

"We're going to have to talk to him," Bud said. "Maybe he can shed some light on this. I hope the motorcycle gang isn't trying to kill you, Anna. While they've been hit hard the last year, they still are dangerous."

"Club," I said, unable to hold back any longer. "It's a motorcycle club and not a motorcycle gang." It was so much better for my brain to focus on something trivial than everything else, especially the fact that those two women had tried to kill me.

Bud looked at me like I'd gone nuts. Yeah, he'd looked at me like that before—more than once. "We'll need to talk to Devlin. Where is he?"

"Right now, I have no idea where he is, but I'm assuming he'll be checking in soon. We are still dating and he doesn't want me dead." I chewed on the inside of my cheek. "He won't know anything, but feel free. Has there been a detective assigned to this case yet?" I held my breath.

"Yeah. Detective Pierce is on it," Bud said. "Somehow he always gets stuck with your situations." Then he drew himself up and looked tall as well as beefy. "I didn't mean it like that."

Geez. Get a guy shot once, and he never lets it go. "It's okay, Bud. No worries." I couldn't really blame him.

Kelsey smoothed hair away from my eyes, and her touch was gentle. "Can I do anything for you? Like call your office and let them know you're out for a while?" She really was sweet, and the concern in her gaze was genuine.

I smiled. "You're kind, but there's nothing to do. In fact, we're still on for your court hearing tomorrow. I'll be fine then. This isn't anything a Tylenol or two won't fix."

My sister Tessa ran into the room, her reddish-blonde hair

flying every direction. She took in the scene, noticed I was conscious and shook her head. "What the hell happened now?"

Bud snorted. "What do you mean? This is a normal Thursday for Anna."

CHAPTER 14

essa helped me out of her car in my driveway just as
Aiden tore up on his motorcycle. He was off the bike
and gently grasped my arms. "What happened? How badly are you
hurt?" His Irish brogue came out full force, and the glittering in
his eyes held danger.

I blinked. "I'm fine. Car accident. We were on the phone,
remember?" Although it was all a little muddled.

"Yeah. I was north of Spokane and got here as fast as I could.
Your phone kept going to voicemail." He looked me over and then
stepped back. "How bad?" His jaw tightened.

"Slight concussion and bruised ribs," I said. They weren't the
worst injuries I'd had the last few months.

Tess shut the car door. "Hi, Aiden," she said dryly.

"Hi." His gaze didn't leave mine. "I want the full story." Without
waiting for a response, he lifted me against his hard chest and
strode around the garage toward my porch.

"I'll just bring her stuff," Tess called out, still sounding amused.
Well, kind of.

We got settled inside the cottage with me on the sofa and
Aiden on the adjacent chair.

Tessa put a hand-crocheted blanket over me and glanced at her watch. "I have a shift in thirty minutes but can cancel it."

"No." I plucked a loose string. "I'm okay. Just field calls for me for a little while until I get my phone back, would you? With the family?"

She leaned over and kissed my cheek. "I already have been. Mom and Dad agreed to stay in Silverville for the night at least. I had to promise you were coming to the family barbecue on Sunday to even get that much from them. I'll take care of the rest of the family and bring you over something to eat after my shift. Don't argue." She patted Aiden on the shoulder as she walked to the door. "Whatever is going on with those women needs to stop, Aiden."

"Affirmative," he said, his gaze not leaving me.

Tessa left and I cuddled beneath the blanket. "What's going on?"

He shook his head. "I'm not sure, but I'm finding out." As if on cue, his phone buzzed and he lifted it to his ear. "Devlin. Hi, Saber. What did you find out?" As he listened, his eyes darkened. "Okay. Make it very clear that Anna is off limits and that I am not happy. Don't be gentle." He hung up.

I swallowed. "What did Saber say?"

"The two women in the truck are old ladies of two of the still remaining Lorde's members. They're low in the organization and thus weren't swept up in either of the raids. Both morons but good for numbers at the moment since I need numbers of members to be interesting to Barensky. Sasha convinced the other women she was still with me, and they were trying to show loyalty by coming after you. Maybe help their men rise in the club since they don't know that most of us are undercover at this point."

I blew out air. "Please tell me this is your last undercover Op as the president of the Lorde's motorcycle club."

"I promise. Chances are the cover sucks, and it's just going to get me shot," he muttered. "We're doing a deep dive with everyone who might know about my affiliation with the ATF before proceeding. I did wear the jacket when we busted that fringe gun group, but we put them all in prison. I'm somewhat certain."

Well, that didn't sound great. "My whole family knows."

"I'm aware," he said. "I've already reached out to your dad, and he's spreading the word to keep it quiet. It's doubtful a bomb-making terrorist has any ties to your family or will run across anybody, but I think your dad can give everyone a heads-up not to talk about me. It's a risk I have to take."

"Why?" My head hurt and my ribs ached, and I needed him in one piece.

He leaned over and pulled the blanket more firmly over my injured side. "When Barensky has been hired for a job, that job happens. Sasha was good at undercover, and her intel was always solid. So this bombing will happen whether or not the Lordes are the pawns or not."

I tried to stay in the moment. "Pawns?"

"Yeah." Aiden kicked off his boots. "Barensky, the nut job, looks at every campaign as a game of chess. He's hired by the King and uses pawns to position the bomb or bombs."

"He's the Queen?" I asked.

"No. He's the chess master. The Queen is the mark or victim, the knights the bombs, the rooks the obstacles. Years ago, the FBI had him in custody, and he was interviewed by a couple of shrinks to determine if he was sane enough for trial. I've been going through those notes again." Aiden rolled his neck and it popped.

I winced. Ouch. "What about the bishops? They're the only chess piece you haven't mentioned."

"They're the unknowns, according to Barensky," Aiden said. "He factors unknowns into every campaign."

My mind was slushy, but I tried to keep up. "Did he win at trial?"

"No. He escaped during transport, and we never caught him

again. I came close and managed to take down the operation he'd created, but we didn't get him last time." A muscle ticked in Aiden's jaw.

"Did Sasha have any idea who hired Barensky to create bombs this time?"

"No. The man has built explosives for anybody with enough money for the last fifty years. He's willing to build explosive devices for bank robbers, terrorists, and just killers." Frustration cut lines into Aiden's forehead. "Sasha didn't get close enough to find out either the client or the bombing site or sites. All she knew was that something was to happen in Seattle."

I snagged the bright blue throw pillow from my side and wrapped both arms around it. The softness felt good against my aching ribcage. "What is Barensky's first name?"

"Norman." Aiden took out his phone and held up the screen. "This is him. Just so you know to keep an eye out, although he shouldn't be anywhere near you."

The guy looked to be in his sixties with thin gray hair, pinched brown eyes, and sallow skin.

"What a charmer," I murmured.

"You have no idea." Aiden's gaze remained intense on mine. "What happened to your car?"

My sweet little car. "Tessa said it was towed to McClosky's Garage. He'll call me with an estimate, and my insurance agency has already been contacted," I said. "I'll drive the Jeep for now." My Fiat was a summer car, and I had an older Jeep Cherokee that I drove in the winter and kept in the garage.

"Good plan," Aiden said.

I watched as the sun sprayed pink and orange across the sky while going down. "How about a glass of wine?"

"You have a concussion and can't have alcohol," he said, lounging in the chair.

I liked it when Aiden got a little bossy. Sometimes. Aiden knew that I liked this. I smiled.

"No," he said. "You're injured."

Darn it.

* * *

I WORE LOOSE BLACK SLACKS, a polka dot black and white blouse, and flats to work in the morning. My head ached, my ribs pounded, and my temper was already up and raring to go. I'd enjoyed my first law firm office meeting with Clark, but now I wished I could go back to bed. Everything hurt as I climbed the steps to the prosecuting attorney's office, where Kelsey waited for me outside. I reached her and forced a smile.

"How are you?" she asked, today wearing a yellow skirt and blouse set. The bandage above her eye only made her look more fragile.

"Okay," I said, turning to look at the bountiful park with the smooth as glass Lilac Lake to the right. The police station, commissioner's offices, and courthouse all faced the park on its northern side, and the community college sat on the west side. I missed working right by the park. "Let's do this."

Kelsey opened the door and we walked inside and up to the receptionist. "Hi, Juliet," I said, glad to see her. "Wow. Those flowers have really grown behind you." The plant had pretty white flowers that smelled sweet, and they'd been tiny buds last time I'd been in the office.

"Thanks." She smiled. Juliet was a sweet young woman and we'd enjoyed working together. "I'll take you to the conference room. You're booked for the smaller one. Can I get you anything?" She stood and led the way down the hall to the conference room, where a water pitcher and clean glasses had been already placed in the middle. "Coffee, soda, tea?"

Both Kelsey and I said we were good, but thanks.

I took a seat on one side of the table with Kelsey next to me. It was odd to be in the office as a visitor instead of a prosecuting attorney. But it'd be nice to see Nick. I'd gotten used to bouncing ideas and cases off him.

The door opened and a young man walked in. He looked to be around thirty with thick blond hair, a swimmer's build, and sharp hazel colored eyes. "Hi. I'm Orrin Morgan." He leaned over to shake hands.

I shook his hand and introduced Kelsey. "I figured I'd see Nick or Alice."

Alice was around thirty-five with a couple of kids at home. We'd worked fine together but had crossed swords with Oliver Duck's case a few weeks ago.

"No." Orrin drew out a chair to sit. "Nick is busy with other cases, and Alice took a job offer in Denver. I was hired to replace her, and this is my case." He wore a smart navy suit with a blindingly white shirt beneath the jacket. "Why are you here, Ms. Albertini?"

I kept my professional smile in place. "I had hoped to talk reasonably about my client. Kelsey didn't know anything about her sister's activities, so charging her with murder is wrong." Sometimes it was easier just to say it out loud in plain English.

"She wasn't charged for murder," Orrin said. "She was charged as an accomplice, and considering she was with her sister all day when Danny Pucci was murdered, it's an easy connection to make. In fact, as I recall, Krissy Walker provided your client with an alibi for that day. They were in the park at a concert together, right? Yet Krissy has confessed to the murder...which means that your client was with her."

"No, I wasn't—" Kelsey began, but I stopped her by raising one hand. She gripped the edges of her chair.

I sat back in my chair and just studied Orrin. For several long moments. He stared right back. Finally, I smiled. "Okay." I looked at Kelsey. "We're done here."

Kelsey fumbled and then pushed her chair away from the

table. She'd gone pale and she sent me a confused look but kept quiet.

I stood and gathered my case file and pens.

Orrin crossed his arms. "Tactics won't work with me."

I smiled. "No tactic here. I just don't have time to waste right now. Things are busy." I gestured Kelsey toward the door.

Orrin still didn't stand. "You're not going to discuss this."

"Nope. Kelsey didn't kill anybody, and she had no knowledge that her sister did. It's that simple, and we aren't going to play games with you. You've got nothing on her, and you know it." I pushed the heavy conference room door open farther.

Orrin cleared his throat. "Your client has been charged with accessory to first-degree murder, evidence destruction and failure to notify of a death. She could get thirty years in prison, easy."

I put on my bored look and partially turned. "Get to it."

"Ten years. She pleads guilty and we agree to ten years. She could be out sooner with good behavior." Orrin still appeared relaxed and calm in his chair.

Kelsey gasped.

I took her arm. "See you in court, Orrin. It was very nice to meet you." I prodded Kelsey down the hallway, smiled at the receptionist, and walked out into the sunny day. A buzz of a lawn-mower echoed through the park in front of us.

Kelsey turned on me the second we hit the sidewalk. "I can't go to prison. Honest, Anna. I didn't know anything, and I really didn't want Danny dead." Tears filled her green eyes. "I can't believe this."

I patted her arm. "It's okay, Kelsey. Take a deep breath. I'm not sure what's going on with Orrin, but we'll figure it out. There's no evidence that you had anything to do with Danny's death. It doesn't matter that you were with your sister for a while that day, and I'm sure Krissy will back you up if needed. Let me handle this." I'd made a tactical decision in walking out of the meeting, and I thought it was the right one for not only Kelsey but for Orrin. He needed to know we weren't going to fold. "We're not going to do anything until your preliminary hearing, where we'll see all the evidence Orrin has. Or most of it, anyway. Before you go, is there anything you haven't told me? Anything they might know that I don't?"

Kelsey shook her head and a tear dropped to her cheek. "No. I didn't help Krissy kill Danny. I'd never do that." Her voice rose and trembled.

I hugged her. "It's going to be okay. Let me get their case file and I'll call you to go over it when it arrives. Until then, just try to relax and stay out of trouble."

She hugged me back and then turned to walk around the rose bushes to the parking lot. I glanced up at the windows from the office to see Orrin watching us, a slight smile playing on his perfectly symmetrical lips. Even though it was a warm day, a shiver ran down my spine.

What did he know that I didn't?

CHAPTER 15

I poked my head in Clark's office on the way to lunch. "We've already forgotten our plan to not see clients on Fridays."

Papers were scattered across his desk and he looked up, circles beneath his eyes. "I know. Just for today. We'll start the new routine next week after we take advantage of your recent notoriety." He shook his head and sat back, looking lawyerly in his purple long-sleeved shirt, deep blue tie, and Monte Carlo style gun-metal glasses. "I can't believe I actually just used that sentence with my law partner." He shook his head. "Do you think we should hire a paralegal?"

"Not yet," I said, leaning against the door frame. "We're having an influx of clients right now, but that might trickle off quickly. Let's give it a month or two, and if work doesn't slow down, maybe we can hire somebody. For now, Oliver and Pauley have things covered." I rocked back on my heels. "You know, we might want to talk to Oliver about attending the paralegal program at the college. We could offer to pay for it."

Clark pursed his lips. "That's a good idea if Oliver is interested in being a paralegal. What about Pauley?"

"We can ask him, but he's focusing on math right now," I said. Since Pauley was only sixteen, he had a lot of time to study a lot of subjects. "He might be interested, but after the two years here, I know he wants to attend a four-year college." I just hoped he was ready for that. But that was something to worry about in two years, after Pauley graduated from the community college. I had enough to worry about right now. "I'm meeting Nonna at Smiley's for lunch. Do you want to come?"

Clark studied me. Man, he was smart. "I don't think so. Not sure what you're up to, but I do know I want nothing to do with it."

It was good that my law partner had a brain, right? "Fine. Want me to bring you anything back?"

His face cleared. "Yeah. Club sandwich and thanks. I appreciate it."

I turned and moved for the doorway to the reception area. Thank goodness we'd created a wall between the offices and the entrance. The room was just as full as it had been yesterday, so I waved to Oliver and hustled out to the office hallway. It was unfortunate we didn't have a back way out. Oh, all of the windows were good exits, and we could get out during a fire, but having a back door would be convenient.

I took several deep breaths as I walked down the sidewalk outside toward Smiley's Diner. Only one building separated the diner from my office building, and Duke's Jewelry Store had been there for as long as I could remember. It was only a one-story building and had an antique clock out front that was protected as a historically preserved sign in Idaho. I ignored the sparkly diamonds in the display window and continued to Smileys.

Smiley's Diner was a Timber City staple. The booths were red, the hamburgers fresh, and the tile well worn. A sparkling and round turret featured the puffed pastries and pies for the day. Fresh ones. My stomach growled, and I hustled past a clustering of tables with wooden chairs, beyond the long counter with fifties style bar stools, to a booth toward the back. "Hi, Nonna."

"Hi." She beamed at me. For her outing, she'd worn a smart lilac-colored pantsuit with no-nonsense gold jewelry. Her hair was up in an intricate bun. "How are you? You look tired. Are you still hurting from the car wreck?"

I started to slide across from her, and she shook her head. "Please sit next to me." .

"All right." I sat next to her, and light jasmine perfume tickled my nose. "I'm fine, Nonna. Just a little bruised." Actually, my ribs were killing me and I'd love a pain pill, but since I planned to return to work, I'd have to make do with more Advil in an hour.

She began to say something and then straightened, waving her hand at the door.

Gerty Basanelli caught her eye and hustled over. She wore a pretty flowered dress with white tennis shoes, and her crocheted shoulder tote bag was big enough to take on a picnic. "Oh, hello, Elda. What are you doing in town?" She opened her cloudy brown eyes very wide and fluttered her eyelashes.

Oh, for goodness sakes.

Nick followed behind her, suspicion already darkening his not cloudy brown eyes. Nick Basanelli was tall, broad, and brilliant. He had topaz eyes, Italian straight features, and dark wavy hair. "Hello."

"Oh, my." My grandma smiled guilelessly. "What a surprise. You really must join us."

"No—" Nick started gently just as his grandmother all but hopped into the booth. He paused. "That would be nice. Thank you." Then he sat across from me and very slightly lifted an eyebrow.

I tried to look as innocent as possible, but my cheeks grew warm. Yeah, I was blushing. "Hi, Mrs. Basanelli."

"Oh, you call me Gerty, sweetheart." Gerty slapped my hand. "It's so lovely to see you. I'm sorry about that unfortunate bar fight the other night. Your sister Tessa wasn't really involved, was she?"

I dutifully shook my head. "No, she wasn't. Not at all." Considering she'd taken on an ATF agent, I might have to go to confession for lying this week. For now, I had two goals. One was to keep my Nonna happy, and the other was to somehow run interference for Tessa, even though this was kind of my fault.

Gerty's hair was cut in a short salt and pepper bob which swished around her face as she talked. "Good. That's what I figured."

Our waitress hustled up and set down bright orange water glasses. She looked to be in her early forties with sparkling eyes. "The specials are on the board, and here are menus." She reached for the counter and turned to give us each a folding menu.

I slowly started to relax. All right. I didn't even know this woman.

Nonna smiled. "You're a sweet person and I hate to be a pain, but could you ask Tessa Albertini to take care of us. She's my granddaughter, and I just don't see her enough."

Nick lowered his chin and stared right at me.

I quickly turned to the waitress. "We don't want to cause any difficulties. If Tessa is elsewhere, we'll just catch up with her later."

The waitress rocked back. "It's no problem at all. We can switch a table or two." She looked toward the other end of the restaurant and gestured. "Here she comes."

Tessa reached us, and to her credit, she looked calm and slightly amused. "Hi, all. The special is the clam chowder with a fruit salad, and I've heard the tuna salad sandwich is exceptionally good today." She caught my gaze and her eyes twinkled. "What can I get you?"

Nonna leaned toward her. "Hi, sweetheart. Is there any chance you can take a break and eat with us?"

Gerty nodded. "You look peckish and should really eat something. What do you say?"

Tessa didn't crack a bit. "I wish I could, but I already had my lunch break, darn it. I ate one of the specialty salads, and it was delicious."

Man, my sister was smart. She'd even offered proof that she'd eaten. Nicely done. "I'll have the special," I said, trying to distract the grandmothers.

Gerty was not to be distracted. "What time do you get off today, Tessa? I really worry that you in the younger generation don't take time to eat properly. I know that Nicolo doesn't. Maybe you could meet and have dinner so your grandmothers wouldn't worry so much about you."

Subtle. Man. I sighed.

"Grams," Nick said.

Nonna tapped her fingernail on the menu. "I'll have the cheeseburger with no onions and an iced tea."

"I'll have iced tea, too," I quickly said.

Tessa looked at Gerty. "How about you? Our burgers are always very good."

Gerty glanced at her menu and then back at my sister. "Don't you need to write this down, honey?"

Tess pushed a wayward strand of her reddish-blonde hair out of her face. "No worries, Gerty. I'll remember the orders."

Gerty shoved an elbow hard enough into Nick's side that he winced. "She doesn't need to write it down. She's a smart one, Nicolo." As if she hadn't just bruised her grandson, she beamed up at Tessa. "I'll have the chicken salad sandwich. Is that a good one?"

Tessa smiled. "It really is. The grapes are fresh and the celery very crunchy. Anything to drink?"

"A Pepsi," Gerty said.

Tessa looked directly at Nick, and damn if she didn't blush a little bit. "Nick?"

"Burger, well done, fries on the side and a Dr. Pepper." He gathered the menus and handed them to her. "Thanks for being a good sport."

She grinned and took the menus, turning and heading back around the counter.

And damn if Nick didn't watch her go.

The grandmothers shared a smile.

I felt like a cat trying to navigate through a carwash. Neither Nick nor Tessa would like to be set up, although they really did make a nice couple. Kind of an opposites attract type of a situation, but they both did have solid cores of strength.

Gerty tucked her monstrous purse by her legs. "Tessa sure is a pretty one, isn't she?"

Nick's eyes narrowed. "Grams? Whatever you're up to, please stop. I'm an adult and so is Tessa."

She elbowed him again, and he tried to move farther away from her, but the booth was only so big. "I'm tired of you taking so long. She's single, you're single, and you're obviously attracted to each other."

Nonna nodded vigorously. "Anna told us you two kind of flirted, so why not?"

Nick swung his gaze to me. "You did what?"

I sucked in air. Saying anything like that to our grandmothers was akin to waving a red flag to an angry bull. "It wasn't like that." Oh, it was exactly like that.

A couple entering the diner caught my eye. They turned toward us and I bit back a smile. It was Kelsey Walker and Teddy Thompson. While his injured arm was still in a sporty black sling, his other hand was pressed to the small of her back. She'd dressed in a light white summer dress with tall blue wedges. "Hi, Anna," she said, hesitantly walking closer.

"Hi." Their meet-cute was the best ever.

She gestured to Teddy. "You remember Teddy?"

"Hi," I said.

"Hi." He had a couple of bruises across his clavicle, no doubt from the wreck. "Um, Kelsey and I were at the station giving additional information about the wreck, and we, um, thought we'd grab lunch." His blue eyes were earnest, and they might be just getting lunch, but the palm of his hand was still on the small of her back, and she didn't seem to mind.

If my job as a lawyer didn't work out—again—I might think about starting a dating service or something. "That's great. Have you heard anything?"

Kelsey's eyes widened and she leaned forward as if she had great gossip. "Yeah. The police found the women who were in the truck, and they were arrested last night. That's why we were asked in to answer more questions and identify them. I'm sure you'll be called in, too."

I probably already had been, but Oliver hadn't gotten a chance to give me all of my messages before I dashed out to meet Nonna for this stressful lunch. "I'm glad you're both okay."

"You, too." Teddy ushered Kelsey past us toward a booth even farther back.

Nonna partially turned her head to watch them go. "They make a cute couple. Isn't that the youngest Walker girl?"

Gerty tsked her tongue. "So sad about her older sister." She looked back at me. "I heard that Kelsey was charged in the murder. It can't be true, is it?" Then she pivoted to look at her grandson. "You'd know, wouldn't you?"

Nick took a drink of his water. "I can't talk about ongoing cases, Grams."

Good answer.

Gerty turned to me. "Well? What do you know?" The sparkle of her silver cross necklace caught the light.

Legal ethics dictated that I couldn't even name my clients, much less talk about their cases. The bell over the door dinged and I turned, hoping I knew who'd entered. Anything to get the topic of conversation away from me. I squinted and then instantly changed my mind.

"Hey!" Yelled the blonde woman who'd smashed her truck into my car. "What were you saying to the police?" She ran toward us, and I began to tense, but she went right by our table to Kelsey and Teddy's table.

The brunette followed but unfortunately recognized me. "It's you," she bellowed, pausing at the counter. "You're all in this together." Her hair was all over and her shirt dirty. It must've been a rough night in lockup. Glaring, she looked frantically around and then snatched a pastry off the turret.

She wound up to throw it.

CHAPTER 16

I ducked, and the pastry flew right over my head.

"What in the world?" Gerty gasped, swiveling in her seat to stare at the brunette.

Not intimidated by her miss, the brunette snatched two donuts and heaved them at me. One smashed into my neck, and the other one hit Nonna's shoulder. Oh, God.

Nonna pushed me out of the seat and dragged her purse with us. Chocolate frosting covered her shoulder.

"No, Nonna," I began, stumbling to my feet and trying to wipe vanilla cream filling off my neck.

"This is not how a lady behaves," Nonna snapped, yanking her wooden spoon from the purse. It was well worn with dents in several places along the handle—mostly from being clanked against pots. Mostly.

I backed away until my butt was against a barstool and I could see everyone at once. Protecting Nonna and Gerty was the only important consideration right now.

The blonde behind me screeched and yanked Teddy from the booth. He slid on the first pastry but pivoted his body to keep his injured arm away from her. Pain and panic widened his blue eyes.

Kelsey immediately exploded from her side of the booth and crashed into the blonde, sending them both spiraling between bar stools and into the counter. Teddy spun and tried to reach for Kelsey with his good arm.

I pushed Nonna toward Nick, who was standing up. A pie crashed into the side of his head, sending whipped cream flying in every direction. He fell into a rapid smattering of Italian that somehow included dead goats and a lot of swear words I'd never heard strung together. When Gerty tried to slide from the booth, he lifted a hand to stop her.

She glared, smacked him with her straw purse, and all but forced him to back away.

Panic grabbed me and my breathing panted out. We had to get the grandmothers out of the way.

A piece of coconut cream pie hit the side of my face with the force of a softball. My head jerked, and I turned toward the brunette while cool cream slid down my cheek to plop on my shoe.

She smiled and was missing one of her canines. "Bitch," she yelled, her fingers covered in frosting. She reached for another piece.

Nick herded his grandma toward mine, putting his body between the brunette and them.

She threw like an MVP pitcher at the same time, and a piece of strawberry cheesecake splashed right into his face. He growled and wiped strawberry goo from his eyes. It extended up into his dark hair and slid along his ear.

Kelsey yanked the blonde up, both swinging.

I yelped and jumped between them and the grandmothers, instantly taking an elbow to the gut. Pain detonated in my stomach and I doubled over, scrambling to ward off blows as Nonna swung her spoon around me and nailed the blonde in the ear.

The blonde screeched and lunged for my grandmother.

Fury roared through me. I have no idea where Tessa came from, but one second she was on the counter, and the next, she was tackling the blonde back into the booth.

I turned to help her just as Kelsey did the same, and we collided, both sliding on the gooey floor and going down hard. She groaned and tried to roll over just as I did the same. More bruises collected on already healing bruises on my body. My ears rang, and it wasn't from the coconut sliding into them.

"The police are coming," somebody yelled from the kitchen.

I grabbed a barstool and tried to pull myself to my feet. My shoes slid on whipped cream, but I managed to gain my balance. Nonna slid a hand beneath my elbow as she tried to help me.

The blonde shoved Tessa off her, and I turned to catch my sister before she careened into Gerty. We slipped and both fell. Nonna smartly released my arm and waited until I had settled on the hard tile before leaning over to help us up.

The brunette threw one more piece of pie and hit Teddy right in the chest. Then she turned and ran out the front door. The blonde started to hurry for the exit, but Nick grabbed her arm and forced her to a stop. She turned, surprisingly fast, and punched him right in the groin.

The sound he made was worse than a furious coyote. He released her and bent over, gasping for air.

Gerty lost it. She careened around him and for the door. "You terrible woman! I'd better still get grandchildren."

I rushed past Nick and reached Gerty, jumping in front of her before she could run outside. "Gerty. Nick is hurt. We have to make sure he's okay. Don't worry. We'll have that woman arrested."

Gerty partially turned. "Elda? Throw me your spoon."

Nonna instantly complied, and I somehow snatched the spoon out of the air before Gerty could get it.

Nick straightened. He was stark pale, and pain glimmered in

his eyes. "Everyone stop it. Right now." His voice was a hoarse bellow.

Gerty hurried toward him. "My baby. Are you okay? How bad are you hurt?" She looked over her shoulder at a trio of waitresses behind the bar, watching us with their eyes wide and their mouths open. "Please get us some ice. Or frozen peas."

"No." Nick held up a hand, still not standing completely upright. "Everyone just stop. Thank you." He glared at several teens over in the table section who held their phones up, catching the entire situation. "Stop filming and stop taking pictures. I mean it."

The teens didn't even twitch.

I looked around at the mess. We all had different frosting or cream on our hair, faces, and clothing. The tile floor was covered with pieces of pie and donut. Teddy helped wipe off Kelsey's face while Tessa shook out her shirt.

Nonna wiped cream off her neck to taste. Her eyebrows lifted. "It's good."

Two uniformed officers walked through the front door and took in the scene. I wasn't sure if I was happy or not that one of them was Bud Orlov.

He looked at me and sighed.

Yeah. I agreed. Chocolate frosting dropped from my chin to my shoe. When had she thrown chocolate cake?

Gerty moved toward Nonna. "I'm not sure this was a good idea."

Nonna's eyes widened in panic. She looked at Tessa and then at Nick. "Oh, this is just one little hiccup." Even she didn't sound sure about that, though.

Bud shook his head and drew out his notepad.

I bit my lip. Hopefully I hadn't just ruined another romance for one of my sisters. I licked my lips and tasted coconut. What a freakin' disaster.

* * *

AFTER GIVING our statements to the police, I watched Nonna drive off after she dropped me outside my office building. The sun beat down on me, and my skin started to itch from the pastries. I wiped my hands off on my skirt again and then fetched my phone from my purse to dial Aiden.

"Devlin," he answered.

"Hey. Where are you?" I asked, wanting to kick off my shoes and wipe off my feet.

Voices echoed in the background. "I'm buying motorcycle parts from Newman's. What's going on?" Newman's was over on Cedar Avenue and just a few blocks away.

"You're in town? Good. I need to talk to you." It was time he got his house in order. Two fights were all I could get Tessa involved in, and right now, it seemed like Nick was running as fast as he could in the other direction. I couldn't exactly argue with him. "I'm outside of my office. How long will you be?"

A motorcycle revved up. "I'll be right there." He clicked off.

Good. I walked over beneath a sweeping maple tree and sat on the wooden bench beneath it. Benches lined up and down most of the streets near downtown. Once seated, I tried to wipe off as much of the pastries as I could.

I heard Aiden's motorcycle before I saw him, and soon he rolled to a stop in front of me. He parked the bike and swung a leg over, watching me carefully. "What happened to you?" he asked.

"If you're in charge of the Lordes, you need to start acting like it." I flicked a piece of coconut off my arm and hit him in the chest.

He cocked his head. In his faded jeans, black tee, and motor-cycle boots, he looked exactly like the badass I knew him to be. "How about you explain what you mean by that statement?"

Oh, I did. In great detail, I told him about the food fight. When he obviously tried to stop a grin, I flicked more coconut at his black shirt. "Tell those women that I'm not to be bothered again." I stood as my temper started to warm to the heated temperature around us. "In fact, tell them to leave Kelsey, Teddy, and my entire family alone. Got it, Devlin?"

His smile was slow and sexy. "Yeah." He wiped his finger along my collarbone and then licked it clean. "Chocolate. Nice." Then he leaned in and licked along my ear. "Mmm. Coconut."

My body performed a full body roll. "Knock it off." I shivered, even though it was in the nineties today.

"Mmm." He wandered along my neck, and no doubt tasted strawberry. "This might be my favorite afternoon ever." He leaned back. "Wanna ride? We can go to your place."

Oh, I wanted a ride. Definitely to my place. "I have meetings this afternoon."

He looked me up and down, his gaze doubtful. "You're covered in food." Then he tugged on my hair. "Is that peanut butter?"

"I don't think so. Maybe vanilla cream filling," I muttered. "I'll wash up the best I can, and then I'll head home after I meet with the clients who've made appointments. What's your plan for tonight?"

Now his smile turned down-right wicked.

I almost ran to his bike and got on. Instead, my thighs weakened and my breath just up and stopped. "You're making dinner, then. After you talk to the Lordes members and their girlfriends. By the way, why are you in town?"

He lost the smile. "I gave bail money to the two Lordes members and didn't know their women were going to cause a ruckus. How did they find you, anyway?"

"They followed Teddy and Kelsey from the police station, it sounded like." I shook my head. "The police are looking for those women again, Aiden."

"I'm sure they've already headed to Washington," he murmured. "Don't worry. I'll take care of it."

I flicked the coconut flakes off his shirt. "So you're back undercover?"

"Yeah," he said softly. "We think we have the cover as solid as possible, but I'm gonna have to stay out of town during the operation to remain off everyone's radar—starting today now that I helped bail out those women."

I pushed my sticky hair out of my face. "This doesn't sound safe. You're dealing with a criminal who likes to make bombs."

"I know, and I have to find out who he's making those bombs for, Angel. It's my job. I deal with explosives more than I'd like." He took my hands and rubbed the dried frosting off my thumb. "As soon as we get a name and a campaign, I'll be out. It's definitely the last time I can use this cover. Or any cover around here, probably."

I didn't like how that sounded. "Okay."

He kissed the top of my nose, and even that heated my blood. "Don't worry. If I go under somewhere else, I'll still consider this home."

The idea of his leaving mixed with the reality that he dealt with bombs and my temples began to ache. It was a huge risk for him to try to keep the Lordes cover, even though he was acting so casual about it. Too many people knew who he really was. "I have to get back to work." I leaned up and kissed his jaw.

"I'll see you at home," he murmured.

A lump settled in my throat and I turned to hurry inside my building.

Aiden Devlin dealt with danger so often that right now, when the world was crumbling, he seemed already at home. What was I going to do with that?

CHAPTER 17

Cream filling squished in my shoes as I walked into my law office. I'd tried to clean up as much as possible at the main restroom in the building, but there wasn't a whole lot I could do. It seemed like a good idea to start leaving a couple sets of clothing at the office just in case. I reached Clark's room. "There was a bit of a scurfuffle at the diner," I said.

Clark looked over my hair and clothing. "Did you get in a food fight?"

"Kind of." I gave him the lowdown, and to his credit, he didn't laugh too much.

Then he sobered completely. "Please tell me there wasn't anybody from the local press there eating lunch. Please."

I bit my lip and still tasted like strawberry. "I didn't see anybody I knew. No photographers or reporters." I shuffled my feet. "But there were some teens who got pictures and video, I'm pretty sure."

Clark's chin dropped. He shut his eyes. "Crap."

I winced. "It's possible nothing will happen."

He opened his intense brown eyes. "Not with your luck. With

your luck? One of those teens is already selling the video and pictures to Jolene O'Sullivan at the paper right this very second."

I swallowed. "The newspaper doesn't have a lot of money."

He pushed documents away from his glass of water, which was set neatly on a coaster. "They have enough money to buy pictures from teens. Besides, I'd bet that Jolene would spend her own money to write a damaging article about you."

That was unfortunately a true statement.

He turned to his computer and typed rapidly, scanning the local news. "Nothing yet. Who knows, maybe we could get lucky this one time."

"Sure." On that note, I squished my way to my office, where I ditched my sodden shoes beneath my desk. I pulled up the calendar system Pauley had installed to see that I had an hour free, so I dug through files to Don McLerrison's so I could scan the papers he'd left. I grinned. The farmer had left not only account numbers but passwords so I could get into all of his accounts. Reaching for a notepad, I started filling out his estate planning documents.

After the hour, I sat back and looked over the notes, my head reeling. Wow. The farm was worth a couple of million dollars, and that was nothing compared to the investments McLerrison's wife had managed. The woman must've been a financial genius. At the end of the day, the estate was worth about twelve million dollars.

I made a call to a friend of mine from law school who'd specialized in estate and tax planning for advice and soon came up with a good plan.

My phone buzzed. "Hi, Oliver."

"Howdy. I have a Mrs. Jennings here to see you. She called and set up an appointment yesterday, and this is the first time I could get her in to see you. Her file is on your desk," Oliver said.

"Great. Please send her back." I rifled through the case file folders and dragged one from the bottom. Then I smoothed my hair back as best as I could and wiped more cream filling off my shoulder.

Oliver appeared with a pregnant young woman. "Here you go."

I stood and gestured to a guest chair. "Hi. I'm Anna." I leaned over to shake her hand. "Please excuse my appearance. There was a pastry incident at lunch."

"I can see that. Sounds like fun?" She was about eighteen with sandy-blonde hair and clear brown eyes. Her belly showed her to be probably about five or six months pregnant, and she wore a pink sundress. "I'm Hailey. It's nice to meet you." Her voice was soft.

"You, too." I hadn't had time to read the form. "How exactly can I help you?"

She shrugged narrow shoulders. "I, well, I want a divorce."

Oh. Family Law. I hadn't intended on practicing it, but I'd help her if I could. "I see." I opened the file and scanned through the little information she'd given Oliver over the phone. "Your husband's name is Darrin, and you've been married a year." I frowned. "How old are you, if you don't mind my asking?"

"Nineteen," she said, rubbing her belly. "We got married right after high school graduation and got pregnant a few months later. It's not working out. So I guess I need a divorce?" She batted away tears. "My mom never liked Darrin, and she's probably right. This is all just so hard, you know?" She looked young and vulnerable in the regular-sized leather chair. "My mom is well off and I can give you a good retainer, if you want. I'd rather pay for this myself, though. If you take payments."

"Yes, we take payments." I shut the case file, wondering at the next best step. The few divorces I'd seen during my life had been messy, and the lawyers had seemed to be just as bad as the clients. So I took a moment. "I have to ask you some questions, okay?"

She clasped her hands in her lap. "Yeah. We don't have a lot of money or stuff to split, and we rent our condo. I'd be fine with joint, um, custody? I watched a couple of episodes of Ally

McBeal before I came in. It's streaming on the older shows channel."

Ally McBeal. I'd totally forgotten about that show. "So you're not afraid of Darrin?" I asked.

Her brows drew up as if I'd surprised her. "Oh, no. Not at all. He's a great guy." Her bottom lip trembled. "Just not ready to be married. I guess. My mom says men never grow up. I don't know."

I took a deep breath. "I just want to make sure you're not in danger and that he hasn't hurt you. Has Darrin ever hit you?"

She laughed and looked even younger. "Gosh, no. Darrin would never hit me or any woman. Or anybody, really."

I believed her. "Are you sure you want to get divorced?" If she did, I'd start the paperwork that day.

She blinked. "I, um, I'm surprised you asked that." She sat back and rubbed her belly some more. "I don't know. I mean, I was mad because we had a fight, and my mom doesn't like him, but I guess I just don't know."

"Why doesn't your mom like him?" I asked just to make sure everything was safe for her.

Hailey sighed. "Because I married him instead of going off to college. But I love him."

My phone rang again. "Hi, Oliver," I answered.

"Hello. A Mr. Jennings is here?" Oliver sounded uncertain.

"I texted him that I was going to have you do the paperwork, and he said he'd come and sign whatever we wanted him to sign." Hailey chewed on her lip. "He wasn't mad but sounded sad."

I slipped my feet back into my now slimy shoes and stood. "All right. Come with me." I walked around my desk and strode down the hallway to the reception area, where a kid with grease on his pants waited. He had brown hair and earnest blue eyes, and by the oil beneath his fingernails, he'd come from work as a mechanic. "Hi. Are you Darrin?"

"Yes. It's nice to meet you." His gaze moved beyond me.

"Do you want to get divorced?" I asked directly.

He cut his gaze to me and his face turned red. "I don't know."

I put my hands on my hips. "Have either of you ever hurt the other? Physically, emotionally, or mentally?"

He looked surprised enough at the question that I instantly relaxed. "No," he said, wiping his hands together. "We'd never do anything like that. Her mom doesn't like me, and it's really hard right now with a baby coming and no money. I'm working two jobs, but it's just hard." He shuffled large boots and looked over my shoulder at Hailey. "I totally get it if you want to move home with her until I get on my feet. I'm really trying, Hay. But your mom's house is nice."

"So is our condo," Hailey whispered.

Darrin shook his head. "It's not what you're used to."

My heart thumped for both kids. "Do you, or do you not, want a divorce, Darrin?" I asked.

He shook his head.

"Good enough. You two come with me." I walked them out of my office and down the hallway to another office that housed Wanda Versaccio's psychology practice, where we moved inside. A young woman sat behind the receptionist desk. She had wiry black hair, even darker eyes, and a stunning smile. She was new.

"Hi. I'm Anna," I said.

"I'm Bess." She held out a hand.

"Wanda is my cousin," I said, shaking hands. My cousin a zillion times removed, but family was family in my life. "Is she around, by any chance?" Wanda was a shrink who was really good at her job.

"Yep." Bess pressed a button on the phone. "Wanda? Your cousin Anna is here with friends." She clicked off.

A minute later, Wanda opened the door set into the wood paneling and walked into the area. Today she wore dark jeans with a light yellow sweater and gorgeous turquoise jewelry. Wanda was in her early forties and had recently streaked her brown hair with pink, giving her a somewhat wild look. "What's up?"

"This is Hailey and Darrin Jennings, and they're having relationship problems. They might want a divorce, or they might not, and I figured it might be nice to talk with you and figure things out." I turned to Hailey. "Wanda also takes payments, and if it ends up you do want a divorce, just come on back down the hall, and I'll start the proceedings." I smiled at Darrin. "I hope you guys figure out what's best for you, and if it is divorce, you'll need to get your own attorney, so you're both fairly represented."

With that, I squished my way out the door and almost made it.

"Anna?" Wanda called out.

I steeled my shoulders and partially turned. "Yes?"

"I haven't seen you in a couple of weeks, and according to the family grapevine, a lot is going on." She looked at Bess. "Do I have any openings today?"

Bess typed into the computer. "No, but you do have Tuesday at noon open."

"Excellent," Wanda said. "Take the weekend and tweak your schedule so you can meet with me on Tuesday, Anna. I'll order in lunch." She smiled. "Don't make me call your mother."

Oh, the ultimate threat.

However, considering both Hailey and Darrin smiled, at least I was helping somebody at the moment. "Fine. This time, order something good, will you?" Last time we'd met, she'd ordered from a new Vegan restaurant. I liked some Vegan food, but the stuff she'd ordered last time might as well have been grass. Even she'd agreed.

"Sure. How about something from Smiley's Diner? You like their food." Her eyes twinkled.

I kept my composure. The gossip about the disaster at the diner had already reached Cousin Wanda? That was a record, even for my family. "Sure. I'll take a turkey sandwich," I said, shutting the door and heading back down the hallway to my office.

The building was at least fifty years old and still had the original wood floor, high ceilings, and decorated trim work. There was something comforting about the entire place.

Our reception area was empty of clients when I opened the door, and I exhaled slowly. "You're doing a great job, Oliver," I said.

He grinned from behind his wide desk. "Thanks."

"You don't have to decide now, but Clark and I were wondering if maybe you wanted to take some paralegal classes at the college. We'd pay for it." Although someday Oliver was going to be a millionaire, which was a fact I couldn't tell him. Also, McLerrison could always change his mind and his will, so who knew?

Oliver sat back. "Really? You guys think I could be a paralegal?"

Sometimes I forgot that not everybody had a family who built them up when given a chance. Hadn't anybody ever just told Oliver he could do it? "Yeah. I think you can do anything you want, Oliver. You're smart, capable, organized, and very good with people."

He blushed so red his cheeks must've hurt. "I, um, thanks."

"Sure." Frosting curdled between my toes. "Just think about it. No pressure." I opened the door to the hallway, saw a couple men meeting with Clark in his office, and headed back to my office to once again wipe the frosting out of my shoes. Apparently I hadn't gotten all of it last time.

CHAPTER 18

J woke up on Saturday morning after having spent the night alone. Aiden had called and said he had crap to deal with and wouldn't make it. The call was quick, and he didn't go into detail with his plans. After a long shower, I relaxed, ate crackers for dinner, and then went to bed early.

My phone buzzed while I was still stretching and trying to decide what to do with my weekend. "Hello."

"Hey, *Aingeal*. Sorry about last night. How about a ride today?" Aiden asked.

I sat up. "Sounds fun. Where to?"

"I thought I'd show you the office in Spokane before I went completely under. Sources tell us that Barensky is still in Denver but is heading this way soon, so this is probably the last couple of days we'll see each other for a while," he said.

I rolled my neck and tried to ignore the panic that created inside me. "All right. Sure. I can be ready soon."

"Good."

My doorbell rang.

I paused. "Is that you at the door?"

"Yep, and I brought lattes," he said.

I jumped out of bed and hustled to the door, almost as happy to see the coffee as I was Aiden. Almost. I sucked it down and hustled to get ready, wearing jeans, a t-shirt, and a light jacket. Within thirty minutes, I perched on the back of Aiden's bike, helmet on, feeling the wind all around us.

There was no other feeling on Earth like riding behind Aiden on his bike with my arms around his waist and my helmet turned against his broad back. It was wild and free, safe and sexy.

I loved it. Had from the first time he'd taken me on a ride, and at that time, I hadn't even known he was on the right side of the law. In fact, there had been ample evidence that he had not been. I didn't care then, and I was happy now.

We rode right through town to I-90 and continued to the older part of Spokane, closer to Gonzaga University. Aiden parked in front of a white columned house that had been turned into an office building with mature trees all around providing much needed shade. I whipped off the helmet and took a good look at the flowerpots hanging on the front porch. "This isn't the ATF office."

"Yeah, they didn't really want us there, so we rented our own office for the SRT." He held out a hand to assist me off the bike and then hung my helmet from his handlebar. "It's better since we're undercover, anyway. Come see it." He took my hand and led me along the quaint stone path and up the wooden steps to the front door.

We walked inside, and the older wooden floor creaked. A massage place was to the left, an accounting firm to the right, and A&E Holdings were straight ahead. He led me to the A&E Holdings door, unlocked it with an old key, and we stepped inside a vestibule with two chairs, a sofa, and a round table holding flowers. One door lay on the other side.

"We have the back suite as well as the entire second floor." He grinned and locked the outside door before heading to the second door, where he slid a wooden panel out of the way and punched in numbers on a keypad.

"All right, James Bond," I murmured. "I take it you guys did some modifications."

"Saber did," Aiden affirmed. "The guy is a genius with security." The door snicked open and he gestured me inside.

I moved past the flowers and into what looked like a control room. Large table, monitors on the walls, computer consoles on the table. Three doors led in different directions.

Aiden pointed. "To the left is my office. On the other side of that wall is a kitchen area with windows looking out back, and to the right is a locked ammunition room. The upper floor holds more offices for my team as well as another conference room." He moved to his right and lifted a blind to reveal a case board with Barensky in the middle, a blank face with a question mark next to him, and Sasha on the other side with a question mark as to who murdered her. "We need to find out who hired Barensky and who killed Sasha—and if the two cases are related. There's a chance they're not, considering her track record of putting away criminals."

I perused the space and tried to concentrate on the danger. "Considering she was killed at my place, doesn't it seem like somebody knows about you and your connection to both Sasha and me?"

He nodded. "Yes, in which case, we have to consider that Barensky already knows we're ATF. In the alternative, there's a chance that Sasha was followed to your house by the killer, so it might not be Barensky."

My throat went dry. "If you think your cover is blown, how can you continue?"

"How can I not?" he asked, looking dangerous next to the case board. "Even if it is blown, Barensky is acting like it isn't, so I have to do the same. He's creating explosives for somebody, and so long as I can keep him somewhat close, we have a chance to stop it."

I shook my head. "It's a game of cat and mouse within a game of cat and mouse." I couldn't do it. All my life, I'd been an upfront type of person who didn't play games. "How do you do this? Stay sane with so much intrigue and danger around you?" This was real.

"It's my job," he said simply.

For the first time, I didn't like his job. "If Barensky killed Sasha, you might be next." I wiped my hand across my eyes. "Or if somebody from one of your cases in the past found her here, they already know you're here, too." It was too much. If you didn't even know who the enemy was, how did you protect yourself?

He reached for me and enfolded me in a hug. "This isn't my first time in this position, Angel. I know what I'm doing."

"So did Sasha," I murmured, my voice muffled against his chest.

"I'll keep you safe, baby." He ran his warm hand down my back.

I swallowed rapidly. "I'm not scared for me." I was terrified for him.

"Don't worry about me. We take all precautions and I have great backup. The team is good—probably the best." He leaned me back to meet my gaze. "Okay?"

"Yeah. Okay." Then I took a deep breath and looked around. "Show me your office."

"Sure." He grinned. "I already have Oreos stashed in my desk."

Yeah, he was the perfect guy. "Prove it."

* * *

I WAS JUST SETTLING into place back on Aiden's motorcycle with my belly happy with a few Oreos in it when his phone dinged. He held it to his ear. "Devlin." Then he waited. "You think so? Okay. It's probably not a bad idea. Anna and I are at the office and will be there in about twenty. Thanks, Saber." He clicked off.

"What's going on?" I paused in setting the helmet over my head.

"Saber called a meeting of the Lordes and thinks I should drop by to make a couple of statements. Having you there will ensure nobody comes after you again." He turned to look over his shoulder at me. "I'd say we should keep you out of it, but every Lordes member already knows you and knows we were dating. So I'm taking you there to get the rest of your stuff from my room, and then Saber is taking you home."

I bit my lip. "Why is Saber taking me home?"

"Because you're no longer my old lady. We're breaking up very publicly in front of the Lordes, and I'm making it clear that you're out of my life and that you're also not to be bothered by anybody. Having Saber take you off property makes that very clear. This is the best way to protect you and the first step in keeping you safe, Angel."

Wait a minute. Heat rose from my chest to my face. "You already had this planned. When you asked me for a ride today, you knew this was going to happen."

"Not really. Saber and I discussed how best to keep you safe, but I didn't know he'd be able to gather everyone today." Aiden turned back around. "Put on your helmet."

I remained still, my mind spinning. "I don't like being left out of the loop." Irritation crawled through me.

"You weren't kept out. We've been moving fast and working hard, and this is one more prong of the plan. Keeping you safe and publicly distancing you from me. I didn't mean to leave you out." He started the motorcycle, effectively drowning out any more conversation.

I slammed the helmet on my head. Oh, if he wanted to show up to the Lordes apartment complex in Idaho with a pissed off woman, he'd succeeded. It was probably part of his plan, darn it.

We drove away from the intriguing super-spy office and toward Idaho. While the Lordes garage was in Washington, their apartment complex was located on the border between the two states on the Idaho side. I'd hoped never to have to see that place again, but soon we were driving right into the parking area between the two complexes. All Lordes territory.

Today picnic tables had been set up in the middle of the lot, with bikes parked on the far side. About twenty members milled around with probably twice as many women, all dressed for the hot weather. A couple of the women even wore bikinis with high heels. I'd never understood that look.

Aiden parked over by the other bikes, and pretty much all eyes turned to us. I conducted a quick scan and didn't see either of the women who'd thrown pastries at me. He got off first and held out a hand for my helmet.

I handed it to him and then swung my leg off.

He secured the helmet. "Look angry and follow me to my room."

"I am angry," I snapped, heading up the outside stairs without waiting for him to lead. I could feel all eyes on us, even though the music from several speakers boomed a hard rock cadence. A couple of grills were hard at work on burgers and dogs, and the smell wafted through the air.

I reached Aiden's door and opened it, stepping inside.

He followed and slammed the door. "I'm sorry about this."

I rolled my eyes. "Whatever." Then I looked at the cheap furniture and scrunchy puke green shag carpet. "I don't have any belongings here."

"I know." He proceeded past me to the bedroom and drew out an old canvas bag, into which he tossed a couple of his T-shirts. "They won't know it's my stuff."

Yeah, I'd sleep in those. I was a total dork. "Okay. What happens now?"

He leaned against the wall, those blue eyes appraising. "We walk out, I motion to Saber, and he takes you home. Then I go down to the barbecue, grab a beer, and make it very clear that nobody is to bother you. It's over, which means you're out of their minds. Period."

I didn't mind being out of the Lordes member's minds. At all. "How many agents do you have here?"

"Ten now," he confirmed. "Ten Lordes members, so we're at twenty total. I just have to keep it together until we get with Barensky." He straightened, and for the first time, a flash of uncertainty glimmered in his eyes. "You're also going to start dating somebody right away."

I drew back. "Excuse me?"

"His name is Kurt, and he's moving into your place." Aiden waited patiently.

I frowned. "I take it I have a bodyguard now?"

"Yep. Named Kurt. He's part of my team, but his only job from now until we take Barensky down is protecting you. That means he shadows you at all times, so you're going to need to figure out a way for him to work at the law firm. I can get him credentials as a PI, if you want. That's a good idea. I'll do that."

Once again, my lungs wanted a different job than allowing me to breathe. "You can't make these decisions for me, Aiden. I mean it. Knock it off."

His left eyebrow rose. "Do you want to be safe?"

"Yes," I muttered.

"Do you mind if I provide a bodyguard until this is all over, considering a dead body was found on your porch?" His reasonable voice was going to get him punched in the face.

I swallowed. "I do not mind." I wasn't a moron, for Pete's sake. I just wanted to be included in the decisions.

"Okay. Then we're agreed. Kurt will be there tonight because he's coming from Montana right now." Aiden dug his phone from his back pocket, swiped the screen, and showed me a picture of a blond guy with a full beard. "This is Kurt. Don't open your door for anybody but him."

Kurt was good looking with a lazy alertness in his hazel eyes. "No problem," I said.

Aiden turned for the door. "Look pissed when we go out."

"No problem," I said, meaning it.

We opened the door and nearly stumbled into Saber.

Aiden paused. "What's up?"

Saber didn't look my way. "Barensky's men are here. Now."

I looked down at the parking lot at the same time Aiden did to see two men there not dressed like the others. They were in dockers and golf shirts, looking like tourists or accountants.

Aiden nodded. "All right. I'll meet with them right now. You take Anna home. This is good. They can see her leave on your bike."

Saber looked at me. "Try to look both angry and sad."

"Throw in scared, and that's exactly how I feel," I said quietly.

"That's because you're smart," Saber said. "Let's go."

CHAPTER 19

S aber dropped me off, and I found my cousin waiting on my porch and reading the paper.

"Quint," I said, hurrying toward him and trying to banish the feeling of impending disaster swamping me. Aiden was meeting with henchmen of a bomber right now, and it was hard to concentrate on anything else.

Quint smiled and stood. "Hey. So. Nice picture." He flipped the newspaper around to show me a front-page picture of the food fight from the day before, and it included Nick leaning over, lines of pain on his face. Tess and I were in the background, both covered with pastries. The headline read: *"Prosecuting Attorney Gets Derailed by Albertini Disaster Train."*

I groaned and took the paper to read about the food fight and my involvement. "Your girlfriend is always so good about mentioning that I'm a partner at the Bunne & Albertini Law Firm." It was as if Jolene wanted to drive the firm into the ground. She really didn't like me. "I doubt we'll have as good as a result from a food fight as we did from a bar fight." And considering Nick wanted to run for office someday, his getting caught in silly situations like this was not good for him. I could see his Grams arguing that Nick and Tessa really shouldn't date.

Quint took the offending paper away. "Jolene is not my girl-friend, and she actually likes you. Unfortunately, this makes good copy. Stop getting in fights and you won't have to worry about it."

"That's easier said than done," I said, walking to my door to unlock it.

Quint whistled and Zena bounded around the cottage.

I gave him a look. "You brought your dog to butter me up?" I allowed Zena inside and then followed her as Quint did the same.

"Kind of. I was hoping you'd watch her for a few days. Jolene and I are going to the hot springs up north." He shut the door and managed to keep a straight face.

I slammed my hands on my hips. "You're going away with that harpy? She's trying to ruin me."

He chuckled. "She is not. You make good copy. Stop it, and the news stops."

"You said she wasn't your girlfriend," I challenged.

"She's not. We enjoy each other's company, and right now, I need that." He set a hand on Zena's head. "I talked to Aiden, and he thought it'd be a good idea for Zena to stay with you right now, anyway. Something about a case he's working on."

I loved the dog and would've watched her anytime. Plus, if Quint needed time to spend with Jolene to help his peace of mind, I couldn't begrudge him that. What if they got married? I hid a shiver.

Quint grinned. "Think of the bright side. If Jolene is up north with me, she won't be writing articles about you."

Now that was a very good point. I wouldn't be able to turn down Zena, anyway. "Fine, but you owe me one." I already had dog food in my pantry for Zena since I watched her once in a while. "I suppose you want to eat lunch here?" I had some good cold cuts in the fridge.

"No," he said. "I need to pack and get on the road. We should be back on Tuesday." He looked at my face. "You have a couple of bruises along your jaw."

"Multiple fights," I murmured.

He grasped my shoulder. "What's up, Anna Banana? Come on. Talk to your tough-guy cousin."

A smile tempted my mouth. "My tough-guy cousin isn't here. Vince is up north, I think."

"Funny. I'm tougher than all of my brothers," Quint said. "What's on your mind?"

The truth blew right out of me. Quint had always had that effect on me. "Aiden, his case, and the fact that too many of us know he's with the ATF," I said. "He's going undercover understanding that his cover is possibly blown, but he's still doing it because it'll get him closer to the, um, bad guy. It's a weird game they're playing." A game of chess. The one Barensky, the bomber, apparently loved to play.

Quint pulled me in for a hug. "Aiden knows what he's doing. He's good at his job, and you have to trust him."

I leaned back. Quint was exactly the right person to talk to about this. His girlfriend had dumped him because of his smoke-jumping job. "I know. I do trust him. Doesn't mean I can't worry."

Quint gingerly touched one of the bruises on my chin. "Worrying doesn't help anything, and you have to find a balance for yourself. If you can't live with his job, let him go. If you can live with it, work on some coping skills. Breathe deep or something." He grinned. "It's not like you don't have enough going on in your own life right now."

He was not wrong.

"All right. Get going on your vacation," I said. "Try not to fall in love with that woman."

"I'll do my best." Quint hustled out the door before I could change my mind, shutting it quickly. "Lock this behind me," he yelled as he headed down the walkway.

I looked at the beautiful brown eyes of the calm black Lab. "He's lucky to have you."

Her tail wagged.

"How about some doggie treats?" I locked my door and then followed the dog into my kitchen, where she stopped to wait patiently by my pantry. She knew what was up. So I dug out some goodies and gave them to the sweet puppy.

My doorbell rang, and she jumped up and ran to it, her body on alert.

I followed and looked through the peephole at a man and quickly recognized him as Kurt. His hair was mussed, but his beard full. I opened the door.

"I'm Kurt," he said, lounging deceptively.

"I'm Anna," I said. "I've never had a bodyguard before."

Zena barked once in warning.

Kurt dropped to his haunches. "Oh, you're a pretty one."

Zena was also well trained. She snarled.

I patted her head. "It's okay, girl. Kurt's a friend."

She immediately relaxed and her tail wagged. Then she stretched her neck toward him, granting easy permission.

He complied by petting her head. "Oh, you are pretty, aren't you?" His accent held a hint of Boston. Then he stood.

I gestured him inside. "Come on in."

He shook his head. "Thanks, but I want to get a lay of the land first. You go about your business while I scout the property for weaknesses." He dug out his phone and scrolled through. "I have a full schematic as well as Aiden's notes on security, but I want to see for myself."

I angled my neck to see his phone. "Aiden drew schematics and a security map for my place?"

Kurt looked up and his forehead crinkled. "Of course. Why wouldn't he?"

Indeed.

* * *

My phone rang just as I sat down to sketch out some preliminary notes for Kelsey Walker's case. "Hello."

"Hey. It's Clark. Detective Pierce called and asked if we could meet for an interview late today. Apparently justice doesn't relax on Saturdays."

I paused. "Talk to me about what?"

"There's an FBI agent who wants to talk to you about Agent Sasha Duponte's death and he's going through the local police right now to help preserve Aiden's cover as a federal agent. As you know, we don't have to talk to him, but I think we might as well get it over with. What do you think?" Clark asked.

The last person I wanted to deal with today was an FBI agent investigating me. "This whole situation is so sticky," I muttered.

"At least the federal agencies are playing well together right now. I think that in the spirit of cooperation, we go in today. Let me do the talking as your counsel," Clark said.

If cooperating meant keeping Aiden safe, I'd do it. "All right. I'll meet you in front of the police station in thirty minutes." I clicked off, finished my iced tea, and tried to figure out what to wear that would make me look both cooperative and innocent. A light summer dress in a blue poppy color and simple sandals were the best I could do.

I let Zena out and then in, making sure she was comfy in the living room before heading to my Jeep Cherokee. It was a darker green color and drove well in the snow. The vehicle was also great in the summer because it had A/C and a connection for my phone to play music.

Kurt was waiting next to it. "Where are we going?"

I'd already forgotten about Kurt. "I'm going to be interviewed by the FBI, and my lawyer will be present. So I can meet you back here."

"Great," Kurt said, opening the passenger side door and

hopping inside. For a big guy, he moved gracefully. Kurt had to be around thirty and was slim but muscled.

I walked around and slid into the driver's seat to start the vehicle. "I'm surprised you don't want to drive."

"I can shoot better if I don't have to hold the wheel," he said easily, pushing the button to unroll his window.

"I doubt you'll have to shoot anybody," I countered, backing out and driving out onto the country road.

He kept his focus outside. "You never know. An ATF agent was murdered on your porch, so obviously there's somebody out there who wants to cause you problems. Or someone who took advantage of a situation and doesn't care if they cause you problems. Unless you're the one who killed her. Either way, I'm ready to fire if necessary."

"I didn't kill her," I said. Yeah, he made some sense. "How long have you known Aiden?"

"About five years," Kurt said. "We've worked together on a couple of jobs, and he requested me for his unit here. My transfer just came in."

"Did you know Sasha?" I turned down another tree-lined road.

"Yeah," Kurt said softly.

I breathed out. "I'm really sorry she was killed."

"Me, too," he said, straightening at seeing a light blue truck parked to the side of the road. He relaxed when two fishermen came into view as they parted high grass to head into the trees. "There must be a creek in there."

"Yeah. It leads to the lake. Good trout fishing if you know where to look." Locals often fished the creek. "It's called Blue Creek, but I don't know why. The water is green like most rivers in Idaho." Rather, the moss and rocks were green, and the water just looked green. I wondered why the creek was called Blue Creek.

"I like to fish," Kurt said, watching the trees speed by. "At least, I used to like it. It's been a long time."

Maybe when all of this was over, we could go fishing with Aiden and Tessa? I liked the idea of Tess and Nick dating, but I might've destroyed that chance at the restaurant. Not that both of them wouldn't do what they wanted, anyway. If not, Kurt seemed like a decent guy. Tessa might be interested in him. Or perhaps she wanted to stay single right now. I should butt out of her love life and I knew it.

We reached the parking area on Justice Road and I parked right in front. "You can't be with me during the interview."

"I know." Kurt jumped out of the Jeep, surveyed the area, and motioned for me to follow.

I grabbed my purse and did so, walking with him toward the main front door. "Have you been assigned bodyguarding duty before?"

"Yeah." He walked up the steps with me and opened the door.

I paused. "Did the body survive?"

"I don't want to talk about it." He ushered me inside.

I stumbled and looked back over my shoulder to see his quick grin. "Funny."

"You're safe in the building. Come out this way, and I'll be waiting." He shut the door, apparently thinking I'd automatically obey.

I shook my head and walked to the reception area to see a uniformed cop behind the main desk. "Hi."

"Hi." He glanced up from a sheet of papers. "Anna Albertini. Sign here, and I'll buzz somebody to come get you. Your attorney is already here and went to the interrogation room."

I reached for a pen. While I hadn't met the guy, apparently he read the paper and had recognized me.

I sighed.

CHAPTER 20

I walked into a familiar interrogation room where Clark sat across from a guy wide enough to be a Buick. They both stood.

"Hi. I'm FBI Special Agent Larry Frankenberry." He held out a beefy hand to shake. "Thanks for coming."

We shook hands and I crossed around to sit next to Clark, who also retook his seat.

Frankenberry wore an oversized gray suit that stretched at the seams. His tie was green and his thin shirt white with bulging buttons. His hair was light gray, sweat dotted his forehead, and his eyes were blue. He looked to be in his late fifties, and by his ruddy complexion, was about a donut away from a massive coronary.

"It's nice to meet you," I said.

"You, too," he said, drawing out his chair to sit. The chair protested with a loud groan.

The door opened again, and a younger man walked inside to draw out a chair next to Frankenberry. He had thick blond hair, deep brown eyes, and a fiercely starched shirt beneath a beige suit jacket. "I'm Ross Stewart, an Assistant US Attorney for the District of Idaho." The guy must be around thirty-five. He glanced at the top of his case file. "You are Anna Albertini, represented by attorney Clark Bunne, correct?" He looked up and we both nodded.

Detective Grant Pierce walked into the room, shut the door, and leaned back against it.

Stewart looked over his shoulder. "I think we're fine here, Detective." It was a clear dismissal.

"Good to hear it," Pierce said, his expression crankier than usual.

Stewart glared. "We do not require your presence."

"That's unfortunate, because I am staying. We have potential state violations as well as federal ones here," Pierce said.

Stewart apparently knew when to stop arguing. "All right. Please run me through what happened the day ATF SRT Agent Sasha Duponte was found murdered on your front porch, Miss Albertini."

Clark shifted his weight. "Miss Albertini has already given a statement, the same one, several times. She is not doing so again. If you have certain questions regarding her statement or require clarification on any points, please ask. If not, then there was no reason for us to meet."

Yep. Clark was wearing his Monte Carlo style wire-rimmed glasses. They were his 'badass' glasses, and now I knew why.

Stewart didn't change expression. "Yet I'd like to run through it again."

Clark pinched his lips together and he looked up at Pierce. "Did you give the statements to the FBI?"

"I did," Pierce drawled.

Clark then looked at Frankenberry. "Do you have the statements?" After Frankenberry nodded, Clark frowned. "Why didn't you share the statements with the state's attorney general's office?"

"I did," Frankenberry said, reaching for a pitcher of water on the table to pour a glass.

Clark then faked a pretty decent look of surprise with a hint of sarcasm. "Have you not had a chance to read those statements, Assistant US District Attorney?"

Stewart flicked his attention to Clark and just stared for a few moments. Clark stared right back and looked like he could do so all day. Finally Stewart cracked first. "Miss Albertini, did you kill Agent Duponte?"

"Of course not," I said.

Clark cut me a look. Oh yeah. I wasn't supposed to talk.

Stewart opened his file to scan what looked like hand-written notes. "Are you in love with ATF SRT Agent Aiden Devlin?"

"That's irrelevant," Clark said, sounding bored.

Stewart looked up. "Love and jealousy are often motivations for murder, as you know."

Clark tilted his head. "I think you know that Agent Duponte was involved in a very dangerous case that got her killed, unfortunately. Anna had nothing to do with it."

Stewart winced as if he didn't like what he was about to say. It almost looked genuine. "Agent Duponte has closed several very dangerous cases without injury, and this is all too coincidental for me. In fact, a smart woman would know that killing Agent Duponte now, during a deadly undercover Op, might create such a sticky situation that it would be swept aside. You're a smart woman, Miss Albertini, right?"

Several smart-ass responses rose in me and I quenched them. There was no need to make Clark's job more difficult than it already was.

Clark pushed away from the table. "If this is all you have—"

"No." Stewart read from his notes again. "We have the report about your car, Miss Albertini. There were no unidentifiable prints on it. Neither were Agent Duponte's prints on your vehicle. How do you explain that?"

"Gloves?" I asked.

"Hmmm." Stewart looked at Clark and then back at me. "We

also have the autopsy report. Agent Duponte was killed by being beaten with the potato bat and then having her head repeatedly smashed against your porch. The attack took time, and the attacker wasn't strong enough to kill with one blow. Seems like a woman did this."

That sounded flimsy.

Clark cocked his head. "Any DNA found on the body?"

Stewart shook his head., "Some but no match yet. We would like your client to submit to a DNA test."

"No," Clark said. "Get a warrant."

"Oh, I will," Stewart said, focusing back on me. "Are you aware that Agent Devlin and Agent Duponte were creating a family?"

I frowned. "With their unit?"

"No. With a baby." Stewart studied me, compassion in his eyes. Kind of. "I take it nobody told you."

"Sasha was pregnant?" I asked, my stomach dropping. I'd gotten in a bar fight with a pregnant woman? I felt sick. She'd died on my porch, and so had the baby? Tears tried to clog up my sinuses.

"No," Stewart said.

"What?" I stared right at him. What kind of game was this jackass playing?

He shook his head. "It's my understanding that Agent Duponte wanted a child and asked Agent Devlin to be the father. A couple of years ago, they agreed upon the timing. Biological clocks and all of that."

"Things have changed since they worked together," I said.

Stewart sighed. "No, they have not. Sasha and Aiden met at the Lordes complex the night before she died, and they both committed to the plan they'd come up with. He agreed to stick with the plan of fathering a child with her."

"Who's your source?" Clark asked.

Stewart shrugged. "Another ATF agent close to Sasha. I don't have to disclose witnesses yet." He leaned forward. "I think Devlin told you about this plan, and I think it infuriated you, and I think you killed her." He shook his head. "It happens in the heat of a moment. She attacked you at the bar and then again in the alley, and I believe you lost it in a moment of passion."

"Bullshit," Clark said. "You're creating an interesting narrative with no facts."

Yet those were all facts and a pretty decent narrative, which was what convinced juries. The room swam around me, and I dug my nails into my palm to keep myself centered.

Stewart continued as if Clark hadn't spoken. "Because of this situation, I'm willing to offer you a plea bargain. We reduce the homicide charge to third-degree with a five year sentence. This all goes away and your boyfriend stays safe in his current assignment. I mean, ex-boyfriend. He was planning a family with another woman, so I doubt you would've continued? Who knows? Either way, this is the best deal you're going to get."

Plead guilty to murder? Go to prison? The ground fell out beneath me.

Frankenberry drank his glass of water in two gulps. "We have witness statements from Sasha's friends, Lordes members, and the women you fought with in the bar, alley, and restaurant. We also have your prints on the murder weapon and the bloody scene at your porch. It does look like a crime of passion to me."

I couldn't believe this. It was all so surreal, and yet, my palms grew sweaty. The edges of the room started to close in, and I fought a panic attack while remaining perfectly still.

"All righty then." Clark pushed away from the table. "Anna, let's go."

Stewart looked directly at me. "You said you'd answer my questions. I'm not finished yet."

Clark stood and pulled my chair back. "That was before we realized you didn't know what you're doing. You're trying to pin a murder on an innocent woman, and we just stopped cooperating. Arrest and charge her, or we're leaving."

They didn't have enough to charge me yet. I didn't think.

"We have enough to charge her," Stewart said easily. "However, the FBI and Attorney General's Office is working closely with the ATF right now to make sure our agents are protected so they can prevent a terrorist attack. Arresting your client puts their mission and lives in jeopardy, so we're not going to do so yet." He smiled. "Regardless, the arrest is going to happen, so you have twenty-four hours to take the deal or any offer is off the table. If it's off the table, when I do charge you, it'll be for first-degree murder. I'll show the jury that you took that potato gun and then lured Sasha to your house to kill her with it. You had motive, opportunity, and ability. In addition, we have physical evidence against you, as you know."

Pierce remained silent but looked so somber my knees wobbled. This couldn't be happening.

It really couldn't.

Clark laughed and the sound made me jump. "You've got nothing. You just mentioned how intelligent my client is, and yet you think she killed her boyfriend's ex on her own porch before calling the police? Right. She also threw the murder weapon, if it really was the weapon, into her own bushes where it would be easily found? Uh-huh." He pressed a hand to my lower back to propel me around the table. "Thanks for the laugh, gentlemen."

Stewart leaned back so he could keep us in his sights. "The autopsy results should be ready on Monday or Tuesday, and when I have them, I'm getting a warrant for DNA. The second that comes in, I'm arresting you and going for first-degree, Miss Albertini."

Pierce opened the door, and I moved into the hallway, where Clark grasped my arm and escorted me down the stairs and out the front door. It was early evening, but the heat still pressed in on me.

I couldn't breathe.

Kurt waited outside, leaning against the bricks. "You okay?"

I shook my head and tried to force air into my lungs.

Clark shoved my shoulders down so I was bent over. "Breathe. Stop the panic and breathe through it. You're okay." He rubbed gentle circles across my upper back.

Kurt's scuffed black boots came into my vision. "What's wrong with her?"

Clark's sigh ruffled my hair. "She's going to be charged with first-degree murder by Wednesday. I think she's gone into a panic attack."

"I don't blame her," Kurt said grimly.

CHAPTER 21

J settled against pillows in my bed and streamed a show about baking. For a Saturday night in August, the lake was surprisingly quiet outside with no boat lights illuminating the waves, although the moon was doing a decent job of it. The blinds to my sliding glass door were open, but it was securely locked with a bar preventing it being opened at all.

Zena had elected to stay up with Kurt because I think he kept slipping her treats. He slept on the sofa outside. Or he planned to, anyway. It was midnight, and I could hear him rustling in the kitchen. Maybe he didn't sleep much.

My three calls to Aiden that afternoon had gone to voice mail. For all I knew, he was in Seattle already dealing with criminals. The idea was keeping me from sleeping, so I gave in to worry and let myself binge-watch the creation of raspberry filled pastries. I wrapped my arms around my knees and waited for the next episode to begin.

The bedroom door opened and I tensed. Then Aiden walked inside.

I blinked once and then again. "I thought we weren't supposed to see each other," I whispered, trying to sort out the cornucopia of feelings slamming through me.

He shut the door and kicked off motorcycle boots. "I took backroads and made sure nobody followed me." He shucked his light jacket and walked over to the blinds to securely shut them. "Rumor has it you had a rough day that included a panic attack outside the police station."

I drank him in, although he was dressed in his usual clothing. "Did you and Sasha agree to have a baby?"

His head jerked. "What? How did you know about that?"

My body jolted like I'd been punched in the solar plexus. Internal pain was worse than a punch, sometimes. My heart ached. "It's true?"

He scrubbed a rough hand through his thick hair and sat at the edge of my bed. "I guess. Kind of. Three years ago, when we were on assignment, we agreed to have a kid if neither of us were with anybody by the time we turned forty. That's eight years away for me. It wasn't a serious agreement or anything, and we were just goofing off talking about it."

I pushed away the second panic attack for the day. "So you didn't recommit to the idea when she stayed the night at your apartment at the Lordes complex?"

"No." He frowned and his jaw hardened. "Of course not. Who told you that?"

I gave him all the details about the interview with the FBI agent and federal prosecutor. "Somehow, the guy thinks you and Sasha had a new plan. Or he was just lying to me and fishing for information."

Aiden's eyes blazed a raw blue. "I want to know who gave him that information. Sasha and I didn't talk about it when she stayed at the apartment the other night." He caught my look. "I slept on the sofa, Angel. You have to know that."

I did deep down. At the same time, we'd only been dating for a little while, and it's not like we'd kept in touch before that. He'd skipped town at eighteen, and I'd only been thirteen at the time. How well did I really know him? Yeah, I trusted him. "I believe you. Who would know about that issue?" I didn't even want to say the word baby in regard to Aiden and anybody else.

He shook his head. "We joked about it on assignment during a poker game. Two other agents were there."

"Was one a friend of Sasha's?" I asked.

"Yeah." He stood and pulled his shirt over his head. "Agent Lila Nelson was there, and she and Sasha were good friends. We were all joking."

That didn't matter. Stewart was willing to use anything against me. "Apparently the investigators on this have dug into both your and Sasha's pasts and even talked to this Lila." There had to be a case or two where an actual criminal had threatened them. "I'm not sure what to do right now."

Except look at his broad and nicely defined chest.

He pulled his belt free.

My breath quickened, but the headache looming over me wouldn't let go.

Then he ditched his jeans and socks before lifting the covers. "Scoot over."

I moved over. "Should you be here?"

"No." He slid beneath the covers and pulled me into his side. "I should not be here, but I wasn't tracked, so I'm staying."

I snuggled into his heat, feeling centered for the first time all day. "They can track phones, you know." Even the bad guys could track a GPS.

"My phone is in the apartment at the complex," he murmured against my hair, looking at the screen. "You're watching the baking show where they compete against each other?" He leaned over me to grab the remote and turn up the volume a few notches. "I love this show."

I stilled. "You watch this show?"

"Sometimes. I'm hoping that kid Nelson wins this time." He

settled down more comfortably around me. "Would it help if I told you not to worry about your case?"

"Not unless you could give me a concrete reason that I shouldn't worry," I admitted. "When Stewart laid out the evidence against me, it was pretty convincing. I can see a jury believing the narrative." It was all so crazy. I'd never kill anybody in cold blood. "I believe in the legal system, but I can't stop thinking that it might go wrong. You know?" The idea of my going to prison was unthinkable.

Yet an assistant attorney general was thinking all about it.

"Yeah." Aiden pressed a kiss to my temple. "We're unofficially investigating Sasha's death while also working on the Barensky case. So far, we don't have anything, and I haven't tied her death to this current mission. If Barensky knows about us, he's not showing it."

I rolled over to face him and gathered the pillow to support my neck. "How did it go with Barensky's two guys you met with at the apartment complex? They looked like golfers."

"They weren't. Both were smart and cagey, and they spoke in euphemisms," Aiden said. "They want us to ride motorcycles over to Seattle in the Pacific Ride a week from now and drop backpacks at designated spots they won't give us until we start riding through town."

"Pacific Ride?"

He nodded. "It's just a motorcycle ride and gathering every year for different clubs. Kind of like Sturgis but a lot smaller, and everyone rides through town—just one street, so we don't clog the whole place up. The final destination is over on the coast for a three-day-weekend and party."

I shivered. "Did the men give any indication or even hint about who hired them or where the explosives are to be placed?"

"Nope. Just said that our business arrangement would net us a million dollars. Any time one of us tried to bring up the packages, they shut it down." He decreased the volume of the TV when one of the contestants started freaking out about burned rye bread.

I flattened my hand on his chest. "That sounds suspicious."

He kept his gaze on the television. "Maybe, maybe not. They might just be cautious, which makes sense. If they screw up, Barensky will end them. He has a solid reputation that way. Otherwise I'd take them in and question them until they gave up the information. Chances are, they don't even know."

My eyes grew heavy. With Aiden next to me, I felt safe and warm. Sleep drew me in quickly, even as he kept watching to see who won bread week.

* * *

I woke up naked with Aiden scooted down on the bed and his mouth between my legs. Delicious sensations wandered through me, and I murmured his name. Aiden Devlin was good at many things in life, and he was spectacular at this. I crushed a pillow over my face with both hands to keep from screaming as the climax took me somewhere else. The waves crashed hard, and I was panting when he lifted the pillow off my face.

"You okay?" he rumbled, satisfaction glimmering in his unreal blue eyes. A lock of his dark hair fell across his brow.

"Gurg," I said agreeably, feeling better than I had in days.

He rolled on top of me. "Good." He took his time, but soon he was embedded all the way inside me, and I wanted to go again. I really liked that about him. "Do I have your attention now?" he asked.

"You've had it since I woke up," I murmured.

"Good." He brushed a wayward curl away from my cheekbone. "Listen to me. You're safe and you're going to remain safe. I'll find who killed Sasha and left her on your porch. I've got you covered." Even though we were in bed, his jaw was hard, and the street showed in his gaze. He'd survived a rough childhood in Ireland, an okay one in Idaho, the rigor of the Marines, and now deadly undercover ops as an ATF agent. His world was one of cunning survival and as far away from my safe haven as imaginable.

"I'm not scared." I ran my hands down the dips and valleys of his arms. A good night's sleep had put everything in perspective. The case against me had holes in it, and it was my job to widen those. "Don't worry."

He grasped my hands and set his over them, palm to palm, holding mine to the bed.

A whole body tremble attacked me.

His grin was more than a little wicked, and he kissed me, his lips firm and warm. I kissed him back, wrapping my legs around his hips. He thrust then and released my mouth. His breath hitched.

That small sound made me feel powerful. I ground my heels into his butt.

"Oh, you're playing today, Angel," he murmured, kissing me again while continuing to thrust inside me.

"I like to play." For good measure, I tried to free my hands.

They remained neatly pinned to the bed. Heat flushed down me.

"Play all you want," he said. "I'll let you know when playtime is over." His eyes glittered in a way that made me feel all feminine and still powerful. Yet caught in a delicious trap. The warning was sexy, but the man was incredible. Need poured off him along with a hunger I could barely tap, and I wanted him more than anything else in the world right now.

Satisfaction curved his lips as he drove inside me. Yet the intensity remained.

He slowed down and tortured me with short and lazy strokes. "It goes without saying that I need you to stick close to Kurt and stay out of trouble. Just until I lock this all down." His eyes flickered with blue fire, showing the dark possessiveness in him I'd only glimpsed a couple of times. It was here in full flame right now. "Got it?"

"Yeah," I whispered, my head digging into the pillow. Desire mixed with need inside me. "I'll be safe."

"For me, *Aingeal*. I need you safe." He thrust in earnest now, going hard and deep. Electricity arced through me, and I curled my fingers through his, holding on for all I was worth. He rocked inside me, so hard and full. So Aiden.

I broke first, shattering and closing my eyes to ride out more waves. He powered even harder and pulsed inside me, dropping his face to my neck. His corded body slowly relaxed, and he kissed up my neck to my mouth.

"You okay?" He nibbled on my bottom lip.

"Think so," I said, my body relaxing into the bed. My legs fell to the side, and I wiggled beneath him. "Are you coming to the family barbecue today?" I knew he couldn't. Still, I had to ask.

"No, and neither are you." He released my hands and balanced himself on his elbows.

I forced my eyelids open. "Yes, I am. I always go to my folks for the barbecue."

"I know." His voice gentled and softened me. "But not this time. This time, you're going to stay home and safe. No driving over the pass and no making your bodyguard track too many people at once. Got it?"

He was cute when trying to be charming.

"No. I'm going."

"You're not." He bit my bottom lip with just enough snap to catch my attention. "You're in my world right now, Anna, and that means I call the shots. Until I find out who left a dead woman on your porch, we're assuming you're in danger. So you remain in lockdown and safe locations for now. It's here, work, here, work..."

He was getting less cute but no less sexy.

"You're not my boss, and my parent's house is as safe as it gets. Family all around." I brushed his hair back from his forehead.

"Ha. Your family invites half the entire town sometimes, especially in the summer when everyone can stay outside. We can do this the easy way or the hard way, but you are staying home today." He rolled his hips, still inside me. "I'm trying really hard to be reasonable here, but you don't seem to be getting it."

It was difficult to concentrate at the moment. "Stop trying to distract me."

"You're in danger and that's that." He started to move again. What was he, a robot? How? It didn't matter. Instead, I held on to his arms. The veneer of civility he often wore began to strip away, leaving pure Aiden in its place. He wasn't going to argue about it anymore. "Tell you what. Last one to the finish line wins," he said.

"You've got it," I grit out, trying to think about anything but his hard body.

He chuckled, and even that was sexy. Then he powered harder and changed his angle, hitting a spot inside me I hadn't realized existed until I'd met him.

Yeah, I got there first. Twice.

It was a good thing I had plenty to do at home that day with Zena.

CHAPTER 22

I felt more like myself when I walked into work on Monday morning, even though Kurt and Zena were both on my heels. I introduced Kurt to Oliver as a private detective we'd just contracted with, which might've been a mistake because Oliver instantly found a new hero.

"I've always wanted to be a private detective," Oliver gushed.

I gestured toward the two boxes on his desk. "What are those?"

Oliver grinned widely. "Our business cards. They just arrived, and I was waiting for Pauley before opening them."

The door to the interior office hallway opened and Pauley walked through. Today he wore tan pants and a red and white striped shirt.

"Hi, Pauley," I said. "This is Kurt. He's our new private detective."

"Hi," Kurt said.

"Hello, Kurt," Pauley said, holding a hand out for Zena. The dog approached and sat, and then Pauley patted her head. "Oliver called me to come to reception. To reception. I'm here in reception." He kept his gaze on the dog.

Oliver pulled a card out of each carton. "We have our cards, dude." He handed a carton to Pauley and then both cards to me. "Thanks for letting us order them. This is my first business card ever."

"Me too," Pauley said.

I smiled. At least something was going right. I looked at the cards with the emblem and office logo I'd created. "Pauley O'Shea, File King?" I read.

"Yes. Like Fisher King, except I am not injured in the leg. I am, however, King of Files and all-knowing." On that zinger, Pauley turned and disappeared back into the office.

Oh, I didn't want to look, but I did it anyway to read out loud. "Oliver Duck, Czar." I frowned and looked up at Oliver.

He smiled. "You said we could choose any titles we wanted."

I flipped the card over in my hand. "But Czar? You're not ruling Russia and it is now post-revolution."

His cheeks looked like ripe apples and delight buzzed in his eyes. "Czar also describes someone who has great power or authority. I rule this reception area and your schedules, you know. I've always wanted to be a Czar."

Well, okay. I had enough to worry about. If Oliver and Pauley wanted to be Czars and Kings, why not? "Has Clark seen these?"

"Not yet," Oliver said.

"Make sure I'm out of the office when he does." I motioned to Kurt. "We have an empty office if you'd like to take it and do whatever you do in it." I led him through the door and bypassed Clark's office since he had a couple of clients in there before walking past the conference rooms, restrooms, and to the twin offices across the hall from each other. It looked like Pauley had more than moved into the one closest to my office.

He looked up from a new desk. "Kings should have offices. My father gave me the desk from his basement." His schoolbooks were neatly stacked in one corner.

"Cool." I turned to the other office, which now held Nana O'Shea's old card table. "Kurt, we can probably find you a desk, but for now, all we have is the table."

"Works for me," Kurt said. "I have my cell phone and have a bunch of phone calls to make. Could I borrow paper and pens? Where's the supply closet?"

I motioned for him to follow me. "Right between my office and the kitchen. Help yourself to whatever you need in either place. We still have a bunch of goodies from our office opening, including some huckleberry cookies from my mom. They're excellent."

Kurt nearly tripped over the dog. "Cookies? I may never leave."

"Then you'll need a better title than P.I.," I retorted. "King and Czar are taken, though." Clark wasn't going to love those business cards, but I'd deal with that situation later. I took my seat and spent an hour hammering out the Last Will and Testament for Mr. McLerrison and then made some notes on a timber trespass case I'd taken.

My phone dinged. "Yes, Czar?" I answered, still typing.

"A Miss Walker is here to see you," Oliver said. "Shall I bring her back?" Apparently Czars used words like 'shall.'

"That would be lovely," I retorted in the worst British accent ever. Why was Kelsey at my office? I looked at the calendar to make sure I hadn't goofed up.

They reached my door and I stood. "Hi, Kelsey. Your hearing isn't until this afternoon."

She looked pale in a light pink dress. "I know. I was hoping we could talk."

Was I about to get fired? I couldn't exactly blame her if she wanted to distance herself from the attorney who kept getting in fights and appearing in the newspaper. "Sure. Do you want anything to drink? We have coffee, soda, and water, but nothing is cold because we don't have a fridge yet."

"No, thanks." She wrung her hands together and stepped inside to take one of my guest chairs.

The Czar kindly shut the door.

I sat. "What's going on?"

Tears filled her pretty blue eyes. "I don't know. It's all so confusing, and I don't have anybody to talk to. My family is still mad about Krissy killing Danny, and they've all scattered. My sisters are all working states away, and now my folks are on a cruise for three months. It's like they all have just buried their heads and I'm so lost."

I took a drink of my water. "I understand, but they wouldn't be much help in your case. None of your family was in town when you and Krissy were at the concert in the park, were they?"

Kelsey shook her head.

"Okay. Then how about we come up with a list of people who can testify on your behalf if necessary?" Sometimes having a project helped when life looked hopeless. "We probably won't need it, but we can do that."

"It's not just my case," she said, tugging on her skirt to settle it better around her legs.

Pauley knocked on the door.

"Just a sec, Kelsey," I said. "Come in, P. I mean, King P."

He opened the door and skirted Kelsey to set a stack of papers on my desk. "From the main printer in the file room. My file room. The King's file room. Like the Fisher King but not. King of Files." He didn't make eye contact and left the room, his movements a little jerky. But he did shut the door.

I gathered the papers into a neat pile, impressed with the heavier bond paper I'd put in the printer for the Last Will and Testament.

"What's wrong with him?" Kelsey asked.

"Nothing is wrong with him." I set the papers to the side to concentrate more fully on her.

She looked over her shoulder at the closed doors. "I didn't mean it like that. Is he autistic?"

"Yeah, with savant qualities." I took another drink of water. "His brain just works the way it works, just like yours does and mine does. All of our brains work differently, and his just has a label for some reason. I've always wondered what the label for my brain organization would be. Haven't come up with anything appealing."

"That's an interesting thought. I wonder what my brain would be called." She seemed to relax a little into the chair. "At the moment it's stressed out and confused about pretty much everything."

I reached for a notepad from the stack by my laptop. "Let's start there. What questions do you have?"

"How do you know you've found the right guy?" she asked.

I dropped my pen onto the paper. "I meant more legal questions." Although, now I was curious. "Are you talking about Teddy?"

She nodded. "Yeah. I mean, do you believe in fate? Some crazy chicks from Spokane ram your car, which pushes us into an intersection where we're hit by an innocent guy just driving his car through a green light to meet his grandma for coffee. Then I meet the guy from the car while a nurse sprays antibacterial ointment on the cut above my eye. How does that happen if it isn't fate?"

"I don't know. So what's the problem? You just met the guy. Take it slow." It was a pretty cool meet-cute.

She shifted her weight. "I kind of have a boyfriend."

Oh yeah. The boyfriend of the purple condom world. "I forgot about that. Well, which one do you like better?"

"I don't know. They both have good qualities and are so different from each other." She rubbed her chin. "I'm sorry to hit you with all of this, but my sisters aren't talking to me, and most of my friends let my calls go to voice mail after my sister murdered Danny."

159

That was sad and unfair. Kelsey hadn't done anything wrong. "It's okay. I think people tell their problems to lawyers all the time because of the confidentiality." I'd be lost without my sisters. "You're also still seeing Dr. Versaccio, right?"

Kelsey nodded. "Yes. She's fantastic, but my next appointment is a week away, and since you and I are going to my hearing today, I figured we could chat."

"Sure," I said. "What are the plusses of each guy?" I took another drink of my water.

"Well, Teddy is funny and sweet, and I like that he has a stable job as a manager of a bank. He's also cute with a great body." She leaned forward, warming to the topic. "And Saber is—"

I coughed and nearly spit out water before rapidly swallowing it. "Saber? James Saber is your boyfriend?"

She flushed. "Yeah. Well, kind of. I didn't tell you because I figured you'd think it was a bad idea. We've been seeing each other since Krissy was arrested. He's hot, sexy, and dangerous. You get that, right?"

Oh boy, did I get that. "Yeah." There was no way Kelsey knew that Saber was an ATF agent. Irritation clacked through my skin. He had better not be using her. "He doesn't have a stable job, does he?"

"No." Her eyes widened. "In fact, I'm not sure what he does is even legal. The Lordes motorcycle club isn't known for being within the law, and they've been busted for both drug and gun-running in just the last few months, as you know. But he's just so...hot."

I frowned. "He seems a lot older than you."

"I'm twenty-one and he's twenty-nine. That's not a big difference," she countered.

"Yeah, but he seems older than twenty-nine. Like with life experiences." I couldn't see Kelsey with him for long. She was too sweet. "How old is Teddy?"

"Twenty-eight," she said. "But he seems younger than Saber, you know?"

"I definitely know." This was none of my business, but Kelsey deserved some stability in her life. "I think you should do a pro and con list for both and then think about it. Maybe fate does exist and put Teddy in your path at exactly the right time. Who knows?"

She drew in air. "You're right. Okay." She stood. "I'm going to take a walk in the park and think about everything. Should I meet you on the courthouse steps after lunch?"

"Perfect," I said.

She faltered. "What exactly do I need to do at the preliminary hearing?"

"Nothing. We just sit there and take notes as the prosecution tries to prove there's enough evidence against you to go to trial. Afterward, I'll make a motion to dismiss due to lack of evidence. They don't have to have much, just so you know, so my motion will most likely be denied. It'll be good to see what evidence Orrin has. He'll have exhibits and might have a couple of witnesses testify. I can ask questions but probably won't unless there's something obvious I need clarified."

She frowned. "So we don't cross-examine or do any of that stuff?"

"Yes, but only to clarify their statements and lock them in. I can also fish for information. This isn't a trial. It's just an evidentiary hearing, so don't worry about it. We're early in this process." I really did want to see what Orrin thought he had as evidence.

"Okay." Kelsey turned and opened the door. "See you in a couple of hours." Then she walked away.

I immediately called Aiden.

"Hey," he answered.

"Hey. What is Saber doing dating Kelsey Walker?" I asked.

He was quiet for a minute. "I try not to get involved with Saber's love life, Angel."

"Is he, or is he not, seeing her to wrap up your case against the gun runners?" I snapped.

"He's supposed to make sure we have all information, but if he's dating her, that's his personal life. He must like her," Aiden said. "Either way, it's none of our business."

It just became mine. That Teddy was looking better than ever.

CHAPTER 23

An hour before lunch, I walked Mr. McLerrison through his options for a trust and his will, having already created the various documents so he could decide. It was good practice for me, and I enjoyed the transactional work. He chose his options, and Oliver would receive payments upon different birthdays until he turned thirty-five and received the remainder of the estate. We used a trust structure to help offset taxes as best as I could.

"All right. Do you want to take these papers and think about it?" I asked.

"Nope," McLerrison said, hitching up his jeans. "I'm ready to sign. Let's do this."

I looked outside my door to see that Pauley had gone to class. He had a couple of summer classes. "Okay. I might need to go find two witnesses." Oliver couldn't be one since he was a beneficiary of the will, and I wanted Clark to notarize it since he was licensed as a notary. "Give me a second." I walked down the hallway and into the reception area, but only Oliver was there typing away. Hmm. Maybe Cousin Wanda and Bess were available. I opened the door and nearly plowed Darrin and Hailey Jennings over.

"Hi," I said, stumbling back. Hopefully they weren't there for a divorce.

Hailey handed over a colorful bouquet of carnations. "Hi. We were bringing you these as a thank you. We decided to keep seeing Dr. Wanda and talk about our problems before doing anything drastic."

Delight filled me. "Great. Thank you." I took the fragrant blooms. "Hey, do you mind doing me a favor?"

"Sure," Darrin said, sticking his hands in his jeans pockets. "What do you need?"

I gestured them inside the office. "I just need you two to witness a client sign his Last Will and Testament. You just sign that you watched him sign, and I'll need your licenses." This was kind of fun. I led them back to the conference room, where we met Clark and Mr. McLerrison. The process went off without a hitch, and soon we had a valid Last Will and Testament with a trust. I thanked the kids and then made a copy for my files and gave the original to McLerrison.

Then it was lunchtime. Clark and I ordered in and ate in the conference room.

"We need to get a table in the kitchen," Clark said, munching on a ham sandwich.

"And a fridge." I'd opted for a bland salad since I was a little nervous before court. Hopefully I'd get over that soon. "Have you had any flak from the article hinting I was a murderer?"

Clark chewed thoughtfully. "Not yet. It'd be handy if Jolene O'Sullivan wasn't out to get you."

"Right?" I said. "I'm glad somebody sees that besides me. Even if I do make good newspaper copy sometimes, she definitely enjoys painting me in a bad light." I glanced at my watch. "Eeks. I have to go. Wish me luck."

"Luck," Clark said, staring at the opening where a fridge should sit.

I fetched my files from my office and poked my head into

Kurt's temporary office. "I have court, but it's just a few blocks away. I'll be back probably in an hour."

He stood and stretched. "We're walking?"

"It's a warm summer day," I said. "Parking at the courthouse is crowded, anyway." Today I'd worn a light green skirt suit, frilly white shirt, and green pumps that were surprisingly comfortable for walking.

"Okay." He followed me out of the office and we both said bye to Oliver. "When you're with me, I'm between the street and you. If I say to duck, you drop to the ground. Got it?"

"Sure." We walked down the stairs into the sunny day. Darn it. I'd forgotten my sunglasses.

The walk was fragrant from the overflowing hanging baskets from the streetlamps, and soon we arrived at the courthouse. There were entrances from the parking lot and the park side, and today we met Kelsey on the steps by all of the cars.

Her face was pale and pinched.

"It's fine," I hastened to say. "This is just a prelim and you don't have to do anything but listen and learn."

"Hi," Kurt said, holding out a hand. "I'm Kurt."

She finally smiled. "Kelsey." They shook hands and she might've perked up more. "Do you work with Anna?"

"He's our private detective," I said before he could answer. It was a good cover, and we should probably stick with it since we'd been telling people that. "I want him in the courtroom to take notes on any witnesses if Orrin has any."

Kurt released her and somehow seemed to step closer at the same time. "I'm also there to make sure you're both safe. If you need anything, don't hesitate to ask." He smiled and a charming dimple twinkled in his left cheek, visible even through his thick beard.

Kelsey preened.

I looked at her.

She shrugged. "I'm young."

That was true. "All right. Let's do this." I walked across the marble steps, and Kurt beat me to the door, opening it gallantly for both of us. I tried really hard not to roll my eyes. "Even though the charges are all felonies, preliminary hearings take place in the misdemeanor courtrooms."

The courthouse was built when the timber and mining companies were prosperous in the area, which meant Italian marble, real cherry wood, and gorgeous sconces. During the eighties, the building had been expanded, and that included a lower level where the magistrate courtrooms were, among other court divisions. I walked down the stairs and proceeded to the first magistrate court, which was decorated in eighties-style salmon colored benches.

Orrin already sat at the prosecutor's table up past the benches and wooden railing. "We're it for today," he called out.

"Okay." I strode up the aisle and opened the swinging door for Kelsey, motioning her to our table. "How long do you need for this hearing?"

Orrin looked up from a stack of papers. "Between one and two hours, I think."

I took out several legal pads and pens with red, blue, and black ink.

Kelsey leaned over. "Can't I waive this part if it's not important?"

I lined up my pens and angled toward her. "Yes, you can waive the preliminary hearing, but it's very important."

"You said we probably won't win," she argued, looking over my shoulder at where Kurt had sat behind us.

"We probably won't," I agreed. "The state just has to show probable cause for this to continue, and that's a pretty low bar to meet. However, this is our chance to see their evidence and lock any witnesses into their testimony. Plus, we're fishing here. It's a chance to start our defense."

She frowned. "You're not going to put on any defense during this hearing?"

I sighed. She wasn't getting this. "If there's a miracle and Orrin has no evidence, I'll put some on so the judge will dismiss. But Orrin is going to have evidence, or we wouldn't be here. So just look at this as part of the process." I gently touched her shoulder. "I know it's hard, especially since Orrin is saying you did something you did not do, but we need to go through this. It'll help you in the end."

She lifted her chin. "All right. Who do you think are the witnesses?"

"One will be a police officer, and other than that, I don't know yet. But this is good because I can cross-examine them for more information." I wondered who the cop would be.

The side door opened and a bailiff with a full beard stepped inside. "All rise."

We all stood and Judge Williams strode to the bench. A light pink blouse peeked through at the top of her black robe. Her salt and pepper hair highlighted the pretty angles of her deep brown face. Her eyes were intelligent and seeking, and she had an air of serenity about her. "Good afternoon. Please sit." She took her seat.

Her assistant walked behind her to sit at a desk next to the judge's bench. She handed over a large case file.

Judge Williams slipped reading glasses onto her nose and read the case name and case number. "All right. Mr. Morgan? Are you ready to proceed?"

"Yes, your honor," Orrin said.

"Ms. Albertini?" the judge asked.

I reached for the black pen. "The defense is ready, judge."

"All right. It appears that the parties have stipulated that Danny Pucci was the victim of a homicide, so those facts are not in dispute here today. The matter in dispute is whether or not the defendant helped facilitate the death. Let's do this." The judge nodded at Orrin.

"The state calls Detective Grant Pierce to the stand," Orrin said.

Another bailiff opened the rear door, and Pierce strode down the aisle to take the witness box, where the bearded bailiff swore him in. Then he sat.

I wrote his name on the notepad. For court, he'd worn a gray suit with a darker gray tie, and with his blondish surf-boy good looks, he appeared earnest and also hard edged. Yeah, he was a good cop.

"He's hot," Kelsey whispered.

I leaned toward her. "You've caught your limit for now."

She grinned. At least she was smiling again.

Orrin ran Pierce through preliminary questions to establish his expertise in the field before turning to the day Danny had been killed. He walked Pierce through the evidence of the case and Krissy's later confession and conviction. "Detective Pierce, what evidence have you acquired that the defendant here today, Kelsey Walker, assisted her sister in the murder of Danny Pucci?" Orrin asked.

I finished the notes with my black pen and reached for the red and blue ones. Red for facts that hurt us and blue for facts that helped us. I'd learned that method during my time with the prosecuting attorney's office.

Pierce's green gaze remained focused on Orrin. "We found Kelsey Walker's DNA on the deceased's body. There were scratches along his back and the side of his neck that have proved to be the defendant's."

I made a note to ask a question.

"What else?" Orrin asked.

Pierce looked believable and authoritative in the witness box. He'd do a good job in front of a jury. "Witnesses attending the park concert that day confirm that both Krissy and Kelsey disappeared for a generous amount of time. Enough time to murder Mr. Pucci and return to the park."

We needed to find our own witnesses to rebut that. So far, I wasn't feeling too badly about this case. I'd ask Kelsey about the marks on Danny's body later. They'd had a turbulent relationship, so that'd be easy enough to explain to a jury if necessary. I might be able to get this tossed out after the prelim, maybe.

I cross-examined Pierce to gain more information about the evidence, how it was collected, and how long he'd suspected Kelsey of working with her sister. "How did you get my client's DNA, detective?"

His eyebrows rose. "Your client voluntarily gave up DNA during the investigation into the death of Danny Pucci. This happened before the arrest of her sister."

Kelsey winced. "I forgot to tell you that," she whispered.

What else had she forgotten to tell me?

I questioned Pierce for another thirty minutes just to make sure I wrung all information out of him that I could. Since this was just an evidentiary hearing, I let myself go into uncharted territory with Pierce. "Detective Pierce, do you think Kelsey Walker assisted in the murder of Danny Pucci?"

"Objection," Orrin said. "The detective's personal views are irrelevant."

I stood. "The prosecution spent a lot of time establishing the experience of the detective, so his opinion is relevant here, your honor."

"Overruled," Judge William said.

I smiled at Pierce. "Please answer the question."

The full force of his green gaze held power. "I don't know if your client helped in the murder. What I do know is that the evidence can be construed with enough probable cause against her."

Interesting. When Pierce was on the case, he was a bulldog with a hambone. Uncertainty from him showed a weak case. By the smile on Orrin's face, he didn't realize that fact.

"Thank you," I said, retaking my seat.

Orrin then called three witnesses from the park to say they lost sight of both Krissy and Kelsey. None of them knew where the sisters had gone, and none had any direct or even circumstantial evidence against Kelsey.

I questioned them so I could lock them in later with their testimony before whispering to Kelsey. "So far, this isn't bad. I'm not sure Orrin will make it past this stage."

Orrin then called his next witness, and Krissy Walker was escorted in from a door to the right of the bench.

Kelsey gasped and partially stood.

I pressed her arm and she sat back down. Crap. There was only one reason Orrin would want Krissy on the stand.

A few weeks in prison hadn't made Krissy Walker lose any of her luster. Her thick black hair wound around her shoulders, and her eyes were clear. Somehow, she looked good in the orange jumpsuit. She was sworn in and then sat patiently, looking only at Orrin.

Orrin stood. "Ms. Walker, let's make this easy. Did your sister assist you in the murder of Danny Pucci?"

Krissy swallowed. "Yes."

Ah, shoot.

CHAPTER 24

*J*t took me nearly an hour to calm Kelsey down in my office after the hearing. After Orrin had finished questioning Krissy, I'd asked many questions to make sure I could lock her in to the statement if we made it to trial. My final question was what the state had given her in exchange for her testimony, which was a reduced sentence.

Now I sat at the conference table with a puffy-faced Kelsey. She was not a pretty crier. "It's okay, Kelsey. If Krissy testifies against you, all I have to do on cross-examination is establish that she's getting a benefit out of everything she says. The jury will discount her testimony."

Kelsey held up a hand. "It's not that." She leaned into Kurt's side as he was sitting right next to her. She fluttered her eyelashes and sniffed delicately, even though her face was beet red from sobbing.

He slid an arm over her shoulders and tucked her close. "What is it, beautiful?"

Geez. Was she a guy magnet or what? Why did men like damsels in distress so much? It had to be biological. I'd always thought that a woman should be able to save herself. Although having a hot guy around was a nice benefit sometimes.

Kelsey hiccupped. "She's my sister."

Oh. Yeah. My heart hurt for her. That had to be excruciating during the hearing. Not once had Krissy even looked at Kelsey during the testimony. "I'm sorry. I'm sure Krissy is just trying to get herself the best deal and hasn't thought it all the way through. She has to be scared."

"Would you ever do that to your sisters?" Kelsey shrieked.

"No," I answered honestly, my ears ringing. "I have to ask you how your DNA got into the scratches on Danny."

Now she blushed even brighter, making her face several colors of red. A motley red. "We might have gotten together the night before, and it was a little wild. The scratches on his back were from sex." Then she lowered her gaze. "We got into a fight after that and he pushed me. I scratched him in response and then ran out. I never saw him again."

I sighed. None of that was good news for her case. "All right. We'll attend the arraignment as scheduled and hopefully we can talk to Krissy before that. If she'd just recant her testimony, this will all go away."

Kelsey stood. "I just want to go eat a gallon of ice cream and then go to bed. Krissy might not recant her testimony, and you know it. The judge said there was enough evidence for us to go to trial. When will that be?"

"First, we'll have a quick arraignment where you can plead not-guilty again and then know all the charges against you. Then a trial date will be set at the pre-trial conference," I said. "With the court's docket right now, I think we're looking at December for trial. Don't worry. That gives us a lot of time to work on this, and both of us will need to go talk to your sister at the prison."

Kelsey walked to the doorway like boulders weighed her down. "Okay. I'll be in touch."

Kurt stood. "You shouldn't drive like this." He looked at me, indecision on his handsome face.

I waved a hand in the air. "Feel free to drive her home. I'll stay here and get paperwork done until you return." I looked toward my office. "I have a nine-millimeter in my drawer and know how to shoot it. If anything goes wrong, I'll take care of it. I'll be fine."

Relief softened the planes of his face. "Okay. I'll just take Kelsey home and be right back. Thanks." He set a hand beneath her arm and escorted her out, even his movements somehow gentle.

Maybe Kelsey would need three columns for that dating pro and con list. Shaking my head, I walked to the kitchen for a warm Diet Coke before heading to my office to conduct some research for my other cases. Zena sprawled across my feet and under my desk. I loved having the dog close. Soon my phone dinged. I glanced at my calendar to see no appointments set for another hour when I'd meet with somebody named Mr. Smith about a land boundary dispute. "Hi, Oliver."

"Hi. Mr. Basanelli from the prosecuting attorney's office is here and says he has an appointment, but I don't see him on the calendar. Did you make an entry without telling me? It's not on there." Oliver sounded slightly peeved.

I searched my memory. "I don't know anything about an appointment, but go ahead and send him back." We didn't have any cases against each other right now, considering Orrin was handling Kelsey's case.

Oliver brought Nick down the hallway and left him at the door.

"Come on in," I said.

Nick looked around the office. He must not have had court today because he wore dark jeans with a blue Lilac Lake Country Club golf shirt. "This is nice."

"Thanks. My uncle is bringing a bookshelf and credenza later this week to round out the place." I gestured to one of the two guest seats. "What's up?"

Nick took a seat and frowned. "What do you mean?"

I sipped my soda. "Why are you here?"

His frown deepened. "You set up the appointment and said to meet here. My paralegal had this on my calendar."

My stomach sank. Right then my phone rang. I sighed before I answered it. "Hi, Oliver."

"Hello. Your grandmother, her friend, and your sister are here to see you," Oliver said, sounding more bewildered than ticked this time. "They said they have an appointment, but again, there's nothing on the calendar."

So much for being a Czar. Oliver needed to learn that not even Czars got in the way of one of Nonna's plans. "Of course they are. Please take them to the conference room, and I'll be right there."

Nick slumped in his chair. "You have got to be kidding me."

"I'll bet you fifty that my Nonna's friend is your Grandma Gerty." I stood. "We might as well get this over with right now. Come on, Nicolo."

Nick looked at the window to the right of my desk. "I think I could make it down that tree."

"Maybe," I agreed. "Although Jolene O'Sullivan is probably lurking around a corner just waiting to take a picture like that. Just think how that would look in the paper." There was no reason to tell Nick that Jolene was out of town with Quint right now. Nope.

Nick lowered his chin. "Tell me you didn't have anything to do with this situation."

"My calendar was clear for the hour, and I had no clue you were coming," I said. If Nick didn't know I'd talked to Nonna weeks ago about what a good guy he'd be for Tessa, no way was I going tell him. "I had no idea they were going to stop by." After making sure Nick showed up.

I led the way into the conference room where Tessa, Gerty,

and Nonna were already seated at the picnic table. Zena trotted along and zipped right toward Tessa. "What a terrific surprise," I lied. Apparently Gerty had gotten over any concerns she had from the food fight.

Tessa spotted Nick behind me and flushed a lovely damask rose. "What is going on, Nonna?"

Ah. Another unsuspecting victim. I purposefully sat next to her so Nick would have to sit across from her. Oh, I loved my sister, but I wasn't messing with Nonna, and she'd no doubt set this stage with precision.

Nonna waited until everyone had sat. Her hair was up in a smooth twist today.

Nick and Tessa looked everywhere except at each other. It was kind of cute, really. So long as neither one of them were mad at me, I could enjoy the moment.

Gerty beat Nonna to the punch. "Elda and I were talking, and we don't do enough for the Silverville community. So we agreed to take over the Elks Christmas holiday party, which serves as a fundraiser for the town, you know. We're co-chairs, and we've filled our committee with the three of you."

As a plan, it wasn't bad.

Tessa tried to get out of duty first. "Oh, I love that idea, but I'm swamped over here in Timber City. The diner has doubled my shifts, and I've accepted, so I can finally put my business plan into action."

Nonna patted her hand. "We can meet here at Anna's office. You certainly don't have to travel back and forth over the pass just to plan a party and charity for needy children. We will make it as easy as possible for you."

Nick's eyes twinkled a deep brown. "I'm down two prosecutors and have at least six trials coming up, Grams."

Gerty smiled broadly. Her new dentures looked lovely. "That's perfect, Nicolo. You're going to need a break from all of that work, and isn't it important to give back? Just think of all the people who aren't as fortunate as you are, and also consider how good something like this will look for a future political career."

Wow. Nick's Grams brought out the big guns. It was impressive, really.

Nonna turned to Tessa. "Tell us all about your business plan."

Tessa's gaze landed on me with a pleading I couldn't ignore. I cleared my throat. "I just have a few minutes before my next client arrives, but I'm happy to help with the holiday party. It's four months away, so we have plenty of time to get things in order." While I was willing to take the attention off my sister for the moment, that was as far as I'd go against Nonna's plan.

"Of course," Nonna said, straightening the Seahawk cloth that covered the picnic table. "Gerty? Should we start an email chain?"

"Yes," Gerty answered. "Or perhaps we should start a text chain?"

"Email chain," Tessa, Nick, and I said in unison. Getting caught on a group text with Nonna and Gerty would not go well for any of us.

Nonna stood. That was one thing about my grandmother. When she won a campaign, she didn't linger. "All right. We'll set up the email chain, and everyone can look at their schedules. Gerty and I believe we should meet once a week, and we're more than happy to work around your calendars. I'll be in touch."

Everyone stood. Okay. That wasn't so difficult.

Gerty looked at her watch. "Oh my. We have to get back, Elda. We have a Lady Elks meeting in forty-five minutes."

Nonna tucked her monstrous purse against her flowered shirt. "You're right. Oh my. Let's go." Then she hesitated. "Tessa."

Gerty gasped. "That's right. We picked Contessa up on the way here. Nick, would you—"

"Sure, Grams." Nick obviously knew when to give up the fight. "I'm happy to give Tessa a ride home."

Nonna clapped her hands together. "That's fabulous since Anna said she has a client coming. We'll walk you two out." Yeah, she was making sure Nick didn't dump Tessa on me. She was one smart woman.

Tessa followed our grandmother and avoided looking at Nick. Zena barked and trotted along behind her. The dog no doubt felt the tension.

Tessa looked down. "I can take Zena, if you want."

It sounded like she wanted to take the dog, and I didn't blame her. "Sure. You go ahead and have fun."

"I'll call you later," Tess said.

Oh, I just bet she would. I kept my smile at bay until they'd left, and only then did I let myself chuckle for a few moments before grabbing a glass of water and moving back to my office. It was surprising that Kurt hadn't returned yet, but I had promised to stay in the office, and Kelsey had been wearing a short dress, so maybe he was offering comfort to her. She had mentioned getting ice cream.

I researched a couple of timber trespass statutes before Oliver called to say my four p.m. appointment had arrived and he'd bring the gentleman back. I was getting accustomed to formality from Czar Oliver. When he arrived at my door with my new client, I stood while setting the water glass down.

"Mr. Smith, this is Ms. Albertini," Oliver said. Then he turned and disappeared down the hallway.

I couldn't breathe. My legs went soft and I nearly fell. In my doorway, plain as day, stood Norman Barensky.

The bomber.

CHAPTER 25

*M*y throat went so dry it hurt. Yet I kept my expression as neutral as I could. "Mr. Smith. It's nice to meet you." I gestured to one of my guest chairs.

Barensky's gray hair looked even thinner in person than in the picture Aiden had shown me. His wrinkled face appeared smaller, and his brown eyes beadier. He sat and smiled with very thin lips. "It's so kind of you to fit me into your schedule." His voice was surprisingly soft.

I sat and forced a smile. "We're building our clientele now, and I'm happy to see you." I had pens and paper on my desk and would need an excuse to open the drawer to my left and get my gun. "I see from your Timber City Golf Course shirt that you like to golf," I said, looking him over to see if he had a weapon.

If he did, it was tucked either at the back of his waist beneath a light beige-colored jacket or in an ankle holster. His pants were a loose gray cotton, and his shoes penny loafers, but there could be an upper calf holster out of sight.

"I love to golf," he said.

"Me, too." I reached for a pen as my mind kept swirling around. Focus, darn it. "My assistant had a notation next to your name that you're involved in a boundary dispute?" Why was he in my office? Did he know I was still dating Aiden? Worse yet, did he know that Aiden was ATF? Or was he just doing due diligence and checking out anyone having to do with Aiden and the Lordes?

This was all way above my pay grade.

Barensky set his hands on his legs, and burn marks wound up his left one into the jacket. "I am having a boundary dispute with my neighbor. He has apple trees, and the fruit keeps falling into my yard, which is a problem because the deer then stomp all over my flowers as they understandably eat the apples."

I tried to proceed as if this was a real case and I wasn't in danger. Did he walk around with explosives just for fun? Why would anybody choose to create bombs? "I see." I drew my paper closer and started taking notes. Going for my gun was possible, but what then? He'd know that I knew he was Barensky, and what kind of danger would that put Aiden in? Also, if the police arrested Barensky, what about the person who'd hired him for this campaign in Seattle? I swallowed. "How long has this been going on?" Sweat gathered down my back. Panicky sweat.

"About three years," Barensky lied.

I dutifully took notes. "How many trees does your neighbor have, and what percentage of the apples end up in your yard?"

"Um, five trees and at least half the apples. The limbs of his trees spread far over our fence." He seemed genuine, and if I didn't know better, I'd believe him. The pink scalp showing through his comb-over hinted at a sense of vulnerability.

"Have you talked to your neighbor?" I asked.

He nodded, his eyes sharp. "Yes. He is not a good man. I believe he has ties to one of those motorcycle gangs."

Ah. Here we go. "I see. Which gang?" I asked.

Barensky leaned forward. "The Lordes. It was my understanding that the Lordes were disbanded because of drug and gun problems, but he still rides a motorcycle and wears a leather jacket with the Lordes logo on it. I'm afraid of him, but I love my flowers. They're all I have."

I set down the pen. "I love flowers, too. Unfortunately, I can't represent you, Mr. Smith." I tried to look properly sad about that.

"Why not?" He fumbled in his jacket and drew out a worn brown leather wallet. "I can pay a retainer."

I tried to smile, but my lips refused to cooperate. "I have a conflict because I used to date a Lordes' member." We really needed to get a conflict check into place with Oliver before Clark or I met with clients. Not that it would've helped in this case. Barensky was fishing for information. "I can recommend several good attorneys in town."

Barensky replaced his wallet in his pocket. "You said you used to date a gang member?"

"I believe they're called *club* members," I said quietly, my hand lightly resting on the drawer pull. "Even though the relationship ended a while ago, I still did have one with a Lordes' member, so I can't represent you. It's unfortunate."

He shook his head. "Well, at least tell me what you know. Are they dangerous? Should I be afraid of my neighbor?"

My shoulders relaxed a fraction. I might be in an enclosed space with a sociopath who liked fire and explosions, but he was just looking for information. "Who's your neighbor?"

"His name sounds like Blade or something like that. I have tried to stay out of his way." Barensky wiped a hand down his face. "Please give me advice, even if it isn't legal advice."

"The Lordes are dangerous," I said. If nothing else, maybe I could shore up Aiden's reputation. "I know a bunch of members went to prison for running drugs, and then more were arrested on some gun charges. How many of them are even left? Maybe twenty?" I shook my head. "That's not many members. Hopefully they don't have any way to make money now and will leave the area. Wouldn't that be ideal for you?"

He smiled, showing yellowed teeth. The guy must smoke.

"That would be perfect. If you don't mind my asking, why did you end the relationship?"

I did mind him asking, but I tried to hide my emotions and sighed instead. "We were too different. I didn't realize the crimes the Lordes were committing, and I'm a lawyer, and everything just fizzled. It was a clean break." Then I pretended to catch myself. "I'm sorry. I shouldn't be talking about personal matters."

Sweat trickled down my back and between my breasts, and my hands tingled. Adrenaline and fear combined into a metallic taste in my mouth.

This innocuous looking guy was terrifying. He stood and edged back to the door. "I'm sorry you can't be my lawyer. I like you."

I smiled. "Ditto."

Then I sat there, unable to move. He left and shut the door, and all I could do for several moments was sit. My hand shaking, I called Oliver at the front desk.

"Hey, Anna," he answered.

"Hi." My voice trembled. "Is Mr. Smith gone?"

Papers shuffled across the line. "Yeah. He left right away and said it was nice to meet me. Why?"

"Just asking." I hung up and immediately dialed Aiden.

"Yo," he answered, engines revving in the background.

I tried to speak, but nothing came out. I tried again. "Barensky was just here."

Silence slammed heavily over the phone. "What did you say?"

I repeated myself.

Aiden burst into a spate of Gaelic that was even scarier than being in the room with Barensky. "Where are you, and are you safe?"

"I'm in my office, and I'm safe," I said, my voice cracking this time. "I have a gun. He's gone. He was just investigating you and the Lordes, I think. There were those newspaper articles about me, and it's known that we dated. I assume he was just gathering intel." Now that I'd started talking, I couldn't stop. "He was old and seemed normal, but he has beady eyes. I couldn't tell if he was armed."

"Where's Kurt?" Aiden asked.

As if on cue, Kurt poked his head into the office. I motioned for him to come inside, and he did so.

"Barensky was here," I said.

Kurt froze. "How long ago?"

"He left about ten minutes ago," I said, my breath feeling funny. Not hot but not cold. Still metallic. The room swam around.

"Give the phone to Kurt," Aiden ordered.

I handed the phone over and reached blindly for my Diet Coke. The soda was now more than warm and definitely flat, but I drank it down like I hadn't had food for years. My temples pounded as the adrenaline started to recede. Kurt's voice was muffled because I was drowning in my own head.

He hung up and I jumped.

"You okay?" he asked, his cheekbones red with what must be anger.

I nodded.

"I'm sorry I wasn't here. It was a bonehead move." He eyed me like he was afraid I'd topple over.

"It's okay. Frankly, it's probably a good thing you weren't here." I forced myself to breathe evenly and convince my body I was fine and not to freak out anymore. "Barensky was just digging for information, and if you had been here, his suspicions might've been raised."

Kurt didn't look relieved. "All right. It's after five, so I need you to gather your things, and we'll get out of here. We're going to hold hands and act like we're together through this building and to your car."

Bile rolled around in my stomach like a tornado had found a home. "You think he'll be watching me?"

"No," Kurt said. "But I'm not going to fall down on the job

again. That means taking every precaution just in case he is watching you. All right?"

I could tell those were orders from Aiden. "Sure." When my legs finally felt solid again, I stood and gathered my belongings. "Should I give Clark a warning?"

"No. Barensky was here to see you and not anybody else." Kurt led the way through the office.

Everybody else was already gone, which filled me with relief. While I didn't think Barensky was coming back, it helped to know that my friends were out of the building for now. In the hallway, Kurt grabbed my hand. It felt weird. I mean, he had a nice hand that was warm and strong.

But it wasn't Aiden's hand.

Aiden's hand was bigger and his hold firmer. Just more Aiden-like.

"Smile," Kurt muttered as we walked down the three flights of stairs and out the back door to the alley.

My cheeks already hurt from my fake smiles earlier, but I forced yet another grin on my face. Then I gently swung our arms and forced Kurt to slow down and look more casual.

The sun still beat down, although it was dinnertime.

His grin seemed more natural than mine felt as he looked down at me near the Jeep. "Do you want to go to dinner tonight? It was a long day."

I chucked him lightly with my shoulder as if playing. "It has been a long day. How about we go to my place and order pizza or cook one of the frozen Irish stews I made last week?"

He opened the passenger side door of my Jeep and grasped my elbow to help me in. "I vote the stew."

My legs were still weak and my head hurting, so I didn't object to his shutting my door and walking around my vehicle to jump into the driver's seat. I didn't even complain when he dug into my purse for my keys.

He tugged on my hair as if we were dating and then started the car to drive leisurely down the alleyway.

"Kurt—" I started.

He planted a hand on my knee. It felt really odd to have his hand on my leg. I barely knew the guy, even if he was Aiden's friend and colleague. "You go ahead and relax, sweetheart. I'll order pizza if you don't want to warm up the stew. But you know I love your Irish stew almost as much as your lasagna."

I frowned. Was he thinking there might be a bug in the car?

He caught my gaze and nodded.

I struggled to stay in the moment and not freak out again. "I think I'd rather have the stew. We can make a salad and open a bottle of wine. What do you say?"

He patted my leg. "I'd say I'm lucky to be dating you."

CHAPTER 26

*K*urt parked the Jeep in my driveway, and I jumped out, numbly heading around the edge of the garage and toward the front porch. There was only a wisp of sound, and a male body slammed Kurt against the side of the garage. I screamed and scrambled into my purse for my gun before I recognized Aiden as the attacker. He held Kurt against the wall with an arm across his friend's neck. "Go inside and lock the door. Your house is secure," Aiden snapped.

I froze. The mask of civility had been stripped completely away from Aiden. His eyes blazed a furious blue, and every muscle in his body was rock solid and rigid.

"Now," he barked.

I jumped and all but fled into my cottage to lock the door.

My whole body shaking now, I hitched inside my cottage. Okay. No way was Aiden killing Kurt. Probably. Either way, it was silent outside. Where had they gone? I risked a peek through the front window and didn't see either man.

Fine. My suit was bugging me, so I went to my bedroom and changed into cutoff shorts and a white tank top. My feet were done after being in heels all day, even though they'd been fairly comfortable. So I walked barefoot back into the kitchen and pulled out one of the bags containing frozen Irish stew I'd made a week before. Then I heated up the oven, tossed a salad, and opened a bottle of Cabernet.

I was on my second glass, and the stew was nicely cooking when Aiden made his way inside by using his key. Leaning against the counter, my glass in my hand, I studied him. No bruises, no ripped clothing. Just pure pissed-off male. My heart rate that had finally calmed now shot into attack range again. "Is Kurt dead?" I quipped.

Aiden didn't smile. His full lips didn't even twitch.

I sighed. We hadn't lived in each other's space enough for me to know how to handle him in this kind of mood—in fact, I'd never seen him in this mood.

Yet, this was Aiden, and I was safe with him. Unlike Kurt. I hoped Kurt wasn't bleeding in my petunias. "Are you hungry?" I asked.

Aiden's eyes flared a rare indigo.

I swallowed, and my heart rate accelerated more with a sense of feminine anticipation I would never be able to describe to my sisters. There weren't any decent descriptions.

So when he started moving toward me, all I could do was freeze on the spot. When he reached me, he shut off the oven, took my wine glass, and drank the entire volume down before setting it to the side.

My breath just gave up. Lungs done. Air over.

He reached for my nape, tangled his long fingers in my hair, and tilted my head to the side. Then he kissed me. I knew the correct term was 'kiss,' but it was so much more than that. Heat, fire, danger and more than a hint of anger consumed us both. He went deep and full, taking as much as giving.

I kissed him back, instantly drawn into his storm.

My tank and shorts flew across the room, and I ripped off his shirt before he helped me with his pants. He dropped to his knees and put his mouth on me, and I was already there. Fast and hard, climaxing and crying out his name. Then he was up and kissing me again, his hands on my butt.

It was fast and crazy and so exciting I could barely keep up. In fact, I wasn't keeping up. He lifted me, and we made it to the sofa, where I found myself bent over, my hair falling over my face. Then he slowly pushed inside me, hard and full. I sucked in air.

Even though we were engulfed in whatever this was, he still went slow and was so damn careful not to hurt me. That, more than anything else, shot my need for him into the stratosphere.

Then he was inside, powering hungrily, fast and hard and nearly out of control.

I broke first, but he was close behind. We both shattered and shuddered, and he was breathing as heavily as I was. When I finally came down, he flipped me around and carried me into the bedroom. My back hit the bed and then he was on me again.

Moonlight cut inside through my sliding glass door, dancing over the impossibly hard angles of his rugged face and illuminating his eyes so I could see the different colors of blue, all glittering for me.

This time, I arched against him and cried out his name.

A while later, after one more time, he curled around me beneath the covers. His hand wandered idly along my arm as he spooned me, and I lazily watched the moonlight play across the lake. "Are you okay?" I asked.

He kissed the back of my head.

Realization tickled through me. Aiden kept fierce control on himself, and I'd never really seen his Irish temper. Oh, I guess I had, but he'd learned to manage it to an impressive degree. When he spoke softly, he was angry. Now, he wasn't speaking at all. That meant he was beyond angry, and even though he was fantastic at expressing himself physically, and I mean out of this world at it, he wasn't so great at the verbal process. I patted his hand. "Come on. I'm starving."

"Go ahead. I'll just wait for you here," he murmured.

Well, at least he had spoken finally. "Nope." I ripped back the covers and grabbed his hand. "That's not how this works." My entire body was sensitized and maybe a little sore, but it was awesome.

He tugged me back into him. "How about we stay here?" He kissed my neck.

"You really don't want to talk, do you?" I was to stay there. "No. I'm sore and probably won't be able to walk tomorrow, and neither one of us has eaten. Whether you like it or not, we have to talk about this, Aiden." I wasn't an expert at relationships, at all, but I needed to go with my instincts here. "Come on. I'll microwave the stew."

His stomach growled.

I grinned. "Come on. Talking about our *feelings* won't hurt you too much."

He groaned and got out of the bed.

I tugged on his discarded T-shirt and snatched a clean pair of panties from my dresser before padding toward the kitchen, where I nuked two bowls of stew. I poured two glasses of wine and two of water. We both needed hydration.

He walked into the kitchen, his jeans unbuttoned, his feet bare, and his black hair mussed.

Maybe we should go back to bed. I shook myself out of it and gestured to the table with the bowls of stew.

We attacked the food like we hadn't eaten in years. Finally, I took a drink of my wine as a thought occurred to me. I wasn't exactly dressed. "When is Kurt coming back?"

Aiden looked up from the food. The messy hair looked good on him, and I had to concentrate not to stare at his bare chest. "Kurt is not coming back."

I paused in bringing my glass to my mouth again. "Tell me you didn't kill him."

Aiden rolled his eyes and took a drink of the Cabernet.

"Aiden, come on. He didn't do anything wrong." As tension started to roll from my boyfriend, I tried another tack. "Okay. Even if he made a mistake, it was a small one. Come on."

Aiden's chin dropped and even half-naked, he looked deadly. "There are no mistakes when it comes to you. None."

Well, that was kind of sweet...and a little scary. My insides went squishy anyway. "Let's talk about this. I handled Barensky pretty well, and your cover is still in place, as much as it was, anyway." I really didn't like how in the dark we were about Barensky's knowledge.

"This isn't about you or what you did. Kurt is gone because of what he did." Aiden took another bite of the food. "He left you alone with a terrorist, Angel. That's unacceptable."

I treaded carefully and tried to find reason. "We thought I was perfectly safe in my office."

"You were wrong."

"Maybe not. I do have a gun in my drawer, you know," I reminded him. When he didn't answer, I tried again. "If Kurt had been there, what would've been different? I assume he wouldn't have tried to interfere and blow your cover."

Aiden finished his wine and turned to his water. "Probably not, but he would've been there if needed, which was his fucking job."

Eesh. Aiden swearing around me wasn't a good sign. I knew Kurt wasn't dead, but there was a decent chance he was out in the petunias gasping for breath. "Aiden, you work dangerous jobs and you have to be used to this. Why are you so upset?"

He looked at me for several long moments. "The only people I've really cared about in my life were my grandparents and now you. I know we've talked about when I helped save you as a kid and how that moment changed us both, but that's not it. I'm not still back in that mode wanting to keep you safe because I did once before."

I took another drink of wine and let him talk.

"It's hard enough making sure you survive your job, and under no circumstances will I allow my job to put you in danger. You're mine. Right in there with my grandparents, right inside me, and you have to stay safe." He stood and placed his plate in the sink, the muscles down his back looking tense. He turned around, bare-chested and mouth wateringly intense. "That's the only way I can explain it."

That was probably the sweetest thing I'd ever heard, and he hadn't meant it to be sweet at all. My heart felt like it swelled and attacked my lungs. If I were a cartoon character, hearts would be streaming from my eyes. I carried my dishes to the sink and tried to think of the right thing to say.

He drew me against him, wrapping his arms around my waist. I rested my head against his chest and listened to the steady thrum of his heart before he spoke again. "I don't want to stand around and explore feelings all night, and I've explained the best I can. I'll give up anybody or anything to keep you safe, and that includes my job. I wish you'd remember that next time you find yourself in a dangerous situation."

"But—" I started.

"I know this one wasn't your fault, and you handled the entire situation perfectly. Better than a trained agent would have. That doesn't negate the reality that you're on Barensky's radar, and he likes to blow beautiful things up. Right now, we're going to continue as planned, and never again will one of my jobs be this close to home. If things go sideways, and I say you're getting out of town, you're doing it. Period."

Ah. Bossy Aiden was back. At least I knew how to handle him, unlike Deadly Silent Aiden. I leaned back and kissed his whiskered jaw. "How about you do your job, put away the bad guy, and we can relax at the lake for a couple of days?"

"Good plan." He kissed me softly on the lips. "Can we go to sleep now? This talking is exhausting."

CHAPTER 27

I dressed in casual slacks, a teal colored blouse, and tan flats for work and planned to get there early before everyone else. There was so much paperwork to do that I was tempted to wear jeans, but I also had some client meetings and needed to look like a lawyer.

As I was rushing to the door, my phone rang and I snatched it off the counter. "Hello?"

"Anna? It's Thelma and Georgiana," yelled a high pitched voice.

I winced. "I can hear you. The phone lines are good between here and London." My friends were currently in London trying to meet the Queen, and my bet was on them.

"Oh." Thelma lowered her voice. "Okay. We were on the *internets* and saw the articles about you. Do you need backup? We can get a plane home."

"No," I burst out. "I mean, no thank you. That's very kind of you, but everything is under control. Continue on your senior tour and have a great time, and don't forget that you promised to bring me lots of pictures to look at when you get home."

The two elderly ladies had become my friends when I'd had a

case against them, and I think they might've adopted me as their granddaughter without filing any paperwork.

"Good. Call us if you need us. Georgiana met a gentleman here, and he's hot. He's Scottish. Gotta go." Thelma hung up.

I exhaled slowly. The last thing I needed was Thelma or Georgiana back in town trying to help me out in a bar fight.

Aiden emerged from my bedroom in clean clothes from his drawer, so he wore jeans and a T-shirt. "Everything okay?"

I nodded. "Yeah. All is good."

He loped his way toward me and nudged my chin up with his knuckle. His unique scent of male washed over me. "I mean it. Are we okay?"

"Yes." I smiled. We'd had sex, talked, and then snuggled. "We're good."

"Good." He dipped his head and kissed me. "We need to go dark for a bit." He walked to the front door and opened it.

Bud Orlov sat on my porch with his legs extended to the ground and his face to the sun.

"Bud?" I moved beyond Aiden as the police officer turned around to face me.

Bud stood and brushed off his jeans. "Morning."

I looked at Aiden as he shut and locked my door. "What's going on?"

Bud rolled his shoulders beneath a worn Nickelback T-shirt. "I'm on Anna duty." He paused. "Again."

I took in his buzz cut and square features. For a guy built like a wrestler, he sure became dramatic sometimes. "I don't understand. Am I being arrested?"

"No," Aiden said, moving beyond Bud to place a kiss on my head. "I called Detective Pierce and said you needed protection. He was able to push the request through because Sasha was killed and found on your porch. You're a person of interest, either as a witness or a suspect, so a protection detail has been assigned to you for the time being."

"Me," Bud said glumly. Geez. Get a guy shot once, and he never lets it go.

I angled my neck to check out the flowers by the garage. No bleeding Kurt was in sight. "What about Kurt?"

"He's been reassigned to another unit back in Los Angeles," Aiden said, his tone not inviting questions. Wow. He had been serious about the no mistake rule. "My bike is hidden up the lake road. I'll see you later." He dodged behind the garage and pretty much disappeared from sight.

Bud flipped his sunglasses onto his head. "While on detail, we take my car. I already secured yours in your garage."

I hefted my bag over my shoulder. "I have enough men bossing me around right now, Bud. You don't want to be another one. Trust me."

"Fair enough." He led the way beyond the garage to a silver Chevy truck with a decent hitch. "Even so, I'm driving, and we're taking my truck because I know how it handles."

I studied the hitch.

"I like to fish. Need to pull the boat." Bud opened the passenger side door.

I stepped up into the truck, sitting and enjoying the plush leather. Who could've known Bud liked luxury? It was too warm outside to use the heated seats, but I was tempted anyway.

"What is the plan for today?" he asked after getting inside and starting the engine.

I plucked my phone from my purse and scrolled through the calendar. "I'm working in my office until ten and then have client meetings for two hours. Then I have a lunch meeting just down the hall with Cousin Wanda." I swiped farther up the screen. "More client meetings afterward, a brief sit-down with Clark, my law partner, and then just paperwork for the rest of the day."

"Sounds simple," Bud said.

"Is that doubt in your voice?" I asked.

He didn't answer.

Fine. I quickly texted Donna and asked if she wanted to meet for coffee at my office around three. She said sure and that she'd bring the coffee, which was what I had hoped. I turned and smiled at Bud.

"What?" he asked, not looking away from the road.

"Nothing." It was time to see if he was going to fish or cut bait. He and Donna had seemed to have a connection when they'd met, and I was tired of waiting for Bud to make a move. Or Donna to make a move. Might as well give them both a little shove. "Turn left there. Tessa is meeting us in front of the diner. She lives above it."

Bud turned and pulled to a stop where Tessa stood with Zena in front of Smiley's.

I opened my door. "Hi, awesome sister who loves me," I said.

"You have got to get Nonna off my back," Tessa burst out. "Please. I can't take it."

I shifted uncomfortably in my seat. The whole situation had started out as my idea, and guilt heated my face. "What am I supposed to do with Nonna? She's determined, and I think Gerty is still on board. I guess we could engineer another very public food fight, and that might make Gerty back off?"

Tessa sighed. "I don't want to get into another food fight. What I want is to be left alone."

"I understand," I said. "How did the ride home go, anyway? Did you and Nick get a chance to talk?"

"Not you, too," she whined.

Now I rolled my eyes. "Oh, stop it. You're not a whiner. I can tell that you're attracted to him, and he's attracted to you, so what's the freaking problem?"

Bud cut me a look and I ignored it.

"We're not a good match," Tessa said, petting Zena's head. "Forgetting the fact that I can find my own dates, Nick and I don't make any sense. He's probably going to be the governor or a US Senator or something."

"So?" I really didn't understand her problem with that.

"So? Can you see me at a governor's ball? Senate confirmation hearing, or whatever they have? Come on."

I focused entirely on my sister and tightened my grip on the inside door handle. "Yes. I see you wherever you want to be. Stop being stupid." Sometimes the gentle touch just didn't work. "You're one of the smartest and classiest people I've ever met. You belong anywhere you want."

"I haven't even gone to college," she said.

"Who cares? If it matters to you, go. If not, stop worrying about it. That doesn't mean anything and you know it." I stretched out my ankles. How were even my ankles sore from the mattress hockey with Aiden the night before? "I mean it. If you don't knock this off, I'm going to tell Nonna."

She was quiet for a second and her face paled slightly. "That's just mean, Anna."

I chuckled. "I am mean. Honest. Now that we're locked in for the Elk's Holiday committee, Nonna will back off a little bit and let you breathe." That was the good news. "However, you might as well get on board because we're going to meet at least once a week. Why don't you explore the idea? What did you guys talk about when he took you home?" Yeah, I was nosy.

Bud's curiosity obviously grew because he lifted an eyebrow and leaned forward to see Tessa beyond me.

"Nothing. I mean, we talked about what pains our grand-mothers were," she said. "That's about it."

"He didn't ask you out?" That was disappointing.

Bud groaned and leaned back in his seat. "Meddling."

"No," Tessa said. "Well, not really. Maybe kind of. I don't know."

"What do you mean?" I asked.

She looked away. "Nothing. I have to go because my shift starts in a minute." She opened the back door and let Zena in. "Bye." She shut the door and hustled toward the diner.

I watched her go. Oh, she hadn't given me all the dish. We were so going to talk about that when we got the chance. If he'd asked her out and she'd refused, I was going to throw her in the lake. Unless she really didn't like him. But I could tell she was intrigued by him, darn it.

Bud pulled away from the curb to drive to my office building. "Is Donna dating anybody?"

Oh, I wasn't helping him out. The guy needed to get off his butt and ask Donna out if he was interested. "Don't be nosy." Yeah. That'd teach him.

He remained silent to the office, into the building, up the stairs, and through the law firm. I flipped on the lights and noted that Oliver had tidied up the reception area before leaving the day before. He sure liked things organized. "This is the firm," I said.

Bud grunted.

I wasn't sure if he was pouting or just being normal Bud who didn't talk much. We walked through the inside door to the main hallway and Zena growled.

Bud pushed me behind him and drew a gun from the back of his waist. I hadn't even seen it. My body went on full alert, and I pulled my smaller weapon from my purse. What was happening? I held my breath and listened, but there was no noise. No hint that anybody else was in the office. All of the lights were off.

Zena ran by me toward my office before I could stop her. At the entrance, she lay down, facing inside.

Bud's shoulders went rock hard. "She's a search and rescue dog, right?"

"Yes," I whispered, chilly fingers ticking along my shoulders. I reached blindly for the wall switch and illuminated the hallway.

Bud walked silently down the hallway, turning and pointing his gun into each room until reaching my office. Then he leaned in and flicked on my light. "Shit."

I followed him to see a woman face up on my carpet, the side of her head smashed. Her blue eyes were lifeless as she stared at the ceiling, and her blonde hair was matted with blood.

"Do you know her?" Bud asked.

My stomach lurched. "Yeah. We were in a bar fight, food fight, and car wreck together." It was the blonde woman whose name I'd never learned. "She's also a Lorde's old lady. You're going to want to call Aiden."

Bud took his phone out of his back pocket. "I need to call this in first."

The coppery scent of blood and death engulfed my once peaceful office.

$\mathcal{J}$ sat at the picnic table in our conference room with Clark and Bud flanking me and Detective Grant Pierce across from me. We'd been there nearly two hours as the crime techs had done their job and then finally gotten the body out of the office. Clark had called both Oliver and Pauley and told them to take the day off.

Pierce finished taking notes.

Bud and I had answered all of his questions about our morning and what we'd seen, heard, or noticed. Zena's head was in my lap, and I stroked her absently, her presence calming me. "What was the woman's name?" I asked, my voice hoarse.

Pierce flipped a piece of paper over. "Bev Martin. We have her prints on file from a DUI three years ago in Idaho."

Bev. It was a pretty name. "I didn't even know her name," I murmured.

Clark pressed both hands on the checked tablecloth. "Do you think this is related to Agent Duponte's murder?"

Pierce shrugged. "Chances are good, considering both women were seen together before the murders. We're bringing in Aiden

Devlin and Bev Martin's boyfriend for questioning this afternoon. I'll see what I can dig up."

"Was Bev killed here?" I asked, my voice trembling now. The sight of her dead body on my wooden floor wouldn't leave my mind.

"Doubtful," Pierce said. "It looks like she was dumped here, which raises the question as to why. She fought with you and injured you in a vehicle accident, and she's connected through the Lordes. If I didn't know who Aiden really was, I'd think he killed her and dumped her as a present."

I wanted to bury my face in Zena's coat but remained upright like a grownup. "You do know who Aiden is, so you know he didn't do this."

"Do I?" Pierce asked.

I kept back a sigh. Pierce had never trusted Aiden, and ATF or not, that hadn't changed.

"I need to know where you were last night," Pierce said.

"I didn't kill her," I burst out.

Pierce's eyes glittered. "I know. If you did, it'd be pretty stupid to dump her body in your office. But if the FBI agents manage to connect this homicide to Agent Sasha Duponte's murder, you're going to be questioned about both anyway. Let's get it over with now, and I'll see if I can provide some cover for you."

I relaxed. Pierce really didn't think I'd done it. He was a friend, albeit a grumpy one. "Thanks, Grant," I murmured.

He nodded. "Get to it. Where were you?"

"I, ah, left work with Kurt, my bodyguard, maybe a little after six and went to my cottage." I scrambled to think what all I could say.

Pierce looked up. "What's Kurt's last name?'

I shrugged. "I don't know. He's an ATF agent who Aiden assigned to bodyguard me."

"Then why did Devlin call me way too late last night to have an officer assigned to you?" Pierce's brow furled.

"Yeah," Bud added.

I rubbed my eyes. "I think Aiden fired Kurt from the job last night. In fact, I know he did."

"Why?" Pierce growled.

Not many men could make a noise that actually sounded like a real growl. Pierce accomplished the feat handily. I sat back in the chair but kept my hand on Zena's head. I wasn't under any sort of confidentially agreement with the ATF, and we were all on the same side, so I told Pierce the entire story.

"The man who's one of the FBI's most wanted was in your office yesterday?" By the end of my story, Pierce's jaw was set so hard he had to be getting a headache. "You need to go take a vacation. Now."

"I can't. The FBI told me to stay here," I reminded him. "Wait a minute. Barensky is one of the FBI's most wanted?"

"Yes," Pierce said. "Guess Devlin left that out?"

I pet the dog. "Not on purpose. He told me how dangerous Barensky is and to stay out of the case."

"Right." Pierce slapped his pen on the table and made me jump. "If Kurt disappeared, who stayed at your place with you?"

"Aiden did," I said.

Pierce pinched the bridge of his nose. "I see. So the president of the Lorde's motorcycle club, the one who would be the prime suspect for this if he wasn't an ATF agent, is your alibi for the night."

Well, since Pierce put it like that. "Yes." I needed coffee. Like now. "But Aiden is an ATF agent, and you know he didn't do this."

"Right. If he had, we wouldn't have a body," Pierce agreed.

I wasn't sure I liked that line of thinking.

Clark tapped his fingers on the Seahawks tablecloth. "The longer you can keep this as a state matter and not federal, the better it is for Anna."

Pierce shot him a look. "I'm more worried about the murdered young woman."

"Me, too," I said.

A uniformed officer stuck his head in the doorway. "Pierce? We're ready to clear the scene."

Pierce stood. "I'll be right back." His phone buzzed, and he lifted it. "Pierce." He listened and then turned to me. "Somebody named Quint Albertini is with Jolene O'Sullivan insisting to be let inside. Something about the dog."

I scratched behind Zena's ears. "Have the officers let Quint in but definitely not Jolene."

"Agreed," Pierce said. "This will hit the papers anyway, but I'm not helping that woman out." He kept talking on his phone as he moved down the hallway, and Bud gave me a look before following him.

Clark sat back. "I hope they take the crime tape off the outside of the office." So far, he seemed to be taking this all okay. "We're going to lose clients over this one. It's one thing to have a bar fight and look tough, and it's another thing to have dead bodies show up in your office. The corporate clients I just signed will be the first to go."

"I'm sorry, Clark," I said.

"Not your fault." He stood. "I'm going to reschedule all of our appointments for this afternoon and will just use the calendar system Oliver set up. We need the afternoon off." Then he opened the door wider so Quint could move in before leaving.

"Anna Banana." Quint was across the room and hauling me up into a hug. He held a red dog toy rope in one hand. "Are you okay?"

"I'm fine." I hugged him back, letting his solidness ground me. "The woman was dumped here and the police are on it."

He released me and dropped to his haunches. "Who's a good girl? Who found the body?" His voice rose.

I stepped back.

He grinned and looked up, letting Zena take the toy and play tug of war. "She found a body and has to be rewarded since that's her job. Playing with me is her reward, and my higher voice is so she knows I'm excited and happy with her. We want her to keep finding bodies when we're searching mountains." He tugged back and dragged the excited dog a foot across the floor.

Her tail wagged wildly.

"I didn't know that," I said.

Quint let Zena pull him a ways. "You did fine by petting her and letting her put her head in your lap. This is my job." He stood but kept a hand on the toy as Zena fought to win it. "I'm staying at your place until we figure all of this out."

I shook my head. "That's sweet, but I have a police detail since Sasha was found on my porch and this woman in my office. The police think I'm both a suspect and a possible witness, so they can justify the overpay." I touched his arm. "What about you? Are you doing better?"

He nodded. "Yeah. Getting away helped, although I'm still having nightmares. Then Chrissy called while I was out of town with Jolene, and somehow that got both of them mad at me. Sometimes I think I should just lay low and do my job with my true love here." He patted Zena's head.

"Well, she's cute but can't give back rubs," I countered. Maybe I should get a dog. Or a cat. I wasn't home a lot, so it probably wasn't fair to a pet, either way. "I'm free if you need to leave Zena again. Any time."

"Did you and Aiden split?" Quint asked.

I paused. "No. Why?" Just the idea hurt, but I wasn't going to show that.

"Nonna called and asked me to invite Nick Basanelli to my poker night next week with the family. I figured something was up."

Oh. Maybe the charity committee was just the beginning of Nonna's plan. "Nonna is trying to fix Nick up with Tessa."

Quint frowned. "Does Tessa know?"

"Oh, yeah. It's a campaign," I said.

Quint's face cleared. "Then I'll invite him. So long as Nonna is concentrated on Tessa's love life, she's not getting involved with mine. It's every Albertini for themselves in this situation." He released the toy so Zena could twirl around with it.

"Keep that in mind, cousin," I said. "I haven't told Nonna that you're dating the woman who keeps writing mean articles about me in the paper."

Quint hugged me again. "Thank you. You're a goddess and I love you."

I grinned. "True. All of that is true."

Bud appeared in the doorway. "I have to go to the office and make another statement. That means you're coming with me. Please."

"Okay." My easy acceptance obviously surprised Bud because he took a step back. Truth be told, the police station was exactly where I wanted to be right now.

Quint reached down and reclaimed the toy from the dog. "I have a dinner tonight, but then I'll be over with ice cream for dessert and a chat. We can figure out what's going on and come up with a plan for you, Tessa, and me. I'll get her on the way." He snapped his fingers and walked out with the happily panting dog right behind him.

Bud frowned. "How come you let him be bossy?"

"He's bringing ice cream," I said.

Bud gestured me in front of him. "There are reporters out the front, so let's go the back way where my truck is. We have the alley cordoned off right now."

"Good." The last thing I needed was another picture in the paper. So I tugged my purse up my arm and reached Bud's truck without incident. He drove us to the station, and we hustled inside. It almost felt like a miracle that I'd been spared. Bud nodded at the cop behind the reception desk. "I have to meet with my captain. Do you mind waiting here?"

"Nope. I'm good." I waited until Bud had disappeared before

moving up the steps to the next level and walking to Pierce's office. It was empty. Then I walked through the bullpen, waved at a few friends, and somehow ended up near the interrogation rooms. Only one had a light on, so I slipped around the hallway and into the observation room, which was also vacant.

Pierce sat with his back to me, while Aiden sat across from him next to a man with a round face, also wearing a Lorde's cut. Aiden was slouching and looked insolent, so he must've been in character.

I flipped on the audio system so I could hear.

"Listen, Carbine," Pierce was saying. "I want to know where you were yesterday and last night. Start talking and now."

Carbine crossed his arms. He had muscled arms, a big belly, and a long beard that was pure brown. No gray. His hair was thick and fell to his shoulders, and it was also brown and possibly unwashed. "I was home."

"What's your given name?" Pierce asked.

Carbine rolled his eyes. "Carbine. That's my name."

Pierce's shoulders stiffened. This was no doubt a voluntary interview, and if Carbine wanted to leave, he could. So Pierce could only push so far. "Did you live with Bev?"

"Not anymore. I kicked that bitch out after she caused the truck accident and food fight." Carbine showed no emotion.

Pierce must've looked at Aiden. "On your orders?"

Aiden shrugged.

I swallowed. Aiden had told Carbine to break up with Bev because of me?

"Devlin, answer me," Pierce barked.

Aiden slowly turned his gaze to Pierce. "I don't get involved in my men's love lives, detective. However, I made it clear that if Bev went after Anna Albertini again, her man would no longer be one of mine or a Lordes club member. He made the decision to either talk some sense into Bev or end things. I couldn't care less which he decided."

Pierce sat back. "Why break up with her, then?"

Carbine scratched his chin. "I needed a change, anyway. Bev was a lot of work, and I was done."

Pierce angled toward Aiden. "I thought you and Albertini broke it off, and you were dating a redhead."

Aiden crossed his arms. "We did end things, but I still don't want anybody crashing a truck into her. We had some good times."

Pierce set his pen down. "I see. You know, a case could be made that you want her back and left her a gift of a dead woman, the woman harassing her, in her office."

Aiden barely smiled. "I'm more of an emeralds or flowers kind of guy, Pierce."

CHAPTER 29

$\mathcal{A}$round nine that evening, I settled onto my sofa with Quint on one side and Tessa on the other after having dished up bowls of ice-cream. The doorbell rang, and Bud hustled from the kitchen to the front door, peering out before straightening. He opened it.

Donna swept inside dressed in cute shorts and a shirt with a bottle of Baileys in her hand. "You didn't start without the Baileys?"

"Of course not." Tess grabbed Donna's bowl off my coffee table. "Here's yours. Bud won't join us."

Donna turned to the already blushing police officer. "You don't like ice cream?"

His Adams' apple bobbed. "I like ice cream." He gently drew her inside and locked the door. "But I'm on duty."

Donna placed her hand on his arm. "You don't have to have Bailey's, but surely you want ice cream." Her voice was smoother than any treat.

Even though Bud had refused a bowl from me three times, he suddenly looked agreeable. "I guess I could have a small bowl."

Tess jumped up and hustled to the kitchen to dish him a bowl. She quickly returned to hand it over with a spoon. "There you go."

Donna sat on the loveseat next to the sofa, and Bud followed after quickly scouting the kitchen with his dark gaze. I wasn't sure what kind of threat he thought might've just entered, but now wasn't the time to tease him. He took a seat next to her and looked as uncomfortable as a guy could get.

Quint snorted.

I partially turned. "Why do you smell like whiskey?"

He hiccupped.

Donna poured Baileys into her ice cream and handed the bottle to Tessa. "Quintino?"

He grinned. "I might've had a few shots with the guys at dinner. Don't worry. I didn't drive here. Jolene brought me, and I invited her in, but she declined."

I accepted the bottle from Tessa and poured generously over my ice cream. "That's too bad." I almost choked on the words. Then I poured some over Quint's bowl.

Tessa laughed. "Bud? Are you sure you don't want Baileys?"

"I'm sure." The officer took a spoonful of the ice cream.

He and Donna looked good together, but maybe he was a little, well, dull for my sister. Oh, he was a nice guy, but perhaps his instinct in not asking her out was a good one. Then I caught him watching her out of the corner of his eye, and I changed my mind. He must be shy.

Donna settled back, crossed one leg beneath the other on the sofa, and delicately took a spoonful of Bailey's enriched ice cream.

My phone buzzed, and I dug it out of my shorts to see it was Aiden. "I have to take this." I set my bowl on the coffee table and stood to head to my bedroom while ignoring my sisters and my cousin making kissing noises at me while I left. "Hi," I answered.

"Hi, Angel," Aiden said. He sounded tired. "How are you holding up?"

"I'm having ice cream with Baileys," I admitted. "My sisters,

Quint, and Bud are all here." It was too bad that Aiden couldn't join us.

"Good. Sorry about the body found at your office. I can't figure out who's targeting you. Targeting us." His voice was hoarse with a hint of anger. "I'm interviewing the real Lordes members to see if anybody thought they were doing you or me a favor by taking care of Sasha and Bev. It's doubtful, but some of these guys are rough and clueless. They might've seen a way to rise in the organization? I don't know. It's crazy as far as I'm concerned."

"Or it's Barensky," I said. "He's involved in your current case, and Sasha was on it, and he came to my office."

Aiden sighed. "I know, but this isn't his style. He loves explosives. When I say love, I mean it in the most sociopathic, desperately-in-tuned way. Smashing heads not only isn't his style, I don't think he could do it, even if he wanted to. If he wanted either of those women dead, he would've killed them with a bomb. With fire and destruction. He's pathological, and so is the way he kills."

I shivered and dug into a drawer for a sweatshirt to put on and zip up. "Then why these two women? I don't get it."

"I don't know, and we can't find Kay Lewis. She's the brunette who was with Bev during the car wreck and the food fight in the diner. She and Crash broke up the same night Carbine and Bev did."

I sat on the bed. "Because of me?"

"No, because of me. Or because they're assholes who'd rather ditch the women they were dating than ask them not to crash cars into my ex-girlfriend. They both wanted out and took the easy way." He was quiet for several heartbeats. "I can't wait until I'm out of this world. The cover should've been ended after the first drug bust."

It was too bad he had to stay the night at the Lorde's complex. "Can you sneak over again?"

"It's too much of a risk," he said.

I looked out at the deep and mysterious lake. "Have you had any luck finding Barensky or who hired him? Surely Sasha knew something?"

"No. She only met with an associate of Barensky's who inquired about a delivery system, and she thought of the Lordes. The name of the associate was Abe, and she didn't have any other information than that. Oh, before I forget. Her autopsy came back, and death was blunt force trauma to the head. There was no foreign DNA on her body, which is surprising since somebody grabbed her head and slammed it onto your porch." Now anger sizzled through the line. "Somebody wore gloves and knew what they were doing."

"I'm sorry, Aiden. I'd help if I could do anything," I said.

"Just be you and that helps everything. For now, I think the lack of DNA works in your favor as a suspect." His phone rustled as he must've moved. "At least something is going our way. Kind of."

I didn't like hearing Aiden so frustrated and down. "I wish you were here," I said quietly. "I'd give you a back rub."

"I'd give you a front rub," he said instantly.

I chuckled. At least I'd lightened his mood for the moment. "I had fun last night."

"Me too."

Now I had his attention. "I meant with the talking, but the rest of it was okay, too." Actually, it was spectacular.

"Just okay?" His voice grew intimate. "Hmmm. I might have to try again."

I smiled into the darkness, feeling happier than I had all day. "I guess I could let you try. I mean, it's the least I could do."

"You're a giver. All right, I have to go. Miss you." He clicked off.

"I miss you, too," I whispered before standing and all but gliding back into the living room. Aiden missed me. He'd said the words. It took me a second to catch the tension blanketing the

209

living room. Even Zena lay on the floor and watched me come closer with soft brown eyes. "What's going on?" I asked.

Donna looked up from her phone and then handed it over. "You're not going to like it."

My good mood evaporated faster than a Nordstrom's gift card. I took the phone and saw the online version of the *Timber City Gazette*. I groaned. "Don't tell me." I scrolled down to see a new article by Jolene about me. I read the headline out loud. *"Local Attorney in Protective Custody: Either as a Witness or a Cold-Blooded Killer."* Shock caught me, and I looked at Quint.

He stood and turned around, raw fury on his face. "I'm sorry. I—"

"You told Jolene?" I asked, my voice quivering. "What I said to you in the office? You told a *reporter?*"

He paled. "I'm so sorry. She seemed concerned about you, and we'd just spent a few good days together relaxing, and I didn't think she was on the record. I sure didn't think she'd run with a story like this."

Zena whined and moved toward him, apparently catching his distress.

I dropped my head and then read the article. Yep. It was pretty bad. Jolene had drawn intelligent connections between Sasha, Bev, the Lordes and me. Thank goodness she didn't know about the ATF involvement. She would've run with that story and helped Barensky get away, no matter who got hurt afterward.

Quint's brown eyes were softer than the dog's. "I'm so sorry."

"It's okay." Even though Jolene had taken some license in quoting an unnamed source, she'd also done her homework and gotten all of the facts. "She would've found all of this out anyway." I reached out and punched his arm. "You're forgiven." I could never stay mad at Quint.

Quint's phone blared and he looked down at the screen. His expression made my stomach ache. It was so angry. And a little wounded. "Excuse me," he said, lifting the phone to his ear and walking toward my bedroom, where he firmly shut the door.

Tessa poured more Baileys on my now melting ice-cream. "Look at the bright side. Not one of us is Jolene O'Sullivan." She smiled and leaned over to pour more into Donna's bowl. "Jolene hasn't met the tornado of Quintino Albertini when family has been hurt. Yep. I'm mighty glad I'm not on the other side of that phone call."

Her words cheered me immensely. I sat and took my bowl. "I wish we could listen."

"No," Donna said. "Not me. I never mind missing a display of Albertini temper." She winked at Bud. "Not that I have a temper because I don't."

Tessa snorted and then caught herself. "That's right. You don't have a temper."

I nodded solemnly. Oh, Donna had a temper and it was ice cold and devastating. "Nope. No temper."

Bud smiled, finally looking relaxed next to her. "I can see that. You do seem to be the calm one in the family." He caught himself and looked at Tessa and then at me. "No offense."

"None taken," Tessa said cheerfully. "I wish we all were as calm as Donna."

Calmly deadly, that was. I again nodded. "Yeah, me too. She's a haven in a turbulent storm."

"Enough," Donna said, sitting back. "Let's talk about anything but me. Like why dead bodies keep showing up around you, Anna. What is going on?"

"I don't know," I admitted. "But at least Bud is here to keep me safe. We do appreciate it, Bud."

Donna turned a full wattage smile on the poor guy. "We do. It means the world that you're protecting Anna."

Bud blinked. Just blinked. Yeah, Donna in full Italian feminine mode was like looking into the sun. With her black hair and mysterious eyes, I'd always thought she was beautiful. Her intelligence and kind heart only made her even more stunning.

"I'm married," Bud burst out.

Ice cream went down the wrong tube in my throat and I coughed wildly, bending over. He was married? Tessa pounded me on the back until I stopped. Tears flowed down my face as I struggled to breathe. "You're married?" I croaked.

He set the ice cream bowl on the table. "Yes. I'm sorry. I'm married. When I asked about your sister before, we were separated, and we were working toward a divorce. There were papers and everything. Then Sheila called last week and wasn't sure she wanted a divorce. I don't know. I'm confused, but I am married."

It was the most words I'd heard Bud speak at once in the entire time I'd known him.

Donna patted his arm. "Relax, Bud. It's all good." She reached for his bowl and handed it to him. "So. Tell us all about it." Curiosity now glimmered in her eyes.

Quint exited my bedroom and stalked toward the sofa to retake his place. "I am very sorry."

"It's okay." I leaned over for his bowl, which was still half full. "You're not done."

He took the bowl. "Oh, I'm done. Jolene and I are no longer seeing each other."

I chucked him with my shoulder. "What a crappy night."

"Amen to that," he said grimly. "Pass the Baileys, would you?"

"Sure." Tessa handed him the liqueur. "We might need a bigger bottle."

CHAPTER 30

The crime scene tape was gone, and the blood in my office cleaned up when I arrived on Wednesday morning. I made a mental note to thank Detective Pierce for that. Bud took residence in the empty office that had briefly been inhabited by Kurt, and both Pauley and Oliver seemed happy to be back at work. Clark had a breakfast meeting, and I hoped it wasn't an interview for a job with another firm—one with health insurance and no dead bodies.

My morning consisted of phone calls. First to cousin Wanda to apologize for missing our lunch appointment the day before, but since she worked in the same building, she was well versed in what had happened. Then to Pierce to see if he could track down the current location of Krissy Walker.

He called me back within fifteen minutes. "Hey. Krissy Walker is still here in custody. They're transporting her back to the women's prison early this afternoon."

"Great. Can you get me in to see her?" If she'd just recant her testimony, then the case against her sister would fold.

"Sure. What's one more favor?" he muttered.

I winced. "You're right. This friendship of ours seems one-sided. What can I do for you?"

"We're not friends," he retorted.

Yeah, we kind of were friends, whether he liked it or not. "We should change that, then. How about lunch today? I'm buying."

"Can't," Pierce said. "I'll get you in to see Walker in an hour, but you need to come early. I have a few more questions about the woman found dead in your office."

Good. That meant he'd kept the case for now, and the Feds hadn't taken over yet. "I'll be there." Then I called Kelsey and asked her to meet me at the station a little before ten and told her to bring anything sentimental to her sister. If I could close out her case, my stress level would decrease enough that I could at least breathe without my chest hurting. It wasn't fair for Kelsey to be hurt anymore in this life.

With Bud protecting me and providing shade from the sun, I stopped by Smiley's Diner to see Tessa on my way walking to the courthouse. She'd had an early shift, and it was in full swing, so I just waved as I waited for the two lattes and pastries to be finished. "Bud? You sure you don't want one?"

He stayed by the door where he could see the entire restaurant. "I don't like coffee."

I knew there was something wrong about him. What was the story with his wife, anyway? I'd have to pin him down later.

A man in the back booth caught my eye and my back stiffened. Kurt. I hurried toward him. "Hi."

He had a black eye and a bruise along his neck but was still breathing. A half-eaten omelet sat in front of him next to a cup of coffee. "Hi."

I hovered near his table. "I'm sorry you were taken off the case."

He shrugged and then winced as if it hurt. "I screwed up. It happens." He looked casual in jeans and a green tee, and his body language appeared nonchalant.

"I thought you were reassigned?" I asked. "To Los Angeles?"

He nodded. "I report on Monday and thought I'd spend a few days relaxing and deciding what to do. Aiden also demoted me, so I'm looking at all options right now. Maybe it's time to hang it up." He frowned. "I don't know."

Demoted? "That's not fair. I'm sorry. I can talk to him?" I shuffled my feet.

Kurt barked out a laugh. "You don't know him that well, then. Once Devlin makes a decision, that's it." Kurt's gaze was appraising. "You might want to keep that in mind. Screw up once, and you're out. Don't fall in love because nobody can meet his standards for long."

I opened my mouth but couldn't think of an answer to that statement. "Well, safe travels. I hope everything works out for you." Looking back at the counter, I could see my lattes and pastries. "Bye, Kurt."

I fetched the goodies and walked outside and toward Justice Road, my mind spinning. I wasn't perfect. In fact, I was so far from it that it wasn't funny. If that's what Aiden was looking for, he wouldn't be with me even right now. The thought actually cheered me and put a hop in my step.

Bud did not hop with me. He kept a steady pace, though.

The August sun was warm, but I was ready for autumn. For the changing of the trees and a slight breeze. Upon reaching the police station, I waved at the cop behind the reception desk and made my way to Pierce's office as Bud went somewhere else in the building. "I brought coffee and scones." I set both down on his desk and plunked onto a guest chair.

Pierce wore a suit today. A light beige one with a blue shirt and tie.

"Nice duds," I said.

"I'm testifying in court today." He tugged on his tie before reaching for his latte. Then he dug into case files at the edge of his desk and unearthed a bright and sparkly yellow file folder. "Here."

I took the folder. "Where do you keep finding these?"

He took a deep drink of his coffee. "There's a box in the supply cabinet and they remind me of you. Nobody else around here wants to use them."

That was fair. I flipped open the folder. "This is Sasha's autopsy report." Surely the FBI had wanted to keep a lid on it.

"Yep. Give it to your attorney," Pierce said. "There was no DNA on her, which helps you, I think."

That was sweet. Oh, I had no doubt that Pierce would be the first to arrest me if I'd committed a murder, but I liked that he believed in my innocence. "Thanks." I rifled through the papers. "When will Bev's be completed?" The killer had somehow carried her through my building to the office, so hopefully, there'd be some DNA.

"Probably not until tomorrow. We're looking at CCTV around town but haven't found anything. You should get security cameras for your building as well as your office." He reached for a pastry. "That Carbine is a pretty decent suspect. His rap sheet is on the bottom page."

I read quickly. "Wow. Assault, battery, assault with a deadly weapon, drug paraphernalia and petty theft. The guy should be in jail."

"Yep." Pierce ate a huckleberry scone and sighed in pleasure. "While you're here, I wanted your thoughts on how somebody got a body into your office. There was no sign of forced entry."

"I don't know. The building is old, so there are probably plenty of keys around. Clark already called a locksmith, and we're changing all the locks and looking into a security system. Those matters were on the to-do list anyway, but this pushes them to the top." I closed the file folder and reached for my latte. "Have you had any luck finding Kay, who was the other woman in the car wreck? She has to be in danger, too."

"We have a BOLO out, but nothing has come in yet." Pierce finished the scone. "None of this makes sense. It's almost as if somebody is just messing with you or Devlin."

"Maybe Barensky knows Aiden is with the ATF." I eyed a scone but didn't really need the calories.

Pierce pushed sugar off his desk into the garbage can. "I agree. But Devlin and the FBI agents investigating the murder have profiled Barensky, and they don't think it's him. He would've included fire or an explosive in the kills. I'm not so sure."

"Not a fan of profiling?" Okay. One scone wouldn't hurt me. I gingerly took one out of the bag.

"Not really. I'm more a fan of going with my gut." Pierce drank more coffee. "Either way, keep your detail with you. The shift changes every twenty-four hours, so Bud is off for now."

I sat back to eat my scone. "But Bud will be back tomorrow?"

Pierce set down his cup. "Yeah. Why?"

"Did you know he was married?" I licked sugar off my finger.

"Why would I know that?" Pierce checked his watch and then his phone rang. "Pierce," he answered. "Okay. Thanks." He replaced the handle in the cradle. "I had Krissy Walker brought up, and you can talk to her in Interrogation Room Two. She's in there now."

"Thanks." I stood with my latte in my hand. "I owe you one."

He scoffed. "You owe me more than one." Then he turned back to his paperwork.

The man wasn't wrong. I left him in peace and jogged down to the main level to see Kelsey waiting with Teddy at her side. They looked right together.

"Hi," I said. "Are you ready, Kelsey?"

She was pale but pretty in a light-weight blue sundress. "No, but let's do it. Can Teddy come?"

Teddy shifted his feet and looked around the police station. With his arm still in a sling and a bruise on his neck from the crash, he looked kind of tough, even with the perfect blond hair cut and beige cargo pants. "I don't mind waiting here so you can talk to your sister. I've never even met her."

"Good plan," I said, drawing Kelsey toward the steps. When

we'd reached the second floor, I whispered, "That seems to be going well." I led her toward the interrogation rooms.

"Yeah. He's sweet and a lot of fun. I'm also seeing Saber on Friday, and Kurt Stockwood asked me out for Saturday night. I figured I needed to stop getting serious about a guy and figure out my life, but there's no reason not to have some fun dating," Kelsey said.

I grinned. "You are so right." Excellent. Kelsey should play the field for a while as she figured out her life. Although, she didn't know that Kurt was an ATF agent, so how close could they become? "How are things with Kurt going?" Just what had the guy told her?

"Fine. I like that he's in private security," Kelsey said. "Doesn't that sound romantic? I'm thinking perhaps I could work with him. I like security."

As much as I loved her positive attitude, nothing was going to work out until we got these charges dropped. "You know your sister better than I do. How can we get through to her?"

"She's a murderer who was running gun parts illegally," Kelsey said. "I don't know her."

Fair enough. I pushed open the door to see Krissy with her back to us, her cuffed hands secured to the table. She wore an orange jumpsuit that was too big for her frame. We shut the door and walked around to sit. The cameras and audio devices were all turned off, as per Krissy's agreement to meet with us.

She looked at her sister. "Hi."

Kelsey fumbled with her chair. "Hi."

I could see the resemblance between them. They both had green eyes and similar bone structure.

Krissy looked down at the table. "I don't know why you wanted to talk."

Kelsey's head jerked up. "Are you kidding me? You killed my boyfriend. Ex-boyfriend. Whatever. You're a killer, Krissy, and now you want me to go to jail, too? How can you do that?"

Krissy stared at her hands. "They offered me a good deal. I have to take it. You don't know how hard prison is."

Kelsey's mouth dropped open. Pain and tension cut lines into her usually smooth face. "So you want me to find out?"

"No," Krissy said, lifting up to meet her sister's gaze. "I don't. The deal is that I testify against you and get time off my sentence, even if you're not convicted."

That was rare. Orrin really had wanted a deal, now hadn't he? I stepped in. "Your testimony is really going to hurt her, Krissy. What if she gets convicted?"

Krissy shook her head. "She won't be convicted. You're good in court. I've seen you."

"You never know what a jury will decide," I retorted. "I can't believe you'd do this to your own sister."

"Please, Krissy," Kelsey said, reaching for her sister's hand. "Mom and Dad are out of town, and our other sisters are too busy to talk, or so they say. You're ruining my life, and I didn't do anything wrong. You know that."

Tears filled Krissy's eyes. "Danny deserved to die. He was a jerk who hit you."

"I know," Kelsey said, also crying.

Krissy had also killed Danny because she didn't want to be exposed for stealing illegal gun equipment from a dangerous fringe group, but there was no need to challenge her right now. I stayed quiet as the sisters talked.

Finally, Krissy went limp. "All right. I don't want you to go to jail, and I'll recant my testimony. I didn't think there was a chance you'd be convicted."

There was always a chance.

My mood lifted finally. Good. Kelsey was going to be off the hook, and hopefully I would be soon, too. I smiled at her. We'd both been falsely accused, and it looked like the justice system was actually working.

The sisters hugged before Krissy was taken away again.

Kelsey watched her go. A plain-clothes officer walked up. I'd seen him before but didn't know his name.

"I'm John Bellingsly, your detail for the next twenty-four hours." John looked to be in his early thirties with blondish-brown hair, intelligent hazel eyes, and a muscular build. He had to be just under six feet tall.

I introduced Kelsey, and I swear, she drew charm on like most women did lipstick. "Hi."

John grinned. "Hello."

Oh, for goodness sakes. Just how many men did Kelsey want to juggle? I started down the hallway and stairs, not caring if they followed.

John beat me to the door and opened it while Teddy came out of the sitting area. The men sized each other up. We walked outside, and Kurt Stockwood was sitting on a park bench, his long legs stretched out and crossed at the ankles. Was he following me or just enjoying the comfortable weather?

Kelsey gave him a little wave.

I had to give it to her. I'd be having a panic attack by now. Then James Saber came around the corner, walking straight at us. Of course. Aiden's right-hand man in both the ATF and the Lorde's organization. Why wouldn't the badass hottie be right here and right now? His dark gaze encompassed everyone at once.

"Hi," I said before Kelsey could. "What's going on?" I was the only person, besides Kurt, who knew that Saber was ATF.

He caught sight of Kurt on the bench. "Just meeting a buddy."

"Oh. All right." I couldn't say anything else without giving up too much information, so I started to move again.

"Hi." Saber looked at Kelsey. "Are we still on for Friday?"

Teddy and John both tensed.

Kelsey nodded.

I just kept walking.

CHAPTER 31

*a*fter a long day at work, I slipped my shoes back on. We'd lost several corporate clients after Jolene's newest article had gone to print that morning. Apparently dead bodies in the actual office was too much for people. I really wished she would move back to Boston. She'd dated Aiden in high school, and she'd been a jerk even then. Apparently the years hadn't made her any nicer.

She made it really difficult to stick to the rules of the sisterhood.

I shut down my office and headed out after sending the documents to Krissy and the court that would hopefully get Kelsey off the hook. I felt good about the case for the first time. Krissy had seemed genuine, and this was one more situation I could put to bed.

John met me at the door and walked me out, his presence mellower than Bud's. We drove home companionably, and after he searched my cottage, he had me lock the doors while he scouted the property. I liked him. Maybe he and Kelsey would go out. Although I liked both Saber and Teddy as well. Kurt, I wasn't sure about. Plus, he was heading back to LA.

My phone rang and happiness swept me as I saw it was Aiden. "Hi."

"Where are you?" he asked, urgency in his tone.

"Home. Why?"

"Do you have a detail on you?" he asked.

I looked around. "I have one here. Why? What's going on?"

"The ME's office and morgue in town just blew up." It sounded like Aiden was on the move. His voice got muffled for a second. "Both Sasha and Bev's bodies were there."

I gasped. "Was anybody hurt?'

"I don't know yet. It's after hours, so hopefully not." The sound of an engine revving came over the line. "I'm hitting the Lordes apartments for my go bag and weapons. You pack a bag for a week. Don't argue with me." He hung up.

I stared at the phone. What did this all mean? If Barensky had just blown up the two bodies found around me, then he knew of my current connection to Aiden and that Aiden was ATF? Was that what it meant? I didn't know. All of it was so crazy. Quickly, I changed into shorts and a tank top before grabbing my duffle bag.

Gunfire from my back porch had me jerking around. Only one shot had been fired. I ran for my purse and pulled out my gun before heading to the sliding glass door. John lay on the ground beyond my deck, and I could only see his feet. I started to turn to reach for my phone when a woman stood on the other side of the door, pointing a Glock at me.

I froze. If I lifted my hand, she'd shoot. Did I have enough time to jump out of the way?

She motioned me toward her with her other hand. I squinted. It was Kay—the Lordes' old lady who'd tried to kill me in an accident. The brunette who'd been with Bev. She cocked her head in warning and then turned, pointing the gun at John.

I tucked my gun in the back of my waist and walked to the door, my heart thundering. Panic tried to catch me, to hold me still, and I shoved it away to slowly open the door. "What are you doing?"

She pointed the gun at me. "I'm not going to let you kill me."

I walked onto the deck and felt the warm heat of an August evening. "Did you kill him?" Without waiting for an answer, I hurried across the deck. Blood covered John's left leg, and he was out cold.

"No. Just shot him in the leg." She pressed the gun to my ribs. "I don't know why he passed out."

I tried to edge away from the gun and think how to handle this. The day fuzzed and I breathed deep to focus. "He passed out because you shot him." Crouching, I ripped off my bra beneath the tank top and wrapped it around his leg. Then I dug his phone out of his front pocket and dialed 9-1-1.

"9-1-1, what is your emergency?" a younger male voice answered.

"Officer down with a gunshot to the leg," I said.

The barrel of Kay's gun pressed against the back of my head. I dropped the phone, leaving the line open, and slowly turned to face her with my hands up.

"Officer?" she hissed, her blue eyes wide.

I tried to see if he was regaining consciousness. "He's supposed to be protecting me."

Panic zipped across her face.

"You should go," I said. "The police are coming."

She took a step back. "You're coming. Now, or I shoot you in the leg, too."

I believed her and wasn't entirely sure she'd hit my leg and not my stomach. "Fine. But you're making a huge mistake."

"I already made it," she said, looking at the prone officer. "Move. Now."

We made it way too quickly around the cottage to her car that was parked down the country road, halfway hidden by trees.

"You drive," she said, her gun still pointed at me.

I entered the driver's side as she did the passenger's, and she maintained a pretty good hold on the gun. After I started the ignition, I slowly drove out onto the road. "Where to?"

"I don't know. Just drive."

The car was an older Chevy with cigarette ash falling out of the ashtray. No music came from the ancient radio, and I kept it slow so the emergency vehicles could catch up. I'd hit one when they got close enough, and hopefully the gun wouldn't go off.

Sirens trilled in the distance, and my muscles stiffened in anticipation.

"Pull over onto that road." Kay shoved the gun in my ribs again.

Pain ticked through my torso. I pulled onto a country road that led to an abandoned church surrounded by a field.

"There," she said, pointing to a side pull-off behind us.

I turned the Chevy around and faced the road, but we were shielded by trees and bushes. Several emergency vehicles roared by.

"Now go." Kay wasn't a woman of many words.

I followed directions. "Get the gun out of my side, would you?"

She pulled back slightly, sweat dripping down her square face. She had to be in her early thirties, and the lines along her eyes showed it hadn't been a smooth three decades. Being a Lordes' old lady didn't seem like a kind life, either. Her brown hair was piled high with hairspray, and her red lipstick had cracked in several places. "Just drive."

"I am." I pulled back onto the main country road. "What's your plan here?" Besides shooting a cop and kidnapping a lawyer.

"I don't know." Her voice rose with a hint of desperation that sent chills down my back.

The stale smell of cigarettes rolled bile through my stomach. "Listen. The cop is going to be okay, and you are obviously frightened. Let's think this through." Fear tasted metallic in my mouth.

"Of course I'm scared. You killed Sasha and Bev. I know I was next." Her legs were long and tan in the cutoff jean shorts. She kicked fast food wrappers out of the way with her flip-flop. "I learned a long time ago to get them before they got you."

"It's a good motto, but I didn't kill Sasha or Bev," I said, pulling onto I-90. "How about I take you across state lines, you drop me off, and then you head to Seattle? It's a big city and you can get lost there." I had to get away from that gun.

"I just shot a cop," she snapped. "They won't stop looking for me."

Yeah, she did. How was I going to get out of this? "It was an accident?" I asked. "He startled you, and you were in fear for your life. Makes sense considering your two friends were just murdered."

"God, you are a lawyer," she muttered. "That explanation might work in your world, but I have a record. I won't be given the benefit of the doubt." Even with the gun, she seemed more sad than scary. "Right now, nobody knows I shot a cop. Except you."

I was wrong. She was terrifying...and correct. I was the only witness. "I didn't kill them," I insisted.

"Then who did?" she yelled.

I jumped. "I don't know. None of it makes sense."

"When they told us to crash into your car, I did it. I always did what I was told because I liked being an old lady. There's good protection there. But why would the Lordes have us hit you if Aiden then got so pissed about it?" She waved the gun wildly as she spoke.

I ducked my head out of the line of fire. "Wait a minute. Some-body told you to ram my car?"

She nodded. "Yeah. Carbine and Crash told us to do it. So we did. I figured you'd killed Sasha, and Aiden Devlin was pissed and wanted revenge. Nobody messes with the Lordes." She gestured with the weapon. "But then Devlin got pissed off and we got dumped. I don't understand."

"Neither do I," I said, passing a truck carrying a mattress. "But

I didn't kill your friends, and Aiden would never order anybody to hurt me."

"None of that helps me right now, does it?" She shook her head. "I'm sorry about this, but there's only one way out."

My body froze. Like literally. Even my toes went ice cold. I'd have to go for the gun. My mind scrambled. "Wait a minute. Aiden Devlin works for the ATF, and he can get you immunity. No problem. But if you shoot me, he'll hunt you down for the rest of his life."

She laughed, the sound high pitched and creepy. "Devlin, the president of the Lordes, is an ATF agent? Right. Good one."

"He's undercover and exceptionally good at it," I said. "Not only that, but he can keep you safe from whoever killed Bev and Sasha. You could go into witness protection." I had no power to promise that, and I wasn't sure Aiden would even go for that or had the power to make it happen. "See? There is a way out without killing me."

She turned toward me. "You are so full of shit."

"I'm not. Let me prove it to you. Where's your phone?" My words came out choppy as I fought a panic attack. Maybe I should just plow into the nearest guardrail and hope for the best. Neither one of us were wearing seatbelts.

"In my pocket. If you think you're going to trick me with my phone, you really are as stupid as Carbine said." She shook her head.

I sped up and passed a couple of logging trucks, headed toward Washington state. There was only one thing to do.

All right. I took a deep breath and swerved down an offramp, punching the gas pedal with all my strength.

Kay screamed. "What are you doing?"

I sped up, going at least eighty and pushing ninety. We careened down the older road with trees flashing by outside. "Hold on, because I'm slamming this thing."

"No," she yelled, the gun aimed at my head.

"You shoot and we die," I yelled back, my hands tightening on the wheel.

She looked frantically around. "No, you—"

I whipped the car into the parking area of the Lorde's apartment complex and swung the wheel in a rapid turn. She crashed against the side of the car, and the gun went flying. I hit the brakes, and we skidded into a bike, crumpling the metal and running it over. Then we teetered on top of it, high-centered.

Screaming, I jumped out of the car and started running.

Men hustled out of apartments, including Aiden and Saber. They ran down the stairs and toward us. Tears streamed down my face as I catapulted myself into his arms.

"What is—" he started.

The ground shook. Then the apartment buildings exploded on both sides of us.

Aiden tackled me to the ground, covering me with his body.

The world went dark.

CHAPTER 32

I was on a cloud. Soft and smooth, the fluffiness around me soothed me. The noise roared in. I opened my eyes to find myself in the back of an ambulance looking up at...James Saber? "Aiden?" I asked.

Saber ducked his head to look closer at my eyes. "Welcome back." He turned and whistled out the open door.

Heavy footsteps sounded along with crackling. A lot of crackling. "Is she okay?" Aiden's brogue was hoarse.

I struggled to sit up and Saber helped me. Then I lost my voice. It was like a scene from an action movie. Flames consumed both apartment buildings while debris and ashes scattered through the air and covered the ground. Fire licked at three vehicles, and several motorcycles lumped in a mangled mess. Emergency vehicles with swirling lights threw red and blue through the haze. "What happened?"

Aiden drew closer. A gash bled above his left eye, and soot covered his face and hair, but he wore an earpiece and an ATF jacket. "Explosives." He motioned a crew toward the brightest burning buildings.

I struggled to center myself. The smell of burning rubber assaulted my senses. "How long was I out?"

"Too long," Aiden said grimly. "You're going to the hospital."

"Not yet." I sat on the stretcher. "I don't understand." My head hurt and everything was blank.

Aiden whistled toward a couple of other guys in ATF jackets. "Get out a BOLO on Barensky and the two men we met with the other day. The names they gave were false, but we caught them on camera."

One of the guys nodded and hustled away from the fires.

"I take it you're no longer undercover?" I croaked.

"No," he said, turning to watch the firefighters spray water. "I don't know if this was an attack against the Lordes by Barensky for some reason, or if he discovered we were ATF, but either way, I'm done. We're going after him and he will give up his client. Period."

Saber patted my shoulder. "The fire is dying down in the northern building. I'll go investigate."

Aiden shook his head. "Not yet. The roofline is too unstable. I'll go in with you as soon as we're solid. Need to see what he used."

I tried to swallow and ended up coughing instead.

"Get her water," Aiden said.

A paramedic jogged up and jumped into the back of the ambulance to hand over a bottle. "Went to get it. You're awake." She was young, and soot covered her brown hair and part of her face. "How's the head?"

"Fine." I accepted the water and drank carefully. My throat felt scalded.

Another ATF agent jogged over. He was tall and blond and looked familiar. "We have four missing Lordes members." It took me a second, but I placed him. He'd been with Aiden during the last time the world had gone crazy. It was during a gunfight, and it was also the first time I realized Aiden was one of the official good guys.

Aiden looked toward the building. "ATF?"

"We're all accounted for," the guy said. "When we heard the car, all of us ran outside."

Must be good training. Oh yeah. I was driving that car.

Aiden swung his gaze to me. "Good timing, Angel."

"She's definitely our angel," the blond guy said. "We'd be dead if she hadn't run over that motorcycle and caused such a ruckus." His expression remained somber. "I'm Drag."

"Anna," I whispered.

A slight grin played on his mouth. "I know."

An engine exploded from one of the cars. Aiden put his body between me and the debris before relaxing. "Which Lordes members?"

Drag eyed the few Lordes members gathered over by a police car. They milled around, looking lost as their home burned. "Jale, Carbine, Crash, and Lewis are all unaccounted for. Nobody knows if they were in the buildings or not."

Carbine and Crash? The night came flying back. "Where is Kay? She had me at gunpoint." I grabbed Saber's arm. "She shot an officer at my house."

Aiden motioned Saber out. Then he stepped up, moving the vehicle. "Kay is on the way to the hospital with a concussion and broken leg, at a minimum. Since she had a gun and you were driving like crazy, I figured something was up, so I sent an officer with her. Are you up to telling me what happened?" He sat on the bench and wiped soot off my chin. His touch was gentle even though his gaze was street hard.

"Yeah." The sound of the fire was unreal. Loud and somehow creepily merry. I could see why Barensky was entranced by it, but right now, fear kept me cold. "Kay thought I killed Sasha and Bev and wanted to get to me before I got to her." I stiffened. "Oh, yeah.

She said that Carbine and Crash told her to crash the truck into my car. The Lordes wanted to hurt me, but she didn't know why."

Aiden cocked his head. "What the hell?"

I shrugged and then regretted it as my neck protested with a jolt of pain.

Aiden leaned toward the door. "Saber? Put BOLOs out on all four Lordes members. We'll assume they're alive for now until we can get into the buildings."

Saber hustled toward one of the state police vehicles.

"Get an update on the cop from Anna's house, would you?" Aiden called after him.

"Thank you." I watched more debris fall onto the Chevy I'd driven. "Why would Carbine and Crash want me hurt?" It didn't make any sense.

"I hope we get the chance to ask them." Aiden watched the northern building burn. The firefighters were slowly getting the fires under control. "I gave the order for everyone to stay clear of you, so it wasn't to gain my favor. They'd better still be alive."

The southern building gave a loud pop, and shingles flew in every direction.

Aiden stretched out of the ambulance and motioned for Drag. "You need to get checked out, Angel. Drag is going to be with you until I can get there."

Drag hustled up to take Aiden's place.

"I think I'm okay," I said.

"Let's make sure. I'll call you as soon as I can." Aiden shut the ambulance door.

Drag balanced on the bench and then reached across my legs. "Hi. I'm Drag."

The paramedic smiled and shook his hand. "Sharon."

I lay back down and closed my eyes. Just briefly. As soon as we reached the hospital, I was going home to rest. Period.

* * *

I HAD to give it to Aiden. He knew me pretty well. My sisters were already waiting at the hospital when the ambulance arrived. While I tried to talk them into taking me home, they were united in their determination to make sure I was all right. So I saw Dr. Springfield, had an MRI, and then settled back in a hospital bed with one of them on each side as dawn finally arrived. We'd been there for hours, and I was done. "I can go home," I muttered, pulling the blanket up to cover the ugly hospital gown.

"Not until we get your results," Donna countered, flipping through a magazine she'd snatched from the waiting room.

Nick Basanelli ran into the room, obviously having just jumped out of bed. His hair was mussed, his jeans threadbare, and his T-shirt inside out.

I blinked.

He looked at the three of us. "Where's my grandmother?"

My mouth dropped open. "Huh?"

He rubbed a hand through his hair and looked out into the hallway. "My Grams called and said something about the hospital and to get here right away. Where is she?"

His grandmother lived in Silverville, and it had a hospital there. What was she doing in town? "Huh?" I said again.

Nick pinned me with a frantic gaze. "She said she was with you and that you were both in the hospital."

Tessa cut her eyes to me. "She wouldn't have."

Donna covered her mouth with her hand. "*They* would have." The sound came out muffled.

"What is going on?" Nick roared.

I winced. "Hey. No shouting. Headache here." Before he could yell again, I held up a hand. "Call your grandmother. She wasn't with me tonight, and I have no idea what you're talking about." There was a chance she was in the hospital, but he should at least call her first.

He whipped his phone from his back pocket and pressed a

button. I could hear it ring, even though he held the phone to his ear.

"Hello?" Gerty asked.

Nick sagged against the wall. "Grams? Are you okay?" He set the phone on speaker. That was decent of him, considering none of this made sense.

"Of course I'm okay," Gerty said. "Did you get to the hospital?"

Nick frowned. "Yes. I'm here. Where are you?"

"I'm at home, silly. Did you check on Anna for Elda? She's so worried, but there's a summer storm over the pass, and I didn't want them to drive over. I said you'd check on her," Gerty said cheerfully.

Nick's chin lowered. "Grams? You said you were in the hospital with Anna."

Gerty chuckled. "No, I didn't. I said I was worried and *wished* I could be there with Anna. You really must start listening better, sweetheart. How are you ever going to be governor if you don't listen to people?"

"Grams—"

"How is Anna?" she interrupted.

Nick swung his gaze to me, looking more bewildered than he had when he'd run inside.

"I'm fine, Gerty," I called out, pressing a hand to my forehead. "Just a little headache. Please tell Nonna not to worry."

"Good. I'll call her right now. Bye." Gerty knew when to get out of a conversation.

Nick stuck the phone in his front pocket. "I cannot believe this."

Tessa blushed a bright red. Like cherry tomato-red and not the lovelier damask shade she often blushed.

Nick swung his gaze to her. "We should just give in right now. I can call a magistrate and have us married by morning. What do you say? We can give them their first great-grandkid by next spring."

Tessa blinked. I swear, she blushed even more. "You're not my type," she retorted.

Nick paused. He turned his body to face her completely. "Excuse me?"

Donna set the magazine down to watch them, and I have to admit, I gazed on totally enthralled.

"Breathe," Donna whispered from the corner of her mouth. "You have a head injury."

Oh. I was holding my breath. In and out. That's right. I watched rapturously, but I remembered to breathe. "Thanks," I whispered.

Donna leaned forward.

Tessa smiled at Nick, and it was the slightly smart-ass—totally in control—sexy smile that I'd never been able to duplicate. "I said that you're not my type, Basanelli. Our grandmothers are adorable, but they'll move on to another project. You're tough enough to wait this out."

"Oh my." Donna's lips formed the words without sound, and I caught it out of the corner of my eye. The other two people in the room were oblivious to us.

Nick cocked his head to the side. I'd seen him make that move in court and it was always like something had intrigued and pissed him off, and he'd accepted the challenge. Then he usually went and won the case. "Oh, baby. Waiting things out has never been my strong suit."

I blindly reached out and grabbed Donna's hand. She held on, tight.

Tessa rolled her eyes. As her sister, I was pretty proud of her holding her ground. As an attorney who knew Nick, I wanted to wince a little bit. Then she spoke. "Not a chance. We do have a cousin who's looking to mate if you really need that kid in time for an election."

"Daaaaammmmnnn," Donna whispered.

"She...did...not," I whispered back.

Tessa kept her gaze on Nick. "We can hear you two dorks."

Nick's phone buzzed and he pulled it out to read the screen. "I have a hearing in an hour." Then he looked at me. "Are you sure you're okay?"

I could only nod.

He smiled at Donna. Then he looked at Tessa again. "We're not done with this conversation, Contessa Albertini. I'll catch up with you soon." He walked out the door.

Donna turned wide eyes on me, and I pressed my lips together. "Wow," Donna said.

I wanted to clap but thought I should keep it cool. Before I could say anything, Dr. Springfield arrived with my test results, and I was fine except for a possible minor concussion. He said I could go home. Thank goodness Donna had brought clean clothes for me. Just as I finished changing, Aiden showed up with Saber and Drag.

"I talked to the doctor and you're cleared. Are you feeling okay?" Aiden asked.

"Yeah." Man, it was good to see him.

He took my hand. "You're with me. Saber's on Donna, and Drag is on Tess for the day, and then the local PD will take over protective detail starting tomorrow. Pierce is making it happen."

I jolted. "What?"

"Until we figure out what's going on, anybody who had contact with Sasha is on lockdown." He smiled at my sisters. "Sorry about this."

CHAPTER 33

"I don't have any clothes," I protested again as Aiden led me into his cabin.

"I prefer you naked," he said, shutting the door behind us.

I grinned. We were way off right now, but he still could flirt. Yeah, I liked that about him. In fact, I liked most things about him, although his mood right now was making my skin itch. He was too calm and too distant, but the flirting helped me to relax a little bit.

The lake tossed whitecaps up as a summer storm started to move in with bruised clouds and an angry wind. The weather had more energy than I did right now. Being reasonable was top of my list right now, but I needed some information. "If I can be here, why can't I go home to at least get my things?"

Aiden locked the door. "Whoever killed Sasha and Bev knows where you live and work. If it was Barensky, he could've already planted explosives if he wanted. If it wasn't Barensky, then I don't know who it was, and you're not safe." He walked toward the kitchen and started taking out mixing bowls. I'd helped him stock the kitchen with a trip to Target the other day. "How about pancakes?" he asked. "We have huckleberries or chocolate chips if you want specialty."

"Huckleberries," I said, having made sure his freezer was stocked. My stomach growled. "Any smart criminal could find you, too. How are we safe here?" My head hurt, my rib cage ached, and I wanted to be home in my bed with a gallon of ice cream and Ozark streaming an entire season.

"The cabin isn't in my name," he said, opening the pantry and fetching pancake mix.

There were three rustic barstools lined up at the kitchen counter, so I limped to sit on one and watch him cook. They were the only furniture, along with a card table and bed, that had been delivered the other day. "What?"

He looked up. "We use a series of companies, LLCs, and dummy corporations to buy our personal homes so they can't be traced to us. Just in case."

Just in case a bomber came looking for him. Right. That's the world he lived in. "I guess it's better to be safe than sorry," I murmured. I dug for my phone, which Aiden had reclaimed from my cottage that morning. Why hadn't he taken some clothes or makeup for me? Men. Just men. "You could've grabbed my toiletry bag this morning," I grumbled.

He folded huckleberries into the batter. "Oh. Sorry. Do you need, ah, products?"

I coughed out a laugh. "No, I don't need tampons, Aiden. I was thinking maybe some makeup."

He grinned. "You're gorgeous without makeup. I didn't even think of getting any."

I shook my head. "You didn't bring me panties, either."

"That was deliberate." He started pouring batter into a pan and they sizzled instantly. Knowing Aiden, he might be telling the truth about that one.

I sent a quick text to Clark letting him know I wasn't coming to the office today. Then I hopped off the stool. "Bathroom." I wandered to the powder room by the front door and then returned.

Aiden's cabin had three bedrooms, three bathrooms, a large great room, and a spacious kitchen with a round breakfast nook. He still didn't have any furniture in the living room, but the bar stools were a decent beginning. I wandered into the smallest bedroom, and it was still vacant. The master bedroom at least had a bed if nothing else. The third room had already been set up as an office with a card table in the middle. I stepped inside.

Aiden caught me snooping. "What's up?" The smell of pancakes filled the air behind him.

I stared at the large board hung on the side wall. A picture of Barensky was in the middle. "Just checking out your murder board."

"Case board," he corrected. "We don't call them murder boards. It helps to have everything in one place."

"I know," I said. I kept a murder board in my laundry room, and I liked thinking of it as a murder board even though I didn't deal in murders. It was more interesting. And I liked to kill it in court, so maybe it fit. At least in my mind it did.

His board was neater. Above Barensky was a blank head and a question mark with the word 'client' written next to it. Below that was Sasha's face as well as the faces of the two guys I'd seen meeting at the Lordes apartment building. Then Bev and Kay, and next to that my picture with a question mark.

I turned to the two guys. "Did you ever figure out the real names of the Barensky representatives?"

"Not yet."

"What all happened when you met with them?" While I understood that he liked to keep his cases private, I had a right to know.

"A lot of double-talk," he muttered. "They used euphemisms for delivery of product and all of that, so they didn't say anything criminal. They talked money to deliver their gifts to Seattle. Five gifts and a hundred k for each. That's it. I hated letting them go, and we tailed them, but they lost the tail. That normally happens in real life—it's not like the movies."

Nothing was like the movies. "How are you going to find out who they really are?"

"We have them on video. Facial rec might help us out, but so far, nothing. It takes a while, though." He secured my hand in his warmer one. "You need to eat."

I studied the board one more time and then went with him toward the kitchen. "I'm surprised you're at home making me pancakes. Don't you have work to do?"

"Yep." He led me back to my bar stool. "I already looked through what remained of the apartment buildings to examine what I could of the devices, and my unit is collecting all of the evidence to send to the lab. We also have BOLOs out on everyone I need to find. I can take the morning off and make sure you're okay before going back to work."

I sat. His ultra-efficient and calm demeanor was starting to throw me off balance, although I appreciated being his priority right now with so much going on. My heart might've twittered a couple of times.

He went back to cooking and expertly flipped a pancake before starting to load up my plate. Syrup and butter was already at my spot. "Peanut butter?"

I shook my head. "No, thanks." I was a butter and syrup type of gal. The smell of perfectly cooked pancakes filled the room with fragrance and my body with anticipation. "What did you find in the apartment building when you looked at the device? Was it still smoldering?"

"The fires were out, but it was still smoldering and smoky. I grabbed a shower at Saber's before picking you up since he lives close to the hospital right now." Aiden filled his own plate. "I didn't find much at the scene."

I paused with the fork to my mouth. Now wasn't the time for him to separate personal and work lives. Whether either one of us liked it or not, I was involved in this thing, considering Barensky had visited my office. "I'm in this, Aiden. Don't try to keep me at a distance. What did you find?"

"Four bombs expertly placed, and all were both explosive and incendiary devices," he said, taking a bite of pancake. "We're talking ammonium nitrate and fuel oil to start with."

I didn't understand much of that and didn't worry about learning bomb talk quite yet. "Was anybody hurt?"

"All four of the missing Lordes members were caught in the explosion and fire," he said. "Carbine and Crash are dead." He rolled his neck. "I wish they hadn't been caught up in this. Neither has family, so we'll take care of some sort of burial. They weren't the best of guys, but they sure didn't deserve this ending."

My stomach ached. While it had probably been a quick death, it was so sad. So unfair. "Do you think they were targeted?" I asked.

His mouth tightened. "Yeah. Based on device placement and where the bodies were found, I think they were probably targeted." He moved for the fridge and took out orange juice to pour two glasses. "They knew something, but whatever it was, I'm lost. None of this is making sense, and I need to figure it out. All of it." He calmly handed over a full glass of OJ. "Drink. You need Vitamin C."

I blew out air. "How do you seem so calm and methodical about all of this?"

He paused with his glass halfway to his mouth. "It's how I work."

It was probably how he had to work with his job. All right. I got that. "So none of this explains why dead bodies have been left for me."

"Nope." Aiden shook his head. "None of that is Barensky's M.O. The disaster last night is exactly what I expect from him." Aiden finished his pancakes. "If I didn't know better, I'd think the two cases weren't related. That somebody was dropping bodies on you as some sort of tribute."

"Tribute?" A chill clacked down my back. Oh, I didn't like the sound of that.

"Yeah. Both Sasha and Bev messed with you."

I finished my breakfast. "There's only one person in the world who'd think that was a tribute," I whispered.

Aiden placed his hand over mine. "It isn't Jareth Davey. We lost him in California, but he's not back here. I have watches on everything, and he's not here. This isn't him."

Someday Jareth and I were going to end things between us. He should've left town years ago after being found not guilty of kidnapping me, and he should've never looked back. Instead, the nutjob sent me cards twice a year. "I feel like he's going to make a move."

"Me, too," Aiden said. "It's time, but this isn't him. When he makes that move, I'll take him down. Fast and hard. I promise. Plus, I'm trying to find him first. Before he can even think about it."

I shivered. "Okay. We agree it isn't Jareth. So who is it? The whole situation is so weird and doesn't make sense."

"That's what I'm saying. Sasha and Bev are both connected to the Barensky case, and you're connected to me, so it has to somehow flow. But I don't see how." He took my plate and moved it to the dishwasher.

"Then it has to be Barensky. He came to my office to check you out, to check us out, and also left the bodies." It was the only thing that made sense, and I hated calling Sasha and Bev 'bodies,' but it was the only way not to completely freak out about this.

Aiden turned around, and frustration cut lines at the sides of his generous mouth. Finally. Some emotion. "I'm telling you that I've met Barensky and I've studied him. I know what kind of explosives he prefers and why he can't help but start the fires. He couldn't kill the way those women were killed, and it doesn't make sense that he'd hire somebody else to do it. If he'd wanted them dead, he would've made a show of it. Period."

I scratched a healing cut on my hand. "We're missing something."

"Yes, we are."

We needed to figure it out before another body dropped. "What now?"

"Now you take a rest." He tossed the dishtowel onto the counter.

I was feeling much better after eating his excellent pancakes. "I'm not tired. If you didn't have to babysit me, what would you be doing?"

He studied me. "I'd be working this case at my office."

The cute house in Spokane. "Let's do that. I can get some work done at the same time. Or we could just go to our respective places of work."

"No. You're with me until we find out what's happening." He ducked his head to study my eyes. "Are you sure you can go to Spokane?"

"Yeah." My head really didn't hurt much. Hopefully it was because my concussion was very mild and not because I was becoming so accustomed to getting a concussion. Didn't the brain just give up from so many bruises at some point? "Maybe I should start wearing a helmet all the time."

"Believe me, I've thought about that." He leaned over and traced my jaw with his thumb. "We'll go work out of my office for a few hours, but if your head starts to hurt or you get dizzy, you promise to tell me. Deal?"

I smiled. "Deal."

CHAPTER 34

I liked Aiden's office building even more when I was working in it. While a storm had been taking Idaho, it was still sunny and pleasant in Spokane. I took over a small part of his office while he worked in the computer room with Drag and Saber. It turned out that Detective Grant Pierce had some juice because protective detail had been waiting for my sisters at their homes. I made a mental note to bake him a huckleberry pie as a thank you once I got back into my house.

An agent named Chelli Wilson had dropped by to say hi, and now she was upstairs in her office. She'd been young and calm, and I'd liked her immediately. Apparently she was the munition expert for the team.

My phone rang and I answered it immediately upon seeing it was my Nana O'Shea. "Hi, Nana."

"Did you get blown up last night?" Her Irish brogue was far more pronounced than Aiden's.

"No, Nana. I'm fine. Honest."

She harrumphed very classily. "I just spoke with Clark, and he said you didn't come into work today. I can bring you some food to tide you over. A smudging wouldn't hurt, either. I haven't cleansed your bungalow lately."

I frowned. "Why were you and Clark talking?"

"We talk all the time. He's a good guy and I cleansed his apartment the other day. What time should I be there?"

I shook my head. The last person I thought would become buddies with my free-spirited, tarot-card-reading, tea-making, air-smudging Nana was Clark Bunne. She'd smudged him the month before after we'd been caught in a crematorium covered in human remains, and apparently now they were friends? "I'm in Spokane working today with Aiden, Nana."

"Oh. Good. That's lovely." Her voice lilted. Yeah, she was happy I was dating an Irishman. "Well then, call me when you are home and want company. Maybe next week?"

"Sure, Nana. Bye." I waited for her to say 'bye' and hang up first because she was my grandma. Then I turned back to draft a quick motion and accompanying brief for a motion to dismiss Kelsey's case if her sister did step up and recant her false testimony, using remote login from Aiden's computer.

The outside door opened and heavy footsteps echoed. "I need to talk to you," a male voice said.

"There's nothing to talk about," Aiden answered evenly. Too evenly.

I winced and leaned way back in the chair to see Kurt facing off with Aiden next to the computer table. Not a good idea. The tension between the men was obvious, even as Saber and Drag watched from next to one of the big screens. Neither seemed inclined to jump into the fray.

Kurt partially turned and saw me. "Tell him I didn't do anything wrong. That it wasn't such a big deal."

Aiden instantly pivoted and put his broad body between us. "Don't talk to her. This has nothing to do with her and everything to do with you disobeying orders, and not for the first time." While his tenor remained calm, the long line of his back showed tension. His dark tee and black cargo pants were intriguing, even without the gun strapped to his thigh.

Kurt's gun was visible at the front of his waist.

I held my breath. They were all armed and it was normal for them. This wasn't scary. Forget the fact that they stood nearly eye-to-eye with dangerous training. Nope. Not scary at all. I stayed in the office and away from them.

"This is bullshit," Kurt burst out. "I was gone for maybe an hour."

Aiden moved toward him. "For an hour when a terrorist came into her office, sat down, and had a discussion. If she didn't have a good brain and a core of solid steel, she would've understandably freaked out and not only ruined this Op but probably gotten herself killed."

"Then it turned out okay," Kurt challenged, also stepping toward Aiden. "She handled it."

"You didn't *know* she could handle it, and you screwed up," Aiden said. "You're out. Report to Los Angeles for a new assignment if you want to remain working for the ATF. If not, feel free to explore other options."

Kurt flicked his gaze to me and then back. "Your personal life is messing with your judgment."

Drag grimaced, and Saber slowly shook his head.

Aiden didn't so much as twitch. Although I could only see the back of him, even I could feel the tension rolling through that room. "You're also free to make any report you'd like to headquarters. If you think my personal life is negatively impacting my team, then file a report. Either way, you're leaving here now."

"You're ruining my career," Kurt snapped.

"I transferred you without a mark to your record," Aiden retorted. "You did a decent job when you followed orders, so you still have a career. Get your ass out of here before I change my mind and file a report with more than one mark. And while you're at it, thank whatever god you pray to that Anna is alive and survived meeting with Barensky."

"Why? Would you have fired me, then?" Kurt asked, all sarcasm.

Aiden took that final step into Kurt's space. "No. Your job would've been the last of your worries had she been hurt."

Even I shivered at the tone of his voice now. I'd never heard it —not like this. He'd never talk to me like that, thank goodness. Even so, I had to swallow over a lump in my throat.

Kurt paused for a second. Then he apparently grew a brain and turned to storm out of the building, slamming the door as he did so.

Aiden watched him go.

Several quiet and tension-filled seconds ticked through the building.

Aiden's phone rang and he slipped it from his pocket. "What?" Then he leaned over to type onto a keyboard. "Okay. I'm bringing it up now. Thanks." The far screen lit up with pictures and stats of the two Barensky henchmen who looked like golfers.

Saber whistled. "Wow."

I stood and walked to the doorway. "Who are they?"

Aiden didn't turn around. "Chuck Velomn and Marc Franks. Guns for hire along with everything else. I can see Barensky hiring them to do the legwork on a job."

Drag stared at the pictures. "Now we just have to find them."

* * *

AIDEN POKED his head in a little after work hours. "You hungry?"

"Starving." I pushed away from the computer. "Want to order pizza or something?"

He shook his head. "There's a great burger joint a block over where a bunch of the Gonzaga law students hang out. If we go now, they won't have taken over yet. I think it's safe enough to stick around here."

"Wonderful." I stood and stretched my back before reaching him. "Any luck finding those two men?"

"Not yet." He took my hand. The more we were around each other, the touchier he became.

I really liked it. I entwined my fingers with his. "Just the two of us?"

"Yep." He locked the door behind us and scouted the area outside like I'd seen him do a million times. I probably needed to learn that skill and pay more attention to my surroundings.

The walk around the block was pleasant as we passed several older homes turned into businesses, all with neatly manicured lawns and colorful flowers. We reached the diner and found a booth in the back. I ordered a cheeseburger and chocolate milkshake, while Aiden ordered a black & blue burger with water.

"No milkshake?" I asked, settling more comfortably in the booth.

"No." He set the menus aside.

Aiden had a few flaws, and a lack of a sweet tooth was one I could work with. "Okay. Why are we taking time to have a burger?"

One of his dark eyebrows rose. "It's dinner time."

"Uh, huh." I studied his serene expression. "If you've brought me somewhere for a milkshake, you're up to something. What is it?"

His cheek creased. "Fair enough. I want you to go on a short vacation with Drag. I need Saber here, but Drag will cover your back."

I figured. "What kind of name is Drag?"

"His name is Mitch Dragoner. Hence, Drag." Aiden sat back as our drinks were placed in front of us.

I stuck the straw in my very thick milkshake. "No. I want to work with you, but I have court tomorrow and need to go." Hopefully I could get Kelsey's case dismissed, and at least that'd be off my plate. "I wouldn't ask you to leave work."

"You would to save my life," he countered, taking a drink of his water.

That was true. "I'll keep a detail with me, but that's it for now. I have to do my job." Then our burgers arrived and we dug in. They were every bit as good as Aiden had promised.

He paid the bill and we walked hand-in-hand back to the office. "I need to grab a few things, and let's head home."

Home. The way he said it sounded so right. Oh, I was in no hurry to get too serious, but I still liked hearing statements like that from him. He unlocked the door and stepped inside, still holding my hand as he punched in the correct code and opened the door to the main computer room. "I was thinking we could drop by the hospital—"

He stopped speaking and let go of my hand, reaching for his gun. He lifted it smoothly.

"What?" I edged to his side and gasped.

Two men lay against the table that held the computer keyboards, one slumped against the other. They were the men from the other day—Barensky's henchmen. Chuck Velomn and Marc Franks. They had small, bloody holes in the center of their foreheads, and their eyes looked sightlessly past us.

My legs shook. "Aiden?"

He swept the room and then his office and the ammunition room. "Anybody upstairs?" he yelled.

Nobody answered. He studied the two dead men. "This doesn't make sense."

I looked closer. "Is that a chess piece?" A pawn was half-hanging out of Marc's shirt pocket.

Aiden stiffened. He grabbed my arm. "Run."

I turned and retreated, hitting the door and running outside into the soft light, leaping across the grass and barreling across the quiet roadway toward the businesses on the other side.

"Keep going," Aiden bellowed, right behind me.

The air thickened and paused. Then an explosion rocked the building behind us. Aiden tucked both arms around me and tumbled us behind a large oak tree in the grass. Debris rained down, and several projectiles smashed into the two-story gray house in front of us that served as a day spa. Glass shattered inward and fell onto a row of bushes outside.

His body jolted as something must've hit him, and he groaned.

I spit grass out of my mouth.

Aiden stayed over me. "Hold still. Make sure there isn't another bomb."

The soft ground hurt my hips. "You're smushing me."

He levered up, flipped me over, and covered me. "Better?"

"Yeah." My hands were trapped between us. "Are you okay?" The shadow on his jaw scratched my nose. Debris rained down, and fire crackled gleefully.

"No. I'm pissed." He waited a minute and then rolled over, coming up with his phone already at his ear, where he gave the details of the explosion. Must've been 9-1-1. Then he pressed a button. "All roll call. Now. Aiden in."

I jumped up and ran over to smash a flame off his shirt.

A series of different voices came over the line, and after seven made it, his shoulders finally went down. "Okay. All accounted for. We've had a breach and an explosion."

Sirens already came from the distance.

He took out his gun and scouted the area. Several people emerged from different buildings, watching the fire and broiling smoke.

I idled next to him. "Barensky?"

"Yeah." The local police arrived. "Wait here and watch for debris." He moved toward the first officer, flashed his badge, and then they talked for a while.

Saber and Drag roared up in an Escalade, both jumping out

and flanking Aiden. Then Saber caught eye of me and hustled over. "You okay?"

"Yes." I was unable to look away from the flames. The entire house was engulfed, and two of the trees out front lit on fire. The firetruck arrived, and the fighters went to work, trying to protect the home/businesses on either side of the rapidly falling building. "It happened so fast."

"It always does," Saber said, feeling solid next to me.

"Those two Barensky men were inside dead," I whispered.

Saber nodded. "The other businesses were closed and the rest of our team was out, thank goodness." His phone buzzed and he answered it. "Hi, Kurt. Just making sure you weren't back at the office. Barensky got to it." He listened for a few seconds. "Yeah. We're all safe. Good luck in LA." He ended the call.

Aiden made his way back to us with Drag at his side. "Well, that answers that," Aiden said.

"What?" I asked.

"Barensky knows we're ATF now for sure," Aiden said.

We all watched as the building burned and then fell.

CHAPTER 35

*I*t was almost midnight by the time we made it back to Aiden's place after being interviewed repeatedly, first by the local police, then the state police, and finally the FBI. Then Aiden had taken back roads and backtracked before driving to his cabin. He and Saber had also run some weird wand thing over the entire truck before we'd left Spokane, checking for explosives as well as trackers. Apparently, the truck was clean.

He pulled into his garage and shut the door with the automatic button.

"I still think you should have a doctor look at your back," I said for the fourth time.

"I'm fine," he said, also for the fourth time. "It feels like a burn but not anything to worry about. This wasn't my first explosion, Angel."

I slipped out of his truck. My head hurt as badly as my ribs, but I was worried about him. "I want to see your back."

We walked into the kitchen and Aiden moved to open the front door, where Saber, Drag, and Chelli waited with bags of chips and soda. They also held computer equipment as well as a bag of what I guessed were weapons.

"The rest of the team will be here in about ten minutes," Chelli offered, moving inside. Her blonde hair was up, and a little soot dotted her chin.

The entire team had shown up at the fire to watch it burn, and then they'd all gone close to examine what remained when it had been safe enough to do so. I'd waited patiently with a police officer, as I didn't know anything about explosives and really didn't need to see what the fire had done to the two dead men. The discussion of 'tissue samples' between Saber and Drag when they'd returned had been enough to make me want to vomit.

Thank goodness nobody but the two dead men had been in the building when it blew.

"The control room is in there now," Aiden said, pointing to the room that had his case board set up. "I'll be a few minutes." Then he took my hand and led me into the master bedroom and shut the door. "How's your head?"

I gaped at him. In the light, burn marks showed on his neck. "I'm fine. Take off your shirt." Without waiting for his agreement, I grasped the bottom of his shirt and started to pull. He ducked his head and let me remove it. "Wow." There were light burns down his arm, and when he turned around, there were burns on his back. Not bad, but they looked painful from the raw bruising that accompanied the burns. "That has to hurt," I murmured, gently touching the skin above the burn.

He shrugged and the bruises all danced. "A piece of wood landed on my back. Nothing is broken, and I just have a couple of bruises." Turning around, he set his hands over my shoulders. "How's your head? I tried to keep you from hitting it on the ground. You already had a concussion."

"I have a little headache," I admitted. Then soot rose from my shirt and I sneezed, turning away. Ouch. That hurt my head even more. "We might need a vacation."

"Oh, we definitely need a vacation." He took my hand and we

moved into the bathroom, where he leaned into the shower and flicked on the water. "Let's get all of this soot off of us, but I'll need to use cold water on my back when we're done with your hair."

I balked. "We can't shower together."

He looked down at me and tilted his head. "Huh?"

I lowered my voice. "Your friends are here.'"

His eyes sparkled as amusement filtered through the various blues. "They know we're dating," he whispered back.

"Yeah, but…" I was being ridiculous, but it had been a tough couple of days, and I wasn't at my best. "You're right." I pulled off my shirt and kicked off my flats.

He ditched his boots and clothing. "Tell you what. If they tease you, I'll shoot them." With that, he tugged me under the spray, careful to keep his back away from the warm water. Then he lathered up and washed me, paying careful attention to my hair. "You're now soot-free," he murmured, pinching my butt.

I slapped an unbruised part of his chest. "Let's do you."

"Yes, let's," he murmured, his voice dark.

I rolled my eyes and soaped him up, washing his thick hair. When I was finished, he was sporting an obvious erection. "No. There are people here," I whispered.

"You sure?" He lifted me right up and pressed me against the side of the shower. His body felt incredible against mine, even with the bruises.

"Your back," I protested. "The water is hot."

He turned the knob and the water chilled. "There you go." His fingers found me the same time his mouth descended on mine, and then there was only Aiden. No danger, no bomber, no burns. Just his mouth and his hands and the rest of him.

I was ready and alive, and when he pushed inside me, I felt safe for the first time all day. He went fast and hard. When I cried out his name, he kissed me, swallowing the sound. I hope.

My legs were rubbery as he let me slide and held me until I

could stand. I shivered as my feet found purchase in the chilly water. "Cold."

He turned the knob until warm water sprayed and then ducked me under it. My body was relaxed and mellow now, and all I wanted was to sleep. Maybe for a couple of weeks.

Warmth glided over me and I sighed as my muscles relaxed again. "I wasn't loud, was I?" I whispered.

"Define loud." His grin was so adorable I couldn't take exception. The water had been on, and the new control room was on the other side of the laundry room, so hopefully nobody had heard me. Right now I was too satiated to worry about it.

I rolled my eyes. "Let's put cold water on your back."

"We already did," he said, turning off the water and reaching for a towel. "Now you need some sleep and I have to get to work."

I wrapped the towel around myself and stepped out of the shower. "You're not going to sleep?"

"No." He dried off, a new glitter in his eyes. An angry one. "We have to find Barensky. Nobody bombs our house."

* * *

I COULDN'T SLEEP. Thunder bellowed outside as the storm hit hard. Rain and wind blew wildly against the windows and tinged off the roof. It was after one in the morning, which meant it was after four in the morning in Detroit. I rolled over and grabbed my phone to press speed dial.

"Morning. Why are you up so late?" Lacey O'Shea answered, her voice chipper.

"Why are you up so early?" I countered like I always did. It was our thing. Lacey was my first cousin and my best friend. "I couldn't sleep and figured you'd be up doing yoga or something silly like that." Actually, I liked yoga. I just sucked at it.

Lacey laughed. "I already finished and was thinking of going for a run. What's up? Nightmares?" She'd been there when I'd been kidnapped, and she'd gotten pushed down but had ignored her broken arm and had run to the campground for help. Without Lacey, I might not have been found.

"Do you have nightmares?" I asked.

She was quiet for a few ticks. "Not about that day, but I have other nightmares. Being a cop in Detroit isn't the walk in the park that was advertised."

I snuggled into Aiden's pillow, surrounding myself with his scent. "Funny. Why don't you come home? You have to be badass city trained by now." While I understood why she wanted some experience away from Idaho, she'd gotten it already. It was time for her to return home and get a job here. "This on-again, off-again romance you have going with Ray is getting old, right?"

"Yeah." Lacey had been dating Ray for a while, then they'd break up, and then they'd get back together. The guy had serious commitment issues, and Lacey deserved better. I'd hoped last time they broke up that it would be the last time. "We haven't gotten back together. Don't worry."

But I did worry. Lacey deserved somebody who thought she hung the moon and then painted it. "Pauley misses you, too."

"I talked to my brother earlier today, and he's fine. I'll come home soon. For now, what's up?" she asked.

I told her everything. From the moment Sasha had shown up on Aiden's front porch to right now. When I wound down, she whistled.

"Well, that's a lot." Movement sounded across the line. "I know I should concentrate on the fact that there's a bomb expert in town, but for a second, I can't believe you're talking to me from Aiden Devlin's bed right now. I mean *right now*. Do you remember the fantasies we used to weave about him?" She chuckled.

I smiled and snuggled deeper. "Oh, yeah. He's better than any fantasy."

"Not fair," she complained. "I had a crush on him, too."

"Everybody had a crush on him," I said. He was the bad boy in high school with an Irish brogue. "Part of me thinks that maybe that's why Jolene keeps writing articles about me." They'd been pretty hot and heavy junior year.

Lacey scoffed. "Probably. Either that or you keep ending up in situations that make good copy. Maybe both reasons."

My eyelids grew heavy. "Probably." I yawned.

"For now, try to see the connections between everything that's going on. It's all there. Look at the situation from a different perspective." A griddle sizzled over the line.

"Okay. I'll call you with a Tessa and Nick update when I get one." I clicked off. Then I let myself lounge for about another hour, but I still didn't sleep. So I got out of bed and padded out of the room. Aiden's shirt covered me to my knees, so I wasn't worried about anybody seeing me.

A quiet peek into the extra room showed Chelli on the floor in a sleeping bag with another woman across the room. Five men sacked out in the living room in sleeping bags, two of them snoring.

Maybe it was a good thing Aiden hadn't bought furniture yet.

I found him in the case room, and I shut the door. He sat with his back to the wall, his long legs extended, looking at the mounted case board. "Hi."

"Hi." The shadow across his jaw gave him the look of a rogue. Lightning zagged outside the window. "Why are you awake?"

"I don't know." I sat next to him, extending my bare legs. They didn't go nearly as far as his did. "Why are you?"

He stared at the board. "I'm missing something."

"What?"

He stood and moved to the board, taking his hand and wiping off the client. "There's no client."

I blinked. "I don't understand."

"No client. This has been a set-up the whole time. We are the job. My ATF SRT unit." He started making notations. "Barensky has changed strategies. He's changed the chessboard and become the King." He scribbled notes. "The rooks are the governmental agencies, and the pawns are the two dupes who ended up dead as well as the Lordes members in general.

I tried to remember what Aiden had told me about Barensky. "The explosives are the knights."

"Yeah." Aiden scribbled some more, making diagrams.

"Okay, so then the Queen would be the SRT unit, and the bishops are unknowns."

Aiden stood back and studied his scribbles. "Not this time. He really did change strategies. The SRT unit would be the bishops because we are unknowns but identifiable. He knows our moves, and he has an idea of what we're doing. Not once did he believe the cover of the Lordes. This has all been the entire game—from the beginning."

It was impressive how much Aiden had been able to get into Barensky's head. "So the Queen is, whom?"

Aiden turned, his gaze dark. "You. You're the Queen in his game, Anna."

I swallowed. It made a really bizarre and kind of creepy kind of sense. "Isn't the Queen often sacrificed in the end?"

"Yes."

CHAPTER 36

J ignored my very cranky boyfriend and carried the flowers into the hospital before work on Friday. Aiden had really wanted me to stay at his place, but I wasn't going to let down my clients. Plus, he was guarding my body for now, and then Bud would be back on duty at my office. I couldn't be safer, really.

We walked to the correct room, and Aiden drew me aside. "Good luck with this. It is a good idea, even if I don't like it."

Yeah, it was a good idea, even if it made me late for work. I didn't have to be in court until ten, so there was time. "Trust me." Without waiting for his answer, I turned and walked into the ex-Lordes old lady's room, leaving him with the officer guarding her door.

Kay lay in the bed with her leg elevated. Her hair was in wild curls around her head, which kind of looked cool. Her eyes widened and her pupils were dilated. "What are you doing here?"

"I snuck in early," I admitted, setting the vase on the counter where she could see it. Actually, Aiden's badge had gotten us in early, and the nurse had assured us that Kay was awake. "I wanted to bring you flowers. I'm sorry about Carbine."

Her eyes watered. "He was an idiot."

Yeah, that seemed to be the consensus. "He still didn't deserve to die like that. I'm sorry."

Her eyes flashed and she looked at the flowers. "Why are you sorry? I held a gun on you and kidnapped you. We aren't friends."

"I know." I pulled a guest chair over and sat anyway. Aiden had confirmed with the police that nobody had visited Kay, and I couldn't imagine being in the hospital and having no one check in on me. "I know that Carbine meant something to you, and I'm sorry he's dead. Aiden and the Lordes are going to have a burial for him, and maybe you can help plan it?"

She slumped in the bed. "I'm going away for a hit and run as well as an aggravated kidnapping. Both against you."

I leaned toward her. "Maybe not."

A tiny sliver of interest lit in her eyes. "What do you mean?"

Oddly enough, I really did want to help her. She'd held me at gunpoint, but I felt sorry for her. Not enough to let her off the hook. But still. The woman didn't have anybody, and that would suck. "If you have information, maybe we can get you a deal."

"What kind of information?" she asked.

"Anything," I said. "Like who told Carbine to have you crash into my car and why."

She frowned. "Why would you want to get me a deal?"

"Aiden really is an ATF Agent and not a Lorde's member," I said. The shock on her face showed she hadn't believed me before. "The truth is out and he's no longer undercover. He is in a position to help you, and you're going to want to take advantage of the moment."

She pushed a button and the bed sat her up. It looked like Kay had a lot more brains than Carbine had. "I'll take any deal. This sucks. All of a sudden, Carbine had extra cash. A lot of it. Then he told me what to do, and I did it. I figured Devlin wanted you hurt, but Carbine didn't say that. I just assumed it."

I sat back. "Somebody obviously bribed Carbine." That didn't sound like Barensky, but if he was moving pieces around on his imaginary board, maybe the King had a bishop of his own. Or knight. Or whatever. "Think hard. Did Carbine say anything about where he got the money? Anything at all—no matter how small."

She pressed a hand against her forehead, jiggling the lines to the saline and drug bags. "He didn't say anything, but..."

"But what?" I leaned toward her again.

She let her hand flop down. "He met with a guy out at Miller's gas station on the west end of Spokane. I was in the truck, and he went inside for a minute, and then he came out in a really good mood. He started throwing cash around the next day."

Anticipation licked through my veins. "Tell me about this guy. What did he look like?"

The sound she made was one of frustration. "I don't know. I wasn't really paying attention. It was a guy inside the garage. Definitely a man, but the truck wasn't close enough for me to really see."

"Okay," I said, trying to sound soothing. "Let's back up. What color was his hair?"

She squinted as if trying to remember. "He was wearing a hat. Like a black baseball cap. Dark clothing, and I think he was as tall as Carbine but wouldn't swear to it. I'm not sure. I didn't see his face."

That was something. "What about build?" I asked.

"Normal, I guess? He wasn't fat or thin...just normal from where I sat in the truck. I really didn't look. I wish I had." Kay yawned. "I'm sorry. I had surgery on my leg, and the painkillers attack at weird times. I was awake all night."

I patted her arm. "It's okay, and it's probably a good thing you didn't get a good look at this guy. He's dangerous." I stood. "I'll see what I can do for you."

She looked down at her hands. "Thank you for the flowers.

Nobody has ever brought me flowers before." Her voice slurred and she dropped off into sleep.

A pang hit my heart. That was just sad.

I turned and headed into the hallway.

"Well?" Aiden asked, a new bruise showing beneath his cheekbone that I hadn't noticed the night before. I think it was from my head when he'd tackled me to the ground.

"See if there are any cameras at Miller's gas station west of Spokane because Carbine met with somebody there and then had a lot of cash," I said, heading down the hallway. "Also, let's try to keep Kay's case a state one and not federal. I'm going to call Nick when I get to the office to see if the county will plea her down."

Aiden sighed. "Softy."

* * *

WHEN I ARRIVED at my office, Officer Bud Orlov was waiting patiently in our waiting room. I smiled. "I guess you're on Anna duty?"

"Yep." Even though Bud was in street clothes, his short hair looked regulation cut. "Since John was shot, I'm on duty."

"That one wasn't my fault, and I called the hospital, and John gets to go home tomorrow." I turned and leaned up to kiss Aiden on the chin. "Have a good day."

He kissed my mouth. "You, too. Stay safe." With a guy nod at Bud, he turned and strode away.

I smiled at Oliver, who was watching everyone with curiosity in his eyes. "Morning. I think I'm in court at ten?"

Oliver nodded. "Yes. I'll call and remind Miss Walker to meet you there. You have three appointments this afternoon that we had to move from yesterday."

"Perfect." I motioned for Bud to follow me. "Do you want coffee? Oliver makes the best coffee around." It was true. I think he added cinnamon and other spices.

Bud remained silent.

"You can work in there." I pointed to the vacant office as I led the way to the kitchen. There I poured mugs of coffee and hot chocolate, handing the hot chocolate to Bud. "So. Tell me about your wife."

He blew on the steaming mug. "I don't want to talk about her right now."

"I gave you coffee." I pointed out.

Bud took a drink and then shut his eyes to hum. "That is good. Man, you were right. This is great." He opened his dark eyes. "Her name is Sheila and that's all I'm saying right now. If I need to talk, I trust you, but right now I just don't want to talk about her." He took another drink.

"I understand," I murmured. I liked Bud. He deserved happiness. "When you do want to talk, I'm here for you."

"Thanks," Bud said soberly. "Speaking of women, is that Kelsey Walker single? I stopped by to see John in the hospital earlier and he wanted me to find out."

I'd forgotten that John had been around when Kelsey had been in the office. "I think so," I said carefully. "She's not engaged or anything, but she might be starting to date somebody. I'm not sure." Or three people. "John should ask her out if he's interested." He seemed like a decent guy.

"Cool. All right. I'll let you get to work." Bud headed for his temporary office.

I looked around. We really needed a fridge. Then movement showed at the door, and Clark entered the room with his empty coffee mug. "Morning," I said.

"Morning." He poured a full cup. "Good news. Well, good news for us. Lola's Cookies over in Rose Lake went out of business, and I bought their fridge and one of their tables. They have character, and they should be here any minute." Then he paused. "I hope that's okay?"

"Sure." I patted his arm. "If you find a good conference table, don't hesitate to buy it. I love furniture with character."

"I figured," he said dryly. "Also, a signed affidavit from Krissy Walker came in this morning recanting her testimony against her sister. It's on your desk."

I gave a happy hop, and my brain cleared. "Awesome. That's such great news." I'd introduce the document at Kelsey's hearing and hopefully get her out of this mess. She deserved to start her new life.

Noise came from the front of the office, and Clark turned as two hefty delivery guys carried a table down the hallway. "Good timing." He opened the door wider so they could get in.

I got out of the way and just stared. The square shaped table was a fifties style with an aqua-blue shiny top circled by crimped silver, and the chairs were silver stools covered with either blue, yellow, or pink tops. The fridge was a matching blue with yellow handles. "Oh, that's awesome," I breathed.

Clark scratched his head. "They're not very professional. You can tell they came from a bakeshop."

"Who cares?" I ran my hand over a plush stool. "We're the only ones back here, and these make me want to have ice-cream. I don't suppose Lola's was selling anything else? An ice cream machine?"

"No," Clark said. "I'll pay the delivery guys." He followed them back down the hall.

I finally made it to my office and read over Krissy's affidavit. Oh, Orrin was going to be ticked.

My phone buzzed and I answered it. "Hello."

"Hey, Anna Banana," Quint said. "The family is worried about you, so I thought your favorite cousin should check in. Do you want Zena to come stay with you?"

Boy, did I. "Not right now, but soon. I miss her." I glanced at the clock. "How are things with you?"

"I'm fine. I'll see you at the family barbecue on Sunday and we can catch up." He hung up before I could tell him I might not make the barbecue. Probably on purpose because Quint was a stubborn one.

I rolled my eyes and stood to gather my papers in my satchel. It wasn't quite a briefcase, but I liked the style of the blond leather laptop bag. Then I straightened my light jacket. For court today, I'd worn a lilac colored skirt with matching jacket over a pale yellow blouse. Yeah, Aiden and I had stopped by Donna's house on the way to work so I could borrow it. Her navy blue pumps looked perfect with the suit.

Sometimes I figured Donna wished she had different sized feet. I, however, liked things as they were.

My body felt lighter than it had been in days, even though I still carried a few bruises. I walked out of the office with Bud protecting my body. In the hallway, Hailey and Darrin Jennings were coming out of Cousin Wanda's office. "Hi, kids," I said. They were holding hands.

"Hi," Hailey said. "We just met with Wanda. Things are good."

Darrin's smile was wide in his young face.

Sometimes things just went right. I knew that if there were any problems, any danger to either one of them, then Wanda would know it. For them to still be seeing her and looking happy, things were working out.

Man, it was a good morning. It really was. I felt like the entire world was looking up, and everything was going to be okay.

Yeah, I should've known better. Sometimes you just don't want to invite fate to kick your ass.

That's a lesson I hadn't quite learned.

CHAPTER 37

I stood at my table in the courtroom with Kelsey next to me after having shaken out my umbrella to place beneath the table. The storm was going full force outside, wind and rain competing to destroy the summer peace. Bud had figured I was safe enough in the courthouse and had gone to run a few errands so long as I promised to stay put until he returned.

Kelsey fidgeted but looked cute in linen pants and a flowy white blouse. Teddy Thompson sat several feet back in the rows, his arm still in a sling. I leaned over. "So Teddy's the winner, huh?"

Her eyes twinkled. "Today, anyway. Saber was supposed to come, but he had to cancel because of work. I mean, what kind of work does a motorcycle club do?"

Huh. Apparently Saber hadn't let Kelsey in on his real job, but they probably hadn't had a chance to talk, considering the team was locked down and hunting for a serial bomber. "Well, they both seem nice. It's good that you're not getting tied down right now. Also, Officer Bellingsly asked if you were single."

"Oh, he's cute," she whispered. "I heard he was in the hospital. Maybe I'll go visit him."

"That's a good idea. If you want, we could grab lunch at my

office and drop by the hospital first," I said, wanting to see for myself that John was mending nicely.

She bit her lip. "I actually have a lunch date with Kurt Stockwood."

"Kurt is still in town?" Wait a minute. He was moving to LA. What was he still doing in town?

She nodded. "Yeah. Why wouldn't he be here?"

Okay. Kelsey needed to stop flirting and start talking to the men in her life. She didn't seem to know anything about them. "What about Teddy?" This shuffling of dates was interesting, although I didn't have the energy for it. Plus, nobody compared to Aiden. If I had extra time, I wanted it with him.

She grimaced. "I'm not sure. I was supposed to meet Kurt at the restaurant later, but I think I saw him in the park outside. He hangs out there a lot, it seems. I think he likes the peace, although he had an umbrella this time."

The storm destroyed any sense of peace out there right now. Even the lake had looked gray and angry.

I was saved from having to answer when Orrin walked inside and took his seat. He looked professionally casual on this Friday in a mint-green suit with brown leather shoes. The shoes were Italian.

The full-bearded bailiff walked through the door to the left of the bench. "The judge will be right in," he said, walking toward us. "I've met Orrin but haven't officially met you. I'm Pete Feliz."

"Anna Albertini." We shook hands. The name fit him.

Kelsey held out her hand. "I'm Kelsey."

Pete grinned. "It's nice to meet you. You're definitely the prettiest defendant we've had in here all month."

She laughed.

I barely kept from shaking my head. Maybe she excreted some special pheromone that men couldn't resist. It was impressive, really. Considering the summer she'd had, it was great to hear her laugh.

The judge's door opened and Pete hustled over to the judge's side. "All rise."

Since we were all standing, only Teddy had to stand. He did so.

Judge Williams took her seat, and her assistant and the court reporter did the same. "All right," the judge said, opening her first case file, all business today. "We're on the record in *Elk County v Kelsey Walker* for an arraignment."

"Your honor?" I asked. "The defense would like to make a motion to dismiss based on new evidence." I handed the paperwork to the bailiff and then gave a copy to Orrin. "Krissy Walker recanted her testimony and took full responsibility for the murder of Danny Pucci."

Orrin sputtered. "You can't drop new evidence on me like this. Your honor, the state has had no warning about the affidavit."

"The affidavit came in earlier today," I said, having also handed over the fax receipt. "It's all legitimate. Without Krissy's testimony, the state doesn't have enough to go to trial. My client is innocent, and this is enough." I turned to Orrin. "You don't even have circumstantial evidence. The fact that witnesses can't place Kelsey at the park at all times doesn't mean anything. They can't place you there, either."

Judge Williams finished reading the documents and looked at Orrin. "It's up to the state how to proceed. Since this was just offered, I'll postpone a hearing to argue dismissal, if you want. But the evidence is pretty clear." In other words, don't waste the court's time and make us come back.

I barely kept from smiling.

Orrin slammed the papers down. "All right. The state will dismiss all charges against Kelsey Walker." He turned and looked at us. "For now."

Kelsey squealed and hugged me, nearly knocking me over. Teddy hurried up, excitement on his cute face. She released me to hug him with the short railing providing no barrier for her excitement.

The judge closed her file folder. "All right. Everyone, have a great Friday. Court is adjourned." She slammed the gavel down.

Almost in unison, an explosion blew the doors in. Fire swished inside.

The force knocked both Kelsey and me into our table while Orrin flew over his. Teddy fell over the railing and his head hit my calf. Pain flashed through me along with an alarming heat.

"Everybody out," Pete yelled, opening the judge's door and motioning for all of us. Panic mixed with the smoke in my throat, and I grabbed Kelsey's arm, shoving us both up off the floor. Teddy rolled to his knees and then his feet, holding his injured arm to his ribs.

An alarm blared loudly.

My shoes slid across papers and I fell, but Kelsey helped me up.

Teddy grabbed her and all but carried her to where the judge, assistant, and clerk reporter had run. Orrin was still down, bleeding from the head and looking dazed.

I reached under his armpits and hefted him up. "We have to run. Now. Come on, Orrin."

Another explosion ripped through the building from the park side. People screamed, and the smell of smoke and burned metal filled the air. The actual smoke was dark and impaired visibility. I dragged Orrin to the door and he regained his balance, finally helping me.

Pete pushed us through and then slammed the door. "Down the stairs. Hurry."

I tripped, but Orrin and I helped each other past the judge's chambers to the back stairwell leading up.

Another explosion behind us propelled us out the door and into the August storm.

* * *

I SKIDDED across the rough concrete sidewalk, scraping both of my knees. My hands flopped down, and rocks cut across my palms. I gasped and tried to turn, but my shirt jacket became caught on the grill of a truck. Rain slashed across my face.

Orrin hauled me up, and I pulled free of my jacket, leaving it hanging from the grill. "Keep going. Get away from the building," he urged. We made our way through vehicles toward Justice Road while sirens erupted all around us and emergency vehicles roared in.

"Over here," Kelsey called, leaning against a yellow truck and partially bending over. Soot covered her head, and blood dripped from her temple as the rain matted her hair against her head.

"You go." Orrin reached the curb where the judge sat, flanked by the bailiff. "I need to sit." He wiped rain off his face.

I turned and limped toward Kelsey, my knees aching and my ears buzzing. Rain soaked my blouse. Emergency personnel swarmed the building. I reached Kelsey. "Are you okay?"

She coughed and lifted up. "Yeah. I think so. Are you?"

I did a quick inventory. Nothing was broken, but my knees really hurt. "Yeah. I'm okay." I pivoted to see Teddy shutting the door of a gray truck parked on Justice Road and hurrying our way. Blood covered the right side of his face. "Eesh. Teddy, how bad is it?"

He blinked blood from his eye and drew a couple of T-shirts out of a bag. "Here are clean clothes to wipe away the blood." His concerned gaze moved to Kelsey. "You're bleeding, honey." He tossed me a shirt. "For your knees."

I caught it and leaned over to press the cotton against the scrapes, patting until I could see better. Small rocks and gravel were embedded in my skin. I winced. It was going to hurt to get those out. I kept patting as Teddy pressed a shirt to Kelsey's face and ignored his own wound. "Teddy? You're going to want to put some pressure on that."

Teddy took Kelsey's hand and put it on the T-shirt on her face, and grabbed another shirt out of the bag to put against his cut. "These are workout clothes, but they're clean." Blood slid over his lip when he spoke.

The day hazed and I shook my head to keep in the moment.

There was so much movement around us. I tried to stay out of the way. Another firetruck lurched to a stop closer to the building. Blue and red lights were everywhere, and ambulances rushed closer to the scene.

A man caught my eye. Kurt Stockwood. I partially turned. His gun was out, and he was moving toward us from the far side of the parking lot.

It all became clear. My lungs jolted and I scrambled to find a cop. Anybody close to us. Kurt kept moving.

I turned. "Run," I whispered, fighting the wind. "We have to go. We have to get away from Kurt."

Teddy moved his bloody rag from his face. "Who's Kurt?"

I rushed toward Teddy and grabbed Kelsey's arm. "It makes sense. He knew about Sasha, he knew about Aiden, and he knows about me. He was by the office before it was bombed. We have to run. Now!" My tone must've convinced him because he grabbed Kelsey's hand.

"This way," Teddy yelled, running toward the gray truck.

"Anna!" Kurt bellowed.

I ran faster and jumped in the back seat while Kelsey and Teddy leaped into the front.

I leaned over. "Just drive over to the front of the police station and we'll run inside. Hurry, Teddy." I turned to see Kurt with his gun pointed at the truck, running full bore through the myriad of vehicles to get to us. I needed my phone to call Aiden. He hadn't thought to look inside his organization for the danger. "My phone is inside the courthouse."

"Mine, too," Kelsey said, her eyes wild and her hair covered in debris.

Teddy punched the gas and whipped onto Justice Road, barely missing another ambulance. He turned left.

"Just drive right into the police station parking lot and up to the front. Hit the sidewalk. I don't care." I turned around to see if Kurt was still coming.

"Crap." Teddy yanked the wheel hard to the right to avoid a motorcycle cop careening toward the scene.

I fell to the side and thunked my head on the window.

Teddy swerved again onto Cedar Avenue. "I'm trying to get back," he muttered.

Kelsey looked over the back of the seat. "I don't understand." She still kept the cloth against her bleeding head. "Why are we running from Kurt?"

I couldn't see him through the back window. "He was coming at us with a gun. It makes sense, right? He's working with the bomber. It's the only way all of this happened." I couldn't see him, but I knew he was coming. Where was he? The further we were from the police station, the more danger we were in. "Teddy? Turn around."

"I'm trying," Teddy snapped. "There are cars coming like crazy and there hasn't been a chance."

"Sorry." I settled back and tried to calm myself. "Do you have your phone?"

He shook his head and peered into the back window. Rain covered it. "I don't see anybody following us."

I had to get a call to Aiden. "Okay. Take a left on Acorn Road, left on Elm, and then we'll hit Justice Road again and go to the police. We have to get to the station." I needed to get to safety and then call Aiden and let him know about Kurt.

Teddy took a left on Acorn Road. "All right. Just hold on." He was going too fast, but I didn't complain. How many people had been hurt in the blasts? I swallowed soot and coughed it out. How long had Kurt been working with Barensky? My head hurt. I really needed an aspirin or something.

I watched Elm Avenue fly by. "Teddy? You missed the road." The guy was probably out of his mind. The wind threw pine needles across the windows.

"Sorry. Willow Lane is coming up." He took the turn to Willow Lane, and the truck bumped, nearly on two wheels. But he turned right instead of left, thus driving away from Justice Road.

"Teddy? Wrong way." I leaned toward him. Had he hit his head worse than I'd thought?

Kelsey gasped and leaned against her door, her pupils dilated. "Teddy?"

His hazel gaze met mine in the mirror. "Yeah. Sorry about that."

I looked down to see that he had a gun pointed at Kelsey's ribcage.

CHAPTER 38

This was unbelievable.

Teddy drove us to the small county airport and parked outside a medium sized hangar. He'd kept the gun pointed at Kelsey the entire drive, so even if I'd wanted to jump out of the speeding truck, I couldn't leave her alone with him.

Shock kept my mind numb, and I had to get control of myself.

He grabbed Kelsey by the hair with his good hand to drag her across the seat and out the door. "Move, Anna. I will shoot her." Gone was the placid and easy-going bank manager with the injured shoulder. A chill lived in this guy's eyes.

I scrambled out of the truck and into the blowing rain, where I set my feet to keep from falling over.

"This way." He propelled Kelsey toward a doorway in the side of the hangar.

I looked around for help, but the area was deserted. The storm prevented anybody from flying right now. I followed, searching for anything I could use as a weapon.

Then we were inside an empty hangar, all dripping rainwater to pool on the cement. There was room for one corporate jet in the main area while a small office sat over to the left. Probably for the pilots.

Teddy gestured toward the outside of the office wall, where a few round hooks had been set into the concrete. The cement around the hooks was a different color than the rest of the wall, showing they'd been added very recently. "Sit there or I'll shoot you."

I reached for Kelsey's hand, and we limped over to sit where he'd instructed. The hooks were above our heads by a couple of inches.

Kelsey looked up at him. "I don't understand."

His gun now pointed at the ground. "That's because you're a moron." His gaze switched to me. "Unlike you. You've got a brain. One I like."

My mouth nearly dropped open, but I remained silent.

Kelsey shifted uneasily next to me. "I have terrible taste in men."

Her statement was so unexpected I burst out laughing. Oh, it was a high-pitched and hysterical laugh, and it surprised even me.

Teddy smiled. "That's a lovely sound."

I stopped laughing. My stomach rolled over as my brain finally began to catch up with my shock. How could Teddy be the bad guy? Meeting him had been an accident—literally. "Wait a minute. The car wreck that hurt the three of us was engineered by you?" It was the only thing that made sense. "You paid Carbine to have his girlfriend ram my car...right when you were driving by?"

His smile held menace. "Now that took some planning. You have to admit, your car hitting mine was the most innocent way we could get together. I bribed some jackass named Carbine and arranged the hit and run so you and I could connect." His gaze flicked to Kelsey and back. "We were watching you, and we had to see how serious you were with Aiden Devlin and his precious special response team." Teddy drawled out the words. "It became apparent you two were together, so Kelsey and I became...friends."

She made a gagging sound. "You are such a dick."

While I admired her sudden spunk, I didn't want to get shot, so I kept him talking. "You're going after the ATF team and Aiden?"

"I am," Teddy said quietly. "His team screwed up our organization, and it has taken this long to track him down and plan. My first hit was the newspaper articles about when he'd been a hero as a teenager. The newspaper articles about you helped, and once we found you, well..."

It had been easy to find Aiden.

I searched for a way out with my peripheral vision. There was the door we'd come in and the large hangar door, and maybe a door that led outside from the office? I couldn't tell. That was it. At the moment, we'd have to go through Teddy to get out. I needed to get the gun from him. Could Kelsey create some sort of distraction without getting shot? "You work for Norman Barensky," I said. Since when did serial bombers work with others?

"No. I work *with* my Uncle Norman," Teddy said. "Partners in the organization. We have our different interests and they often combine." Now he sounded downright creepy and not so businesslike.

I gulped. "Your interest is pounding women's heads into the ground?"

"It really is," he said congenially. "That nosy Sasha deserved to die after harming our organization five years ago, and she was the easiest way to get to Devlin until you came along. I left her as a present for you. You're welcome."

I was going to throw up. "What about Bev?"

"Who's Bev?" he asked, flicking a glance at his wristwatch.

"The woman found in my office," I blurted out. "The dead one?"

His eyes cleared. "Oh, yeah. She's one of the women who

crashed the truck into you. They were witnesses, and I figured she'd make a good gift to you as well. Sorry, I didn't get the third woman, but there's always time now, I guess. You're welcome again."

"Did it occur to you that I might not want dead women as a present?" I snapped, my hands freezing on the chilly concrete.

He shrugged. "It was part of my uncle's game as well. He likes to play chess, you know."

"I've heard," I whispered, flashing back to the bombings today and the parking area afterward when I'd run from Kurt. "Is Agent Kurt Stockwood working with you?"

"I don't know Kurt," Teddy said. "But I owe him one. Whoever he is, he got you to my truck today without my having to pull out my gun. I would have, though. Either way, we would've ended up right here and right now."

Kelsey wiped more blood off her face. "What happens now that we're here?"

He barely looked at her. "To be honest, you're no longer needed."

"Wait. Don't shoot her," I said, tensing to cover her.

"Why not?" he asked, not lifting the gun.

I swallowed. Why not?

He smiled. "Don't worry. I'm not going to shoot her."

A burst of relieved air came out of Kelsey.

"I'm going to bash her head against the floor." He ignored her gasp and looked at his watch again. "Or I might give Kelsey to my uncle. He deserves some fun."

I blinked. "Your uncle likes to blow things up."

"Exactly," Teddy said. Then he walked closer and dropped to his haunches next to me. His gun rested on his thigh, and the barrel pointed directly at my ribcage. His eyes sparkled, not looking quite right. "I'm quite fascinated by you. Most women bore me. They use their looks to hurt a man. Every time. But you?

I think you're different. When you were kidnapped as a child, were you harmed?"

"Is that why you bash their heads in? So women aren't as pretty and can't hurt you?" I wasn't a profiler or a shrink, but I was happy to keep him chatting until help arrived.

"I don't have time for introspection right now, and I'd much rather learn more about you," he said. "Tell me if being kidnapped changed who you are. It had to. You're a lawyer, so others can't get off like your kidnapper did, right?"

I laid my head back against the wall and just looked at him. He wasn't getting anything out of me.

He tilted his head. "I was kidnapped as a child, too. Isn't it fascinating how two unrelated events from so long ago led us both right here to this moment?"

"What are you talking about?" I asked. The longer he kept talking, the more alive Kelsey and I would remain.

"You were kidnapped, Aiden saved you as an adult, he took down my uncle's organization, my uncle needed my help, we hunted down Aiden, and I found you." Teddy traced a circle on my thigh. "See? We're all connected. The minute I found those articles about you as a child, about you being kidnapped, I knew we were meant to be together. Two halves of a whole. Don't you feel it?"

I shook my head. "Listen, buddy. I already have one sociopath leaving me love letters twice a year. My plate is full."

Teddy smiled, looking like we shared a joke. Man, he was nuts. "Jareth Davey, right?"

"Yeah," I said. "How did you know?"

"He was your kidnapper, according to the news reports. Then his case was dismissed, so that makes sense." Teddy leaned in, and he smelled a little like pepper. The baking kind and not the spicy chilly kind. "I can kill him if you'd like."

"Sure," I said, calculating the speed I'd need to get the gun out of his hand before he could fire it. I didn't have time with him in his current position. "Go ahead and kill him if you can find him. So far, he's done a great job of staying under the radar." This time I showed my teeth. "Tell you what. Why don't you go take care of that now, and Kelsey and I will wait here?"

He laughed and patted my thigh. "You are unique, Anna Albertini. Some would think that's a bad thing, but I believe it's fate. You and I are going to have fun together in this world." He leaned in. "Maybe our first adventure will be to hunt down Jareth Davey and break his head open like a watermelon."

"Sure. Let's go right now," I said. "We don't need Kelsey with us. She can stay here quietly." Just how crazy was he?

"We'll go soon enough," he said, looking at Kelsey intently. "You're right. Kelsey will stay here very quietly after I've finished with her."

She pulled her legs up and wrapped both arms around them. Her body shook so hard that I could feel it. "Don't do this, Teddy," she whispered.

"I have to," he said, almost hypnotically.

"Teddy," I snapped, drawing his attention back to me.

He frowned. "What?"

"Tell me about your kidnapping," I said. "You brought it up. Who kidnapped you?"

He gulped a couple of times as if drawing back to the moment. "My grandmother. She took me from my mother, who had a drug problem."

Okay. I got his train of thought off Kelsey for now. I couldn't let him kill her. "I see. I take it your grandmother wasn't loving toward you?" I tried to make my voice sound sympathetic, but my voice was hoarse from fear.

He nodded. "She was beautiful—like a snake. So mean. She didn't want me but didn't want my mother to have me."

That was sad, but a lot of folks had sad childhoods. "Maybe you just need help? Let me get you help," I said.

Teddy stood. "I don't need help. Believe me, I know exactly

how to silence the demons in my mind. Kelsey is going to under-stand what that means very soon."

She sucked in her breath but didn't say anything.

The outside door opened and Norman Barensky walked inside, shaking out a clear umbrella decorated with large blue polka dots. He smiled, showing yellowed teeth from cigarette smoking. A large black duffel bag had been slung over his narrow shoulder. "Well, isn't this fortuitous? It's lovely to see you again, Anna Albertini."

CHAPTER 39

I wanted to stand up and face Barensky, but Teddy still had his gun held loosely in his hand. "I take it you blew up Aiden's office the other night?" I asked.

The wind had moved Barensky's thin hair to the side, leaving bald spots where strands had combed over. He dropped his shoulder and the duffle bag fell to the floor. "I did. Figured it was a good way to dispose of those two pawns as well as let the ATF know where we were on the chessboard. It's almost checkmate, and it was only fair to give them warning."

I shivered. "I didn't think serial bombers had partners."

Barensky glanced at his nephew. "Family is family. We have different interests, but for this occasion, we came together. I would've preferred to blow Agent Sasha Duponte's head off her shoulders instead of just leaving her on your porch, but in a partnership, one makes concessions, no?"

Kelsey gave a soft sound of distress.

My breath heated down my throat, and panic edged into my thinking. I shook it away. There was only one way out of this, and I hadn't found it yet. There was always a way. Until there wasn't.

Barensky looked at his nephew. "Of course, the deal was for the agent and not the other woman. She was to be mine."

Teddy huffed like a spoiled toddler. "I said I was sorry about Bev. She seemed like a romantic present for Anna."

I frowned. Something was off between those two. Besides the fact that they were nuts. "How did you get Bev's dead body into my office, anyway?"

"Your security stinks," Teddy said, watching me. "I'll take better care of you when you're mine."

I stilled. "Excuse me?"

"Haven't you been listening? You're my payment," Teddy said. "I spent so much time studying you for the last month, and the newspaper articles really helped. I haven't been able to get you out of my mind. When that happens, I can't stop. Until you're mine."

Kelsey reached over and took my hand. I squeezed hers.

The longer I kept them talking, the more chance we'd have for somebody to find us. If Kurt was a good guy and not the killer I'd thought for a moment, then surely he'd called reinforcements.

"What's your plan here, Norman?" I asked. It looked like Barensky was in charge.

"It's time to move the pieces on the board." He reached into his bag and drew out cuffs to toss at our feet. "Anna? Please cuff Kelsey to the wall." He stood and his back cracked. "Getting old is difficult." Then he smiled. "I put those hooks in just for you a week ago."

So this was planned. Right here and right now. There was only one thing Barensky liked to do, and I wasn't cuffing either one of us to the wall. "No," I said.

His eyes lit up. "Excellent." Then he reached over and secured the gun from his nephew. "Kelsey? Teddy is going to cuff you, and if you fight him, I'm going to let him take you out back and break open your head."

Kelsey squawked and squeezed my hand so hard it hurt.

Teddy faltered. "I thought I got to take her, anyway. But this is good. You can do what you want with Kelsey, and then I can take Anna with me."

"I like my head in one piece," I snapped, my lips trembling.

"It will be for a while." Teddy gave what would've amounted to a charming smile if he wasn't talking about smashing my head. "There's something special about you and I need to figure it out. First."

Second came death.

It was now or never. I stiffened to charge Barensky.

He pointed the gun at Kelsey's head. "Stop moving."

I sank back down. What the heck was I supposed to do? Barensky angled to the side so Teddy could cuff one of Kelsey's wrists to the wall. She didn't fight him and instead watched the gun.

I coughed. "The explosives at the courthouse didn't hurt us. You could've killed us."

"Yes, but that wouldn't have gotten me farther on the chess-board. Not really," Barensky said. "Those were tiny little blips to get you where I needed you to be. There was barely a fire, and I doubt anybody died. Maybe a burn or two." He paused and looked into the distance. "The fire was lovely though. Beauty snuffed out too quickly."

Man, he was crazy.

Teddy finished securing Kelsey to the wall.

"Anna, too," Barensky said, gesturing with the gun.

Teddy reached for the cuffs and looked over his shoulder. "I'm taking her. You can have the other one. I know it's a change to the plan, but I need this."

"I know," Barensky said. "Just cuff her until I get everything ready, and then you can take her."

So there'd be a chance to get free. How was I going to free Kelsey at the same time? Since Barensky had the gun pointed at my head now, I let Teddy enclose my wrist with the cuff before attaching it a couple of inches above my head to the wall. It was definitely uncomfortable but not painful. Yet. I gave an experimental tug. Since the hooks had been added, maybe they weren't as secure as Barensky thought.

Then Teddy patted my face. "I like your skin." He leaned in.

Panic caught me hard. Instinct had my knee raising, and I nailed him right in the groin. He stilled and his eyes widened as he grunted in pain. Then he scrambled back. "Bitch."

Barensky smiled. "I like her."

Teddy stood but still stayed a little bent over. "You're going to be very sorry you did that." He moved closer to his uncle. "Hurry up so I can take her out of here. There's a well-equipped cabin toward the valley where we're going to spend a lot of time."

Barensky sighed. "I know you have needs, nephew. Unfortunately, I'm the King here." He shoved Teddy into the office, where Teddy fell. Then Barensky fired the gun three times toward the floor.

Blood slid from the office and across the cement floor.

* * *

Kelsey screamed.

I jumped and fought to pull the hook out of the wall, using all of my weight. Nothing. It remained firmly attached. My wrist and damaged hands protested, but I kept struggling.

Barensky slipped the gun into the front of his waist. He wore old man dockers that looked too loose to keep the gun in place, but it stayed there. "Now then, we can get started."

Tears streamed down Kelsey's face, and she wiped them off with her free hand. "He was your nephew."

Barensky shrugged and reached into the bag to draw out what looked like a very bulky knee brace. "Ah, there we go." He moved toward me.

I pulled my knees up, prepared to kick.

He was ultra-careful with the brace. "I wouldn't move if I were you."

I couldn't move now if I wanted. "Wh-what is that?"

He set the brace next to me, and I stared at it, horror slithering through me like poison. Without a word, he slid the skinny part beneath my leg and zipped it up the side. Whatever he had in the homemade pockets was heavy against the top of my thigh.

I winced. "That's too heavy."

He chuckled, the sound high and creepy. "That's the least of your worries, Anna." His familiarity with my name split anger through my terror.

"Why are you doing this?" I asked.

Kelsey cried quietly next to me.

"Because you're the Queen. The fire needs to kiss you, which will then force Devlin to scramble his pieces." Barensky craned his neck. "It's beautiful, don't you think?"

I looked down at the knee brace. It was a dark blue with a hole for my knee, and it extended up my thigh and a little way down my calf. A heavy solid was located in a pocket on my thigh, and it looked like the only way to reach into the pocket was on the underside, which was pressed against my leg. Coppery little wires spread out in every direction, and they were expertly wound throughout the zipper. "What kind of bomb do you have in there?" I asked, my lungs squeezing painfully.

He looked up, his eyes brilliantly clear and brown. "The most special kind. You will feel the fire and dance in the flames, Anna Albertini. I'm so jealous."

"Then you take it," I snapped. "I don't want to blow up." This was insane. There was a bomb on me.

"You will," he promised. "The moment right before, when the world goes quiet, is just for you. Only for you this time. Do you know how special that makes you? I've given you the best gift in existence. Fire. Your fire."

Insanity obviously ran in their family. "The little wires?"

His face flushed. "Those keep the baby intact. If you move your leg or try to unzip the brace, well then. Everything speeds up to right now." He stood and stepped back to survey his handiwork from afar. "Very nice."

"Why are you doing this?" I asked.

"I've already explained to you. Why aren't you listening?" He frowned. "Because of the fire. Do you not understand the beauty of the explosion? That moment—the second before the fire lives—where all is silent? That moment is everything. You will feel it and you will understand."

Kelsey sniffed. "Please don't leave us with a bomb."

"It's not just a bomb," he said, almost gently.

I sneezed. "Why do I smell...hydrogen peroxide and, um, gunpowder?"

"I must've spilled a bit," Barensky said, his tone almost teasing. "Sorry about that."

Kelsey gulped. "Hydrogen peroxide? The stuff you use to clean earrings?"

"It's also an explosive material, right?" I asked, twisting to see if there was any way to loosen the brace on my leg. The thing was solid.

"Yes," Barensky said proudly like I was his prized pupil. "I'd like to stay and chat, but I must get going. This first real strike against Devlin must happen now." He took out a phone and dialed a number. "Hello. Please connect me to ATF SRT Agent Aiden Devlin. I have his girlfriend attached to an IED." Then he winked at me.

It took a couple of minutes, but I finally heard Aiden's voice. "This is Devlin."

"Hello, Agent Devlin. It's so enticing to play against you." Barensky switched on the camera and pointed it at me. "The timer is already set and we're in the fifth hangar at the Timber City Airport. You have fifteen minutes until the fire wins. Goodbye for now." He tossed the phone over his shoulder, and it broke into pieces on the cement when it hit. He moved toward the device.

I stiffened and tried to edge away.

Then he pushed the bottom of the protruding pocket. "There you go. He might make it in fifteen minutes. The game has to be fair, after all."

"No." I shook my head. "You don't want it to be fair." I scouted the area again. "How many devices do you have planted here?" If he wanted maximum casualties, he'd have secondary devices ready to go when emergency crews arrived.

He patted my head. "You are smart, aren't you?"

I jerked away from him. "Take Kelsey with you. She's not involved with the ATF or Aiden's team. There's no reason for her to be here."

"She's a pawn. Pawns are always sacrificed." He leaned over and tossed his duffel bag on his shoulder. "Good luck." Then he jogged out into the storm and slammed the door shut.

Kelsey jumped.

I tried not to move too much since I was attached to a bomb.

CHAPTER 40

"Okay." I tried to keep from freaking out. How stable were the explosives? "Kelsey? We have to get you free. Pull on the hook with all of your strength—away from me. Try not to nudge me at all."

She flipped around, twisting her arm. Then she put both feet against the wall and shoved, grunting with the effort.

Nothing happened.

She fought wildly, kicking and pulling, crying and grunting. Finally, she hung her head and sobbed, her arm over her shoulder. Then she twisted back around and sat, straightening her legs. "The cement is solid."

My leg was starting to twitch. It had to stay still. "That didn't work. Next plan? Let's scream," I said. Maybe there was somebody around the airport checking on their plane or something.

"What about sound vibrations?" she asked wearily, putting her head back on the wall. "What if vibrations ignite the bomb?"

I tried to keep my breathing even so I didn't hyperventilate. "That's a good point." What about sound vibrations? "I don't know."

Thunder roared outside.

"Nobody is out there, anyway," Kelsey said quietly. "Yelling is too much of a risk." She looked sideways at me. "Do you have anything in your hair that we can use to pick the locks?"

"No," I said, looking down my body. "Nothing. Wait a minute." I barely shifted my shoulders. "What about underwire? My bra has some."

"I'm not wearing one." She shifted onto her knees and faced me with her arm still over her head. "Front clasp?"

I shook my head. "Back."

"Okay," She whispered. "Best scenario is that I take the bra off and try to work it without bumping you."

"Agreed." The less movement I gave, the better. How many minutes had passed? I leaned away from the wall, careful not to jostle my leg. "Go for it."

She gingerly reached beneath my blouse in the back and unclasped my bra. "All right. Bring your free arm toward me." When I did so, she slid down the strap and freed part of my bra. "I'm going to unroll the strap of the other side." Holding her breath, she leaned over me and tugged at my shoulder strap.

I closed my eyes and forced my body to stay as still as possible.

She pulled free with a triumphant grunt. "Got it." She set my frilly beige bra on her thigh.

I reached over with my free hand, even though my raw skin was stinging pretty badly. "I'll hold it still and you work the underwire free."

She picked at the fabric. "Ug. We need something sharp."

"I've got it." Just moving my arm, I brought the bra to my mouth to bite through the small fabric at the base of the cup. The silk shredded, and I used my teeth to latch onto the wire and pull it free. The bra fell to my lap. "Here you go. Do yours first." I handed the wire to Kelsey.

She took it and leaned away so she could see. "Do you have any tips?"

"Nope. Just put the wire where the key goes and try to work it all around." I set my head back again.

She tried several times with no luck. Then she tried again, and something clicked. "I'm free." She swung wide eyes to me. "I can't believe that worked." She rolled out her now free arm and then scooted around my legs to my other side. "I'll try not to move you. Just hold still." She leaned closer and her hair brushed my face. After several tries, my lock clicked and my arm fell to the floor.

I shook out my hand. "Nice job." We both wore half a cuff, but at least we weren't attached to the wall. I grabbed her arm with my free hand. "You have to go. Find help. Go, now."

Indecision crossed her pretty face. "I can't leave you."

I'd known she was a sweetheart with a strong backbone. Even though I wanted to smile at her, my lips weren't working. "Go find help, Kelsey. It's our only chance," I said. We probably had about five minutes left before the bomb detonated, and there was no reason for both of us to die. My body began to tremble and I couldn't stop it. "Please, go. Find somebody. Find a phone."

Sirens suddenly sliced through the rain outside. The sound of screeching tires coincided with another lighting strike.

Kelsey hovered near me. "Help is here." Tears tracked down her face.

The door burst open and Aiden ran inside, his phone in his hand, an ATF jacket dripping rain from his shoulders. He took the scene in instantly and was at my side. "Kelsey, get out of here," he said.

Chelli, Saber, and Drag ran inside followed by several uniformed police officers.

"I'm staying," Kelsey said, the bra wire still in her hand.

Aiden ducked his head to study the wrapping on my leg. "Saber? Clear the vicinity. Everyone to the far end of the runways at minimum."

Drag looked over his shoulder. "That won't pack enough to go much past this building."

Aiden dropped to his haunches and set his bag next to me, his blue gaze on my leg. "Barensky would've left secondary devices throughout this place. Once this one goes, the whole building will follow. Clear it. Now."

Saber knelt on the other side, his focus on my knee. "This is a two person job. Chelli and Drag, clear it."

Chelli turned and ran back to the officers while Drag grasped Kelsey's arm.

"No," she protested, fighting him. "Anna and I are in this together."

I swear, I loved her right there. Whatever happened, we were going to be good friends forever. I hoped forever lasted beyond the next couple of minutes. "Kelsey? You have to go. We can't let Barensky win like this."

She set her chin.

"Drag?" Aiden said.

Drag lifted her right off the ground and tossed her over his shoulder to stride toward the doorway, where Chelli had already cleared everyone out.

The door shut with a bang of finality.

* * *

Saber pointed a bright flashlight at the bomb. "Nice threads."

"Yeah." Aiden reached into his bag and pointed some device at the bomb, read it, and nodded. "All right." He took out a small set of scissors and then looked at my face. "You've been doing a great job, Angel. Now I need you to hold on a little while longer, okay?"

Tears pricked the back of my eyes, and I tried to stop breathing. "Teddy is in the office. Barensky shot him three times, and then there was blood."

Saber leaned over and looked into the office. "I see a body."

"Need to concentrate on this," Aiden said. His hands were

shockingly steady as he moved over me and meticulously cut the bottom of the pocket.

"Wh-what about the coppery colored wires?" I whispered.

"The added pocket isn't secure enough to have the wires throughout," he murmured, cutting up both sides. Then he removed the cloth and tossed it over his shoulder.

I looked down at a round metal cylinder with a multitude of wires connecting it to the other side of the brace. "I don't suppose you could cut those wires?"

"No," Aiden said, angling his head down to see better. "Flash the light on the right quadrant."

Saber moved his position.

"That's good," Aiden murmured.

"How much time is left?" I asked.

Aiden reached in his pack and drew out another light, but this one shone a red beam. "Approximately two minutes."

I shut my eyes and swallowed. "You guys have to go. Get out of here." The last act of my life wasn't going to be watching Aiden Devlin die. "Tell my family I love them. But go."

"I'm not leaving you, Angel." He didn't look up at me. "Be quiet for a second, would you?"

Saber leaned closer to the bomb. "Talk it out as we go."

"Affirmative," Aiden said, his voice a calm thread through the chaotic day. "The size of this is big enough to include enhancements. Based on a study of Barensky, it'd be colored glass fragments, most likely genuine depression ware glass."

I didn't care about glass. "If it blows, is there a chance I'll survive? Maybe lose a leg?"

"No," Aiden said. "We have a silver container housing the initiator, switch, and main charge."

Saber nodded. "Can we get into it?"

Aiden stretched out flat on the ground with his face eye-level to the bomb. "I smell gunpowder and peroxide. The man does like a good fire." He looked up, his blue eyes intense. "Hold still, Angel. We're getting out of this."

I couldn't breathe. We probably had less than a minute left. "Please go, Aiden."

He reached in his pack. "You ready, Saber?"

"Yep." Saber set the flashlight on the ground. "Twenty seconds left. I pull, you cut?"

"Affirmative." Aiden gently twisted the bottom of the cylinder.

Saber reached out and let Aiden set the metal barely on his hands. "I see the timer. Fifteen seconds."

Aiden pulled something silver out of his bag. "Need to cut off the igniter. That'll give us time." He moved steadily, his hands sure.

"Seven seconds," Saber said calmly.

Tension roiled around us, but they seemed so serene. I shut my eyes and tried not to breathe. Was this what they did for their jobs? Diffused deadly explosives while talking it out? Who were these guys?

"See it," Aiden said. "Hold steady."

"Three seconds," Saber said.

I inhaled Aiden's scent. Man, motor oil, and leather with just a hint of an Irish storm. The scent I'd take with me forever.

Something clicked.

My eyes shot open.

"Move, now," Aiden said, unzipping the brace and gingerly setting it to the side. Then he stood and caught me up in his arms before I could move. "Run, Saber."

Saber was already ahead of us, opening the door. We ran into the storm and rain lambasted us. The emergency vehicles and personnel were visible at the far end of the runway, blue and red lights slicing through the storm. Aiden turned and ran into the forest with Saber at his side.

The world stilled. A moment of silence, pure and calm,

descended. Then the wind roared through the trees, pulling us toward the building.

The explosion rocked the storm. Pieces of debris flew between the trees, and smoke billowed into the sky. The force knocked Aiden off his feet, and he turned mid-air, landing on his back with me on his front. We landed with a hard thud, and he groaned. He immediately rolled over me, holding me to the wet and dirty ground.

Mini-explosions rocketed out from the bigger one, and even the earth moved beneath me.

I turned my head and coughed out dirt. But I lay still, totally spent beneath Aiden. So long as we were both in one piece, I didn't care how heavy he was.

The rain hit the fire with a mutinous hiss of steam. I shivered.

Aiden lifted up and set me with my back against a tree. He wiped rain and dirt off my face. Mud covered the side of his jaw. "You okay?"

I couldn't move. Every bone in my body turned to liquid. Tears leaked down my face. I'd never, in my entire life, been that terrified.

He lifted me right onto his lap and held me close. Heat, male, and strength surrounded me and helped ground me. Kind of. "You're okay," he murmured. He looked over my head at Saber, who sat against a tree with a burning piece of wood next to him. "Told you there'd be other explosives."

Saber grinned.

I shook out my legs because I could. "Barensky got away."

Aiden tightened his hold. "I know. We'll get him. There's a net around town, and we have blockades up. I've got you."

I mulled over the entire situation while being held safely by my badass. "He thinks the Queen is dead," I murmured, playing through the chess game in my head.

Aiden leaned back, his expression alert. "True. What's your point?"

I rubbed more dirt off my neck. "The Queen is the protector. In chess, when the Queen is no longer on the board, every piece is in danger, especially the opposing King, which would be you. It's king against king, and you've lost too many pieces. It's the time for checkmate. You're about to be vulnerable, and he knows exactly where you're supposed to be tomorrow."

A slow smile tipped Aiden's lips. "You're right. You're a genius, Angel."

CHAPTER 41

J hunkered down in Aiden's truck, partially hidden behind a sweeping oak tree. The rain had softened to a light patter but bruised, and swollen clouds still covered the moon, giving us perfect darkness. "We've been here for two hours," I murmured.

"Stakeouts aren't fun," he said, peering through his binoculars. "There's probably something wrong with me, but I've always found cemeteries at night to be peaceful. Even comforting."

"There's definitely something wrong with you." I reached into the potato chip bag for more chips. It was odd, but I was comfortable wherever we were, so long as we were together. What was it with Aiden? There was something just so solid and tough about him, and yet, he had a great brain. More than that, he trusted my brain. I liked that. A lot. "What if I was wrong about Barensky?"

Aiden took a drink of his soda. "Then we'll figure out another way to get him."

I looked out at the different shapes, all marking graves. Round gravestones, square ones, even a few spherical ones. A huge gravestone across the cemetery held a cross up to the darkened sky. I guess it was peaceful. The quiet was calming, even with the rain. I yawned and tried to keep my buzz of excitement going, but it had been a long day. My leg still felt the bomb strapped to it, even though that had been hours ago.

He took another drink. "It's against protocol to have you here, so remember your promise. No matter what happens, you stay in the truck until I signal otherwise. Got it?"

"Yep." I'd had enough excitement for one day and had absolutely no trouble staying in the warm truck and out of the rain. The chips were the good barbecue kind, too.

Aiden's phone dinged, and he handed it over to me so I could field a phone call from my sister, Donna. The family was trying to keep my involvement in the earlier explosion a secret, but soon word would be out. The next article from Jolene would be landing, no doubt. Hopefully she would at least double-check her facts this time and not make things up.

Donna sighed. "Why are you still with Aiden? I thought the three of us were going to have a sister's night. Tessa is already asleep on my sofa."

I grinned. "It's hard to keep her awake unless we're doing something. We're still here. Let's do a sister's night next weekend."

"I got the scoop on Bud from Cal Carisea, who works in the courthouse. Bud is definitely married, and his wife is a spitfire who's now in town. I'm hoping we get to meet her," Donna said.

"Me, too," I agreed. "Sorry he's married, though."

"I'm not. It's a good thing. We can't be with a guy who's scared of our family." Donna sounded cheerful about it.

Good. She was right, too. Family was always around.

"Are you sure you're safe?" she asked.

"Yeah." For now, Barensky didn't know I was alive, and I was fine with that. "I'll call you tomorrow. Bye."

She said 'bye' and hung up.

For now, I needed to say a couple of things to Aiden. "With us scrambling all day, I didn't get a chance to thank you for staying with me and diffusing the bomb earlier. I've never seen anybody be so calm in a situation like that," I murmured.

"It's my job to stay calm in situations like that." Aiden lowered the binoculars and stared out the side window.

I tried again. "I know, but I'm more than a job. I mean, it meant everything that you stayed." Yeah, he probably would've stayed for anybody, but he was my boyfriend. "I just wanted to say thank you."

He turned toward me, and even through the darkness, the brilliance of his blue eyes shone. "You're my angel. I'm not going to leave you alone in danger, and I'm sure not going to let a bomb get you."

My heart turned over. Probably twice. His sweetness was so natural. "Also, about Kurt. He was running toward us with his gun out," I said, reliving the day.

Aiden nodded. "Kurt saw you leaving the courthouse after the bombing and went on instinct. He was trying to protect you."

I stared into the darkness. "So I guess he's back on the team?"

"No, he's still going to LA, but I gave him a commendation." Aiden chewed on a chip. "We're solid, but he still screwed up in the one area I can't allow. You."

Man, his sweet side was killing me.

His radio crackled. "We have movement coming from the southern gate. One individual. Suspect parked outside the fence and is proceeding on foot inside. Saber, out."

"Received," Aiden said, lifting his binoculars again to peer through them. "No visual as of yet."

Anticipation rushed through me, and I leaned toward the front window, squinting to see through the rain. A dark figure, barely visible, moved toward the open grave only yards from us. The grave had been dug just that morning, and outdoor green carpet had been laid over the hole to keep the rain away. A small tent protected chairs that would be brought out for the funeral this coming morning.

"Everyone hold tight," Aiden ordered through the radio.

The figure, hunched over with a duffel slung over his bony shoulder, ducked his head from the rain. He methodically walked between grave markers until finally reaching the carpet covering the open one. Leaning over, he gently lowered the dark duffel bag to the ground before straightening and looking around.

Aiden pressed the button on the radio. "Move in. All move in." He flicked the lights on his truck to bright, illuminating the grave. Then he jumped out of the truck and slammed the door.

Even though the rain, I could hear "ATF, stop," coming from every direction. The team moved in swiftly, lights on, guns out like a coordinated dance.

With the lights on, it was easy to identify the figure as Norman Barensky. He whipped around with nowhere to go. When he caught sight of Aiden coming at him, his shoulders went back.

Aiden reached him and flipped him around so fast his thin hair flew. Then Aiden had the bomber cuffed in seconds.

Barensky said something that had Aiden's mouth tightening. Aiden shook him and leaned down to say something in his ear. Then my badass ATF SRT agent boyfriend looked at me and gestured that it was safe for me to approach.

Oh. Okay. I moved to the driver's side of the truck and stepped down, tucking my coat around me as I walked toward Aiden and the open grave.

Barensky's mouth dropped open. He looked like a sad old man in the rain and not a deadly bomber.

I reached them and smiled. "Checkmate."

EPILOGUE

*I*t had been a week since Norman Barensky's arrest had hit the paper, and Jolene's article about the situation and me was relatively positive. She'd interviewed Kelsey, who had gushed about bravery and what a good lawyer I was. That had to bug Jolene so badly. In addition, the article had nicely cleared me in the death of Sasha.

I smiled at the thought as I sat back at my usual table for the family barbecue at my parent's house in Silverville.

A large tree shielded the table from the sun. We were close to the river and away from the busy porch and tables spread throughout the yard. Usually Pauley sat with me, but today he was inside playing the new PlayStation with Oliver, who'd agreed to come to the barbecue. So my sisters sat on either side of me, which frankly was the most comfortable position for me.

The August sun beat down, and the air was clear after a week of rain. The smell of freshly cut grass and a lot of delicious food filtered around with the sense of home and family.

Tessa drank Prosecco to my right and Donna drank Merlot to my left, and I sat between them watching the family. A boisterous game of darts sprang up on a tree on the other side of the deck, and our Nana seemed to be winning.

Donna breathed deep. "I can't believe you had a bomb strapped to your leg."

I winced. "Shh. Don't say those words out loud again. I barely got mom to stay home this week and not with me."

Tessa clucked her tongue and gestured toward Clark. "Please tell me you drove him over the pass and can drive him back to his apartment."

Clark was currently doing shots with our Uncle Sean, who disliked lawyers but really liked Clark, considering he was the best golf partner Sean had ever found. Right now, Sean was trying to talk Clark into opening a fishing business with him and giving up law. They seemed to be arguing while also drinking Irish Whiskey.

"Aiden and I drove him over, and we'll make sure he gets home," I said. "Uncle Sean needs to stop trying to take my law partner away."

Donna sipped her wine. "Don't look now, but Nick Basanelli and his Grams just sat down at the main picnic table. Nonna should be coming to get you any time, Contessa."

Tess sighed. "You know? He's sexy and smart, and if everyone would leave us alone, maybe I'd ask him out."

Donna cut me a look. "I think Tessa has a crush."

"I think Nick has a crush," I countered, seeing his gaze searching the backyard and landing on my sister. "Yep."

Nonna winked at me from across the lawn. I winked back, truly enjoying the moment. It seemed like Tessa had finally stopped thinking Nick was beyond her. That was so stupid. Tessa was amazing, and any man would be lucky to even be friends with her. "Nonna has a good eye for romance, but you're going to be off the hook soon. I think she has Quint in her sights."

Quint sat over at a table with my dad with Zena on his feet. She was such a sweet dog.

Aiden loped down the deck steps with a bottle in one hand and a plate of food in the other. In his basketball shorts and tee-shirt, he still looked tough and dangerous. When he caught sight of me, his expression softened.

Tessa chuckled. "He is too much."

"Agreed," Donna said.

Then, in unison, my sisters deserted me. Aiden grinned as he approached and took Donna's seat. "Was it something I said?" He refilled my wine glass. I'd opted for a Chardonnay today.

I snagged a wing off his plate. "No. They think you're cute."

"Nobody has ever called me cute." He took a drink of my wine. Apparently we were sharing. "*You're* cute and brave and strong." He leaned over and kissed my cheek. "I'm hoping everything will calm down now."

"Me too." I snuggled into his side. It had to.

Right?

SANTA'S SUBPOENA

ORDER THE NEXT ANNA ALBERTINI NOVEL NOW!

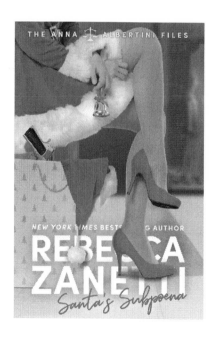

Preorder Santa's Subpoena Now.

HOLIDAY RESCUE

AN ALBERTINI FAMILY ROMANCE

Chapter 1

A wet nose touched Heather's, and she opened her eyes to see the prettiest brown eyes imaginable. Large and soft with a sparkle of puppy adoration and triumph in them. The dog licked her chin, sat on its haunches, and barked three times.

Heather blinked freezing snow out of her eyes and sat up straighter against the solid tree trunk, trying to get her bearings. Her butt and legs were chilled from the frozen ground. She must've drifted off beneath the sweeping pine boughs after pressing her personal locator beacon for help. Pain ticked through her head, and she gingerly tried to move her injured ankle, biting her lip at the agony. That's right. She looked over her shoulder at the rocky and icy terrain she'd fallen down after slipping on the trail near the top of the mountain. Her pack was next to her, and she patted it, wincing as wet snow splashed up. Then she focused on the quietly panting Black Labrador. "Hello."

The dog's tail wagged across the snowy pine needles. It wore a bright red Search and Rescue vest along with a wide collar with a box that had a blinking red light. Heather had fallen into some sort of gulley, surrounded by trees with one very rocky edge heading back up to the main trail. The rocks were black slate, icy, and sharp.

A whistle sounded from up above, and the dog barked three more times before laying down with its nose on its paws right in front of Heather. Snow scattered.

"Good girl, Zena," came a masculine voice. "Hello? Can you hear me?"

Heather angled around the tree and tried to look up and beyond the jagged rocks. "I can hear you."

"What are your injuries?" The man was tall against the rapidly darkening sky, and his face remained in shadow.

Heather swallowed. "A few bruises and I think a broken ankle." There was no 'think' about it. "It's broken for sure," she yelled, trying not to shiver. Was she going into shock?

"All right. Two of us are coming down, so stay behind that tree in case we loosen rocks or ice," he called down, his tone remaining calm.

"Okay," she yelled. Then she hunkered down behind the tree. Oh, she'd definitely expected danger to come her way, but not out by herself scattering her grandma's ashes on the mountain top. She'd worry about her disastrous life later. For now, she studied the rescue dog, which had the loveliest black coat she'd ever seen. "Zena, huh? You do look like a warrior princess."

The dog kept perfectly still, watching her as if she didn't want her prize to wander away. Her brown eyes were alert and smart, and she vibrated as the rescuers maneuvered down the large rocks toward them. Her training was as impressive as her obvious intelligence. Snow landed on her nose.

Heather listened as sure steps made their way down the craggy rocks, and soon a man stood before her. She'd been wrong. *He* had the prettiest eyes she'd ever seen. They were a tawny brown, lighter in the middle of the iris, the color spiking out into deep chocolate rims. "Hi." He dropped to his haunches to study her face.

Maybe she was still unconscious because no way was this guy real. Dark and mussed-up hair swept away from a rugged face with more than a couple days of whiskers across his edged jaw. His chest was broad, his hands wide, and his gaze intent. "Hi," she whispered.

The dog perked up and moved to the man's side, tail still wagging.

He patted the dog's neck. "You've already met Zena, and I'm Quint Albertini. Want to tell me what happened?"

Albertini? Yeah, he looked Italian. "I was hiking down the trail and slipped." Then she'd tumbled over the rocks, bruising herself, until landing next to the tree. "I think my ankle is broken."

He reached for a flashlight in his pack and shone it at her foot, which she'd already wrapped before putting a warmer at her toes and struggling to wear another sock over it all. "Looks like a solid wrap." He looked at her hiking boot, which was near her pack. "Good idea taking the boot off before the ankle got too swollen."

Another man jumped from a rock and landed. This guy was also in his late twenties, maybe early thirties, and had dark brown hair and strong features. Like Quint, he wore hiking clothing, a red Search and Rescue vest, and a backpack. "What do we have?"

"Broken ankle," Quint confirmed. "Her eyes are clear and I don't see signs of a concussion." He leaned toward her. "Are you hurt anywhere else?"

"Just bruised," she admitted. "I'd walk but can't put any weight on the ankle." There was no way to hop back up the rocky embankment to the trail.

Quint looked over his shoulder. "This is Rory, my brother."

"Hi. I'm Heather," she said, the cold starting to get to her. She shivered.

Rory grinned. "Great job taking the PLB with you. Most hikers aren't that careful."

"I was hiking alone," she said. "So I figured having a personal locator beacon was just smart." She'd hit the panic button the second she'd landed and regained her pack.

Quint looked closer at her ankle. "As well as boot warmers, extra socks, and granola bars?" The remains of a wrapper stuck out of a pocket of the backpack.

"I like to be prepared," she murmured, trying not to feel like a dork.

The wind sped up and splashed water off boughs toward them.

Rory peered up at the bruised looking clouds. "I know we've had a really late and light winter, but hiking Storm's Peak in mid-December is a bad idea. There's another storm moving in, and we need to get going." He reached for a radio and told somebody that they'd found the hiker. Then he paused. "Do we need the litter?"

She knew from her research that a litter was the stretcher rescuers used to carry an injured person down a mountain. While December wasn't a good month to hike, she'd had to wait to get the permits for her grandmother's ashes, and it had looked like the storm would hold off for another couple of days. The local weather forecast had been incorrect.

Quint looked her over, and her body somehow warmed. "I'd prefer not to use the litter. The terrain is too rocky and slick." He leaned in. "In cases like this, it's a lot easier to piggy you out. Are you up to it?"

Her eyebrows rose. "You want to give me a piggyback?"

Rory chuckled. "It is the easiest way, and we do it all the time. The question is if you can hold on."

"I think you're going into shock," Quint said, eyeing her snowy and wet jacket.

She could handle this. "I'm okay. I can hold on."

"Good." His gaze lightened. "It'll be a lot easier to climb up these boulders if you're on my back."

She breathed out and tried to sound cool and not like a love struck teenager. He was going to carry her out? Flutters wandered through her abdomen. "All right. Let me take off my other boot."

He held up a hand. "You can keep it on."

"No." She tried to sit up straighter. "It'll be easier for me to balance with both boots off, and that way, I won't keep kicking you." She winced. "I'll apologize now for the late season huckleberry milkshakes I've been eating all week. I'm sure I was five pounds lighter last Monday."

His smile warmed her enough to push the sense of shock away.

* * *

Order the Holiday Rescue today.

TAKE A PEEK AT THE FIRST ANNA
ALBERTINI BOOK!

DISORDERLY CONDUCT - CHAPTER 1

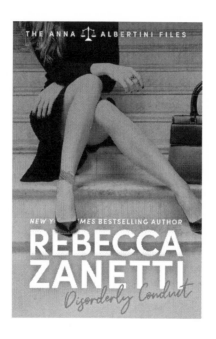

My latte tasted like it was missing the flavor. It might be because I had less than a week until I received an anniversary card from a sociopath, and the waiting was painful. Sighing, I took another sip. Well, the brew wasn't so bad, and the prosecuting attorney's office was fairly quiet this morning, so I could get caught up on paperwork.

The outside doors burst open, slamming loudly against the traditional oak paneling. What in the world? I jumped up and ran around my desk, skidding to a stop at my doorway to see a cluster of men stalk inside. Weapons were strapped to their thighs. Big ones.

It felt like a blitz attack.

The receptionist in the waiting area yelled, and a paralegal walking while reading a stack of papers stopped cold in spiked pumps, dropping the papers. Her name was Juliet, and I'd just met her last month but didn't know much about her except she liked to use colored paperclips when handing over case files.

She sidled closer to me; her eyes wide. Even though I wore thick wedges, she towered over me by about a head.

Six agents strode inside, all big and broad, all wearing blue jackets with yellow DEA letters across their backs. There should be a woman or three among them. Why just men? More importantly, why was the DEA invading the prosecuting attorney's offices?

The shortest agent slapped a piece of paper on the reception desk, and the other five stomped around her, prowling down the long hallways and past my office which was the nearest to the reception area. Being the most junior of all the deputy prosecutors, I was lucky to have an office, if it could be called such. I waited until the grim looking agents had passed before walking across the scattered papers to read what predictably turned out to be a warrant.

An arrest warrant.

I tried to digest that reality when the tallest agent, a guy with light blond hair and light-refracting glasses that concealed the color of his eyes, escorted Scot Peterson, the prosecuting attorney, out of the office in handcuffs. My boss was around sixty-something years old with thick salt and pepper hair, bright blue eyes, and a sharp intelligence that had won him cases at the Idaho Supreme Court on more occasions that I could count.

He didn't look right cuffed. I finally burst out of the fuzz of shock, and heat slammed through me. What was happening? Scot was a decent guy. He helped people and even taught for free at the local community college. The agent led him out the door, and then he was gone without having said a word.

The office went deadly silent for about ten seconds. Then pandemonium exploded. The remaining DEA agents started gathering manila files, case files, and random pieces of paper.

I cleared my throat and read the warrant again. It was for Scot's arrest and any documents pertaining to...the distribution of narcotics? "Wait a minute." I interrupted a tug of war between the nearest agent and the receptionist over a picture of her with Stan Lee at a Comic Con. She was in her early twenties, blonde, and very chipper. Right now, she had tears in her usually sparkling brown eyes. "That's outside the scope of this warrant," I protested. No doubt any warrant. Come on.

The agent paused. He sighed, his lips turning down, as if he'd just been waiting for an argument.

I nodded. "Yeah. You've just raided an area ripe with attorneys." Yet in looking around, I was it. The only attorney on the floor. A pit dropped into my stomach, and I struggled to keep a calm facade. I'd only been a lawyer for a month. What did I know? The other attorneys were elsewhere, including my boss, who'd just been arrested.

I swallowed.

"Do something," Juliet muttered, her teeth clenched.

I blinked. "What?" There wasn't much I could do at the moment. While there should be a sense of comfort with that realization, it felt like I *should* do something.

"Anna." Clarice Jones, the head paralegal, rushed toward me with two case files in her hands. She shoved them my way.

I took them instinctively and tried to keep from falling backward. "What's going on?" If anybody knew what was up with Scot, it'd be her. They'd worked together for decades.

"I don't know." Clarice's white hair had escaped its usually too-tight bun to soften her face with tendrils. She'd gnawed away half of the red lipstick customarily blanketing her thin lips. "Worry about it later. You have to take these felony arraignment hearings. Right now."

I coughed as surprised amusement bubbled through me. "You have got to be kidding." I'd been an attorney for a month and had only covered misdemeanor plea bargains to date. Plus, my boss had just been arrested. "Get a continuance. On both of them." I tried to hand the files back.

"No." She shoved harder than I did. Her strength was impressive. "These cases are before Judge Hallenback, and he'll just dismiss if we don't show. He's not playing with a full deck lately, but he's still the judge. You have to take the hearings while Scot gets this mess figured out." She tapped the top folder, which seemed rather light in my hands. "Just follow the notes on the first page. Scot sets out a strategy for each case. The defendant will either plead guilty, in which case you ask for a sentencing hearing sometime in the next couple of weeks. Or they plead not-guilty, and you argue for bond—just read the notes."

District Court? I was so not ready for district court. I looked frantically around the mayhem surrounding me. How could I possibly go to court right now? "Where is everyone else?"

Clarice grabbed my arm and tugged me toward the door. "Frank and Alice are up in Boundary County prosecuting that timber trespass case. Melanie went into labor last night and is still pushing another one of her devil children out. Matt is with the police investigating that missing kid case. And Scot was just dragged out of here in cuffs." Reaching the doorway, which was still open, she tried to shove me through it. "That leaves you."

I dug my heels in.

The agent who'd been so determined to get his hands on the

Stan Lee photo rushed my way. "You can't take documents out of here."

Relief swept me so quickly I didn't have time to feel guilty about it.

Clarice turned and glared. "These are just two case files, and the judge is waiting for the arraignment hearings." Flipping open the top one while it settled precariously in my hands, she tapped the first page with her finger. Hard. "Feel free to take a look."

Ah, darn it. The agent scrutinized the first page and then the too few other pages before looking at the second file folder. I should've protested the entire situation, but my knees froze in place. So did my brain. I really didn't want to go to district court. Finally, the agent grimaced. "All right. You can take those." He moved back to the reception area like a bull about to charge.

I leaned in toward the paralegal. "Call everyone back here. Now." I needed somebody with a lot more legal experience than I had to deal with this.

Clarice nodded. "You got it." Then she shoved me—pretty hard —out the door. "Go to court."

The flower-scented air attacked me as I turned and strode down the steps into the nice spring day just as news vans from the adjacent city screeched to a halt in front of my building, which housed the prosecuting attorney's offices, the public defender's offices, and the DMV. The brick structure formed a horseshoe around a wide and very green park with the courthouse, police station, and county commissioner offices set perpendicular to my building. Directly across sat Timber City Community College, which stretched a far distance to the north as well. The final side held the beach and Lilac Lake.

Ducking my head, I took a sharp right, hit the end of the street, and turned for the courthouse. The building had been erected when the timber companies and the mines had been prosperous in the area and was made of deep mahogany and real marble brought in from Italy. Instead of walking downstairs like I had the last two weeks, I climbed up a floor to the district court level. It even smelled different than the lower floors. More like lemon polish and something serious. Oh yeah. Life and death and felonies. My knees wobbled, so I straightened my blue pencil skirt and did a quick check of my white blouse to make sure I hadn't pitted out.

Nope. Good. I shouldn't be too scared, because the pseudo-metropolis of Timber City had only 49,000 residents, roughly the same as a large state college. But compared to my hometown of Silverville, which was about fifty miles east through a mountain pass, this was the big city.

My wedges squeaked on the gleaming floor, and I pushed open the heavy door and made my way past the pews to the desk to the right, facing the judge's tall bench. My temples started to thrum. I remained standing at the table and set down the case files before flipping open the first one.

A commotion sounded, and two men strode in from the back, both wearing fancy gray suits. I recognized the first man, and an odd relief took me again, even though he was clearly there as the defendant's attorney and on the opposite side of the aisle as me. "Mr. O'Malley," I murmured.

He held out his hand. "Call me Chuck, Anna." He was a fishing buddy of my dad's and had been for years. "They've thrown you into District Court already?"

I shifted my feet. "It's a long story." That would be public shortly. "The DEA took Scot away in handcuffs," I said.

Chuck straightened, his gray eyebrows shooting up. "Charges?"

"The warrant said something about narcotics." We were on different sides right now, and Chuck was a phenomenal criminal defense attorney, but the truth was the truth and would be out anyway. "He probably needs a good lawyer."

"I'll check it out after this hearing." Chuck's eyes gleamed the same way they did when my Nonna Albertini brought her apple pie to a community picnic. He nodded at his client, a guy in his late twenties with a trimmed goatee and thinning hair. "This is Ralph Ceranio. He's pleading not guilty today."

Thank goodness. That just meant we would set things for trial.

Chuck smiled. "Unless you agree to dismiss."

I smiled back. "I'd like to keep my job for another week." Probably. "So, no."

Chuck turned as the bailiff entered through a side door by the bench and told everyone to stand, even though we were already standing. Then Judge Hallenback swept in.

Oh my. My mouth dropped open, and I quickly snapped it shut. It was rumored the judge had been going downhill for some time, and I was thinking that for once, rumors were right. While he had to only be in his mid-sixties, maybe he had early dementia? Today he wore a customary black robe with a charming red bow tie visible above the fold. It contrasted oddly with the bright purple hat with tassels hanging down on top of his head. A bunch of colorful drawn dots covered his left hand while a grey and white striped kitten was cradled in his right, and he hummed the anthem to *Baby Got Back* as he walked.

He set the cat down and banged his gavel, opening a manila file already on his desk. "Elk County vs Ralph Ceranio for felony counts of fraud, theft, and burglary."

I swallowed.

"My client pleads not guilty and requests a jury trial, your honor," Chuck said, concern glowing in his eyes. He and the judge had probably been friends for years, too.

"Bail?" the judge asked, yanking open his robe to reveal a Hallenback's Used Car Lot T-shirt. Oh yeah. The judge and his brother owned a couple of car dealerships in the area. If he retired now, he'd be just fine. "Hello? Prosecuting attorney talk now," he muttered.

I quickly read Scot's notes. "Two hundred thousand dollars.

The defendant is a flight risk, your honor. He has access to a private plane and several vehicles."

"Everyone has a private plane. Heck. I even have one." The judge shook his head before Chuck could respond. "Fifty thousand dollars. How many days do you need for trial?"

I had no clue. I didn't even know the case.

"Probably a week, Judge," Chuck said, helping me out.

I could only nod.

"All right." The judge reached for a calendar and announced the date six months away. "See ya then."

Chuck patted my shoulder. "I'll be in touch."

I swallowed again, wanting to beg him to stay with me for the second hearing. But I had to at least act like I had a clue what I was doing. The bailiff, a brawny guy whose nightstick somehow looked thicker than usual, moved for the door he'd emerged from earlier and opened it. He grabbed an arm covered by an orange jumper while I shuffled the files and looked down, trying to read Scot's mangled notes. Hopefully I could get caught up quickly.

The judge slammed down his gavel again. "Elk County vs. Aiden Devlin for narcotics possession and intent to distribute."

I stilled. Everything inside me, from thoughts to feelings to dreams and hard reality, just halted. I slowly turned to face a tall man dressed in an orange jumpsuit. Oh my God. "Aiden," I whispered, the entire world grinding to a harsh stop.

He smiled, his eyes bluer than I remembered, his face much more rugged. "Hi, Angel."

ALSO BY & READING ORDER OF THE SERIES'

I know a lot of you like the exact reading order for a series, so here's the exact reading order as of the release of this book, although if you read most novels out of order, it's okay.

THE ANNA ALBERTINI FILES

1. Disorderly Conduct
2. Bailed Out
3. Adverse Possession
4. Holiday Rescue novella (Albertini Family Romance)
5. Santa's Subpoena

* * *

DEEP OPS SERIES

1. Hidden (Book 1)
2. Taken Novella (Book 1.5)
3. Fallen (Book 2)
4. Shaken (in Pivot Anthology) (2.5)

5. Broken (Book 3)
6. Driven (Book 4)
7. Unforgiven (Book 5) - 2022

Dark Protectors / Realm Enforcers / 1001 Dark Nights novellas

1. Fated (Dark Protectors Book 1)
2. Claimed (Dark Protectors Book 2)
3. Tempted Novella (Dark Protectors 2.5)
4. Hunted (Dark Protectors Book 3)
5. Consumed (Dark Protectors Book 4)
6. Provoked (Dark Protectors Book 5)
7. Twisted Novella (Dark Protectors 5.5)
8. Shadowed (Dark Protectors Book 6)
9. Tamed Novella (Dark Protectors 6.5)
10. Marked (Dark Protectors Book 7)
11. Wicked Ride (Realm Enforcers 1)
12. Wicked Edge (Realm Enforcers 2)
13. Wicked Burn (Realm Enforcers 3)
14. Talen Novella (Dark Protectors 7.5)
15. Wicked Kiss (Realm Enforcers 4)
16. Wicked Bite (Realm Enforcers 5)
17. Vampire's Faith (Dark Protectors 8) *****A great entry point for series, if you want to start here*****
18. Demon's Mercy (Dark Protectors 9)
19. Vengeance (Rebels 1001 DN Novella)
20. Alpha's Promise (Dark Protectors 10)
21. Hero's Haven (Dark Protectors 11)
22. Guardian's Grace (Dark Protectors 12)
23. Vixen (Rebels 1001 DN Novella)
24. Rebel's Karma (Dark Protectors 13)
25. Vampire (Rebels 1001 DN Novella)
26. Immortal's Honor (Dark Protector 14)

27. Garrett's Destiny (Dark Protectors 15)
28. Warrior's Hope (Dark Protectors 16)

*** The Dark Protectors/Reese Brothers 1001 Dark Nights novellas (Teased, Tricked, Tangled) can be read any time after Marked. Even though it features Chalton and his family there's no crossover.

* * *

SIN BROTHERS/BLOOD BROTHERS spinoff

1. Forgotten Sins (Sin Brothers 1)
2. Sweet Revenge (Sin Brothers 2)
3. Blind Faith (Sin Brothers 3)
4. Total Surrender (Sin Brothers 4)
5. Deadly Silence (Blood Brothers 1)
6. Lethal Lies (Blood Brothers 2)
7. Twisted Truths (Blood Brothers 3)

* * *

SCORPIUS SYNDROME SERIES
**This is technically the right timeline, but I'd always meant for the series to start with Mercury Striking.

- 1. Scorpius Rising (Prequel novella - was actually written after Mercury Striking and shows how it all started)
- 2. Blaze Erupting (Scorpius/Brigade novella, 1001 Dark Nights)
- 3. Power Surging (Scorpius/Brigade novella)
- 4. Hunter Advancing (Scorpius/Brigade novella)

Scorpius Syndrome NOVELS
1. Mercury Striking (Scorpius Syndrome 1)
2. Shadow Falling (Scorpius Syndrome 2)
3. Justice Ascending (Scorpius Syndrome 3)
4. Storm Gathering (Scorpius Syndrome 4)
5. Winter Igniting (Scorpius Syndrome 5)
6. Knight Awakening (Scorpius Synd. 6)

* * *

MAVERICK MONTANA SERIES

1. Against the Wall
2. Under the Covers
3. Rising Assets
4. Over the Top

ABOUT THE AUTHOR

New York Times and *USA Today bestselling* author Rebecca Zanetti has published more than fifty romantic-suspense and dark paranormal novels, which have been translated into several languages, with millions of copies sold world-wide. Her books have received Publisher's Weekly starred reviews, won RT Reviewer Choice awards, have been featured in Entertainment Weekly, Woman's World and Women's Day Magazines, have been included in Amazon best books of the year, and have been favorably reviewed in both the Washington Post and the New York Times Book Reviews. Rebecca has ridden in a locked Chevy trunk, has asked the unfortunate delivery guy to release her from a set of handcuffs, and has discovered the best silver mine shafts in which to bury a body...all in the name of research. Honest. Find Rebecca at: www.RebeccaZanetti.com

Made in the USA
Middletown, DE
28 March 2021